A Monstrous World Novel

Faeling
A Fantasy Monster Romance

S. E. Wendel

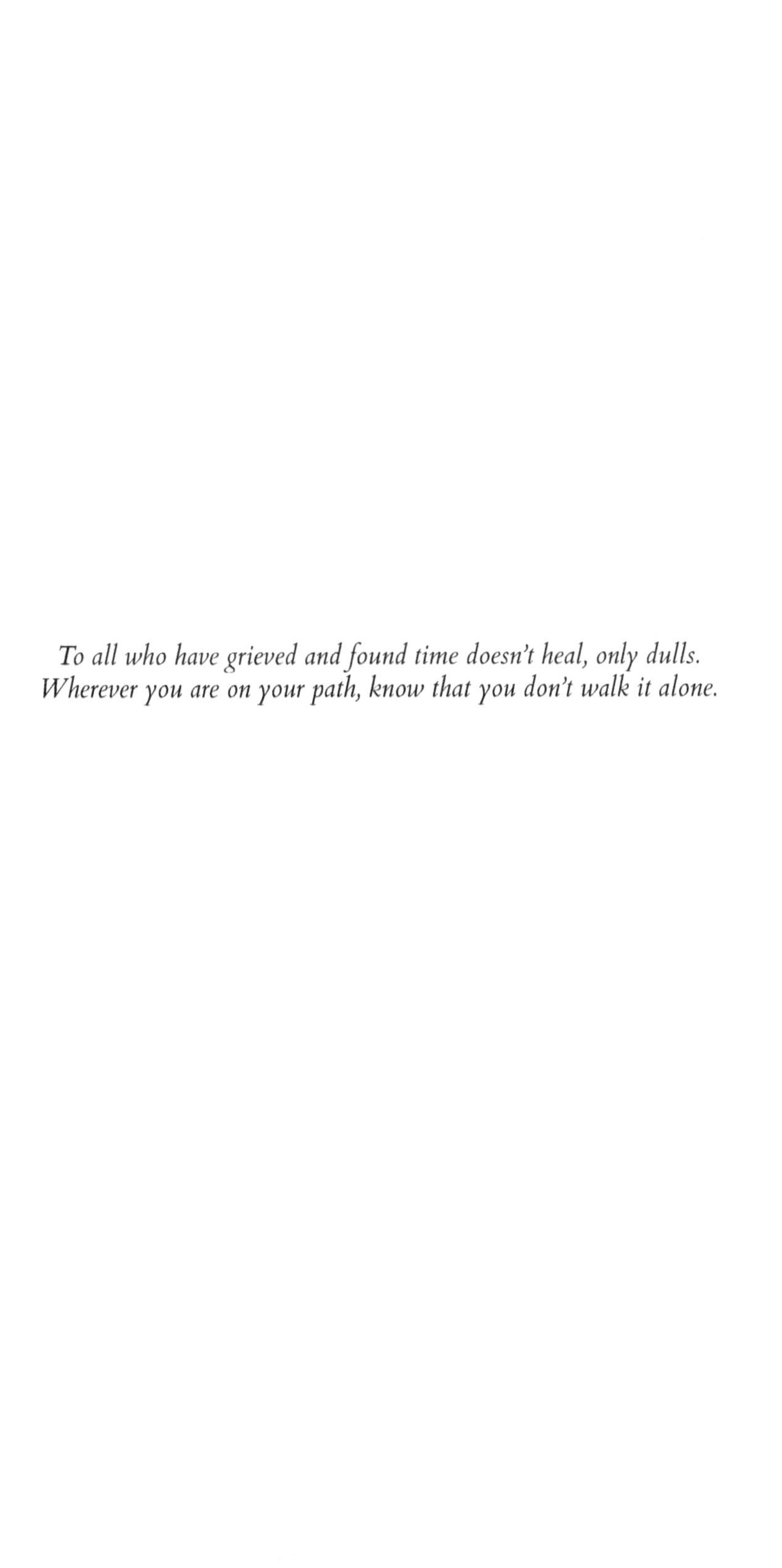

*To all who have grieved and found time doesn't heal, only dulls.
Wherever you are on your path, know that you don't walk it alone.*

The Fish
Culda
Larach
Shanago R.
Sca
Northpoint R.
Kilkarach
Bandaraugh R.
EIREA
Granach
Calca
Middlerun R.
Casholl
Rathcaran
Brigg
Southford R.
The Scales
Gray Knolls
Kinv
FAELANDS
Lune R.
Griegen Mountains
FALLORIAN
Kaldebrak
The Twins
Holdur
ORCISH
TERRITORI
BALMIRRA
Innrin
DRAGON KINGDOM
The
MONSTROUS
WORLD
HIGHHOME
The Drople

HD
2024
CALEDON
Glendown
INSLEY
The Gates
Bellbee
Intersea
Larkspur
GLEANNA
Adrigoll
Threepoints
Abbon R.
Kilgaran
GOLD SEA
BORDERLANDS
LYCEA
rrin
ne-Skin
amp
PYRROS
Irynian
Delta
CONQUERED
CONFEDERATION

Before You Begin...

I hope you're excited for *Faeling!* A few things before you begin:

This is book 4 of the Monstrous World series. The book stands on its own but will be best enjoyed after book 3, *Sweetling.* Although, it will draw from all three previous books, so being totally caught up will offer the best reading experience.

A few content/trigger warnings: our heroine Ravenna has lost her parents and is dealing with her grief in self-destructive ways. Our hero Vallek can be bossy and pushy. You can check my website for a full list of TW/CW; take care of yourself!

The book includes a glossary of people, places, pronunciation, fae, and medieval terms in the back. Don't be afraid to flip back and forth, but don't spoil anything for yourself.

All righty, here we go!

What's Come Before ...

Just a quick refresher for you before you begin! In the first book of the series, *Halfling*, a woman named Sorcha is betrayed to slavers, who kidnap her from her family's estate and sell her on to a splinter camp of orcs, the Stone-Skins. Orek, a half-orc whose own mother was a human slave purchased by the clan decades before, frees Sorcha and agrees to take her home. The two fall in love along the journey, and Orek joins Sorcha's large family.

Upon their arrival, they report what's happened to the liege lord of the land, Merrick Darrow. It is Merrick's son and heir, Jerrod, who sold Sorcha out to the slavers after she rejected his romantic advances. Merrick gives Sorcha the choice of what should happen to Jerrod. She decides he should be banished to the Ward, a castle converted into an infirmary, run by monk wardens. He is also stripped of his inheritance and position as heir, which is given to his older sister and Sorcha's friend Aislinn Darrow.

Orek and Sorcha's story spreads throughout the land, and otherly folk (orcs, fae, dragons, manticores, harpies, and sirens) begin arriving in the Darrowlands hoping to start a new life in peace and find a human mate.

In the second book, *Ironling*, Aislinn grapples with her new responsibilities as heiress, as well as her growing attraction to the new castle blacksmith, a half-orc named Hakon. Their friendship soon grows into more, although they are unsure how they can be together. Aislinn's brother Jerrod reemerges with an army of mercenaries to try taking back his inheritance. Among her own force, many non-human warriors fight on her side, including a fae warrior named Allarion and his unicorn steed, Bellarand. In order to secure his participation, Hakon offers a promise to Allarion, to be named at a later date. Aislinn's forces defeat Jerrod's, who himself is killed in the battle, which secures her place. She and Hakon marry the following spring.

Throughout, Aislinn has sought to help otherly folk settling in the Darrowlands, including Allarion, who purchases an abandoned estate called Scarborough. In the third book, *Sweetling*, Allarion often visits the Darrows' city of Dundúran, where he ends up finding his *azai*, his fated mate, Molly. A barmaid, Molly works at her uncle's pub and keeps the business going.

In a series of misunderstandings, Allarion essentially purchases Molly's hand in marriage from her uncle, soon taking her to the eerie Scarborough estate. It takes Molly quite a while to warm up to the sentient house, strange land, and unfriendly unicorn Bellarand. Through his mating with Molly, Allarion hopes to hasten his magic bonding to the land.

As they come to know each other, a deep bond forms, and Molly comes around to the idea of a strange fae husband and his even stranger estate. They are just beginning to find their rhythm when Allarion's past threatens them: having fled the faelands, the cruel Fae Queen Amaranthe sent scouts to try finding Allarion and Bellarand. The fae knights are eventually defeated with the help of Hakon, Orek, and the otherly village.

Once his bond with Molly and the land are established, Allarion secrets back south, where he left his friend Ravenna in the deep sleep. The halfling daughter of his old friend Maxim and his human *azai* Aine, Ravenna has the gift of foresight and has seen the death of Amaranthe. The Fae Queen has sought her ever since, even slaughtering Maxim and Aine when they wouldn't give her up. Allarion helped Ravenna escape, and after finding and making safe a place for her, he's returned to where he left her to bring her to her new life.

Except, upon reaching the bower where she laid, Allarion finds it empty . . .

Prologue

Despite all her father's careful planning, despite the sacrifice he and her mother made to keep her safe, Ravenna's long sleep wasn't so long at all.

She'd been told that the long sleep was a dreamless, peaceful thing. That time and the outside world meant little to a sleeping fae. Her body would need neither food nor drink, her mind would not mark the passage of time.

But Ravenna wasn't a true fae. A halfling, the daughter of a human mother and fae father, Ravenna and her magic had never acted as her father, Maxim, had predicted. A creation of two worlds, her magic was unpredictable, wild. It took years of honing to forge it into something manageable for Maxim.

Yet, it defied him. One last time.

Ravenna awoke from her deep sleep far sooner than he'd designed. Hers hadn't been a dreamless sleep, either, instead filled with vivid but incoherent images. That was often the way with her gift, her foresight. Given the chance, with her usual defenses dulled, all manner of disjoined visions had unspooled one after the next, a jumbled pile of thread to detangle.

—the burn of saltwater in her eyes—the pass of warm green skin over hers—white lashes catching the sun—the screaming whinnies of unicorns— sprite—all hail all hail all—

Ravenna's eyes peeled open, her true vision blurry with disuse. Her mind quieted almost immediately, her gift receding behind the careful ramparts she'd made for it.

Reality pierced the protective cocoon her father had constructed for her, and Ravenna felt nothing but relief.

As her vision slowly refocused, she started to rouse her body, one little bit at a time. She began with her toes, wiggling each before rotating her ankles. Working her way up, she tested each joint, carefully easing sensation back into her corporeal form.

By the time she was ready to sit up in her bower bed, her body only creaked a little. Although only fifty-two, barely out of adolescence by fae standards, it took long moments before Ravenna felt secure enough to stand. As she waited, she tested her hands on the textures of her bedding and her nose on the warm scents of summer outside the bower.

Her hand found and clutched her childhood blanket, drawing it onto her lap. The batting had long gone flat, the embroidery frayed and bleached with time, but when she held it to her nose, she still caught a waft of her childhood—sea breezes with the tang of salt, sugar and lemon mixing in a bowl, thyme and rosemary drying on the windowsill.

The blanket was all softness and comfort, just as her mother Aine had been.

That knife of reality sank a little deeper, finally pricking something that hurt. She quickly put down the blanket and her softness.

Maman is dead.

A sheep led to slaughter.

Angry tears blurred her vision, and Ravenna quickly wiped them away. There had been enough tears already; more wouldn't bring her mother back.

When she felt able, she pushed herself up to standing, her knees only wobbling a little. The door to the bower her father had built into the side of a grassy knoll creaked on its unused hinges, opening to a quiet summer afternoon. The air was warm and fragrant, a contrast to the cool bite of late winter when she'd first entered the deep sleep.

Ravenna stopped a few paces from the bower door, regaining her bearings. The world was so vivid, every shaft of light blinding, each scent overpowering. Her fingers and toes prickled as blood flowed back into her extremities, and her wings slowly unfolded from her back to spread in the light.

As blood and feeling flowed back through her body, so too did the memories. Her heart pounding as she ran. Her mother's cry in her ear. *"Run! Run, Crow!"*

Ravenna had run, as fast as she could. All her life she'd lived with the fear of the evil Fae Queen coming to claim her—when it finally happened, it hadn't seemed real. That her whole life should come crashing down just by chance, bad luck—it was unbelievable. That she and her mother should happen upon a handful of fae knights on a commonplace walk through the forest, foraging for mushrooms, truffles, and wild onions.

Maman had wanted to make truffle soup, her father's favorite. For when he returned.

There would be no return. Flinging their baskets away, she and her mother had fled at the first sight of the fae knights, their ghostly pale armor flashing between the trees. For a moment, Ravenna hoped they hadn't been spotted. For a moment, she hoped they'd gotten away.

"Run! Run, Crow!"

Ravenna had run, as fast as her feet could take her, back to their cottage by the sea, surrounded by a wall of wards set by her father. She'd returned alone. Too late, she realized her mother had drawn them off. Too late, she realized the fate she'd dreaded was coming to pass.

It wasn't until weeks later that the fate of both her mother and father was confirmed. Her father's friend Allarion Meringor had come for her, as planned. He brought with him the terrible news—the culmination of Maxim's own morbid prophecy. Her parents had died protecting her, refusing to give her up.

Now it was time for Ravenna and Allarion to play their parts in the plan. To secret away to lands unknown, seeking a life of anonymity and possible safety. It was the final gift her parents gave her—and Ravenna didn't want it.

She was an ungrateful, angry, guilty daughter.

Maman's blood is on both our hands, papa.

The sound of hasty hoofbeats broke her concentration, and from the eastern tree line burst a silver blur.

You stubborn thing, Oberon scolded, *what are you doing up?*

Ravenna squinted at the question—it was a good one. She'd always meant to wake up before Allarion could come to fetch her, of course. How or when hadn't been so precise, however.

But Oberon, her father's dread-mount, his bonded unicorn war-horse, wasn't finished.

Get back to sleep, Crow. It isn't safe.

His silvery head turned, those velveteen ears she'd loved to pet as a child flicking back toward the trees.

Ravenna's skin pricked with gooseflesh. A breeze shifted the dry leaves and branches of the grove, a chill of awareness brushing against her cheek.

Maxim had added layers upon layers of warded magic around the bower. Only Allarion and his dread-mount Bellarand, Oberon, and his herd could pass through.

Still, something was close.

What is it? she whispered to him. Although most unicorn stallions only bonded with their dread-riders, forming a magical and mental link, that bond could sometimes extend to family members. Such had been the case for Oberon and her mother, but female fae had entirely different bonds with the unicorns. Mares were too wild and temper-amental to ride, a trait Ravenna admired deeply, yet they could often speak with fae women with or without a bond.

So it was with Oberon's dam, who came trotting from the grove.

Callistix had once been the same dappled gray as her son, but in her regal age, she'd gone nearly white, only a spatter of silvery spots on her withers hinting at her former coloring.

They come closer, Callistix huffed, tossing her graying mane. She turned her ferocious gaze on Ravenna, her bright gold eyes snapping with frustration. *What are you doing awake?*

My question exactly, agreed Oberon.

Who's getting closer? Ravenna asked instead, although she thought perhaps she already knew.

For years, the same vision had haunted her thoughts.

—a traveling band of green-skinned warriors—a camp of burgundy tents—the burning blue eyes of a warlord—

Ravenna didn't know how to explain *knowing*; her father always said a gift such as hers was often beyond explanation. It only made sense to the one who bore it. She doubted Oberon and especially Callistix would appreciate that answer, but all Ravenna knew was that she needed to be awake. That the vision was coming for her, and all she could do was meet it.

Her visions had never been wrong. She didn't see threads of possibility like other fae seers of legend, for which she was grateful. Such sight often led the mind into the oblivion of possibility, never to return to the safety of what already was.

Instead, she saw fragments, images, that often needed stitching together to make any sense, if at all. Many visions hadn't yet come to fruition or didn't affect or include Ravenna at all.

She wished she'd never asked her father what they meant. In the way of children, she'd asked what it could mean when she saw the white-haired queen resting on the rocks of the sea. The vision, one of her first, had upset her—her young mind couldn't comprehend that the queen didn't rest, she hung impaled. She sought her father's comfort and wisdom, but she should have held her tongue.

Her father and many of his family had heard her sobbing, babbling about what she'd seen. Everything changed that day. Maxim put plans into motion that could not be undone. He moved Ravenna and Aine from the faelands, hid them behind a fortress of wards and magic. His family was sworn to secrecy, but whispers of the queen's death still found their way back to her ears in Fallorian.

Because of her gift, because she couldn't keep her mouth shut, Ravenna had been hunted by Queen Amaranthe all her life. Because of her, her parents had sacrificed themselves, taking her location to their deaths. Because of her, Allarion had broken from the faelands in search of a safe haven to spirit her to, where Maxim envisioned her living in quiet peace, safe from Amaranthe and her own visions.

Because of this, Ravenna learned not to share what she saw.

She didn't tell her father she wouldn't sleep through their sacrifice, waiting to be saved. She didn't tell him that she'd known for decades that one day she would wake from her deep sleep and make her own way.

Which began with an orc camp of burgundy tents.

Callistix pawed the earth in agitation. *Orcs approach. They fell trees for their infernal fires.*

Ravenna's heart skipped a beat. She couldn't describe the sensation at her back other than the hand of the fates giving her a push.

She wouldn't wait to be saved. She wouldn't live the life her father planned for her.

Ravenna was the daughter of slain parents, a woman robbed of her life, and she would have her revenge. A nocked arrow fired from the bow didn't care if it would split upon impact; neither did Ravenna care if she survived her vengeance. Only that Amaranthe wouldn't.

Be it the wind, her visions, the hand of some faceless goddess—it didn't matter now what had woken Ravenna. Her chance had come to find her, and she had to meet it.

Looking between Oberon and Callistix, she said, "Take me to them."

Although she had a long name, one that implied many branches of an ancient family tree, Ravenna Broch-Illyinia rode out to meet the orc camp and her fate alone. Her mother had had a large, jovial extended family, made up of her many cousins and great-great-grandnieces and -nephews, but that warmth always cooled whenever Aine's fae husband and halfling child accompanied her to visit. Ravenna had few memories of the imperious Illyinia clan, although she'd spent her youngest years amongst them. She'd only a handful of memories of each family, a few impressions that weren't enough to forge the bonds that made blood thick.

So she rode out alone, not to any of her remaining family. Her family was dead. She was a clan of one, an orphan, and—

Please, Oberon huffed, *spare me the indulgent melancholy. You are* not *alone.*

Ravenna grinned despite herself. Leaning over his back, she reached to gently pet one of his velvety ears. It'd taken a long argument—and a few threats—to get the dread-mount to agree. She hadn't meant for him to come along, nor his whole herd to follow behind, but he refused to let her wander off toward, as he put it, *a murderous pack of axe-swinging idiots* by herself.

He'd promised her father. He'd promised her mother. And so he deigned to let her sling saddlebags full of supplies and a few cherished bits she couldn't leave behind over his sides before mounting his broad back.

They left the bower behind, Callistix and her herd melting into the shadows of the trees to follow them. Ravenna didn't know how she would hide or explain a whole herd of unicorns—they and orcs had a history of enmity, after all. But that was for later. For now, they would find the camp and the warlord there.

Patting his neck, Ravenna replied, *That's true. I have my old friend Oberon.*

Indeed. But call me old again and you'll be walking your way to these orcs.

I

Vallek Far-Sight of the Broad-Back clan had earned his moniker in recent years for his vision of the future. Of a united orc kingdom, strong in the face of incursion and outside threat. Too long had the clans squabbled and skirmished amongst themselves, weakening what they could be strengthening.

While the other chieftains, of clans great and small, fought over scraps of territory, the growing Pyrrossi Empire encroached from the east, the dragons grew bolder in the south, and the tentacles of the faelands crept across the waters of Dyfan Bay. The orcs had sailed to their lands long ago, claimed the high peaks and steppes of the Griegen Mountains when none other had the courage. Yet, at this rate, they would be thrown back into the sea if something wasn't done.

Vallek understood that. He saw what the others refused to see.

Strong as they were, bigger and more intimidating than all the other races except perhaps dragons, with their towering mountain cities of stone and steel, the orcs were nevertheless weak: Should any of their neighbors ally together to strike a killing blow, there was little the orcs could do to stop it.

That was why, in his eighteen years as the chieftain of Balmirra, the strongest, most ancient of the orcish cities, he'd run across the territories hundreds of times, feet pounding across thousands of leagues. Most recently, it'd been to quell a border dispute with a growing Pyrrossi mining colony on the southern Shanago River.

With that headache taken care of, Vallek returned to his city with no small amount of relief, the familiar spires, towers, and peaks spearing the sky. The sight always made him proud—his city was the biggest, most impressive of the orcish cities, where the ancestors had first dug their roots into these mountains.

Dusty and sweaty from the run, Vallek slowed to an easy trot as the city crested along the horizon. His men behind him, an elite unit of warriors specially selected for their skills and loyalty, gave a great cheer to see home. Known as the berserkers, his men fought hard and deserved all the awe and privilege their rank afforded them.

Vallek turned to his left, but he needn't have bothered. Mattias, captain of his berserkers, was already pulling his horn from his belt. Putting his lips to the horn, Mattias blew, announcing their return.

A moment later, an answering trumpeting thundered across the plain before the mighty walls of the city. The berserkers gave an answering roar, and their pace picked up again, closing the last distance to the city wall.

Their feet pounded across the drawbridge overhanging the wide moat, through the tunnel of stone into the four-tiered curtain walls. The five portcullises rose before them one after the other, metal teeth disappearing into the stone curve of the tunnel as they passed.

The cool of the tunnel quickly gave way to the burning afternoon sun, the column of berserkers pouring into the city streets. A crowd quickly gathered, applause following them as the column began to climb the mountain higher, to the citadel. Orc-kin called out warm welcomes, clapping and hooting as the impressive force ran by.

They didn't slow until they finally met the walls of the citadel itself. The main limestone promenade of Balmirra switched back and forth, climbing to the citadel at the very top. A cluster of towers, spires, and great halls, the citadel had been the house of government and home to Balmirra's chieftain since the very first ancestors. As sacred as it was ancient, Vallek felt the weight of his forebearers as he passed beneath the final portcullis, entering the wide, lush courtyard of the citadel.

Late apple blossoms sweetened the air, loose white petals releasing their perfume as they were crushed underfoot on the flagstones. Flowering rhododendrons and manicured junipers lined the white limestone walls, offering some shade from the summer sun. Vallek eased into a walk as he came to the steps leading up to the great double doors of Ninevar's Basilica, the first building constructed on the citadel.

Mounting the first three steps, he turned to face his men. The last of the two-hundred elite warriors came jogging through the gate, leading the unit's small herd of takin. The hearty goats were perfect for the rugged terrain of the territories, and their wool was spun into all manner of cloth throughout the cities.

Although tired from the days of running, their wide chests heaving beneath their dusty breastplates, his men all looked to him.

Grinning, Vallek unhooked his double-bladed axe Hormhím and raised it high above his head. Every chieftain of Balmirra helped forge their own axe, a symbol of their reign that lasted as long as they kept their throne. From start until end, the axe was their emblem; it could be repaired but never replaced. Its strength and craftsmanship foretold the new chieftain's resolve, and so Vallek had poured himself into the blades, and eighteen years later, he still hefted the weapon high with pride.

"Warriors!" he called through the courtyard. "I thank you for your company—and fast pace." A rumble of laughter went through the ranks. "I know we're all looking forward to our cups and a real bed. Be off with you, then!"

"Hear, hear," the men cheered, knocking spears and hilts into their breastplates to create a deafening din.

The orderly lines of their ranks began to dissolve as the men disbanded. From the front, Mattias, Vallek's second Ulrich, and the four guardsmen who followed him everywhere split from the group to head with him into the basilica.

The great cedar doors opened on a silent *whoosh*, their metal plating glinting almost gold. The door bearers bowed their heads as Vallek crossed the threshold, and waiting just inside was his trusted steward—his elder sister Eydis.

Bobbing her head just enough to be respectful, she greeted him with a brilliant smile. "Welcome home, *breddah*," she said.

Little brother, she called him. No matter that he hadn't been littler than her in some thirty years. To Eydis, he would always be *breddah*. Which was good; it kept him humble—according to Eydis.

"It's good to be home," he sighed, leaning down for Eydis to kiss his cheeks.

Discreetly wiping her mouth with a kerchief, she muttered, "You've brought half the road in with you."

When she held out her fist, Vallek offered his open palm. In it she placed the ceremonial key to the citadel, bestowing him with mastery of his domain once more. Hooking the damn clunky thing onto his belt, Vallek offered his sister his arm. She took it—once she'd given his vambrace a quick pass of her kerchief.

Vallek chuckled, in no doubt that he was filthy. "I'm bound for a bath," he assured her.

"That's what you think," Eydis laughed.

He groaned. "They've—?"

"Oh yes, Lady Silvia has seen to that."

Vallek sighed again—and steeled himself to be greeted by his court. He walked arm-in-arm with his sister out of the vestibule into the basilica to the resounding echo of applause.

It thankfully wasn't the whole court; not even Lady Silvia, the niece of the previous chieftain, could organize so many people in the time it took to run from the east gate to the citadel. Still, at least three dozen finely dressed paladins awaited him, their fine leathers and furs and silver filigree catching in the warm amber light of the basilica.

They formed a gauntlet for him to run, standing on either side of the aisle between massive red limestone columns. When Eydis slowed to stay a half-step behind him, he trapped her hand in the crook of his elbow.

"Oh, no," he warned, "we face them together."

Eydis snorted.

The first to greet them was Lady Silvia herself, of course, her eyes artfully lined in kohl and the neckline of her silk tunic plunging. She bowed to him in a way that neither broke eye contact nor let him ignore the swells of her breasts, generous for an orcess. Lovely as always in the deep burgundy and gold of the Broad-Back clan, she fluttered her lashes as she straightened.

"The gods bless us to have you home so soon, my king."

Vallek inclined his head at her welcome. The epithet of *king* was a new thing, one he'd introduced himself. Orcs had rarely had kings in their long history, the few who'd claimed the title rising to unite the territories into one kingdom of orcs. There were over a dozen chieftains throughout the territories, some of whom still hadn't pledged him their fealty, but Vallek meant to unite them all under one banner and one cause.

Whether they wanted it or not. They would thank him one day, when the Pyrrossi incursion ceased and the dragons went back to their islands.

Lady Silvia had been one of the first to use the new title as he began amassing oaths of fealty from the other chieftains. It was a clever move for her, since she wanted to be a queen.

"It is a blessing to see your loveliness," Vallek replied, speaking a little louder over the sound of Eydis gagging.

Lady Silvia blushed prettily, stepping closer to lay gentle fingers on his free arm. A dozen rings glinted on her fingers, and a matching set of dangling headdress, earrings, and necklace glittered with silver and diamonds, encasing her in sparkle. A sign to all that though her family had been ousted from the throne, she still possessed wealth and influence.

"You must be tired from your journey," she said, voice dropping to an intimate tone. "Perhaps I can—"

"*Breddah!*"

To his immense relief, Lady Silvia had to sidestep out of the way before catching an armored elbow to the tit. Asta, his younger sister, bounced on the balls of her feet, smiling impishly up at him.

"Sorry, milady, didn't see you there," she said without looking at Silvia. Spreading her arms wide, she threw them around Vallek's neck. "Welcome home."

Eydis coughed delicately. "Is that really becoming of a captain of the royal guard?"

Slipping back to her feet, Asta turned a wolfish smile onto their sister. "Hello, sister. You're looking haggard today."

Eydis merely sighed. "Keep moving," she whispered to Vallek, "or you'll never get your bath."

Rumbling in agreement, he caught Asta's arm, keeping her nearby as they continued down the line of nobles and notable orcs. With a sister on either arm, there was nothing for anyone to catch and hold him in the basilica, so once they got their momentum, the crowd passed quickly. He saw his minister of coin, his master of beasts, his chatelain and seneschal, and all manner of heads of houses and state. He nodded and greeted them all, sure not to give one too much of his attention. They would get all of him—tomorrow.

After a bath. And a long sleep in his magnificent bed.

Once the crowd had thinned, Vallek, his sisters, Ulrich and Mattias, and his four guardsmen bypassed the imposing throne set at the head of the hall. Carved from a single trunk, the back was set with dozens of rubies and garnets, common rocks in Balmirra and the first good that had made this city her fortune. Liquid copper had been set into engraved designs along the legs and head, meant to catch the light of the many stained-glass windows that let in the sunshine in shafts of saturated color.

A door tucked into the back of the basilica led to the chieftain's private entrance, where their little group caught the maze of corridors that exclusively serviced his wing of the citadel.

As they walked, Eydis dutifully listed everything that would need his attention. "Rats were spotted in the southern silos again, so I've ordered a dozen more cats be employed. And Minister Bellos wishes to speak with you about repairs to the lower city cisterns . . ."

Vallek listened just as dutifully, making notes in his mind for what he meant to do about each. When he'd first fought and won the throne of Balmirra, he'd no notion that leadership was mostly the minutiae of everyday life. His people cared much more about clean water and a constant flow of grain than they did about battles—although they loved a good brawl, to be sure.

Since challenging the old chieftain, Mordis, for the position nearly eighteen years ago, Vallek had barely known a day's peace. Between politics, city planning, and protecting the realm, his attention was always needed somewhere.

Although training with his men and clobbering their enemies with Hormhím was his favorite, he still found the administrative duties fulfilling. It helped to have someone as competent as Eydis by his side, of course. Balmirra was always in good hands when she held the ceremonial key.

It was because of Eydis, in fact, that he was chieftain at all. Mordis hadn't been a kind man. His rule had been tyrannical, his mind fractious and petty. He relished pitting houses against one another and intimidating their allies. Many had tried before to challenge his rule, but none had succeeded. Not until Vallek.

There'd been nothing truly special about him and his challenge. He wasn't the first outraged young warrior to challenge for the throne, promising a fairer, kinder regime. What had set Vallek apart was that he hadn't wanted to be chieftain. Not truly. All he wanted was to protect his sisters, and the only way to do that, to ensure they wouldn't be married off to horrid males or thrown into the arena to fight wild beasts, had been to become chieftain.

Such a horrid male had been chosen for Eydis. The old chieftain's son had been particularly odious, a male who forced himself on women and men alike, who thought nothing of the feelings of others, and thought the strength of his sword arm made him right. Eydis was not a warrior. Her talents were in politics and management, and her brilliant mind would not only have been wasted but broken by such a husband.

That was likely what the old chieftain intended. Vallek wouldn't allow it.

What made him victorious where so many others had failed and lost their heads was simple—Vallek couldn't lose.

His sisters needed him to win, and so he had.

He made safe his family and rose to the honor of chieftain. His first years were marked with more challenges by supporters of Mordis, and it had been a particular pleasure to cut off the head of his son. Hormhím had dripped with blood for many moons, but Vallek kept his seat.

He never wished to return to such a time. If he could have his way through diplomacy and politics, he would. Bloodshed was messy—and took him far away from his truest love.

His big, soft, magnificent bed.

His body ached just thinking of it.

Soon enough, they were at the doors to his personal quarters. Two of his guardsmen opened the doors and did a quick sweep inside, ensuring it was just the servants preparing his bath within.

Brynhíl, his personal housekeeper and the one in charge of all the servants who directly served him and his household, looked up and smiled gently. The soft lines around her eyes crinkled with fondness to see him and his sisters.

"Welcome home, my king. Your bath is almost ready."

"Thank you, Bryn. Much obliged."

Gathered in the wide front vestibule, Vallek turned to Mattias. "See that the men are rested tomorrow. But keep them ready, we will soon need to leave to handle the clans in the east." To Ulrich he said, "Ensure the ministers are ready to give me their reports tomorrow and see to the supplies for our next departure."

"Yes, my king," they said.

Mattias and Ulrich were good men, none more loyal. Ulrich had been by his side since before he challenged Mordis, standing as his second in their duel. Mattias was a hard man, one who'd earned his place rising through the ranks, and the men respected him for it. Between the three of them, there wasn't an enemy gate they couldn't crack.

Stepping into his quarters, Vallek shrugged off his cloak and unbuckled his heavy belt. "Good. Now everyone get out, I'm having my bath."

The warm water lulled him into a pleasant doze. Afternoon bled into evening, a rosy sky visible through the leaded diamond panes of his windows. The southern Griegens stretched out on the horizon, a few of their peaks holding onto the last layers of snow. Balmirra would never be called a warm place, but still, the snows melted most years, feeding the many rivers and streams that flowed into Lake Lovath.

The narrow strip of water was deceptively deep, and legend said that sirens still lurked in the darkest depths. The cold waters lapped at Balmirra's southern walls, providing water and fish for the people, as well as quick passage by boat north to its sister city of Holdur.

The waters of his bath were far more pleasant, even as the steam evaporated and the temperature fell to lukewarm. His muscles relaxed, he was loath to leave the comfort of his deep copper tub. He could descend the spiraling staircase to his own personal hot springs, deep in the mountain, but he didn't fancy all the stairs.

No, this was perfectly pleasant.

Until he remembered he'd been expecting a visitor.

A gentle knock on his door reminded him.

"Yes?" he called.

The door opened a crack, one of his guardsmen announcing, "It's the soothsayer, my king."

"Ah, good, send her in."

With a sigh, Vallek stood from the tub, rivulets of water sluicing from his body.

"You sent for me, my—ack!"

2

Ravenna spun around, pulling the hood of her cowl lower over her eyes to hide her blush—and her avaricious gaze from the perfect backside of the orc king. The moment offered a chance to claw back her composure, and she took it.

By the time she heard the slosh of him stepping from the tub, her glamoured mask was firmly back in place.

"Forgive me," she begged, "I thought—"

"Indeed, I did," he said in that brusque, deep voice of his. "My apologies, the afternoon slipped away from me. You're punctual as always, *kone*."

"Far be it from me to keep a king waiting."

He chuckled, the sound rich and resonant. Ravenna's toes curled in her old boots, and she cursed the little flutter of her heart every time he spoke to her like that. Intimate. Warm.

Such a tone featured often in her dreams. She heard that voice of his tell her a great many things, from mundane to wicked, and she listened raptly. The human fates and fae goddesses were all cruel cunts for blessing him with a body and voice made to make a woman come apart.

Straightening her heavy cloak, Ravenna ruthlessly squashed such thoughts. Orc noses were sensitive, and she didn't need him sniffing out her consuming lust for him. No need to give him a reason to laugh at her.

"I'm decent now. Your modesty is safe," he teased.

Ravenna turned to find a luxurious robe draped from his shoulders and tied loosely around his thick waist. Sumptuous white fur lined the collar, and the rich burgundy of the robe matched the other trappings of Balmirra. As he crossed from the tub to an ornately carved set of table and chairs, Ravenna kept her gaze at his shoulders or higher—she definitely didn't try to sneak a peek at what lay hidden beneath the red folds.

"You must save your flirting for a younger woman," she chided, "my poor human heart can't take it."

He smiled roguishly as he poured two cups of mead into golden goblets inset with rubies. "As king, I take my flirting very seriously. I know I'm safe with you, *kone*."

Kone, he called her. Seer. Although it was her position within his household, he didn't say it like a title. No, the way he said *kone,* he might as well have called her *my darling* or *sweetheart*. That was the way with him, that informality, an intimacy. It wasn't hard to understand how he'd gathered so many clans already to his cause without having to use force.

In truth, Vallek Far-Sight didn't need her and her power. He'd been called Far-Sight long before she presented herself before him, offering her services as a soothsayer. His own vision and confidence had seen him succeed where most others would fail—she supposed her little predictions were merely a nice reassurance.

That was all right. She didn't need to be more. She couldn't be more.

He extended one of his huge green hands toward the empty seat across from him. "Come join me," he invited, although it wasn't a request.

Bowing her head, she acquiesced. Someone had already anticipated her arrival, leaving a cushion and step stool for her. In the human world, she was a perfectly adequate height—to the orcs, she was positively puny.

Stepping up to take her seat, she settled on the cushion, sure that her cloak draped over as much of her as possible. Although she pushed the cowl back enough to reveal her face, she didn't let it completely fall from her head, as the shadows offered a little more protection for her pointed ears.

She'd had enough practice by now to hold her disguise without the cloak, but only having to mask her face and hands made it much simpler. As a half-fae, her grasp on magic had always been more erratic. At the home she shared with her mother, in the territory claimed and saturated with magic by her father, it'd been easy enough.

Now, though, far away from the little life she'd once had, surrounded by stone and steel and orcs, it took concentration to utilize her inherent magic in such a focused way.

When he smiled at her over his cup, he would see an older human woman, perhaps in her forties or fifties. A little weathered but still clinging to some of the beauty of happier times. The glamour hid the soft lilac shade of her skin, replacing it with the bronzed color of a woman who'd worked long hours outside. Her dark hair held streaks of gray, and her eyes were muted from their usual violet to a grayish blue.

Nothing like the striking lapis-lazuli blue of Vallek's intense gaze.

She had tried to make herself plain, simple, unremarkable. What her glamour became, what was easiest for her to hold, though, was something she knew intimately. And that was her mother's face.

So when the chieftain grinned over his cup, it was a facsimile of Aine's face he smiled at.

Ravenna's heart hurt to think on that too deeply, but she did like the notion that Aine's face wasn't forgotten. That this mighty king would remember it, even if he never knew how important she truly was to him.

Opening a lacquered box on the table, Vallek began pulling out the pieces for a game of *talfon*. The board was set between them, a beautiful thing of polished black walnut, the diamond-shaped places inlaid with gold. He lined up his pieces on the board, each figure a single piece of exquisitely carved stone.

"You're not too tired to play?" she inquired. She'd heard he and his berserkers had only just returned that very afternoon.

"Never," he said, "unless you mean to rally and present me a real challenge."

Ravenna guffawed in offense. "It's rude not to let a king win."

"And imprudent," he agreed, winking before he slid the box of pieces over to her.

Talfon was a game of strategy played between two parties. They each had the same number of figures, each with their own strengths and weaknesses. Although a bout was between two players and two sets, there were four sets to choose from, each with its own unique traits.

As always, Vallek had chosen the black set, built for speed and lateral movement.

Ravenna preferred the pink quartz set, at least when she played him. Much stronger in its defensive traits, she enjoyed making him test her defenses and find ways to make her bend.

Today, she chose the set of gold. This one was less maneuverable but powerful. She smiled to herself to see how one of his heavy brows arched in interest at her choice.

With the pieces all set, they began. Vallek always let her have the first move, and she always enjoyed squandering it. She often moved her pieces randomly in the first few moves, just to see how he would react—and she knew it vexed him.

Were he born with fae blood, she might have thought him gifted with a magical propensity for reading people. Behind his affability and charm was a ruthlessness she admired; through his smiles and banter, he was already reading his opponent, always looking for how to gain the upper hand.

This was on display most when he played *talfon* and when he played politics. Elsewhere, the signs were far more subtle. He was good with others in a way that made her almost jealous. He saw their needs and wants, could rise to fulfill them or use such desires against them with the skill of a politician far older.

She supposed, with how young he'd been when he first sat upon the throne of Balmirra, he'd had to learn. Quickly.

Ravenna admired him for it. It spoke to a will to survive, one born of desperation and impossible chances.

She knew such a fate well.

Although she'd told him as little as possible about herself, perhaps he still sensed this understanding. Perhaps it was why he sought her company.

A king such as him didn't need to share an evening mead and bout of *talfon* with his soothsayer. She'd tell him her visions with or without his friendship. That he offered it, inasmuch as a man of his position could to an old human woman, remained inexplicable.

Ravenna could hazard a guess, but that guess would indeed be hazardous. Whatever he might feel toward her, whatever bond they might share, it didn't matter. It couldn't.

She was using him, after all.

Not that he wasn't using her right back, of course, but she suspected he'd be at least a little grumpy to know she intended to help him unite the orc clans, to build them up into a strong nation, and then aim their armies at the faelands itself. She hadn't quite worked out the logistics on that last part, but she had time. An opportunity would present itself, she was sure.

Building the orcish kingdom had already taken Vallek some ten years, and she'd been with him for almost three of those now. It would likely take just as many to finally solidify the alliances between the holdout clans and force the more intransigent ones into line. She reckoned she'd have to give the new kingdom about a year for Vallek to put the final pieces in place.

After that—who knew, perhaps a war with the fae would be exactly what the new kingdom needed to rally together.

And while the orcs and the fae clashed, Ravenna would take her revenge. Whether Amaranthe would lead her armies and prove an easy target, or Ravenna would have to secret herself to Fallorian and strike while her armies were away, remained to be seen.

No visions nor opportunities had presented themselves to elucidate that part of the path, but again, Ravenna was patient. She was right where she needed to be, that she knew.

As their pieces moved about the board, Vallek regaled her with meaningless talk of his travels. This most recent journey had been to the southernmost border of the orcish territories, along the southern Shanago River. Mining operations had popped up all along the river; the human kingdoms had long been covetous of the minerals and ores found in the Griegens, and although these camps weren't officially on orcish lands, the water they used flowed downstream to orcish villages.

"So what will you do about them?" she asked, moving her raven piece up the board.

He huffed disdainfully. "We burned their camp and threw the equipment down a ravine. Even if they wanted to return, it would take months to rebuild."

Ravenna bit the inside of her cheek to keep from smiling. It wasn't that she delighted in violence, but she could appreciate the expediency. As charming as the orc king could be, there was no mistaking him when he issued a threat.

The fae would find him a formidable opponent, and Ravenna relished the thought.

She intended to cause the Fae Queen as much trouble and grief as possible before she drove a knife between that hag's fourth and fifth ribs. Although the fae had long lived on magic alone, they did still have hearts. Amaranthe's shriveled little organ would know Ravenna's blade and vengeance.

The Fae Queen would pay for what she'd done to Maxim and Aine.

One day, she would fall. Ravenna knew this as surely as she knew that Vallek Far-Sight was her mate, her *azai*.

She could only have one, though. That she knew, too.

And she chose her vengeance.

That was the choice she'd made when she first laid eyes upon him. Leaving Oberon and his herd a league away, Ravenna had walked the rest of the way to the orcish camp not far from her bower. Using a little magic, she'd slipped through the tents as a shadow. Orcs hardly ever thought to look down for long, and so she made it deep into their camp before she was noticed.

The elite guardsmen had stopped her, of course. They were trained to look everywhere. She explained loudly why she was there, loud enough that Vallek himself had come from the tent to get a look at the strange human woman claiming to be a soothsayer.

As he'd considered her, a bolt of recognition struck Ravenna. A white-hot light enflamed her very being, and she'd known with a clarity so intense it was blinding—*azai*.

But he saw only what she wanted him to see, her false face. And so Ravenna had put away her realization for later, mustering through a demonstration of her powers for him. Through that, and several more correct predictions in the days to come, she'd earned her place in his household. Taken by the orcs back to Balmirra, she'd been given a room in his own quarters, kept near in case she saw anything important and timely.

Her plan had worked perfectly. So much so, Oberon had been more than a little annoyed.

Don't be so smug, he'd tell her from where the herd followed behind the orcs from a distance. *It isn't becoming.*

In truth, though, Ravenna wasn't smug. Not really. Pleased with herself—a little. But that first march to Balmirra had been hard, both on her body and her heart. Long nights she spent awake on her pallet, desperate for sleep but her body burning for her mate. Her fangs ached to bite him, her magic reached out to bond to him.

It was only through sheer will, and his leaving again soon after installing her at Balmirra, that she was able to shore up her defenses. Over the intervening years, between his absences and her own dogged practice, she grew stronger. She could deny them both, for to do anything else would only bring ruin.

The thought brought her little joy, and she hoped he couldn't spy her sudden melancholy through the glamour. It was silly, really, to mourn what she would never have.

Still, the grief of never having nor claiming her *azai,* her one true mate, sent by the goddesses themselves the fae said, was a thistle beneath her skin. Every instinct inside her cried out to him. Yet, whenever she looked for recognition in his eyes, she crushed the hope mercilessly.

She could bear the grief precisely because she didn't know what it was to have an *azai.* To know and give it up, to lose it . . . that could not be borne.

And so Ravenna kept her disguise and her peace.

It was enough to play *talfon* with him on a quiet summer evening. To glimpse his sharp, ruthless mind and indulge in his attention was a gift.

He would never know what she was to him, and she would never know the loss of him.

She would use him and his armies to obtain her revenge. Ravenna had no illusions that she would survive the ordeal. Although she never quite knew where her visions came from in time, none were from later in her life that she could tell. She wouldn't grow old. She wouldn't build a life for herself beyond her father's usurped plans.

Even if her soul might rail against that truth, this was the way it had to be.

What Ravenna could give her *azai* in return was his own vision. She would help him make the kingdom he sought, realize the vision of a united orcish people. Yes, she would use it to her advantage, but Vallek would lead them through it.

She would make sure of it.

Sipping from his goblet, Vallek moved his leopard piece into position, readying his trap.

Ravenna feinted consideration before moving her horse piece two diamonds left, negating his trap. She enjoyed the little incensed tick above his brow as he leaned forward to rethink his strategy.

"Have you had any visions?" he asked. "I mean to bring the eastern tribes to heel by winter, and it would be helpful to know what I'm walking into."

Sitting back in her seat, Ravenna peered down into her goblet. Although she'd been sipping throughout their game, the goblet and portion of mead were both orc-sized, so there was plenty left in her cup to swirl. The rhythm of the liquid lulled her mind, and she let herself fall into a vision.

—stone circles set in a maze—leather tents clustered around a bonfire— smoke obscuring stars—yes, my king—loyalty and an eye—

Ravenna clutched her cup tighter, her hand gone suddenly cold. She set it down on the table before it could spill.

Vallek hadn't moved, and his posture remained relaxed, but those vivid blue eyes pierced her with their intense curiosity.

"What is it?" he breathed, familiar now with the process of her visions.

Pulling in a breath, Ravenna fussed at the folds of her cloak as she gathered her thoughts. She had trained long enough with her father that she could call a vision forward and aim its focus. At least for others. Visions of her own future still only came to her suddenly or in her sleep. Though, Ravenna wasn't sure she wanted to know her own fate any more than she already did.

"They will bow to you," she confirmed, "although not without some dissent."

"Hm." He eased back in his chair, pleased with the news. "As long as they bow, I don't care what comes before."

She hoped that was true. Even if life was easier with her handsome *azai* out of the city, she still worried for him while he was gone.

Before the night grew too late, Ravenna sabotaged her own strategy and let him win. He knew this, of course, and while he might always like to win, she enjoyed that it annoyed him to know she'd let him.

"After all this time, I still cannot decide if you're a master at *talfon* or horrible at it," he mused before bidding her goodnight.

She couldn't say, either, only that it pleased her to play with him. And that she and her mother had spent long hours playing the game, wiling away the days when her father was away.

As Ravenna retreated down the dark corridors of the royal quarters, she couldn't help musing that she now spent her life much as her mother had—waiting for her *azai* to return.

It was a life Ravenna had resented. Aine was all goodness and kindness and patience. Her love was vast, warmer than the blankets she knitted and sweeter than the cakes she baked. They were often left alone in that seaside cottage, her and her mother, and together they got up to all manner of things.

Aine taught Ravenna about the moon and tides and how to weave a net. They hunted for abalone and sea glass together, keeping the shells to decorate the path up the cliff to the cottage and the sea glass in little bottles on the windowsills to catch the light. They spun yarn and darned socks and knitted caps, and Aine taught Ravenna how to embroider the cloth with every color of thread.

Aine made everything she touched beautiful. It was no wonder that her goodness had caught the likes of a fae warrior.

Ravenna still hadn't forgiven Maxim for sacrificing such goodness. *They didn't have to die.*

Since foolishly voicing her vision of Amaranthe falling, Ravenna's life had been honed into a sharp blade for survival. Maxim had insisted that one day, Amaranthe would find them. He hadn't needed Ravenna to see that the Queen would destroy any in her path to foil the prophecy and procure herself a seer.

In so doing, Maxim made his own prophecy, one he fulfilled himself. He readied Ravenna for life as a fugitive. He readied himself and Aine for sacrifice.

"One day, she will come for you. We will stop her."

Ravenna had pleaded that this didn't mean her secret must die with them. They could all go away, far away. Make lives somewhere new, where the fae and their magic could never hope to reach.

But Maxim thought this impossible.

He planned and prepared. Many days he sat at the cottage's kitchen table with Aine and his old friend Allarion, detailing how Ravenna would be made safe. *Planning how they meant to die.*

And so it was decided. Ravenna would be hidden away when the time came. Maxim and Aine would defy the Queen and lose their lives.

Done. Sorted.

Ravenna refused to accept that still. *"It is the only way,"* her mother would say, but she didn't believe it. She didn't *see* it.

Her mother, soft and beautiful, deserved better.

Better than to be left waiting for months at a time as Maxim visited the Illyinia lands to keep up the ruse and throw off suspicion. Better than to be kept with a foot in the human world and the other in the faelands, never to be accepted by either. Better than to be slaughtered like a lamb in sacrifice.

Ravenna would avenge her mother.

And she would have revenge on her father, too. All his plans, his own sacrifice, for nothing.

She never wanted to walk the path he'd set her upon, and so she meant to make her own. That that would lead to her own ruin, well . . . even better.

You're being morbid again.

Ravenna rolled her eyes under the cowl of her cloak. *And you're eavesdropping again.*

I can't help it that you think so loudly, Oberon complained. *Leagues between us and still I'm plagued with your tortured thoughts.*

You could try harder not to listen in.

Alas, if only that were true. But no, I must listen in, to ensure my most difficult foal doesn't get herself killed. At least not too soon, of course, he added acerbically.

I'm not going to get myself killed, she argued.

No, you're just going to fall into Amaranthe's claws willingly.

Don't you have anything better to do than—

Ravenna skidded to a halt on the flagstones as a big body rounded the corner in front of her. Righting her cloak, she bobbed her head in deference without lifting it to meet Ulrich's odious gaze.

The lord commander of Balmirra, the king's second in command, had never liked her. Ravenna didn't overly care, she hadn't come to the orcish territories to make friends, but it did put a wrinkle in the weave of her plan.

"And where are you skulking off to?" he grumbled. A bit shorter than most other orcs, he was still heads above Ravenna and stout with muscle. Although Ravenna believed lord commanders of orcish strongholds usually stayed to help the stewards in the running of the cities, Ulrich never let Vallek go anywhere without him.

Fresh from their return and apparently the baths, his long hair stuck to his skull, his long pointed ears gleaming with gold hoops marking his rank and accomplishments. He might be considered handsome if he'd stop scowling for a moment. As it was, he was always on the lookout for enemies and threats. Ravenna wouldn't mind that had he looked a little less at *her*, hypocritical as that might be. Yes, she meant to use and manipulate Vallek, but no more than any courtier. She wasn't his enemy.

"I was speaking with our king," she answered, failing to keep the acid from her tone. It was late, she was tired, and she wanted to drop her glamour.

"Spinning your tales, I see."

"Indeed. Reassuring the king that his instincts are correct." She smiled evilly. "Do you mean to imply you don't consider the king's instincts correct, lord commander?"

His lip pulled back into a snarl. "A spider spinning its web is what you are." Leaning down to put his face in hers, Ravenna shuddered to feel his hot breath on her forehead. "I won't let the king fall into your trap."

Ravenna sighed. "I truly wish I had even half as marvelous a plot as you seem to think I do, but alas, I'm merely a woman making her way in the world. I am of use to our king, and so I serve him."

Ulrich snorted, ruffling her cowl. Ravenna worked to keep her glamour perfectly still as the lord commander glared down at her, his eyes casting an eerie gold in the lamplight of the sconces.

"Be off, wench, and remember, I'm—"

"Always watching, yes yes, I know. Pleasant dreams, lord commander."

Sidestepping around his great bulk, Ravenna ignored how his head turned to follow her. She kept her pace measured as she turned the corner he'd come from, down a flight of steps into the quarters of the king's personal household.

With the hour so late, she slipped into her room without any more interruptions.

Closing the door to her small chamber behind her and locking it, Ravenna smiled to herself. It wouldn't be too difficult to gather a few spiders from around the citadel and put them all in the lord commander's room . . .

Don't antagonize him, Oberon groaned.

You never let me have any fun.

I promised to keep you alive, the stubborn unicorn retorted, *not to have fun.*

Ravenna rolled her eyes. Striding further into the room, she unpinned the brooch of her cloak and pulled the heavy garment from her shoulders. The cloak had been spun by her father's people, renowned weavers and dyers, and imbued with his magic. It kept her warm and dry no matter the weather, helpful for the craggy mountains of Balmirra, so high that even in the depths of summer, it was rarely ever hot.

Sighing with relief, she let her glamour fall, and the cool night air kissed her warm cheeks.

Don't forget to set your wards, Oberon reminded her. They wouldn't stop someone from getting into her room—after breaking the lock, of course—but it would hinder them the needed moments for her to throw on her glamour.

Yes yes, nanny goat.

Oberon huffed. *Only two legs and yet, somehow, you are by far the most troublesome of all my foals.*

3

Vallek had barely taken his throne before the delegation from Kaldebrak was led into Ninevar's Basilica. Punctual, as always. He expected nothing less from Chieftain Kennum's people.

The second-largest of all the orcish cities, Kaldebrak was another marvel of orcish engineering. Built straight into its mountain, the city was a trove of iron ore, copper, and silver. The smiths of Kaldebrak rivaled those of Balmirra, tooling exquisite filigree and forging mighty blades.

That Kennum had allied with him without a single crossbow bolt being fired Vallek considered one of the most important achievements of his reign. If anyone could have opposed Vallek and his vision, it was Kennum in Kaldebrak.

The two united cities, occupying the northern and southern orcish territories, made a compelling argument for all in between to join their ranks.

The Balmirran court had gathered to see the delegation from Kaldebrak, most of the empty space between the thick red limestone pillars crowded with finely dressed orcs. The wealth of the city was on display, every paladin dripping in fine silks and silvers, expertly tooled gorgets and torques round their necks declaring house and rank, and there were hardly any earlobes to be seen, every ear studded with golden hoops announcing achievement and position.

Although he found the whole display a tad pompous, Vallek himself rarely standing on ceremony outside of official functions, the sight of the court still stirred his pride. They were rich and content, and it wasn't just the nobles and officials who benefitted from Balmirra's prosperity. Even in the lowest quarters of the city, Vallek's people were cared for. Everyone was clothed and had shelter, all had access to water and food. Those who needed it were given work through the city's many industries; those who required it were given medical aid in any one of over a dozen healing houses.

His people paid him with their loyalty and hard work. He repaid them with his care. They wanted for nothing.

That was what the delegation from Kaldebrak saw as they entered the basilica—a prosperous city, full of successful orc-kin. And at the very top of it all was him, Vallek Far-Sight, ready to welcome all to take part in the success. The price was loyalty—not an unreasonable fee, in his opinion.

Three officials sent by Kennum walked at the head of a retinue of Kaldebraker warriors. Several of them carried boxes and baskets, no doubt full of gifts, and one official had a set of scrolls tucked under her arm.

The party halted at the foot of the steps leading up to his throne, and as one the group bowed low to him. Vallek nodded, acknowledging their deference.

"I welcome you to Balmirra, my lords and ladies. I trust your journey was swift."

Straightening, the frontmost and eldest of the officials, an orc Vallek knew as Rulf said, "Indeed, my king. Our chieftain sent us off with fine weather, and we bring it with us to you."

"Much obliged. The people will thank you for the break in thunderstorms; we're all sick of the hail."

Rulf and his underlings made the appropriate noises of commiseration, and a few more pleasantries were exchanged before the old orc waved for the boxes and baskets to be brought forward.

"Please accept these gifts from our chieftain, a token of our cities' continued friendship."

Five warriors brought their loads and placed them on the dais steps. Lids were lifted to reveal the glitter of gold, gems, and breathtaking metalwork. Vallek leaned down to inspect, lifting a particularly large sapphire from a box. Cut and polished, it took up most of his palm, and holding it up to the light rendered the red banners of his hall a deep plum.

"Exquisite. Please write to your lord conveying my thanks. These will be the treasure of Balmirra."

Like most gifts he received, some would be added to the citadel's coffers, while the rest would be given to the people. He would be sure to tell the officials who passed out the wealth to inform the people of the gift from Chieftain Kennum.

Fostering good relations between not only him and Kennum but also their people was vital.

They were all orcs. Kin.

"I most certainly will, my king. Thank you." Holding out his hand to the assistant on his right, one of the scrolls she carried was placed in Rulf's waiting palm. Unfurling it, he said, "Our chieftain wishes to offer one more gift, if it would please you, my king."

"Indeed. He's already been far too magnanimous." With a nod, he invited the official to speak.

"Our chieftain has been blessed many times over with the gift of his seven daughters. As a sign of our friendship and alliance, Kennum Green-Fist offers you the hand of one of his four unmated daughters to take as your queen."

Vallek could feel Eydis's gaze fall on him from where she stood to the side of the dais, but he didn't meet it. More than a few gasps and murmurs fluttered through the court, although Vallek found it hard to believe anyone was truly surprised by the news. He certainly wasn't.

With so many unmated daughters, it was only a matter of time before the old fox positioned one of them to rule alongside Vallek.

He and Eydis had talked many times over this very scenario, predicting that it was likely why Kennum had been so amenable to an alliance in the first place. Installing one of his daughters as queen would ensure Kaldebrak's continued influence throughout the territories.

In all their discussions, Vallek had never found himself entirely opposed to the idea. Surely, he could find at least one tolerable.

He'd never come close to mating or marrying, but as he continued to rally more clans and banners to his side, the question of who would sit beside him on the throne only grew.

Eydis had warned him he would soon need to choose.

Kennum's offer was a good one. A smart one. However, Vallek anticipated a similar offer to come from Chieftain Hrothgar of Innrinhom any time now. Well, perhaps it was little more than wishful thinking, but Vallek was willing to give the old battleaxe a bit more time to pull his gray head out of his arse.

Innrinhom was the most serious threat to Vallek's unification, its chieftain a sly old soldier who never bowed to anyone. Vallek wasn't the first chieftain of Balmirra to seek unification of the clans, but Innrinhom always proved a holdout.

Though not as large as Balmirra or Kaldebrak, Innrinhom was still formidable and occupied an important strategic territory near the Shanago River. Built atop a steep escarpment overlooking the river plain below, it was sheltered deep within an ancient forest. Innrinhom had the unique distinction amongst orcish cities of never having been sacked, by orc nor any other race. Hrothgar's line traced itself all the way back to the ancestors who first stepped from the ships, unbroken through the centuries as it ably ruled the eastern territories.

The Innrini were proud and stubborn. Vallek didn't relish the thought of trying to take that which had never been seized by force.

He'd much rather find a diplomatic solution, and if that meant taking an Innrini bride, he was at least open to the idea.

An Innrini bride and queen would mean that none of Kennum's daughters sat on the throne, though.

There had been those chieftains who took multiple spouses, of course. And it wasn't rare to find bonded mates of three or even four. Still, he doubted Kennum or Hrothgar would appreciate his rationale.

Rubbing his jaw, Vallek said, "I know Chieftain Kennum is fond of all his daughters—to offer to part with even one is more than generous. I will consider it with the gravity it deserves."

He could almost hear Eydis's sigh of relief. They needed to discuss this and form a plan of action. Prevarication wasn't Vallek's preferred strategy, but he had far too much to lose now. He wouldn't risk unification and all his work on the wrong bride.

Another evening, another goblet of mead, and another bout of *talfon* with his soothsayer. Vallek enjoyed his meads and sweet wines, but a king needed his wits about him, and so only indulged in one cup a night, once all the day's business had been sorted. He let the honeyed liquid rest on his tongue a moment, savoring the lush richness of its buttery base and notes of elderflower, before swallowing it down.

He was savoring the game, too. He wasn't sure when exactly he'd begun his bouts with the soothsayer; something in him had recognized the sharp mind and wit she hid beneath that thick cloak of hers. Vallek admired boldness, and it required heaps of such nerve to have marched into his camp demanding a position in his court.

He still couldn't say precisely what had convinced him. Her little predictions that night in the camp could have easily been parlor tricks. Ulrich certainly had been in favor of leaving her tied to the nearest tree as they decamped the next day, and Vallek rarely if ever broke with Ulrich. They had been of one mind since they were young warriors, training together under the tyranny of Mordis. Cantankerous as he could be, Ulrich was loyal, and that was what counted to Vallek.

Still, he couldn't deny the allure of a soothsayer. Halfway through their journey back to Balmirra, she proved her worth, predicting an attack from a band of outlaws. The human bandits quickly turned tail and ran when they saw how great a force Vallek had at his back—he never traveled anywhere with less than a hundred of his berserkers. So while they may never have been in danger from a roving band of human buffoons, the soothsayer had proven her skills.

Each new vision had only solidified her usefulness. She correctly predicted where Pyrrossi settlers would encroach on their eastern borders, as well as over a dozen particularly bad storms. Given the notice, Vallek could dispatch his troops to drive off the settlers as well as warn his people to take shelter.

She'd been invaluable time and again, and Vallek was grateful to her for helping hasten the unification, as well as keeping his people safe.

None of that meant he needed to form a friendship with her, though.

That had come of its own accord—and as quite a surprise to him.

Vallek hadn't formed such an attachment without a bit of information, of course. Eydis watched over the soothsayer carefully, and he knew Ulrich was always suspicious. Between the two of them, if the human meant Vallek, Balmirra, or any orc any harm, they would have known it by now.

So, not too long into their acquaintance, Vallek had invited her to play *talfon* with him.

Perhaps at first it'd been a way to figure her out. Vallek understood the critical importance of information, and he had to know everything about those closest to him. Assassination was more the style of the dragons, but it wasn't unheard of within the orc-kin. And he was no ordinary chieftain. He'd more than a few enemies within his own kind, let alone outside his borders.

Much could be gleaned about a person based on the way they

played *talfon*. Some had no patience for the game at all. Which set they chose to field often implied underlying character traits, such as who might be more cautious. How did they handle the ebb and flow of the game—and most importantly, how did they handle losing?

Seeing how she lost every bout they played, Vallek would say his soothsayer handled it admirably.

Perhaps what had him coming back was an itching fascination. Why did she not use her gift to predict his moves? Did the gift not work like that, or was it that such predictions sapped the thrill from the game?

Whatever her reasons, he enjoyed her company. And that he won. It was another burning question of his whether she always let him win—he'd begun to keep a tally of games he won outright and which he suspected she threw.

According to the tallies, they were evenly matched.

Peering at her over the rim of his cup, Vallek considered his opponent.

She may have been beautiful once, to human eyes. She was soft in the way humans seemed to favor, with downturned eyes and a small mouth. Fine wrinkles lined her forehead and fanned from the corners of her eyes, hinting at her age. Her skin was a deep tan, but he couldn't say whether that was because of years in the sun or hailing from more southerly climes.

He couldn't say much about her at all, really. She never spoke of her life before, other than a few allusions to a lost family. Eydis suspected from her accent that she'd grown up along the western coast, perhaps even amongst the islands known as the Scales. Ulrich despised not knowing more of her story, and perhaps Vallek too should have been bothered by it.

He just . . . wasn't.

Nothing about her seemed threatening to him, and she'd proven her loyalty and usefulness tenfold. What he'd come to learn about her from their evenings spent playing *talfon* was that he enjoyed her conversation, relished her cutting wit, and looked forward to watching her sharp mind at work.

After years with only Ulrich and his sisters as friends, it was an indulgent pleasure to have something of a friend in his soothsayer. He need not be king or chieftain, and she need not reveal her painful past. They could leave that all behind for a few pleasant hours, chatting and drinking.

Would he enjoy the company of his bride like this, he wondered?

The thought was unwelcome, but it stuck to his mind like a burr to a boot.

In truth, he hadn't much considered marriage or mating. There had been far too many things to do to secure the safety of Balmirra and the orcish territories. Like most orcs, he hoped that his mate, the one who stirred the inner beast all orcs had—a base set of instincts they feared and revered, one that goaded them to fight and to fuck—would find her way to him someday.

A mate would certainly ease the sticky business of marriage. However she came to him, finding her and feeling his beast clamor for her would settle the matter—orcs respected the mate-bond above all things. There was little more fearsome or feared in this world than a bonded orc defending their mate.

Having his own would put to rest any ambitions others might have of gaining a throne through his bed—others like, say, Lady Silvia. It would also ensure that he could trust his queen. She wouldn't be a princess from another territory, loyal first to her city and people—she would be *his* mate, loyal to *him*. Because they were mates.

Vallek liked the simplicity of it. He also liked the idea that fucking one's mate was the highest pleasure any orc could hope to achieve.

The smallest purr rattled in his chest at the thought. Yes, he liked the idea of fucking his own mate, of spreading her out on his big, magnificent bed and mussing the sheets. His bed was plenty big for two.

He'd indulged in a few discreet liaisons through the years, of course.

There was nothing like returning home triumphant, high on victory, and sinking his cock into a warm, welcoming cunt as the orcess screamed his name. And there had been plenty of other nights when he was merely lonely, his arms restless to hold another against him as he slept.

A mate would be all of those things and more.

Sighing, Vallek slumped back in his seat, swirling the mead in his cup. All these thoughts of mates . . . perhaps he was getting lonely again. He hadn't taken a lover in . . . gods, it'd been years now. Perhaps that, with the delegation's proposal of a bride, had him wanting.

Marrying a daughter of Kaldebrak or Innrinhom would present possible . . . complications if he ever did find his mate. Or, perhaps, could the gods bless him one last time, could he dare to hope that one of them might stir his beast?

Now there was a thought.

As the golden liquid swirled, Vallek seriously considered it. What if he had all the daughters of Kennum and Hrothgar brought before him? Surely neither chieftain would protest his choosing the daughter who stirred his beast. If none did, well then, they could resume their negotiations.

But if one did . . .

"It's your turn, my king."

Vallek looked up from his ruminations. His soothsayer sat patiently as she always did, her face open and neutral.

He could . . .

But did he dare?

Catching the nail of his thumb on the rim of his cup, he considered it.

"I wonder, *kone* . . ."

Her brows lifted with interest. "Yes, my king?"

"Have any of your visions been of my bride? Of who I will take as queen?"

A choked sound erupted from her throat, although he hadn't seen her drink. She clapped her hands over her mouth, her eyes wide in horror.

Shaking her head, she dropped her hands and his gaze.

Intrigued by the sudden shift, Vallek leaned forward in his seat, folding his arms on the table before him.

"Well?"

Her head rose suddenly, her cowl falling backwards in her haste. A mysterious fire burned in her eyes, and through pursed lips she told him succinctly, "No."

"No, what?"

"No, I don't see your bride." She almost spat the last word, as though it were an insult.

"You didn't even look." He didn't know much about her power or how it worked, but he knew what she looked like while she had a vision. It only took a few moments, but in that short span, she was gone entirely. Eyes distant, face relaxed. Her expression had been nothing but pinched since he'd asked.

Her little nostrils flared in a huff. "I haven't seen any bride in my visions of you," she amended.

"But you could look."

"No."

"No?" She'd never refused him before. "No, you can't? Or no, you won't?"

Her jaw worked, and for a moment, Vallek thought she wouldn't answer him at all.

Finally, her shoulders dropped from where they'd scrunched up to her ears, and she closed her eyes. Quiet fell between them, but it wasn't one of the comfortable silences he'd come to enjoy, where they mulled their next move.

He couldn't quite tell, with her eyes closed, whether she truly used her gift. Her body went a little more lax, but otherwise, she sat still in her chair.

It was a long while before she spoke, and Vallek waited impatiently. He couldn't decide which disturbed him more—her denial or her defiance. She'd shown him neither before, and both displeased him.

Finally, she lifted her head, although when her eyes opened, she wouldn't meet his gaze.

"I don't see anyone, my king."

"No one at all?"

Chewing her cheek, she admitted, "None."

Vallek frowned and stood from the table. No bride? Could that really be true?

Turning from their game, Vallek put some distance between him and his soothsayer. He'd never disliked one of her fortunes—or lack thereof—before.

So accustomed now to successes and triumphs, disappointment sat bitter at the back of his tongue. He didn't want to swallow it.

"It's late," he said. "You may go."

Still refusing to look him in the eye, the soothsayer stood. She didn't jump from her seat and dash away as he half-expected her to, but she did flee after a polite bob of her head.

"Goodnight," she muttered and then was gone.

Vallek stood in place for a while longer, not wanting to face the possibility of what this could mean. The idea of a life alone stretched out before him, a vast emptiness that his soul raged against.

No. No, that couldn't be true.

Could she be wrong? Or perhaps not have had a vision yet? Perhaps her gift wasn't as precise as she'd led him to believe.

Perhaps if there wasn't a bride in his future . . . could that mean there was a mate instead? Why would she not tell him if so? She'd never requested he be precise in his semantics before.

A tendril of suspicion brushed his cheek. Did she lie? And if so, had she lied before?

His beast rumbled unhappily and unhelpfully, the questions roiling inside him worse than heartburn. He could ask her, he supposed. Whether she saw a *mate* in his future.

But did he want to know her answer?

4

"It was just sudden is all. He's never asked about anything like that before. I don't know that he's even taken a lover in years." Ravenna hoped, the more she prattled on about the other night and the awkward way it'd ended, that she might start to believe it was less disastrous than it felt.

She was deluding herself, of course. The moment the question fell from his lips, the possessive fae inside her had viciously hissed a denial—*there's no one for you but me*. It'd taken all her will to keep her magic from leaping across the table to wrap itself around him in a proprietary vice. Honestly, if he hadn't dismissed her, she might have fled of her own volition.

Perhaps it was for the best. She could serve him and oversee her goals without nightly games wherein she found and hoarded every new little discovery about him. She would miss his company, but she didn't *need* it. Or him.

Oberon blew her hair back in a smug huff. *You're jealous.*

Ravenna looked up from her lap, where she'd been stringing daisies together into a little flower crown, to glare at the chortling stallion bastard. "I am *not* jealous."

Oberon dipped his horn in a mocking gesture. *You're so very jealous.*

"No. I was *surprised.*"

The unicorn had the audacity to throw his head back and whinny a great horsey laugh. Ravenna pouted as he made a fool of himself, prancing around and laughing. The rest of the herd looked on in amusement as they selected tender grass from the tufts bursting out of every rocky crag and crevice.

Over a league out from the city, the rocky hills and windswept plains could be a dangerous place. Snow leopards occasionally came down from the mountains, and wolves were known to prowl the plains, but amongst over a dozen unicorns, Ravenna had nothing to fear. So far, all she'd seen were a few marmots poking their heads from their burrows and an eagle circling above looking for easy prey.

And the big dumb unicorn, of course.

"How father ever rode into battle with *you* is beyond me," she muttered.

Your father knew to respect his elders and listen to good advice. Pawing the rocky ground with a hoof, Oberon told her, *You are too stubborn for your own good, Crow. Tell him who you are to him.*

"Absolutely not," she argued. "A man like Vallek will want to have his way. He'll only get in the way of my plans."

Someone should, he grumbled.

Ravenna rolled her eyes. "I don't want to argue about this again."

I think between a rock and your head, the latter is the harder of the two. Oberon shook out his mane in exasperation. *Goddesses deliver me from idiotic foals.*

"I'm not an idiot for wanting revenge."

No, but you are an idiot for throwing your life away on it. You have found your azai. He's strong and can protect you. Make a life for yourself with him, put aside your revenge, and live. It's what your parents would want.

That was all true, of course, but Ravenna wouldn't give him the satisfaction of admitting it. Sighing, she turned her true face up to the summer sun, relishing the warmth on her skin. She always enjoyed visiting Oberon and the herd, even if it came with a lecture. Getting out from the confines of the city, letting her glamour drop, was an indulgence she never took for granted.

"I may not be able to visit for a while," she said, ignoring how Oberon's ears swung backwards at her obvious avoidance. "With the king back in the city, there are more eyes."

Mostly two, both of which belonged to the lord commander. Ugh. She didn't know what'd gotten Ulrich's kilt in a twist about her, but he was determined to root out all her secrets.

How long do you intend to keep up this ruse? Oberon demanded.

"As long as it takes. It's not so bad."

The unicorn huffed. *And do you—*

Leave the foal alone, Obi. Callistix came to stand alongside her, nudging Ravenna's shoulder with her muzzle.

Someone has to talk sense into her, mother.

Head bobbing, Callistix asked, *Who is more senseless—the one who seeks revenge or the one who keeps trying the same argument to no avail?*

Ravenna giggled under her hand as Oberon's tail swished. *I'm merely keeping my promise to her father to keep her alive.*

Here she is. Alive. Callistix hooked the shaft of her horn beneath Ravenna's chin, lifting her head so she could see more of her. *Looks to be healthy.*

For now, Oberon groused. *That's liable to change the longer she denies her* azai *and continues down a path that leads to Amaranthe.*

We will sort that out when we near it. There's no use fussing over it now.

Ravenna patted Callistix's leg. "Thank you, grandmare," she said, lifting her woven flower crown to hook over the unicorn's horn.

Callistix let the flowers fall onto her forelock, and Ravenna swore the mare stood a little taller.

Perhaps it was unorthodox to call a unicorn *grandmare*—and even more so for the unicorn to allow it—but Callistix was the closest thing to a grandmother Ravenna had ever known. As a halfling, she'd hardly been tolerated in her mother's human family. It didn't help that all the human kin Aine had known had already passed long before Ravenna was born; Aine's great-great-grandnieces and -nephews found her and her halfling child at best an oddity.

It only isolated Aine in that seaside cottage further. Ravenna became Aine's whole world, her bulwark against the tide of sadness whenever Maxim had to go away.

A soft breath ruffled her hair, and Callistix dropped her head, allowing Ravenna to pet her velveteen muzzle.

You're my favorite, you know.

Ravenna grinned smugly. "I know."

Mother—

Now, tell me more about this plan of yours with the spiders.

It was difficult leaving the herd. Two new foals had been born just that spring, and there was always news and gossip to learn whenever she visited. However, the hour grew late, and the sun began to drop. The longer summer day granted her a little more time, but eventually she had to follow her feet back to Balmirra.

Bidding farewell to the herd, Oberon and the new foals walked with her part of the way, but she sent them back when they neared the bend in the path that would make them visible to the city garrison. The watchtowers glittered in the sun with the many scopes pointed in every direction, hunting for incoming threats, and the enmity between orcs and unicorns was ancient.

Please be safe, Oberon said before turning back.

I will, I promise.

He huffed an affectionate breath in her face, warming her cheeks, and she kissed his muzzle.

Good evening, Crow.

Goodnight, Oberon the Put-Upon.

You aren't funny! he called after her, but she only laughed and waved.

The path she followed was a small one that wended and wove around the shallow rises of the craggy scrubland that characterized the land to the east of Balmirra. Hares bounded and wrens fluttered about in the late afternoon, and she thought she spotted the triangular ears of a fox not far off the path.

As the great shadow of the city fell upon her, Ravenna lifted her cowl and put on her false face. Although there was nothing truly corporeal about the glamour, it still stuck to her like a film, a layer she could sense just above her own skin. She'd gotten so used to wearing it now, she hardly felt it anymore, and maintaining it for long periods wasn't so taxing.

Thankfully King Vallek didn't require her presence for more than a few meetings with his generals and their evening games of *talfon,* so, alone in her room, Ravenna could wear her own face for a while. However, she was always careful to eat and bathe at times less popular with his other staff, and whenever she ventured into the city proper, she kept her face hidden deep within her cowl.

Of course, her height marked her as other. But the orcs of Balmirra had grown used to her presence by now, as she was a common sight in the lower city's bazaars. The king paid her a tidy allowance, which she used to buy threads for embroidering, sweet-smelling oils for candles and lotions, and once in a while little honey cakes or sugar cubes for the herd. Between the embroidering and pack of cards she'd brought with her from the bower, she kept herself fairly entertained in her comfortable little room in the royal quarters.

She couldn't say she'd made any friends or allies in the city per se; most were wary of her, worried perhaps that she might tell them an inauspicious fortune. Still, her money was good, so she procured what she wanted. The bazaars were also excellent places to gather information, and she always kept her ears out for news of the faelands.

The orcs and fae had always been fractious neighbors, but it was a time of at least tenuous peace, so some trade was managed at the borders. The king and his warriors may have gotten round the kingdom, but it was the merchants and traders who knew the land best. They brought commodities and stories, each more valuable than the last.

Nothing of real note had come up in her eavesdropping, but she was hopeful. The everyday orcs of the bazaar knew and spoke of things never mentioned in Vallek's court, so it was worth visiting whenever she could.

The city loomed above her, her little path spilling into a wide packed-earth road that led right to the formidable curtain wall. The rounded scalloped edifice of the wall was broken only by the eastern gate, manned by a contingent of guards. The wall itself was four layers thick, successive additions by different chieftains. The third wall included crenellated ramparts for guards and archers, and conical watchtowers had been built into the fifth wall. Each layer combined into an impregnable defense, making Balmirra nigh on invincible. The bridge was drawn and the portcullises lowered at night, but she wasn't too late to hurry back inside the city.

At the gate, a guard stopped her. They all knew her on sight by now, but she still dutifully lifted the brooch at her neck, the crossed double axes of the king done in silver filigree. The guard nodded at it and waved her past.

She hadn't gone a handful of steps before she was stopped again.

Her breath caught in her throat as she looked up and up into Ulrich's sneering face.

"Out for a walk, were you?"

Ravenna hid her trembling hands within the folds of her cloak. She'd never faced him down outside the citadel before.

Had he followed her?

"Is that a crime now, lord commander?" she asked.

His nose wrinkled, and without warning, he tugged the cowl from her head.

"Don't touch me," she spat, hurriedly stepping outside his reach.

It would take more than that to break her glamour, but the sudden invasion of her space rattled her enough that she had to actively think about maintaining the disguise. Her mother's face glared right back at the lord commander, an expression Aine rarely if ever made in her own life.

Ulrich only grunted, eyes squinting as if to try and peel away her glamour.

Her guts went cold with the unnerving thought—*does he know?*

No, that was impossible.

He could suspect whatever he wanted. He couldn't prove anything.

"Jumpy," he accused.

"Do you often go around accosting women, commander?"

"You didn't answer my question. Where were you?"

"You asked me no such thing."

A tendon in his jaw ticked. "I'm asking you now."

Ravenna opened her mouth to tell him he hadn't, in fact, asked her then either but thought better of it. She *had* promised Oberon, and keeping herself safe didn't start with a night in the citadel's dark, dank dungeon.

"As you say, I went for a walk."

"All day?"

Ravenna smiled nastily. "Anxious for my return, were you?"

"You test my patience, wench. You may have the ear of our king, but that means nothing if I believe you to be a threat."

"I'm no such thing," she hissed. "I have only ever been loyal to our king. I've served him faithfully."

Ulrich grunted again, nostrils flaring. "Perhaps. Perhaps not."

Ravenna refused to rise to his bait, for she knew she'd done nothing to endanger or threaten King Vallek. Claimed or not, she would *never* seek to harm her own *azai*.

Ulrich was all hot air. The more concerning thing was why he made his threats and insinuations now?

"I don't know how to convince you, lord commander. That is something between you and your conscience. Now, are we done? I'm tired from my walk."

Leaning down, he leveled his gaze with hers. "Next time, don't go out so far or so long."

Biting her cheek so hard it nearly bled, Ravenna nodded.

He didn't move from her path, but he also didn't stop her when Ravenna righted her cowl and resumed walking, leaving a wide berth between them.

—mountain mist—a hundred thundering feet—blood sprayed upon the cliff-face—a commander's cry—

Ravenna halted as quickly as she'd started, the vision passing over her sight. It was a more enigmatic set of images, but she could extrapolate enough that she turned to meet his scowl again. The smile she gave him was downright evil, and she relished how his scowl slipped just a little with unease at the sight.

"I would avoid cliffs in future if I were you, my lord. Good evening."

Vallek was just finishing his work looking over missives from the townships around Lake Lovath when Ulrich found him. It was already fairly late, and Brynhíl had been good enough to bring his dinner to where he worked in the smaller council chamber. The remains of his food sat further down the table, his papers arrayed before him.

Fishing estimates were good, with hearty numbers of trout and pike, and taxes were flowing smoothly. Only a handful of criminal cases had needed his attention, as well as a few proposed town laws. All in all, the region of the southern Griegens was thriving, and Vallek was damn proud of it.

So when Ulrich came marching through the door, that burr-in-his-boot look on his face, Vallek could only sigh and bid his good mood farewell.

Pouring himself an indulgent second cup of his preferred sweet wine, Vallek said, "Good evening, lord commander."

For some reason, his greeting made Ulrich's eye twitch. Still, his friend was nothing if not a stickler for protocol and quickly regained his composure, bowing his head. "My king."

"Drink?"

"No, my king, but thank you."

Vallek arched a brow. "Well, out with it. What have you to say?"

Ulrich's lips thinned between his tusks in the way they did whenever he was about to tell Vallek something he didn't want to hear.

"I am newly returned from the wall, my king. I received word that the soothsayer left through the eastern gate late this morning."

Vallek set down his goblet, the wine in his belly turning acidic. "Where is she now?"

"She's returned to her chamber."

He nodded, not quite understanding where his second was going with this information. "And is this the first time she's left the city?"

"No, my king. She seems to venture outside every few days."

"And what did she have to say about her adventures?"

A sneer twisted Ulrich's lips, an expression Vallek found disturbing. His second was usually so composed and matter-of-fact, so to see such a venomous look alarmed him.

"Nothing of use, of course. She's slippery, never giving a straight answer."

Vallek made a noncommittal noise in his throat. He wasn't surprised, given how little the soothsayer liked his second. For whatever reason, the two of them had never liked each other. Vallek didn't require his friends and allies to like each other, but they did have to work toward their common goal. If that was compromised by rivalry or enmity, then it became his problem.

Considering his second carefully, he asked, "What is it you suspect her of?"

Face pinched, Ulrich admitted, "I don't know yet, my king. But there is something about her I mistrust." Straightening, he met Vallek's gaze gravely. "I ask for your permission to question her further and again send inquiries to our contacts in the border villages about her."

His immediate instinct was to deny the request. The rejection clamored in his throat, far more vehement than it had any right to be. Ulrich's reasoning was sound—it had always been Vallek who'd been less careful about the soothsayer. Anyone else would have required far more inquiries into her background to be allowed so close to him.

That wasn't to say Ulrich hadn't already made such inquiries. He had—and found nothing. Suspiciously nothing.

Eydis too had sussed out what she could about the human seer and gotten just as far. Yet, she'd never harbored any great suspicions about her. *"I like her well enough,"* she'd once said, *"and if she meant you any harm, we would have found out by now."*

So Vallek had grown complacent, choosing to ignore any possibility that his soothsayer was anything but a kindly human woman in his service.

He liked her.

That was the root of it.

But, as he should well know by now, fondness and affection couldn't supersede caution and good sense for a king.

"You truly think she's a threat to me?"

Likely sensing hesitation where there hadn't been before, Ulrich's eyes gleamed, and he stepped forward, nodding zealously. "I cannot yet say whether she's a true threat, but there is much she hasn't told us.

We must know if anything in her past could pose a danger to you."

Again, Vallek wished to tell Ulrich no. To leave it alone.

And yet, he couldn't get the previous night from his head. *No, I don't see your bride.*

How could she not see? Or why did she choose not to look? His beast wouldn't let him believe he was destined to occupy his throne and bed alone forever, and neither did his mind. The position of queen, of ruling beside him, was perhaps the single most influential political tool he had, and he couldn't afford to waste it.

So why didn't she see?

"You may ask her more questions and look further into the matter," he said. "But you will do so discreetly and with all due respect."

He hated the words the moment they left his mouth, even softened as they were with his caveat to be civil.

Even more, he hated the triumphant grin Ulrich wore. Vallek wanted to punch it right off his face.

Reaching for his goblet, Vallek downed the rest of his wine in one gulp. He needed his magnificent bed and a long night's sleep if he was truly wishing to strike his oldest friend over a matter so small.

But even with the wine and Ulrich's departure, Vallek and his beast found no solace from the prickle of regret already itching beneath his skin. Grumpily, he suspected he wouldn't until the matter was resolved.

5

The late summer night was stiflingly hot, even for Ravenna. There was little to do other than open the latch of her narrow window to coax in even the slightest breeze. Laying on her cot with a damp cloth over her face in only her night shift and trying to move as little as possible was her best strategy. She wanted desperately to fall asleep, for there was no chance of entertaining herself with embroidery or reading in this kind of heat, but such escape eluded her.

Is the herd all right? she asked Oberon, desperate for something to focus on other than how sweat slid down her temples and pooled between her breasts.

Quite so. It is pleasant outside of those musty rooms you two-leggeds insist upon. We found a lake nearby to soak in.

Ravenna groaned with jealousy. *That sounds like perfection.*

She could have stolen down to the baths, of course, but in the wake of Ulrich's questioning, she didn't dare. Especially since she hadn't been summoned to another evening of *talfon* with King Vallek in over a fortnight.

Which was all right. Just fine. It wasn't that she minded or missed him. Not *at all.*

It was just worrying, the coincidental timing.

So best to stay in her room and expose herself to as few risks as possible. No doubt the king would leave again soon, taking Ulrich with him, and they could all put these suspicions and questions of his future bride to bed.

Ravenna groaned again at *brides* and *beds* in the same thought. The heat did nothing to help her constant lusting after Balmirra's ruler. She'd been told all her life what a blessing finding one's *azai* was—how it didn't happen for all fae. Her mother and father had shared a uniquely beautiful love story, according to them and Allarion, although Ravenna had never wished to find a mate and relationship like her parents'. Ravenna wasn't soft and patient in the way Aine was; Ravenna was spiteful, prideful, and quick to temper. She'd always tried to quell these traits, at least in front of her mother, and never relished the idea of having an *azai* who scolded her for it as her father did.

Something told her that Vallek wouldn't mind her fire. Perhaps that was fantasy; perhaps he preferred soft, obedient partners. But this was Ravenna's fantasy, and she based her guess on how he seemed to enjoy their exchange of wit over the game board.

That smug grin of his was always her undoing. How it stretched between his sharp tusks, a complement to his brow arched just so and a twinkle of amusement in his intense, uncanny eyes. The way he filled up his chair, limbs spread in a loose show of comfortable confidence, thick wrists laid on the table, big fingers playing with the gaming pieces.

How would those fingers feel on her skin?

Ravenna sucked in a needy breath and closed up her link to Oberon. He could batter through it if truly needed, but for now, he didn't need to know just how much she missed her mate.

She blamed it on the heat, of course, as she gathered the hem of her thin nightgown to her waist. Her skin was supple and damp with sweat, and when she reached between her legs, she found her cunt already slick with want of him.

Damn it all, she cursed as her fingers began to move. She'd promised herself she'd stop doing this—at least to thoughts of him. Her need was always worse when he was home in Balmirra, knowing he was only a few corridors and staircases away.

Her fangs ached something fierce as her fingers deftly skated over her needy flesh. Sweat gathered behind her knees and under her breasts, but she couldn't stop now. Overheated and agitated and bored, there was nothing for it than to give herself to her imagination.

He would lay her down on that great big bed of his, careful of her wings. She'd fill her hands with the meaty muscle of his chest, digging her claws into the supple green skin. He wouldn't come down to her immediately, oh no, he enjoyed leaning over her, seeing her squirm with need of him too much. Balanced on one arm, he used his other hand to gather her skirts and hike them high. The whisper of fabric over her skin left her shuddering and gooseflesh in its wake. He would rumble, pleased at the sight she made.

"Touch me," she'd tell him, for she refused to beg. Yet.

"In good time," he'd reply, those lapis-lazuli eyes dancing with heat and pleasure.

His big hands made gentle passes up her legs, feeling how her muscles jumped beneath her skin at his touch. His nostrils flared, no doubt catching the thick scent of her arousal, of her need for him—*thick fingers slid inside her, first one and then two—a big hand grabbed the back of her knee to spread her wide, wider than she'd ever been—her wings fluttered beneath her, a strange melody—azai—and he rumbled with pleasure.*

"That's it," he'd say, "come for me."

And Ravenna did. Her fingers worked frantically over her clitoris and cunt, stringing out her pleasure for as long as she could bear it. She didn't know where fantasy ended and vision began, but it didn't matter. She came and came, body spasming with release, his name on her lips.

The thought of him left her in a sweaty heap on the bed, her hand still tucked against her weeping cunt as it throbbed in aftershocks. Hair plastered to her scalp and her shoulders with sweat, Ravenna panted for breath.

Fates, she was weak. Too weak. He needed to leave again, and soon. For both of their sakes.

She'd just rolled to her side and reached for a fresh cloth to clean up when something smashed against her door.

Ravenna sprung from the bed and turned her back to the door.

"Open up, in the name of the lord commander!" a male shouted on the other side.

No chance.

Ravenna used the precious few moments she had to set her glamour. It wasn't perfect, sitting uncomfortably on her sweaty skin, but when the door burst open, splinters raining from where the lock had once been, it was Aine's face that stared at the incoming soldiers in shock.

At least five warriors poured into her tiny room, taking up all the air, before the lord commander himself strutted in.

"What is the meaning of this?" she demanded.

Ulrich lifted the lamp he carried, shining it into her eyes. Ravenna glared at him, not sure if they were hers or her mother's eyes, but she was too angry to care.

The lord commander's nostrils flared, and to her horror, she realized all the sensitive orc noses could scent what she'd been doing. Still, she refused to flush or pale or flinch. This was *her* room, she could do as she liked.

"Search it," Ulrich commanded his men.

Ravenna watched as the warriors went to work stripping and tearing apart her room. The mattress was upended, every sheet and blanket pulled away. The pillows were ripped from their covers, every scrap of clothing she owned was pulled from her small trunk, and her handful of books were each tossed onto her small table for Ulrich to rifle through.

Clenching her fists, she made herself stand still as the big bodies buffeted her. But when someone pulled out her cloak, the midnight blue fabric gleaming in the low lamplight, Ravenna couldn't bear it.

"Don't touch that," she spat, grabbing the cloak out of the warrior's surprised hands.

"Everything must be searched," Ulrich said in an almost bored tone.

Clutching the cloak to her chest, she bared her teeth at the lord commander. If they wanted it, they'd have to pry it from her scratching, vicious hands.

"How dare you?" Ravenna demanded, using her outrage to quell her tears. "You can't just—"

"I *can*," Ulrich corrected. "I am lord commander of this city, and the king's safety is my most sacred duty."

"I'm *not* a threat to the king."

Ulrich spared her a glance. "Everyone is subject to inspection."

"This isn't inspection, this is intimidation."

"If you like."

A furious noise erupted from her throat, but there was nothing Ravenna could do. Forced to wallow in her helplessness, she watched on as every single one of her things was touched, shaken, pored over, and even ransacked.

Eventually, one of the warriors came for her cloak. She backed up into the wall, shaking her head.

"Don't be difficult, mistress," the warrior said, not unkindly.

Lips pursed, Ravenna held up the cloak for him to see, turning it back and forth and shaking it out. "It's just a cloak, nothing t-to see," she said, horrified when her voice began to break.

The warrior, perhaps not unsympathetic, allowed her to hold it up as he quickly ran his hands over it, checking for secret pockets. When he found nothing and stepped back, Ravenna snatched the cloak to her chest again, shielding herself with it.

With so many bodies crammed into her tiny room, and with very little to truly inspect, the process took less than a handful of minutes. It felt much longer.

Seething, Ravenna glared again at the lord commander—only to jump forward when she saw what he had in his hands.

Her mother's grimoire.

Leatherbound and far more well-loved than her other books, the grimoire was her most treasured possession apart from her cloak. She and Aine had painstakingly filled the pages together with recipes, knitting patterns, instructions on how to do the many things Aine had taught her, and even little spells and incantations to help Ravenna remember how best to use her magic.

It was all her mother's knowledge, bound up in one precious book. And now *he* held it.

"Give that back," she said, knowing that it was a mistake but unable to help it.

Ulrich arched one imperious brow. "This is a strange book," he said. "I'll need to confiscate it for further inspection."

"No! It's nothing, just recipes!"

"Then no need to fret. If it's truly so benign, it will be returned to you soon."

The look he cast her was vicious, even though he grinned. His triumph over her was ugly, and Ravenna clenched every muscle in her body to keep from setting upon him like a beast. He was her enemy now—she'd carve it into her very flesh and bones. One day, she would see his downfall.

Her magic snapped against her fingers, desperate to be unleashed, but she buried her nails in the cloth of the cloak.

Not yet. Not yet.

A time would come.

"I won't ever forget this, lord commander," she said, satisfied when more than one warrior shivered at her words.

Ulrich only frowned. "You're in no place to be making threats, woman."

"It's not a threat. It's a promise."

"Hmph." Looking over her head, he nodded at his warriors. "Fall out."

The warriors left in a neat line, a sharp contrast to how they'd entered and the state they left her room in. Ulrich made up the rear, stopping only to grasp the broken door.

"Expect to hear from me soon," he said before pulling the door shut.

It didn't close, the latch broken off, leaving a crack of space and a hole on the side where the lock had been.

Ravenna stood shaking, alone in her ruined room. Voices muttered out in the hallway, no doubt the entire staff awoken by the noisy raid, but no one dared to knock on her door.

That was all right. She didn't need anyone's pity.

Alone amongst her ruined things, tears streamed down her face, angry tears that burned hotter than the summer heat. Knees buckling, she knelt on the floor and buried her face in her cloak.

She would make him pay for this. The lord commander would be getting far worse than spiders in his room, so help her.

6

Over the next three days, Ravenna's already tiny room, as well as the very walls of her already compact world, began to shrink. Although she never saw the lord commander, she felt his presence everywhere she went.

Whenever she left the violated, false safety of her chamber, it was under obvious surveillance. A guard didn't necessarily dog her steps, but one followed several paces behind wherever she went. To eat, to walk. When she tried to slip out to her favorite bazaar, one of the guards actually intercepted her. "Best to stay within the citadel for now, *kone.*"

A polite way to say she was under house arrest.

Ravenna bristled at the constraints, skin crawling with all the eyes on her. It wasn't just the guards. The staff looked at her askance now, when otherwise they might not have even noticed her walk past. Round every corner, in every room, all eyes darted to her, full of suspicion.

No doubt just what the lord commander wanted.

He intended to make her slip up.

Well, Ravenna hadn't come this far to lose to a worm like Ulrich. She made herself as unnoteworthy as possible, quiet and meek. She kept mostly to her room, despite Oberon's pleas for her to leave and come join the herd.

Ravenna even started sleeping in her disguise. She couldn't be sure she kept it in her sleep, but until she drifted off, she kept the glamour in place. It was exhausting, but she didn't dare let it slip. She couldn't even chance going down to the baths, and so in her small, overwarm room, Ravenna slowly cooked herself in her temper.

She blamed her exhaustion and smelliness for barking at whoever dared knock on her door one afternoon.

"What is it?"

The door, already open a crack since no one had bothered to come fix the lock, creaked as it opened wider. Into her room stepped King Vallek's elder sister, Lady Eydis. Dressed as she usually was in smart robes with crisp draping folds, her belt jangling with keys and pouches, and her hair swept behind her pointed ears into a neat plait that fell down the length of her back, she was far too elegant for Ravenna's small cell. Although never ostentatious, Lady Eydis still exuded dignity and affluence, several golden hoops glittering from both ears, a ceremonial gorget displaying her rank laying on her chest, and silver threads gleaming along the hems of her robes.

The sight of her here was so surprising, Ravenna forgot what she was meant to do for a full moment.

Finally gaining her feet, Ravenna bowed. "Forgive me, my lady, I wasn't expecting you."

"Quite all right." Eydis looked around the room, her keen gaze landing on the broken door. "There's a good story to this, I assume?"

Ravenna bit the inside of her cheek. She liked the king's sisters, clever Eydis and lively Asta, but wasn't sure where she stood anymore within Vallek's household. His sisters were just as loyal to him as Ulrich, if not more so, and Ravenna couldn't help but worry that the lord commander's sudden tightening of the screws were on direct order of their king.

If so, she couldn't count his elder sister as an ally.

Still, her confusion over the broken door seemed genuine.

Choosing her words carefully, Ravenna said, "The lord commander thought it the most expedient way of searching my room a few nights ago."

Lady Eydis's lips thinned. "I see." Looking over the door more critically, she said, "Some of the other staff have mentioned the greater . . . attention he's been paying you."

Ravenna just held onto her snort of derision. "It's hard to miss. I'm not sure what the lord commander hopes to find." A lie, of course, but Ravenna didn't care. If she could turn someone against Ulrich, she would.

"Ulrich is . . ." Lady Eydis sighed. "He's a determined man. He's actually why I'm here."

Ravenna's shoulders tensed, her folded wings trembling against her back.

"The lord commander has requested both of us for a meeting."

"Now?"

"It would seem so."

Trying not to pull a face, Ravenna nodded and took up her cloak. She couldn't hide her grimace as easily as she slipped on the heavy fabric and drew the cowl over her lank hair. The garment was stifling, but it helped with her disguise and hopefully masked some of her smell.

Perhaps not enough, though, as Lady Eydis couldn't hide her expression when Ravenna followed her out of the room.

"Forgive me, *kone,* but . . . have you not been shown to our baths? The ones beneath the citadel are open to all staff."

Ravenna's cheeks burned even through the glamour. Clearing her throat, she muttered, "I haven't felt comfortable going to the baths with the lord commander paying me so much attention."

Lady Eydis's brows snapped down into a forbidding frown. "That won't do." Stepping further out into the corridor, she called, "Bryn?"

After a moment, one of the older housekeepers appeared from her room. Brynhíl was the king's own housekeeper and oversaw all staff who served him and his family directly. She was as dignified as she was strong, her arms thick with muscle and her dark mane woven with streaks of silver. Kind brown eyes took the both of them in as she approached.

Bobbing her head in deference, Brynhíl asked, "My lady?"

Lady Eydis nodded at Ravenna's door. "Please see that this is fixed by tonight. And send for a hipbath to be put in her room and filled." Turning to Ravenna, she said, "It won't be warm, but it will be a bath."

Ravenna shook her head. "No, my lady, it's perfect. Thank you! You're too generous."

The orcess grinned ruefully. "I'm not, you just stink."

"I'm afraid to say you do," agreed Brynhíl.

A laugh burst from Ravenna, and although her flush of embarrassment only deepened, she didn't mind the teasing. As much as she'd never forget Ulrich's violation, she'd also never forget the orcesses' kindness.

"Thank you, still. I might never get out once I'm in."

They bid farewell to Brynhíl, on her way to find the citadel's locksmith, and instead turned to climb to one of the higher levels.

With every step, Ravenna lost her good humor. She chewed on her cheek and whether to ask if Lady Eydis knew what exactly this meeting was about.

Instead, the king's sister asked, "Do you mean to tell Vallek about all this?"

Ravenna sucked in a breath, considering. "No," she said finally, "not yet." She wasn't a helpless damsel, running off to plead for help at the first sign of trouble. She wasn't defenseless and intended to stand her ground.

And there wasn't an insignificant chance that Vallek had himself ordered it.

"I would consider it if this continues," Lady Eydis advised her. "Of course, I support keeping my brother safe, but you've given us no reason to doubt you. If Ulrich continues to be heavy-handed, tell the king."

"Wouldn't he already know?" Ravenna asked quietly.

Without hesitation, the orcess answered, "I doubt it. If Vallek has suspicions or doubts, he tends to meet them head on. Subterfuge isn't his way."

Well, that gave Ravenna a little heart. She didn't know if she believed it, for Ulrich didn't strike her as the type to do anything without the king's permission. He was too loyal, too obedient.

As if her mind had gone down the same path, Lady Eydis added, "I will say, though, to not make an enemy of Ulrich. He will protect my brother at all costs. If he finds a threat, he gets rid of it."

Ravenna could only nod. She didn't intend to heed Lady Eydis's warning, for she suspected she and the lord commander were already far beyond that line. Ulrich considered her a threat and hunted for evidence to prove it. Ravenna waited for a moment to exact revenge.

In the meantime, she would be patient. There was nothing for him to find.

Probably.

Her mother's grimoire was the only thing she could think of that might have the smallest scent of the suspicious. She knew it'd been a risk to bring with her, but the memories and knowledge it held were too great a value to leave behind.

The grimoire was written mostly in Eirean, the language of her mother. However, there were plenty of fae words peppered throughout. Ravenna could only hope that the lord commander wouldn't know the difference.

Vallek's curiosity over the request for a meeting with his lord commander only grew when his sister walked through the small council chamber door—with the soothsayer behind him. Ulrich didn't have to bother calling a meeting; if he had something to tell Vallek, he usually just did.

Standing up from his seat, Vallek exchanged puzzled looks with Eydis. It seemed she didn't know what this was about, either.

He didn't miss how the soothsayer stayed near the door. She was in her usual cloak and cowl, and although she'd always been markedly shorter than him and all other orcs, something about the way her wary gaze bounced between him, Ulrich, and Eydis made her look so much smaller. Reduced.

Vallek's curiosity bled into suspicion, which he preferred to focus on rather than the niggle of guilt nipping at his chest. He'd learned long ago that as a chieftain who aspired to kingship, he couldn't afford guilt. Not outwardly, at least.

"Is this all of us?" asked Eydis, her tone mild but her eyes sharp on Ulrich.

"Indeed, my lady." Striding around the great table where Vallek's council met every week to discuss the business of the city and kingdom, Ulrich stared down the soothsayer as he closed the distance between them. Without looking away, he locked the door, barring any quick escape.

"This is highly unusual, lord commander," Eydis complained.

"It's necessary," said Ulrich.

From a satchel slung across his shoulder he retrieved—a book. Placing it on the table, he opened the old, battered thing, revealing pages of browned ink. What looked like lists, songs, and sketches took up every bit of available space, the pages paying no heed to organization or margins.

"With your permission, my king, I confiscated this from the soothsayer's personal belongings. She claims it's just a recipe book, but it's full of spells and magic. There are faethling words."

The tanned skin of the soothsayer's cheeks paled. She held perfectly still, staring at the open grimoire.

"Her visions are magic," Eydis reasoned. "Is it not to be expected she'd have spells? She might even have a fae in her lineage."

"Fae are the enemy," Ulrich growled. Again he turned to loom over the soothsayer, blocking her in.

Vallek's feet moved before he could think, rounding the table carefully and drawing Eydis behind him. He wasn't sure which he thought more of a threat—his own lord commander, a gleam of obsession in his eye, or the accused soothsayer, her shoulders rounding at Ulrich's intensity.

"I am *not* an enemy," the soothsayer said, her voice quiet but firm.

Ulrich's upper lip peeled back, revealing the full length of his tusks. "You are a liar. A spy!"

Grasping her cloak, he ripped away the fabric, the brooch holding it closed flying across the room to clatter on the other side of the table. The soothsayer could only gasp before Ulrich held her up by the throat.

"Who are you?" he demanded, shaking her violently.

"Ulrich!" Eydis cried.

"Enough!" Vallek demanded.

But Ulrich was too lost to his rage, snarling up at the soothsayer.

He shook her again, her small hands clawing at his forearm as she dangled helplessly. Vallek stepped forward to stop—

Her face *flickered*. There and gone again. Leaving Vallek's eyes with only the impression of the palest purple and stopping him short in surprise.

"I knew it!" Ulrich crowed. "Reveal your true face, snake!"

He shook her again, his fist clamping tighter around her neck.

Feet wheeling uselessly and her clawing hands ineffectual, the soothsayer's bulging eyes clenched shut. From one moment to the next, her face changed.

Gone was the older human woman with lines around her eyes and graying hair.

In her place, Ulrich held a beautiful young woman by the throat. Skin a pale lilac, hair a dark, lustrous black. Eyes like violets snapped open, sparkling with rage, and her rosebud lips pulled back to reveal a set of little fangs.

Eydis cursed under her breath and Vallek—

Mate!

Vallek's beast roared to life.

His own rage closed its jaws around him, and he was across the room, knocking Ulrich away. His second staggered back with a heavy *oof*, letting the woman fall from his grip.

Vallek caught her in his own grasp, his hands looking so huge against her slim shoulders. His lungs worked like great bellows, and yet he felt lightheaded, all his blood rushing past his ears. With every breath, her scent punched through him—incense and nighttime, jasmine and cloves. Sweetness and spice and *female*.

Big violet eyes stared up at him, rimmed in white and terrified.

No, no that wouldn't do.

He needed her away from others. He needed her to himself.

Without word or warning, he ducked down to catch her middle with his shoulder. Throwing her over his back, he caught her behind the knees and turned for the door.

Vallek ripped open the lock, his hands shaking with haste, as Ulrich and Eydis tried to reason with him.

"My king, she's dangerous!"

"Vallek, wait!"

But they and their concerns didn't matter. Not when he'd found *her*. Not when he finally had *her* within his grasp.

Heart thundering, he could hardly discern between its pounding and how her little fists and feet beat against him. She was a wild thing, thrashing and spitting, her will to survive obvious and thrilling.

A strong mate. Good, very good.

He took the stairs up to his quarters three at a time, not slowing for anything—not the angry woman in his arms, not his sister and friend jogging behind him, not the startled looks of the servants they passed.

Vallek made his door long before any others and kicked it open— then shut it behind them. Flipping the lock, his beast rumbled with pleasure.

Alone with our mate.

Hands beat at the other side of the door, and he bellowed, "Leave us!"

Passing through the front chamber then central hall, under the archway into his bedchamber, he lost little time depositing his angry mate on his big bed. She bounced on the mattress, her dark hair spread across the silk bedding.

A purr rattled to life in his chest at the sight. Yes, this was exactly where she belonged.

She made herself smaller, less of a target, but those violet eyes burned with defiance. He suspected that if he got too close, she would bite.

A fresh wave of carnal need surged through him at the thought.

Fuck, he was hard just from the sight and smell of her—the idea of her sinking those precious little fangs into his arm nearly had him wetting his trou.

The orcish mate-bond was as revered as it was finicky. They didn't believe mates to necessarily be fated or decided by the gods, like the fae and the dragons did. There was some level of choice in the matter, their bonds forming over a prolonged courtship. Orcish mate-bonds were forged through time and connection, not just pheromones.

That was all well and good, but Vallek found himself in one of the rarer categories, not unlike what the fae and dragons must feel.

An immediate, searing *knowing*. An aching sort of need he'd never experienced.

She hadn't even said anything, just glared up at him with those plush rosebud lips pursed, and already he was monstrously pleased.

He shouldn't be, of course. This was a complication he didn't need.

All his hopes of an orcish princess mate went right out the window—along with his sanity, it seemed, because he just didn't care about any of it. The only thing he needed to know, the only desire that consumed him was—

"Your name?"

Those lips thinned further, as if she meant to deny him.

Oh no, no that wouldn't do, either.

Leaning over her, he balanced his weight on an arm while he traced the pert point of her chin with the other. He shuddered to feel her soft skin, her pulse fluttering wildly at her elegant throat.

"I will have it, *skala*. It's mine now, just like the rest of you."

Those intelligent eyes narrowed, and she looked just like the clever raven he called her, with her dark hair and shrewd assessment. Her eyes measured his distance from her before flicking lower, gauging the distance to the door.

He chuckled low in his throat. "That isn't wise."

Her nostrils flared, and she searched his face for something. He didn't know what. He wished to give it to her, whatever it was, but his instinct rode him harder with every heartbeat.

Claim. Conquer. Fuck.

Clear, simple needs.

The beast wanted her and didn't care about the ramifications or what needed to be done.

Dipping his head lower, one of the many braids that held back the sides of his long mane fell onto her chest. The bead at the end glittered against her skin, and Vallek's purr deepened. He wanted her to smell of him. Now.

But first, he needed a name.

"Your name. Please."

It wasn't quite begging, Vallek was too proud and not quite desperate enough for that yet. But he could be soft, if it got him what he wanted.

Her jaw worked against some unseen struggle before, reluctantly, she said, "Ravenna."

The world around him spun, every instinct and desire refocusing on her. It was a harrowing ordeal, plans and wishes torn apart and remade in the space of a few breaths. His soul cried out against the violent realignment, but his instincts overrode all.

Until the bond was sealed, there was nothing and no one but her. Ravenna.

Lowering his head even more, he touched the tip of his nose to nuzzle hers. Orcs preferred nuzzles to kisses, what with the obstacle of their tusks, but the nearer he got, the more tantalizing that rosebud mouth became. Especially when she frowned at him so mightily.

"Ravenna," he breathed. "My *mate*."

7

Ravenna . . . needed a new strategy. One that got her out from under the purring orc looming over her, his pupils dilated and his expression so hungry he might devour her whole.

Her treacherous body wasn't opposed to that. Oh, no. If she didn't keep her limbs clenched close to her chest, she might just let her legs fall open in welcome.

Which wouldn't do.

Her mind hadn't quite caught up with the whirlwind of the past ten minutes, but she knew enough to understand that things had taken a dangerous turn—and she needed to get away from him. Before she did something irreversible, like bed him.

Of course, that part of her mind, the rational one with plans of revenge and a will to survive, was fighting an uphill battle against the onslaught of her own lust. Instinct ravaged her, burning its way through her innards to focus in a throbbing ache between her thighs.

Awful and shocking as it might be, her *azai* looked upon *her* now, her true face, and purred. With just one look at her true face, he knew her immediately and took her to his bed. It was inordinately flattering—and distracting.

Beneath her, the delicate membranes of her folded wings began to quiver. The sensation had Ravenna sucking in a quelling breath—wings only vibrated and hummed like that for *azai.* The harmony was said to be an alluring call to one's mate, a temptation they couldn't resist.

Do not *hum for him, that'll only make it worse,* she scolded herself.

Don't hum for who? questioned Oberon suspiciously. *What's going on?*

We may have a problem . . .

Through the bond, the unicorn sent the lengthiest, most dramatic sigh that had ever been breathed. *Now what?*

There wasn't time to explain, not with her handsome orc leaning down to touch his nose to hers. She'd seen orcs nuzzle before, knew it was a sign of romantic affection. His claiming was sweet, a small combining of their scents, and Ravenna almost let out the little moan of pleasure building in her throat.

Sweet as the gesture was, those predator's eyes never left her. He seared her with his intensity, that purr almost violent with how hard it shook the both of them.

"What were you doing hiding yourself away?" he demanded, although gently, his voice still that low, coaxing tenor that was made for candlelit nights and warm afterglows.

Ravenna ran her tongue along her lower lip, a movement his eyes tracked from one corner of her mouth to the other.

"It's been for my safety, nothing more," she lied.

"You think I cannot keep you safe?" That was a trap if she ever heard one. His hand lowered from her chin to cup the side of her neck, a wholly proprietary hold that sent another throb through her cunt. "No one touches what's mine."

"I didn't say that," she said carefully. Glorious as he was like this, gaze riveted, chest heaving with purrs, she knew this wasn't the Vallek she'd come to know. This was someone different, someone far more dangerous to her. Someone she needed to get out from under. "It was to keep me safe from everyone. Especially you."

A tendon twitched in his neck, and a modicum of clarity began to bleed into his eyes. "You knew?" Without waiting for her answer, his face fell again to hang above hers, their noses just grazing. The heat of his breath seared her lips, and the outer curve of his tusks teased her cheeks. "You would deny me?"

Wetting her lips again, she said, "I had my reasons."

Vallek rumbled, the sound less pleased than a true purr. "They don't matter now. I've found you, *skala*. I don't give up what's mine."

He said it more as a threat than anything else, and yet Ravenna's treacherous body thrilled at his words. Others may have balked at his possessiveness, but all the broken things inside her only wanted to draw closer to him and his claim. To be the obsession, the focus, the *mate* of such a man . . .

"You may yet," she whispered. "A mate such as me will only bring you grief."

One of his heavy brows arched. "Is this one of your visions?"

"No. But a prediction nevertheless."

"Do you mean to betray me?" Tightening his hold at her neck, he lifted her torso off the bed to press her forehead to his. "Do you mean to stab me in my sleep or poison my wine?"

"No!"

"Then I see no reason why a mate as small and delectable as you should cause me any grief," he said with an infuriating grin.

Ravenna snorted. "You don't know me very well. And your people will never accept it."

"They will. I am their king and you are my mate. They will accept this. I'll make it so."

His arrogance was breathtaking—and arousing.

Grasping at any other argument she could, she said, "Your rule is too fragile to assume that."

"*You* don't know *me* very well," he said, repeating her words back.

"Nothing about me is fragile. And it will be my pleasure to prove it to you."

"They will think I'm an enemy," she yelped, growing desperate, "a *spy*."

His lips thinned between his tusks at the word, and he levered himself up, offering her a little space to breathe.

"Spy or not, it doesn't matter anymore. What you are is my mate."

Ravenna bit back a growl of frustration. "Your own lord commander has accused me. Others will, too." The mention of Ulrich cooled the air between them, and faster now, Ravenna's mind caught up with all that had happened. All that Ulrich had said.

"You let him raid my things," she accused, realization dawning. Her arousal shriveled up, and her wings fell silent.

Of course, she'd suggested he had, even if Lady Eydis disagreed. Ulrich answered only to Vallek.

It made sense for him to investigate her, but that bit of reason didn't quell her growing ire. Shoving his hand away, she rolled to the side and leapt off the bed. With the terror and excitement wearing away, she was left with an aching neck. Memories of how Ulrich had gripped her round the throat assaulted her, and she touched her neck gingerly, feeling how the hot skin had already begun to bruise.

A look at Vallek found him following her movements, and a thunderous frown crashed upon his brow when he truly looked at her throat.

"We had to be sure," was what he said, nothing close to an apology.

"Well now you know," she spat.

That frown didn't leave him as he followed her back out into the central hall.

He reached for her again, but before he could say anything, a key scraped in the lock. The door to Vallek's quarters burst open, Eydis, Ulrich, and Brynhíl rushing inside. They brought with them a cacophony of noise, their questions piling atop one another.

Lady Eydis, ever the diplomat, raised her hands, asking for calm, but it was Ulrich who Ravenna watched closely. The lord commander's furious gaze found her, and his upper lip curled, as if to accuse that the king making off with her was her own fault.

Ravenna couldn't help peeling back her own upper lip to reveal her fangs. Although not nearly as impressive as orc tusks, she let the lord commander know she could bite back.

Understanding her threat, Ulrich's nostrils flared and he began to barrel toward her.

He'd gone perhaps three steps before Vallek intercepted him, catching his lord commander by the throat. Ulrich stumbled backwards, and Vallek used his momentum to slam the other orc into the stone wall, making the sconces quiver. Ulrich sputtered, eyes wide with horror, as Vallek snarled in his face.

"You *ever* look at her like that again, I'll carve out your eyes with my tusks."

Ulrich's eyes bulged—whether from the shock or Vallek squeezing his throat so tightly, Ravenna didn't know. Or care, really.

"Vallek, let him go," Eydis said calmly, as if he wasn't about the choke the life out of his second. Still, the orcess's eyes creased with worry as she looked between Ravenna and the scuffling orcs.

"He threatened my mate. This cannot be allowed."

"Your mate?" Eydis gasped, and Ulrich made a similar sound of astonishment.

"My beast recognized her the moment I saw her true face," Vallek confirmed.

Eydis took a long look at Ravenna, which she met head on. Although she'd no clue where she stood at the moment, Ravenna knew it was wise to have the king's older sister as her ally. Eydis's sharp mind whirled behind her eyes, blue like her brother's but a lighter hue.

"Ulrich didn't know," Eydis said, not looking away from Ravenna. "Not even you did."

Vallek bared his teeth at the sound logic, and after another moment, he released his second. Ulrich slumped back against the wall, gasping for air and rubbing at his throat. Ravenna had to keep a tight hold of her magic, the power itching beneath her skin to reach out and finish what Vallek had begun. Her own bruised throat demanded vengeance.

But if anyone believed his throttling would stop Ulrich, they were wrong. "She cannot be your mate," the lord commander wheezed. "She is *fae*. She must have bewitched you."

Vallek snorted. "She had many opportunities to do so before and didn't."

"My king, you cannot—"

Slashing his hand through the air, Vallek growled, "*Enough,* Ulrich. I've heard enough poison from your mouth today. What's done is done." Although his stance remained ready, his gaze tore away from his second to find Ravenna. "She is my mate. My beast has decided."

With her hands held up in a gesture of peace, Eydis stepped forward. "Let us all take a moment to breathe. This complicates everything and tempers are high."

"I'm fine," Vallek grumbled, stalking around her to stand before Brynhíl. "Have her things moved into my chambers. My mate sleeps with me."

Brynhíl bobbed her head. "Of course, my king."

"Wait!" Ravenna yelped, halting the older orcess.

Marching up to Vallek, she insisted, "There's no need for that. My staying here will only raise suspicion."

"You are my mate," he bit out. "I will have you in my chambers."

"I don't need to stay in here with you, not when—"

"This isn't up for debate, *skala.*"

"—you cannot just *decide* to—"

"I can and I have—"

"—just your beast's instinct, you will have a clearer head and see—"

"—*I* am king here and—"

"—need not know, I can resume my position. I could leave—"

Snarling, Vallek struck quicker than she could see, catching her by the waist to haul her into his massive body. Pressed close to him, his heat enveloped her, and she couldn't help a gasp to feel just how large he was compared to her. She had to look up and up and *up* to meet his glare with her own.

"You will *not* leave. You will stay here. With me. Where you belong." Vallek looked up long enough to nod at Brynhíl, sending her along to have Ravenna's meager things brought.

A sound of pure outrage erupted from her throat. Struggling in his grasp, Ravenna argued, "Nothing good can come of this!"

"Listen to her, my king," Ulrich insisted.

"Oh, now I'm to be listened to?" Ravenna spat.

A vein in his forehead throbbed, but before the lord commander's expression could grow too withering, a growl from Vallek had him rearranging his features.

"There will be no way to hide this, not forever," said Eydis. "A fae for a mate will complicate everything. We need time to think about this, Vallek. To plan."

"I am only half-fae and have no love nor loyalty to them," Ravenna admitted, not wanting Eydis to think less of her.

Brows arching in surprise, Eydis nodded.

"She will be kept safe. Secret," said Vallek. "With me."

Ravenna pushed against the heavy slabs of muscle that made up his chest. "You cannot just keep me prisoner in here!"

Snarling, he growled, "Watch me."

"She will stay here," agreed Eydis, her voice gentle and soothing, "until we get this figured out. For now, come away, Vallek. Let clearer heads prevail."

The arm wrapped around Ravenna tightened for a moment before, finally, he released her. Her instinct was to spin away and get as much distance between them as possible—well, that was one instinct, the other was to sidle up to him and pet that glorious chest—but she thought better of it. He watched her with that predator's stare once more, and any sudden movement would likely see her caught again.

He considered her for a long moment, no doubt deciding how she might try to escape his imprisonment, when Brynhíl returned with the battered trunk holding all of Ravenna's possessions.

Frowning at it, Vallek asked, "That's it?"

"Yes," Ravenna hissed.

A different kind of consideration overcame his expression, one that had her belly flipping.

Nodding he said, "Help her settle, but she isn't to leave. You will see to her yourself, Bryn."

The older orcess nodded. "Of course, my king. It will be my honor."

Apparently satisfied, Vallek motioned for Ulrich to proceed him out into the corridor. The lord commander went, storm clouds gathered around his shoulders, opening the chamber door to reveal two guardsmen stationed on the other side.

Eydis offered what Ravenna hoped was an encouraging lift of her brows before following him out.

Before he left with them, Vallek pinned Ravenna with those lapis-lazuli eyes. "The door is under guard. You aren't to leave."

Ravenna curled her lip. "Such a pretty prison."

"And comfortable, too," he said, not rising to her bait. "Bryn will take care of you. You and I will speak when I return this evening."

Then her *azai* turned on his bootheel and *left,* confident that she would stay put.

Now alone with Brynhíl, the sudden silence echoed in the chamber.

The orcess looked Ravenna up wend down. "Please don't make me chase you. You'll be caught eventually, and my knees aren't what they used to be."

Ravenna bit her cheek. She wanted to refuse, to rail and complain, but none of this was Brynhíl's fault. The orcess had only ever shown her kindness and competence.

"Come along." Brynhíl nodded at the bedchamber. "Let's put your things away."

"There's nothing to put," Ravenna muttered, grudgingly following Brynhíl into the next room.

Placing her trunk on the far side of the room, the orcess opened the trunk lid and whistled. "You're right, there's not. Well, I'm sure our king will have that sorted soon. In the meantime—" she lifted one of the three plain kirtles Ravenna had, the second of which she wore "—perhaps we can . . . launder these?"

Ravenna shrugged, cheeks flushing with embarrassment. They were the homespun disguise of a plain, unassuming human woman. The kirtles were meant to hide her, to discourage attention. Held up in the orc king's bedchamber, though, surrounded by his lavish four-post bed layered in sumptuous silks and brocade, the thing looked downright drab.

Perhaps sensing her chagrin, Brynhíl replaced the kirtle and closed the trunk.

"You were meant to have a bath after your meeting," she said. "Would you like to do that instead?"

Ravenna couldn't help her skepticism. She was sure Vallek would just *love it* if he came back to a washed, sweet-smelling, docile little mate.

She glared at his luxurious bed and furnishings, considering whether she shouldn't roll around in her days of sweat and grime. He certainly wouldn't want to sleep in the same chamber, let alone the same bed with her stink.

Brynhíl sighed. "Think of my knees."

A surprised laugh escaped Ravenna before she could stop it.

The orcess smiled kindly, walking over to one of the polished doors in the bedchamber. Opening it revealed a closet full of linens, bedding, and what looked to be some of the king's everyday attire.

An evil idea sparked in her mind. No fires were lit due to the summer heat, but it wouldn't take much to light a little one in his closet.

Even just the idea, the notion of defiance, made her feel a little better.

Brynhíl reemerged with arms full of fluffy bath sheets and ceramic bottles.

"What should I call you?" she asked. "Surely your name cannot be *kone*."

"No. It's Ravenna."

"Ravenna," the orcess repeated. "Very pretty. Well, Ravenna, shall we go down to the baths? The king's private bath is quite spectacular."

She held out a moment longer, but the chance at a proper bath was too much. She needed to scrub her skin, and hopefully, the steam and warm water would help clear her mind and make room for a plan.

She was in dire need of a new one.

"Very well," she said. "But I'm not doing it for *him*."

"No indeed," Brynhíl agreed, "you'll do it for me." The orcess winked, earning another laugh from Ravenna. "Besides, if you must confront something, better to do it clean and smelling pleasant."

8

In the end, Vallek hardly made it past sundown. After abandoning Ulrich's arguments and Eydis's advice, he made his way into the training yard for his berserkers. A few of his most unfortunate men were treated to a thrashing in the pit, Vallek unleashing the might of his beast and throwing himself into a fray.

The exertion helped—for a few moments. But by the time his blood began to cool, his beast was still loud in his mind. He'd succeeded only in tiring his limbs and shocking his men. He sent them back to the barracks with word to Mattias to give everyone the day off tomorrow.

Instinct drove him back up into the citadel. He climbed two stairs at a time, his beast gnashing its teeth to be near her again.

However, when he nodded at the guards at his chamber door, he'd no plan, no solution. Beyond that door lay the true challenge. The brutal sparring in the training yard hadn't prepared him for a mate like Ravenna.

He wasn't sure anything could have.

A half-fae mate.

It was almost too fantastic to believe.

The rational part of him agreed with Eydis—this complicated everything. The fae were longtime enemies of orc-kin. Many ancestors had met their deaths at the end of a unicorn horn or fae blade. Although outright war hadn't been declared between them in centuries, their borders were always places of tension, and suspicion ran deep.

The only thing worse than a half-fae mate would've been a full-fae mate.

But the gods, the fates, whatever it was that oversaw the universe, cared little for politics, it seemed. There was a reason for all of this, Vallek just had yet to see it.

None of that, however, was comforting as he opened the door to his quarters.

What in the name of the Ever-Father will I do with a fae mate?

His beast had more than a few ideas, none of which were helpful. If he was honest, he'd hoped taking Eydis's advice to leave, to breathe, to be *away* for a few hours, would clear his head. While he might have clawed back a scrap of his sanity in the training yard, the moment he strode into his quarters, it was forfeit.

The faintest hint of jasmine met his nose, and a purr immediately sparked in his chest, rattling his battered ribs.

Satisfaction as sweet as ambrosia flooded his veins to smell how their scents were already combining within his space. That buzz of pleasure soothed the worst edges of his misgivings, and he strode purposefully further inside, seeking out his wayward mate.

Instead he found Bryn, her arms full of ugly fabric that smelled of his mate. Her soothsayer disguise, no doubt.

"I'm off to the laundress with these," Bryn said. "Is there anything else before I retire?"

"Please have our dinner sent up." He nodded at the bundle she carried. "I won't be aggrieved if those find their way into a fire."

"Perhaps not, but your mate might." Looking over her shoulder into the adjoining room. "She's a spirited one, your mate."

"Indeed," he sighed.

Chuckling, Bryn patted him fondly on the arm before taking her leave.

When the door *clicked* shut behind her, Vallek resumed his search.

He found Ravenna sitting in a chair on the far side of his den. A spacious chamber, it was stuffed full of plush furniture meant for reclining and relaxing. Gathered in a semicircle around the cold hearth, the red sofas and benches and chairs were well-loved, his sisters often joining him for long bantering conversations. There was little better than sitting in his favorite chair on a winter's night, watching the crackling flames as he sipped his goblet of mead.

Ravenna hadn't taken any of the comfortable seats, instead dragging one of the wooden chairs from the six-seat dining table over to one of the windows. He contented himself that the window was far too high to offer an escape.

Although, weren't fae women supposed to have wings? He looked carefully as he approached but saw no sign of any such limbs on her back.

All he saw was loveliness.

Gone was the dowdy brown dress. Instead, she sat in the finest cream linen, the fabric draping around her lithe form like water cascading from the pitcher. Her hair had been washed and brushed to a high shine, black waves softer than the night sky. Her lilac skin seemed to glow in the hushed light of the sconces, and the gathering moonlight just touched the gently tipped points of her ears.

The breath rushed out of him in a harsh exhale. Gods, she was exquisite.

She could do with a less dour expression, though. Those violet eyes were sad as they turned to watch him approach. Her rosebud mouth was downturned, her hands folded delicately in her lap.

He didn't believe her show of docile tragedy for a moment, not after the fight she gave both him and Ulrich.

"Good evening," he said.

"Good evening." Her soft voice had gooseflesh breaking out across his neck and arms. Gods, he needed her whispering like that while he sucked on her pert lilac tits. He assumed they were lilac, anyway. What color would her nipples be? A deeper purple hue or perhaps more pink like human skin?

His cock twitched with interest at the thought.

He watched as she stood from her seat. She regarded him thoughtfully for a moment—and then her face shifted. Between one blink and the next, he stared at the soothsayer he'd known for years.

His beast roared in outrage. *Give her back!*

"This doesn't have to mean anything," she said in that soft voice. "We can go back to how it was before. No one need know."

Vallek growled, closing the distance between them. To her credit, she stood her ground, even when he caught her chin with his thumb and finger to tilt her face up.

"In these quarters, with me, you will wear your own face."

His sensible side reasoned that it might be wise for her to maintain her disguise, at least for the time being, but he wouldn't have it now. Not with him. He demanded her true face and all of her loveliness. Even when she was glowering at him—as she was when the glamour fell.

Lifting her head out of his grasp, Ravenna skirted around him.

Disliking her retreat, Vallek demanded to know, "Why do you wear a false face?"

When she gained enough distance from him, Ravenna turned to answer succinctly, "This world is dangerous for halflings."

That was true—but it also wasn't everything.

Halflings were more common than many realized or preferred to admit. Although smaller and weaker, humans were far more numerous than other folk. They bred like rabbits, and their soft bodies were appealing to some.

"Why not stay with your kind? Human or fae?"

Those berry-red lips pursed. "I'm both and neither. Living with humans or fae would be far more dangerous for me."

Vallek wasn't sure he believed it. Although he couldn't claim to have seen many fae, he didn't consider her very different from the handful of fae women he'd spotted before. Perhaps more lilac than gray. And less skeletal. There were fae who looked like walking skeletons, their grayish skin pulled taut over prominent bones.

His Ravenna was all healthy curves and colorful flushes. His beast rumbled in approval.

What he couldn't approve of was how much danger she'd thrown herself into.

"So you thought an orcish stronghold would be safer?" It defied belief.

"As a human, yes. Nowhere would be safer than the orc king's court."

Pride pricked his heart, but he didn't let it swell to his head. "I fail to see the logic."

She merely shrugged. *Shrugged.*

Before she could turn and walk away from him, Vallek's arm shot out to grab hold of her hand. A tempestuous frown met his efforts, and he swore he felt something slide between his fingers. There was nothing to see to confirm it, but still he sensed something wedging between her hand and his, as if to force him away.

Her magic?

Vallek held on tighter.

"You will explain this to me, *skala*. I must know everything if I'm to keep you safe."

"No."

He blinked at her. "*No?*" he repeated. "That wasn't a request."

"There's nothing to tell. And besides, I'd been managing just fine before you let your hound go sniffing through my things." Her tone oozed venom, and Vallek knew he would have to see about Ulrich and his raid.

"A human soothsayer amongst orc-kin warranted investigation," he reasoned—perhaps more to himself than her.

"I've served you loyally for years. I've done nothing to earn this treatment." Genuine hurt sparkled in her eyes, and Vallek hated to see it. Defiant as she was, it seemed his and Ulrich's actions had truly wounded his little faeling.

"Perhaps. Perhaps not." Reeling her in with the hold he still had on her hand, he said, "Did you truly see no bride in my future, sprite? No one at all?"

Color suffused her cheeks, answer enough when she only shook her head.

A seductive purr grew in his chest as his hand slid to the small of her back, easing her into the protection of his body. *That's right. Just where you belong.*

"Were you jealous at the thought of another? Did you see yourself at my side?"

A tendon jumped in her cheek as she clenched her jaw. "No and no," she ground out.

Vallek chuckled. "I don't believe you." Daring to run his hand up the narrow span of her back, he coaxed, "You need not deny the both of us any longer. Tell me, *skala,* tell me what you have seen of us."

Chin jutting in defiance, she grumbled, "Just because you made yourself king doesn't mean you get everything you want."

"That's exactly what it means," he purred, leaning down to run his nose along the crown of her head. "You will not deny me again."

Jerking out from under his lips, she bared her teeth in the facsimile of a smile. "*Watch me,*" she taunted.

Frustration and arousal, a potent mix, punched through Vallek. His nostrils flared, drawing deep of her scent, and his cock began to rise with agonized interest.

By the Ever-Father, and the All-Mother, too, he shouldn't find her defiance so alluring. His instinct-addled mind caught on the idea of what it would be for her to score his hide with those little fangs of hers. What would it be to have her wicked claws scrape down his back? Small as she might be, he'd no doubt she'd leave an indelible mark upon him.

Dark and dangerous, like the flowers of the belladonna.

His cock throbbed at the thought, tenting his trou.

Finally, Vallek clawed back some of his sense and released her. If he set upon her now, she would fight him. And while he enjoyed an active partner in bed, he also required enthusiasm. While his pride insisted he could persuade her, he also understood that in these first few hours, their bond was fragile.

He had a spitting hellcat of a woman glaring at him right now, and he'd rather she not scratch his eyes out.

Easing away without turning his back on her, Vallek offered her a conciliatory grin. "We shall see. I'm bound for the bath if you'd care to join me."

She didn't dignify that with a response, just crossed her arms over her chest below her impressive tits. While not huge for a human or fae, they were large compared to an orcess, even Lady Silvia, and his gaze immediately dropped to the enticing curves she created with her forearms.

She huffed in offense and lowered her arms.

Vallek took pity on her and headed for the bath, his body already anticipating the soothing warmth of the water. He'd much rather she joined him, of course, at least so long as she didn't try to drown him.

Still, as he jogged down the steps, at least he could content himself with stroking his cock to thoughts of her. His mate. With her little fangs and sharper tongue.

When he returned from his bath, steaming and covered only in his linen breeches, Vallek reentered the den to find two platters of food laid out on the dining table. One already had its white porcelain lid taken off, about half the portion of seasoned quail, sautéed squash, and roasted apricots eaten.

Vallek sat in his usual chair, drawing his own plate to him. Lifting the lid revealed a full portion—except all but one of the apricots had been eaten.

My little hellion, he thought fondly.

Tucking into his meal, he remained acutely aware of how she watched him from the corner of her eye. Ensconced again at the window, she made an effort to appear as though she ignored him, but they both knew differently.

"Join me," he said as he cut into his quail.

"I've already eaten."

"Hardly. There's still a feast here."

"I require less than you do."

Well, that might be true. She was a slight thing, her head barely coming to the center of his chest. Honestly, if he let himself think too much on how small she was compared to him, he might start to break out in a nervous sweat.

Such a little thing . . . he would have to take great care with her.

Which started with ensuring she'd eaten plenty.

"You could still sit with me," he cajoled. "Keep me company."

"I could," she replied. *But won't.*

Vallek bit back his sigh with a mouthful of squash. Chewing thoughtfully, he regarded his faeling mate, not bothering to hide his stare. Muscles loose and relaxed from the bath, he found the eventful day weighed on him. Their sparring could wait until morning. For now, he knew it was too much to try to persuade her into more carnal pursuits, but he hoped they might at least talk civilly.

"Where are you from?" he asked, keeping his tone light. *There, sprite, a question, not a demand.*

"North of here."

Well that was obvious. She'd found their camp years ago in the northern Griegens.

"How old are you?"

"Fifty-five."

It took effort not to choke on his mouthful of quail. He stared at her in surprise, although her poorly hidden smugness at his shock wasn't such a surprise.

Vallek wasn't a good judge of human ages, but he'd have guessed her to be half that, perhaps even less. Certainly not older than his thirty-eight years. Of course, the fae were long-lived. Few knew just how much so.

Resuming his meal, he asked, "Where did you grow up?"

"By the sea."

Hmm, so not inland Eirea or Pyrros. He knew the northwestern coasts were nominally claimed by the human kingdom of Eirea, although it was far less populated than the fertile, rolling hills and forests of the hinterland. A fishing village, perhaps?

"And who was your father?"

"A fae."

"Your mother?"

"A human."

"I see. So our children will be quarter-fae and quarter-human."

A strangled sort of choking sound caught in her throat, and Vallek looked up from his plate to see her bulging eyes.

"We will *not* discuss children," she wheezed.

"Fine. Then you choose a topic, *skala*. I've been carrying this conversation anyway."

She loosely crossed her arms and shot him with a frown, seeing how easily she'd walked into his trap.

"Let us discuss my imprisonment, then," she bit out.

Vallek shrugged before pulling her plate closer to finish off her food. There was no sense in wasting it. Although his family were of noble blood, they were a relatively minor name in the list of Balmirra's paladins. He and his sisters had had a happy enough childhood, wanting for nothing, until Mordis came into power. He demanded all paladin sons be conscripted to train as warriors, and Vallek had spent his late adolescence and early adulthood in the harsh conditions of Mordis's camps. Boys fought for food and slept on soiled straw.

To make them hard, said Mordis.

To break them, more like.

And so no food went to waste with Vallek. He indulged in good food and his one goblet of mead or wine, every plate and cup another defiant insult to Mordis's hated memory.

Spearing a chunk of cooling squash, Vallek sighed. "We've already discussed that at length."

"We *have not!*" Jumping to her feet, Ravenna marched to stand before him, her fists planted on her hips. "You merely declared you were king and would have your way."

"I am, I did, and I will," he agreed. Catching another piece of squash, he lifted it to touch Ravenna's lips. "Just a few more bites. For me."

"I will not be fed like a baby," she seethed, eyes narrowing when he pushed the bite past her lips before she'd fully finished speaking.

"No, not a baby. A cherished, well-spoiled mate."

He was inordinately pleased when she took a second piece, chewing speedily as she glared daggers at him. He'd accept this, and his beast was pleased to see her fed by their hand.

As she finished chewing, Vallek poured them both a goblet of wine. "Drink with me?"

Ravenna took the cup he offered and raised it to her unsmiling mouth. Without dropping his gaze, she drank the wine in three great gulps. Placing it back on the table, she sneered, "Finished. May I be excused now?"

Not waiting for permission, she turned on her heel and flounced back to her seat.

Vallek pressed his lip to his tusks, holding back his laugh. Hellion indeed.

He didn't rush his evening cup, sitting before the cold hearth in his preferred chair. More than once he tried to coax her to sit somewhere more comfortable, but every time she refused. Although he admired her determination to spite him, by the time his lids grew heavy with sleepiness, he was ready for her capitulation.

Rising from his seat, Vallek stretched out his back. His body and mind a pleasurable kind of tired, he stalked over to his wary mate. She squinted up at him suspiciously, confirming his instinct not to bother asking if she'd accompany him to bed.

Instead, he leaned down and gathered her up in his arms. She could do little more than gasp and sputter as he held her high on his chest and walked from the den into his sumptuous bedchamber.

Ravenna had just started protesting when he laid her gently upon the rich bedding. She looked so right there, and one day soon, he vowed she'd look up at him from these very sheets with warmth and welcome in her eyes.

For now, he had to contend with the spitting hellcat again.

"I will make but one more demand," he said. "As my mate, you will share my bed tonight and all nights hence."

Before he could cage her in with his arms, Ravenna's dainty foot landed hard in his vulnerable middle, pushing him back. Using her momentum, she rocked into a backwards somersault and began to roll across the bed. He watched her go, not sure whether to be amused or horrified or annoyed. Perhaps a bit of everything.

She landed gracefully on the other side of the bed, well out of his reach.

"I will not," she growled. "I'd rather sleep on the floor."

"Fine then," he growled right back, his annoyance winning the day.

Lips pursed in an expression he was getting far too familiar with, Ravenna snatched at the thin coverlet and began pulling it closer. Vallek thought about jumping on it to stop her, but in truth, he was tired.

He matched her glare as she gathered up the bundle of bedding, ridiculously larger than her, and made to walk around the bed.

"Oh, no, my hellion, even if you will not share my bed, you will still sleep in my chamber." *Where I can keep an eye on you.*

Her nostrils flared as she glowered, but after a moment, with great huffs and puffs, she made a little nest for herself with the coverlet on the floor, near the foot of his bed.

Vallek resented how cozy she ended up looking.

Before he could give into the temptation to snatch her up again, he busied himself preparing for bed. After throwing back the remaining sheets, he dropped his linen breeches to toss them onto the bed for morning. In her full view, of course.

Two wide violet eyes watched him from under the coverlet as he went about dimming the sconces and snuffing the lamps.

When the room was dark, he eased onto his big, comfortable bed. A noisy sigh of contentment filled the room as the bed molded to his body.

If she wanted to keep her pride and stubbornness with her on the floor, then fine. He'd slept on floors and packed earth and rock too many times to ever give up his comfortable bed. Even when he left the city, he brought along a luxurious camp bed for his tent.

His beast, and indeed his own pride, chafed at knowing his *mate* lay on the floor, at the foot of his expansive bed. She should be beside him. If not under him crying with pleasure, then at least in his arms. Or if not that, then comfortable and warm in his bedding.

That's her choice, he reminded himself.

She won't hold out for long, he promised himself.

Even as quiet permeated the chamber, sleep eluded him, although that wasn't a surprise. Part of him was curious to see if she would try to sneak off somewhere or even stab him in the back as he slept.

She did none of those things, however. In fact, after a while of tossing and turning, she grew quiet. Quiet enough that he had to sit up and crane his neck to see over the edge of the bed and confirm she was still there.

Ravenna made an achingly small lump in the pile of his coverlet. A lock of dark hair slipped from behind her pointed ears, framing her face, soft and serene in her slumber.

Slumping back, Vallek stared up at the ceiling of his bedchamber, more than a little befuddled.

What am I to do with a faeling mate?

9

Ravenna wasn't truly surprised when she awoke to find herself laid comfortably on Vallek's bed. Annoyed, yes. Surprised? No.

She'd had a feeling something like that might happen. The orc king had held his throne for almost eighteen years; he wasn't used to being defied.

Apparently, her magic hadn't considered him a threat. Usually it was good about warning her of danger while she slept, but it seemed her magic was more than ready to recognize Vallek as her mate. An *azai* wasn't a threat—they were one of only a select few a fae woman allowed close. Trusted with her magic and her wings.

Her heart and mind weren't ready to extend such trust, however. No matter how her heart *pitter-pattered* at the thought of his beast recognizing her immediately. No matter how her mind concede that taking a strong orc for an *azai* certainly had its benefits.

Ravenna kept still, letting her ears tell her what they could. She didn't hear him breathing, and a small tendril of magic across the bed told her his place was cold. Long abandoned.

She peeked over her shoulder to confirm that she was alone.

Sighing, she scrubbed her hands over her face. Fates, what a mess.

She could hardly believe the change a day made. This time yesterday, she'd been merely a human soothsayer in the orc king's employ. Today, she was his mate and prisoner. Not exactly an improvement in conditions, but big changes nevertheless.

A presence poked at her mind. *Oh, good. You're awake. Tell me everything,* insisted Oberon.

I already told you everything, she reminded him. Left with a little time to think as Brynhíl brushed out her damp hair, Ravenna had informed Oberon of the developments. The unicorn didn't seem to know whether to be alarmed or smug.

Tell me what's happening now.

I just woke up.

In his bed?

Ravenna made a face at the far wall. *I'm not telling you.* Talking about anything of the sort with him was almost as bad as discussing it with her father.

In his bed, Oberon confirmed, and Ravenna could hear the echo of his gleeful whinny. *Well, go on. What kind of mate is he?*

An overbearing one. Like someone else I know.

Good. Perhaps he will finally talk some sense into you.

I don't intend to tell him, nanny goat.

Ravenna—

Severing the connection, she disentangled from the coverlet and threw her legs over the side of the bed. It wasn't an insignificant hop down to the ground; the bed was sized for an orc, a big orc, and so the mattress with its bedding rose to her chest. She'd likely need steps to get back in it—or a running start.

Not that she'd be getting back into it, of course.

Straightening out the linen robe Brynhíl had put her in after the bath and finger combing her hair, Ravenna padded silently around the bed to peek past the threshold.

Vallek's quarters were luxurious and included several rooms, all branching from a short central hall. The four main rooms—the bedchamber, den, the front antechamber that he used as a meeting room, and what she presumed was an office of some kind—were clustered like clover leaves around the hall, with a door to a smaller space in between their arched thresholds. One such door led down to his private bath, another to a garderobe, the third into an expansive closet of all his finery, and the fourth was the door leading outside.

Ravenna couldn't help peering long and hard at that most elusive door. It wasn't even that far away. She could likely reach it before he even thought to catch her. The problem was, she'd run right into the waiting arms of the guards posted on the other side.

She'd have to find another means of escape, then. What she planned to do beyond that . . . she didn't truly know. Leaving Balmirra entirely was out of the question. She'd spent too much time on this plan; everything was already in motion. And . . . she wasn't sure how long her mind would last against the gnashing instinct to be near him.

It'd been one thing when she was hidden away. Seeing him now and then for a friendly game while touching herself to thoughts of him had seemed to be enough. Now, though, that all changed. Now, her instinct drove her out of the bedchamber in search of him.

Before turning into the den, the sound of voices met her ears. Ravenna stopped by the side of the archway leading in, concealing herself in shadow.

Her mother always said listening at doors was rude, but Aine likely never imagined her daughter in such a situation.

She could tell by the happy way her magic hummed inside her that Vallek was near. Two female voices accompanied his within the den, and Ravenna held her breath to hear better.

"It certainly complicates matters," said one voice. Definitely Lady Eydis.

"I don't see why," said the other. "All kin know the beast has the final say. No one will argue with it." This one took Ravenna a moment, but she guessed from the easy way all three of them spoke that the second voice was Captain Asta, Vallek's younger sister.

"They will argue when they see she's a fae," said Eydis.

"Half-fae," Vallek corrected.

A pause, in which Ravenna could imagine Eydis shooting her brother the kind of look only eldest sisters managed. "Half or not, she *looks* fae. There will be suspicions. Ulrich is already against her, even knowing she's your mate."

Asta huffed. "Ulrich has always had a stick up his—"

"He's *loyal*," Eydis interrupted. "That's what matters."

"Perhaps too loyal," Vallek ruminated.

"There's no such thing."

"There is too," insisted Asta. "I agree with Vallek. These past few years, Ulrich has been . . . fervent in his loyalty."

Another pause, then Eydis said, "We aren't discussing him right now. More important is your new mate."

"She can glamour herself, right? Just have her wear a human face. Or even an orcess's!"

"And keep up the ruse for the rest of her life?" Eydis scoffed.

"Fine. Then get some cosmetics and make her the right complexion."

"These are good suggestions," Vallek said diplomatically, "but will only bandage the wound, not heal it. There must be something more definitive."

Ravenna made a face at being referred to as a wound.

"Well," sighed Eydis, "that is your decision. What are we to do about her?"

"Shall we ask her?"

Ravenna's heart dropped to her stomach, and for a breathless moment, she didn't know whether to reveal herself or race back to take a running leap at the bed.

Vallek didn't give her a chance for either, appearing around the threshold to take up her vision. Those linen breeches from last night were back, searing her mind with the memory of watching them drop to reveal the taut green flesh of his backside. Now he also wore a sleeveless linen tunic, stretched wide over his massive chest.

Her magic pooled at her feet and crept along the flagstones to wrap around his ankles.

One of his heavy brows lifted in interest.

"Good morning, Ravenna."

"Good morning."

"Join us for breakfast." Not waiting for her answer to his not-a-question, he lightly laid his hand at the small of her back, ushering her forward.

Ravenna stepped quickly into the den, avoiding letting him get too close to her back. Although her vulnerable wings were folded high up on her back and hidden beneath her robe and hair, his hand was enormous.

The den was much the same as the night before, food spread on the dining table, the hearth empty. Two orcesses looked up to mark her entrance, though, their eyes wide with interest.

She'd seen more of Eydis, the elder sister, than she had Asta. The younger sister was tall like her siblings, but where Eydis was lanky for an orcess, Asta carried thick ropes of muscle across her back and chest and down her arms and thighs. A leather cuirass molded to her form, oiled to a high shine, and an ornate golden gorget hung round her neck, denoting her rank. Fine leather trou had been tucked into knee-high boots, and her long mane of inky black hair had been scraped back into a sleek tail.

Asta looked every inch the warrior she was, so the wide, almost girlish smile she lobbed at Ravenna was startling.

"Well now," she whistled, "here's the half-fae herself." Reaching out her much larger hand, she took hold of Ravenna's forearm in a sign of greeting and respect. "I'm Asta, the best looking of the siblings. Thank you for taking our brother off our hands."

In her surprise, Ravenna didn't think to tell the orcess she'd no intention of doing that, but she did manage to give her name.

Asta nodded. "So I hear." A sudden frown creased her brow. "Are you sure you're fully grown?"

"Asta!" hissed Eydis.

"I'm only wondering! She's just short, is all."

"I'm a perfectly average height for a human," Ravenna groused.

Asta shrugged, apparently content with that answer. "Just be sure he prepares you before—"

"*Asta!*"

"What! I want her to survive!"

A hand at Ravenna's back urged her toward the dining table to choose her breakfast.

"I'm perfectly capable of taking care of my mate," Vallek grumbled as he passed his sister.

Cheeks burning, Ravenna blindly loaded a helping of fruit and bread rolls onto her plate before retreating to her isolated chair across the room. All three orcs watched her go with raised brows, as if they expected her to choose a more comfortable seat amongst them.

"Now look," chided Eydis, "you've scared her away."

Lifting her hands in a gesture of capitulation, Asta moved one of the other wooden chairs and placed it near Ravenna's. Sitting down beside her, Asta smiled toothily, showing off her gold-capped tusks.

"I'm sure you've an opinion on all of this," she said. "What should be done about you?"

"Asta." This time it was Vallek who warned her.

Ravenna shot him a withering look. At least Asta cared to ask.

"We go back to how things were," Ravenna said. "I resume my disguise—*and* my chamber in the servants' hall. This can all just be an . . . inconvenience."

Perhaps it was a stubborn, even naïve, plan, but Ravenna held fast to it. While parts of her thrilled at the idea of having Vallek for her mate, she had to be practical. Her revenge became increasingly complicated if she was introduced as the mate and queen of the orc king. Eventually, Amaranthe would find out.

That could mean putting Balmirra under threat, and while she intended to utilize Vallek's army to take on the hag on the faelands throne, she couldn't stomach the thought of bringing misery to the whole city. She would take her battle to the faelands.

And . . . petty as it might be, Ravenna had already had most of her life decided for her by her father. She wasn't about to let another male swoop in and decide what her life would now be. Even if that meant denying her heart and her *azai*.

Her life was hers. If she wanted to dedicate it to seeking revenge, well then, that was her right. Her father couldn't stop her, and she'd be damned if she let her mate try.

Her suggestion, however, was met with utter silence. Even by Asta. A quick glance at all three siblings revealed that it had likely been the wrong thing to say.

"The mate-bond isn't an inconvenience," said Eydis. Her tone was calm, measured, but Ravenna immediately sensed she'd offended the orcess. "It's a blessing. The timing may be inconvenient, perhaps, but never the bond."

Vallek moved to stand before Ravenna. Seated as she was, he loomed even larger above her, and she had to crane her neck to meet his serious gaze. He lifted a hand to tip her chin even further up with his knuckle before running a feather-light touch down the length of her throat.

"What's done is done, *skala*. The beast has decided. There's no going back."

That may be true, but it was also true that Ravenna refused to be anything to him just because he said it was so.

"Fae also feel a mate pull, do they not?" asked Eydis.

Ravenna swallowed hard. "They do."

"And?" said Vallek, although his hard face told her he already knew.

Wetting her lower lip, she reluctantly admitted, "You are *azai*."

His nostrils flared and his chest swelled, the prideful triumph obvious in his intense blue eyes.

"Then we must move forward, not back," said Eydis, far too reasonably.

Leaning down, Vallek caught a lock of her hair to curl around his fingers. "That means you stay with me, *skala*."

"*Skala?*" Asta laughed. "That's the least romantic thing I've ever heard, *breddah*."

"Yes, I'm sure your many paramours in the garrison are far more creative with their pet names." Eydis rolled her eyes.

"Just because you're old and married doesn't mean the rest of us are dead and dusty." Asta met Ravenna's scandalized look with a wink.

Were all siblings this . . . antagonistic?

"Ravenna will stay within my quarters until a plan is formed," said Vallek.

Eydis nodded. "We will need to deal with several matters before she's introduced as your mate. Most of all, Ulrich. For now, we will say the soothsayer is ill and being tended at a hospital in the lower city."

"Leave Ulrich to me," Vallek said. Pointing at her full but untouched plate, he said, "Now you must eat."

Ravenna's eyes narrowed, but before she could say anything cutting, Asta knocked her shoulder gently with her own. The orcess pulled a face at her brother's order. "Best do what he says," she teased, making a rude gesture at Vallek.

"Don't test me, either of you. She's my mate, I must know she's cared for."

Her soppy heart might want to flutter and swoon at such a statement, but Ravenna had locked away that heart long ago. It'd survived decades of living with the imminent death of her beloved parents, and then the devastating aftermath when their demise came to pass. Perhaps there might have been a romantic inside her once, but that person lay dead alongside her parents and whatever hopes she might've had for her life.

So instead, she glared at her bossy mate, telling him without words that she put an apple to her lips not for him but for her.

It was an awkward handful of moments as they all fell silent, the only sound Ravenna's chewing. Whatever Vallek thought to gain, he seemed determined to stand there and watch her take every bite.

It was Asta who finally broke the silence. "If she can maintain the disguise, I suppose she could do that outside your quarters for now. I can assign her own guards—I'll pick the men myself."

The captain was quickly becoming her favorite sibling. Ravenna rushed to chew her bite, anxious to agree with Asta's suggestion, but—

"No." Vallek's denial was swift and firm.

"It's a reasonable compromise," said Eydis.

Yes, she knew she'd always liked Eydis!

Slashing his hand through the air, Vallek growled, "No. She will not leave my sight."

True ire sparked in her belly, and Ravenna stood to face him, leaving her plate behind on a sideboard. She channeled all her frustration and fury into a volley of ferocious pokes to his damnably magnificent chest.

"You insufferable—" *poke* "—bullheaded—" *poke* "—inconsiderate—" *poke* "—swine! I will *not* be your prisoner!"

He opened his big mouth to meet her very clever, very judicious protests when a heavy knock echoed through the den. One of the doors to the quarters opened, and a guard poked his head in.

"Forgive me, my king. There's an urgent message for you."

Hrothgar's sudden arrival sent the citadel into something of a frenzy. Ulrich and Mattias were dispatched to the southern gate with a handful of berserkers in full regalia to escort the wily old chieftain and his retinue through the city. Preferably taking the long way up.

In the meantime, Asta gathered Balmirra's court as Eydis rallied the staff to ensure Ninevar's Basilica and comfortable accommodations were ready. For his part, Vallek dressed in his kingly best with Bryn's help fastening buckles and tying straps.

His grumpy mate hovered nearby, unwilling to participate but curious enough to watch him prepare. He wasn't too proud to show off his form in his regalia—a golden breastplate polished to a mirror shine, fine leather boots trimmed in fur, his summer linen burgundy robe embroidered with gold thread, gauntlets of leather and iron, a gorget studded with rubies, and gold ear and tusk caps.

As he turned to leave his quarters, he offered Ravenna a grin. "I will return soon," he promised.

"I'll be here," she sneered. Although she meant it as a barb, her words put him at ease. His beast wasn't so agitated knowing that she would be safely tucked away in his quarters. He even left Bryn to see to Ravenna's every need.

By the time Ulrich and Mattias led Hrothgar's party into the basilica, Vallek sat upon his throne to receive them, Hormhím's handle resting against the outer side. The Balmirran court lined the central aisle, looking on in interest at the orcs from Innrinhom.

The grizzled chieftain led his retinue, mouth pulled into a scowl around his tusks. The delegation's arrival wasn't so surprising—he and Eydis had debated whether Hrothgar would send his own after hearing of Kennum's offer. What was astonishing was that Hrothgar had come himself. He wasn't known for leaving his stronghold, let alone leading peaceful delegations.

As the Innrini approached, Vallek met Hrothgar's scowl with a smile of welcome. Sitting tall in his throne, he extended his arm in greeting.

"My friends," he boomed, voice carrying through the basilica, "welcome to Balmirra."

The Balmirran court bowed their heads in respect to both him and Hrothgar. The Innrini, however, were more scattered in their response, only some choosing to bow their heads in deference to Vallek.

Hrothgar wasn't one of them. Instead, he stepped forward, his leather armor creaking, as if he meant to climb the dais steps but stopped at their foot. Even in his old age, Hrothgar was a formidable orc, his wide shoulders still rounded in muscle. His mane and neatly trimmed beard had gone silver, and one of his eyes had gone milky with rheumatism. His jaw and forearms were littered with little scars, a brutal history of his long reign.

"This is some hill you've got," he said by way of greeting.

Vallek's smile turned sharp. Balmirra was a mountain, one which Hrothgar had visited before.

"Indeed. I hope it didn't prove too steep for you."

Hrothgar snorted. "These old knees have a few steps in them yet." Squinting his rheumy eye up at Vallek, he said, "Well, no reason to belay the point. I heard you were in need of a queen, and so I've brought you one."

Even though she stood off to the side of the dais in her usual place, Vallek could feel Eydis's smug satisfaction to hear she was right.

"That is most gracious of you," said Vallek.

"You will be spoiled for choice," agreed Hrothgar.

The old chieftain stepped to the side, waving forward three orcesses, all dressed in gleaming green silks with silver thread, the colors of Innrinhom. Each was lovelier than the last, one tall and buxom, another with enticingly wide hips, and the third with beautiful ringlets of mahogany hair, a rarity amongst orc-kin.

"These are my daughters, Yphella and Yngrid," he said, gesturing at the first two orcesses, "and this is my niece, Birgit." *She of the beautiful hair.* "Any of them would make a fine queen."

The orcesses all bowed their heads in respect, smiling up at him with silver-capped tusks and low-cut tunics. His blood rushed hotter at the sight of such bounty, his eyes hardly knowing where to look first. Many a male would kill for such a choice.

"And what would you hope to gain by such a union, my friend? To part with any of your kinswomen is a high price."

Hrothgar harrumphed, as if this part needed to be dislodged from his throat. "An Innrini queen would . . . unify our kind."

"So you would recognize my position?"

The old chieftain's lips thinned between his yellowed tusks, but eventually he said, "Aye. I'd treat with you."

Vallek hid his triumphant smile behind his hand, instead nodding gravely at Hrothgar's offer.

It was just what Vallek had wanted. The reticent chieftain of In-nrinhom had come himself to barter for peace. This was everything he and Eydis had been working toward. A peaceful, diplomatic end to eastern resistance to his kingship. Finally, he would have a unified orcish kingdom, strong enough to meet the Pyrrossi threat.

He should have enjoyed it. He should already be considering which of the three orcesses would suit him best.

Except, he thought none of that. No, his thoughts were only for the angry faeling in his quarters.

The All-Mother was known for her cruel sense of humor. Just when Vallek had everything in his grasp, it seemed she would make him choose.

The east without bloodshed. Or his fae mate—with perhaps a little bloodshed.

Gods, this was truly a mess.

10

It was a long, long time before anyone returned to the king's quarters. In fact, it was nearly sunset by the time Vallek returned, with Eydis in tow.

At the sound of someone entering, Ravenna jumped up from where she'd been lazing about on one of the plush sofas in the den, halfheartedly embroidering between intermittent naps. She hurried to the threshold but stopped just before they came into view, not wanting to appear *too* eager.

Breezing confidently through the archway, Ravenna came to stand in the middle of the central hall to meet the siblings. Vallek's gaze immediately found her, and although he nodded in acknowledgement, his attitude was markedly cooler than that of yesterday.

Ravenna turned her attention instead to Eydis, watching the orcess closely as Vallek shrugged out of his robe and began to pull the caps from his ears and tusks.

Eydis nodded politely at her, too, although she wouldn't keep her gaze.

Something had happened.

Looking between the both of them, Ravenna's suspicions only grew. Their shoulders were too tense, their gazes too flighty.

"I assume the city isn't under attack," she said. The great horns of the citadel would have sounded across Balmirra if that were the case, of course, but she wanted to get them talking.

After a whole day by herself—she'd long ago released Brynhíl from having to babysit her—she was anxious to hear the news. Were she free to don her disguise and move about the citadel as a human sooth-sayer, she could've easily found out everything in the servants' dining hall. All the best information was to be had there.

Instead, she'd been cloistered in his quarters with nothing better to do than embroider and plot. For an hour she considered turning all of his socks, trou, and undershirts inside out, but that would likely only create more work for Brynhíl. Then she considered setting fire to his regalia, but there again, that would only annoy him and create work for someone else.

Hanging her head out of one of the windows had confirmed what a sheer drop it was to the citadel courtyard below. If she tied all of his fine bedding together, it might be long enough to get her down—right to the center of the courtyard with dozens of guards waiting to nab her again.

If she could fly down, she would. However, her little wings had always been too small and weak to sustain true flight. On a particularly strong updraft, she might be able to glide, but as far as getting four stories down, her wings would only slow her fall enough so that she'd perhaps break an ankle rather than a leg.

A whole day with nothing to show for it—except wild schemes and growing anxieties without a clear release. Oberon was no help. Although he assured her the herd would attack Balmirra's gates to free her if she wished, he thought it much wiser for her to give in and claim her *azai*.

Fucking over fighting? Other unicorns would be scandalized to hear it.

No they wouldn't, he scoffed. Then, after a pause, *And you won't tell them.*

It was difficult to reach Callistix from such a distance. Although her grandmare likely would have been happy to slash and skewer orcs on her horn, there were foals now in the herd to consider.

For now, Ravenna was on her own. And that meant she needed information. Starting with whatever had happened today that made these two orcs unwilling to look her in the eye.

"The city is secure," Eydis confirmed, but she wouldn't say more, her gaze shifting back nervously to Vallek.

Stripped down to just his trou, Vallek stepped forward. "You and I have much to discuss."

Well, that sounded ominous.

Perhaps she should have delighted in his careful tone. Maybe he'd reconsidered or was willing to see reason. Still, she couldn't help the stone of dread weighing down her stomach as he gazed gravely down at her.

To Eydis he said, "Thank you for your counsel today. Please have dinner sent up, and my regards to Hilde."

His sister nodded and looked more than a little relieved to beat a hasty retreat. Ravenna watched her go with a frown, which she turned on her suddenly taciturn *azai* as the door *clicked* closed behind Eydis.

Vallek raised his arm to usher her into the more comfortable den, but Ravenna stood her ground. She suspected she'd need to meet his news standing.

"What news?" she asked, wanting to get this over with.

He searched her stern face a moment longer before admitting, "Hrothgar of Innrinhom has come with his daughters and niece. He offers peace if I were to take one as my bride and queen."

None of that should have been surprising—Ravenna was aware of the political game Vallek played throughout his new, fragile kingdom, as well as his desire to seek unification without violence. A marriage of alliance was certainly a tidy solution.

Still, the stark truth of it, that such a reality had come knocking that very day, sank like stones in her gut.

He's been mine a day and already some orcesses are trying to steal him away? The thought sprang up from some primal part of her she'd denied these past years, and its vehemence unnerved her almost as much as knowing he stood on the precipice of taking a wife—who wasn't *her,* his mate.

"I see," she said through numb lips. She couldn't think of anything else to say.

His thick brows descended into a forbidding frown. "I see?" he repeated. "That's all you have to say?"

Ravenna could only shrug, meeting his frown with her own to hide how her eyes stung. "What else can I say? It's been made abundantly clear that my opinion isn't of any value."

His nostrils flared in an exasperated huff. "I've said nothing of the sort. You put words in my mouth."

She bit her lips together to keep from spitting something insulting at him. An angry fire ignited in her chest, and it was all she could do to keep from storming away.

"How else am I to feel when I'm kept prisoner here?"

Vallek sighed long and with feeling. "You are not a prisoner. This is only temporary."

Ravenna bared her fangs in a harsh smile. "Until you take a wife, you mean? Which orcess will you choose?"

"It isn't so simple," he growled.

"It was two days ago."

"Indeed it was," he spat, "but two days ago, I didn't know my own mate hid herself right under my nose." Closing the distance between them, he loomed over her as he demanded, "Why hide yourself from me? We could've had three years to sort this out."

"I didn't mean to be so inconvenient to your political timetable. I meant to stay entirely out of the way. *You* have decided I must be an obstacle to overcome."

"You're not—" He shoved his hands through his mane in a gesture of utter frustration. "You put words in my mouth again."

"I am an inconvenience," she insisted. "We both know it. You hoped to marry one of these orcesses, even to find your mate amongst them. It would've been so simple, so easy. And now . . ."

His expression turned desolate, and Ravenna's stomach flipped to realize just how true her accusation was. Being right about it didn't feel good. It was awful, in fact.

"The beast decides the mate. All orcs know and respect this," he said.

"None of that will win you an alliance with Hrothgar."

Vallek didn't immediately respond, his gaze turning pensive as he searched her face. One of his large hands rose to gently touch her cheek with his fingertips, sparking flutters of pleasure in her chest. Even now, amidst an argument, his touch so easily pleased and aroused her. That was perhaps the most frustrating thing of all.

"Why did you hide from me?" he asked, tone gone low and serious.

There were so many answers to that. None of which she wanted to tell him. So she didn't. Ravenna stood there silently, biting down on the inside of her cheek.

When he realized she didn't mean to answer, his expression hardened, his eyes going flinty. Although his fingers were warm at her cheek, his touch nevertheless turned cold.

"What will I do?" he asked as his thumb stroked her cheek. "I will find a way to keep a wife and a mate, I suppose. Kings are supposed to be selfish, are they not?"

Ravenna's insides curdled, and she moved her head away from his touch. "Don't be cruel."

"I'm being practical, as any king should be. You as my mate will satisfy my beast. Hrothgar's daughter will fulfill the unification." He said it so flippantly, as if it made so much sense, that she knew he meant to rile her. She'd hurt him with her nonanswer, and now he sought to hurt her in return.

It worked.

Not only did her eyes sting, but pressure gathered between them.

She *hated* the tears that threatened, almost as much as she hated that sardonic expression he wore.

"That wouldn't be fair. To your mate *or* your wife." It made her sick to even think about.

"The gods aren't fair, and neither are politics." He laid his hand on her shoulder, and it was big enough to span both her shoulder and up the side of her neck. He kept her still as he leaned down into her space to say, "I will have my unification, *skala*. But I won't give you up."

Ravenna sneered in his face. "Do you expect a wife in your bed and a mate at your feet?"

He chuckled humorlessly. "I'd much rather have you both in my bed."

Without thought or care, her palm *cracked* across his face in a vicious slap. "How *dare you?*" she growled, that jealous, feral part of her roaring in her ears.

"I will dare," he growled right back, "because *you're mine.*"

Her magic snapped around his wrists, holding him in place as she rose onto her toes to grab his chin in her claws. "Fae do not share *azai,* and I will not share you."

"Then claim me," he dared her, "don't hide away."

She didn't know if he leaned down or she pushed up, but in the next moment their mouths crashed together in a fiery, angry kiss. His tusks pressed into her cheeks as his lips hungrily moved against hers. She met every nip, every pass of his tongue, twining hers with his as he plundered her mouth.

When he bent to pick her up, she jumped into his waiting arms, coiling her limbs around him. *Mine. You're mine.* Digging her nails into his glorious mane, she held on as he surged forward, taking them somewhere—she didn't care.

All she felt and saw and tasted was *him.* She drank him down in great greedy gulps and went back for more, body aching to be closer to him even though she was wrapped around him. It still wasn't close enough, how would she ever be close enough, and her body and soul and magic cried out for more.

Her back hit the soft give of his bed, and then he was above her, claiming her mouth again as his hands delved through the voluminous fabric of her linen robe. She scored him with her fangs, urging him faster, closer, her hands almost frantic as they mapped every inch of his glorious chest. Nails scraping down his pectoral, she caught his flat, dark green nipple between two fingers and pinched.

A hiss puffed against her lips, and the purr in his chest ratcheted higher, nearly shaking them both in its violence.

Ravenna gasped when his scorching palm found the bare skin of her thigh. There was no teasing or hesitation, it ran up her flank to trace her hipbone before pushing between her legs. She let them fall open, murmuring enthusiastic nonsense against his tusks as his fingers skated through her slick.

He ran two fingers up the seam of her cunt, finding her clitoris with the aim of a skilled hunter. He caught it beneath his calloused thumb, beginning a merciless rhythm of circles that had her seeing starbursts.

Digging her nails into his shoulders, Ravenna's hips began to buck.

"So slick for me," he rumbled, his voice the one she so loved, the one of intimate evenings and sweet wine and soft fire glow. "You need this."

Ravenna could only moan, clutching at him as he hurtled her toward oblivion.

Her magic pooled around them, a warm ethereal caress. She felt how he shuddered as it ran gentle touches along his back. She claimed his front with her hands and lips, tasting the salt of his skin on her tongue as he nuzzled the crown of her head.

Pleasure so sudden and overwhelming it was nearly painful punched through her when he slid one long finger inside her. She wept and gushed for him, soaking his hand, and he purred in encouragement, easing deeper and deeper inside.

"You're tight," he breathed against her cheek. "So tight. But with a little practice, you'll take my cock, won't you?"

Ravenna could only thrash her head back and forth on the bed as he found a spot inside her that made every muscle in her abdomen contract.

"You will," he insisted, "you were made to take me. My hellion. My mate. You're mine."

His words kept time with his incessant pace, his finger sliding in and out of her cunt to wet her thighs as his thumb drove her mad. He nuzzled her temple and neck as she panted and wordlessly begged for more.

"Tell me. Tell me you're mine."

"Yes!" she howled. "Yes yesyesyes!"

Ravenna burst. Everything she was and knew came apart at the seams, unravelling her. He overwhelmed her, his fingers, his big body, his words all conspired to push her past limits. She was lost to him and the orgasm he claimed, body frozen in a rictus of pleasure so acute, she forgot to breathe.

She *throbbed,* her cunt clutching him tighter even than her hands in his mane. He coaxed wave upon wave, unrelenting, until spots danced around the edges of her vision. His purr buzzed against her chest, teasing her sensitive nipples, prolonging—

—unicorns screaming—salt burned her tongue—the smell of iron and blood—water in her nose—you're mad, you know—maman—

—the pleasure until she just couldn't bear it.

Ravenna gasped, senses failing her. She saw and heard and smelled nothing but him—he was all she knew as her orgasm and vision bled into one. Pleasure mixed with a hurt so deep, it seared her soul.

When both released her, she slumped to the bed in relief.

The world around her swam as the sweat cooled on her skin.

For a singular moment, Ravenna lay still. For a moment, she lay in the arms of her *azai,* safe and satisfied.

Then, one by one, her realities came back to her.

She gasped again, this time in horror. *What have I done?*

Sitting up, she pushed his hand away, wincing at how her own slick gushed down her legs. Worse was how she ached for him, immediately bereft without his touch. Still she retreated, flinging herself from the bed.

"Ravenna!" he called after her.

But she didn't stop. Only drew her arms around herself, her linen robe loose about her shoulders.

She stopped only when she made it to the den, to the chair she'd placed by the window. Into it she climbed, drawing her knees up to her chest.

What have I done? What have I done?

II

Vallek . . . might need a new strategy. That assumed he'd had one to begin with, which he couldn't truly say he did, but after the unmitigated disaster of the previous night, whatever he'd thought the plan was clearly needed to go.

The haunted way she looked at him . . . he wore it as a wound on his soul.

Everything had felt so good, so right; feeling her hot, lithe body in his arms as she came apart fulfilling a very male, very ancient need in him. Nothing had ever satisfied him the way witnessing her glorious climax did. He wanted it again. Forever. Would've made her come on his hand all night if she hadn't pushed him away.

But she *ran* from him. Literally ran away.

His own *mate*.

It was a dagger to his pride, and for long moments afterwards, he'd sat alone in his bed, stunned silent. Her slick cooling on his hand, his cock still throbbing in the confines of his trou, his mind hadn't been able to comprehend what'd just happened. Where he went wrong.

Pursuing her into the den hadn't yielded any answers. If anything, it only made everything worse. Seeing her curled up on that chair, looking for all the world like a wounded animal and at him like he was the very hunter who'd hurt her, had shriveled up his lust faster than cold water and thoughts of his granddam.

He didn't know what was wrong, but he didn't need to ask to know she wouldn't tell him. With how she looked at him, he thought he'd be lucky if she ever spoke to him again.

Vallek hadn't known what to do. His beast whined inside him, a desperate, clammy feeling overcoming him as he hurried to fetch her a cloth to clean herself and then his coverlet to wrap round her. She sat there stiffly, not moving at all, and Vallek could think of nothing to say.

He retreated alone to his bedchamber, convinced that while he might have won their sparring, goading her with his talk of wives, he also may have lost something far more important.

There was little sleep to be found that night, marking the second night he went with hardly any rest. His tactician's mind pored over what they'd done, every word and expression, searching for an answer to what went wrong.

Through the dark hours, he couldn't pinpoint a precise moment to focus on. The deeper the night became, the more he suspected he should apologize—but for what he didn't know.

When predawn light began to filter weakly through his bedchamber window, Vallek quit the field. Rising from his bed, he grabbed only a tunic and boots before heading for the door.

A quick glance into the den revealed that Ravenna had at least moved to one of the sofas. His chest ached peculiarly to see what a small lump she made under the coverlet, just the very top of her raven-black head visible against the scarlet fabric of the sofa. The need to hold her, to gently place her on his bed as he had the previous night was a visceral thing, lodging just behind his heart.

Instead, he padded silently across the hall to the door. Not a retreat—a strategic withdrawal for now.

The guards on the other side of the door were surprised to see him, but they were too well trained to do anything but watch on in silence as he slipped the tunic over his head and stepped into his boots. He left them guarding her, quietly descending through the citadel.

No one but the night watch was awake at this early hour, not even the cooks. Vallek had the citadel to himself.

He sat in the basilica as the sun rose, watching how the light crested over the eastern mountains. Morning rays slanted into the basilica, catching on the flecks of pyrite running through the red limestone. The great panels of stained glass cast shafts of colorful light onto the checkered pattern of the flagstones, purples and greens and reds.

It was a dazzling, beautiful display, a reminder of the genius and might of Balmirra and his forebearers.

And it was lost on Vallek.

Regaining his feet, he left the basilica behind, a restless despondency taking root in his chest. He didn't care for the feeling at all.

His feet brought him to the training yard, and he contented himself with wearing out his body. A few of his berserkers were about by now but all gave him a wide berth, no doubt remembering his fury in the pits.

No matter how hard he beat the straw-stuffed dummies with his wooden practice sword, Vallek couldn't seem to shake his dejection.

Is she awake now? Was she disappointed to not find me there—or relieved?

Whack went his sword against the dummy, old straw bursting from a fraying seam.

His thoughts circled like birds in an updraft, spiraling higher and higher. The harder he beat the dummy, the greater his frustration. Sweat soaked his linen tunic and matted his hair to his skull, but he didn't want to stop. To stop was to face whatever this was, whatever he did.

But how could he face what he didn't know?

The sun rose above the citadel wall before Vallek finally stepped away, chest heaving. Wiping the sweat from his eyes, he noticed Asta standing off to the side observing him.

Grinning cheekily when she realized he'd seen her, she jogged over to meet him. With her thin sleeveless tunic and loose braid, she wasn't yet dressed for the day. Still, she took up another practice sword, clacking their weapons together.

"Care for a partner who can fight back?"

He rarely denied Asta; sparring with her was always a delight, for she made an agile opponent, testing his strength and cunning.

And yet, "Not today. I'm in a foul mood."

Asta hummed, making a show of looking closer at his face. "Yes, you do look pretty haggard."

Vallek huffed. "You're not helping."

"Who said I was?" She grinned again, but when she saw her usual charms weren't working on him, she sobered. "What is it, *breddah?* You know you can tell me."

He didn't want to. Gods, he didn't want to admit his own mate had run from him as though he'd struck her rather than pleasured her. His pride was far more battered than the dummy he'd pulverized, and it shrunk away from revealing what a hit it'd taken.

Yet, there was no one else Vallek trusted more than his sisters.

Pressing on the bruise, he admitted under his breath, "She resists me."

Asta's brows rose. Looking around the yard to mark the growing number of warriors gathering, she caught his arm to pull him under one of the thatch awnings that provided shade for those training.

"Tell me," she said, all her boisterousness gone.

In as few words as possible, Vallek explained how the previous two nights had gone with his faeling mate. How she fought him at every turn. How his beast yearned for her as much as it was bewildered by her.

"She's known all this time, Asta," he sighed. "Yet she hid herself from me. Denied our bond. She still does."

Twirling the end of her braid with a finger, a habit she'd had since girlhood, Asta asked, "Have you asked her why she hides?"

"Of course," he said, "but she gives me nothing. Anything I get must be fought for."

"You wouldn't like it if it was easy," she teased gently. "We both know you'd be bored with a simpering orcess within the month."

Vallek harrumphed, not liking that she was right. "Perhaps, perhaps not. But why must everything be a fight? She's known all this time, has sat with me for many evenings over *talfon,* and yet she doesn't trust me."

"She agreed to play *talfon?* More than once? Yes, you're well suited." Sighing profoundly, she slapped her hand onto Vallek's shoulder. "That time before, she wasn't your mate. She was someone else. Whatever you had then, it must have felt safe enough for her. What you have now is different."

"She has seen me for who I am all this time," he argued. "Yet she still hid away. She still runs from me."

"What have you done to reassure her? To win her over as your *mate?*"

Vallek's mouth opened, but nothing came out.

There had to be something.

"I have told her she's safe," he insisted, although he didn't need Asta rolling her eyes to tell him what a weak answer it was.

"Told her, yes. You've told her many things. Ordered her about, too, I'm sure. What have you done to prove it?"

Vallek had no answer for that. *I'm her mate,* his beast insisted. For any orc-kin, that would've been enough. The knowing they all felt, it was a foundation to build upon. The beast knew, and the beast inside was their truest selves. It might be wrapped up in pretty, divine platitudes, but at its core, the beast was the intrinsic self of every orc-kin.

He *knew* Ravenna, knew she was for him.

Why wasn't that enough?

Seeing his inability to answer, Asta groaned dramatically. "I swear, you and Eydis claim to be great lovers of women, but you hardly seem to understand them." Gripping his shoulder hard, she rocked him back and forth, as if to gently shake sense into him. "You must reassure her, *breddah*. She's a fae amongst orcs and must have a good reason for it. But she won't tell you until you've earned her trust."

If he hadn't done that in the three years he'd known her, how was he to start now?

"My king!"

Vallek and Asta looked up to find Ulrich hurrying toward them.

Ducking under the awning, the lord commander rushed to say, "Forgive the intrusion, my king, but we just received urgent word from Toksfinge."

The name immediately sharpened Vallek's attention. Although not a large place, Toksfinge was nevertheless an important fishing village along the southern coast of Dyfan Bay. Toksfinge was one of a collection of villages and outposts that ringed the southern curve of the bay, marching up to the Spearhead, a squat peninsula overlooking the estuary that led from the western sea into Dyfan Bay.

Toksfinge was one of the southernmost of these villages and the nearest to Balmirra, about two days' hard run away.

Already anticipating what Ulrich would say, Vallek asked, "How many?"

"One fae ship," Ulrich answered. "It came ashore just west of the village."

The fae and orc-kin had long vied for control of the bay, as well as the estuary leading into it. With the major strongholds of Kaldebrak, Holdur, and Balmirra all within just a few days of the bay waters, maintaining it was vital to the security of orcish territories. With the fae rimming the northern coast and their capital of Fallorian overlooking the mouth of the estuary, keeping control of the south, especially the Spearhead, was imperative.

No incursions could be tolerated.

"Find Mattias and prepare the berserkers," Vallek ordered. "We leave by noon and we run through the night."

Ulrich's gaze flared with eagerness. "Yes, my king."

"Vallek, you can't just leave," Asta insisted. "The beast won't let you."

"You've given me much to think on. The days' run will do my mind good."

"Indeed," agreed Ulrich, "there is time yet to get this soothsayer business sorted. There are more important things that demand the king's attention now."

Asta turned a rare withering look upon the lord commander. "There's nothing more important, more sacred than the mate-bond."

"She will still be here when we return," Ulrich grumbled. "The bond is still new, a little distance can be withstood."

Ulrich spoke Vallek's own mind, and yet, hearing the words aloud, they grated against him. The very idea of leaving his mate now, in the early days of their bond, went against every instinct. His beast roared at him for even considering it.

"Find Mattias," he ordered Ulrich.

Startled by Vallek's shortness, Ulrich's lips thinned before he bowed and turned to fulfill his orders.

"Vallek, you can't really—"

Lifting his hand, he silenced Asta's objections. From his belt he pulled the ceremonial key to the citadel and handed it to her.

"See that this gets to Eydis. She knows what to do. And have her tell Hrothgar; he will understand the delay." The old chieftain had himself fought many a skirmish against both fae and Pyrrossi incursions.

"Send Ulrich to handle it since he's so keen," Asta argued.

"I lead by example, Asta, you know that."

"A chieftain would see to it themselves, yes. But you're more than that now. A king is pulled in many directions. You can't go charging off any time something arises."

"The people expect it of me. Hrothgar will expect it. You want me to lose face in front of him? Now, when an alliance may have to be negotiated without a marriage?"

Asta's look was dark as she said, "You complain that she runs from you, and yet here you are, running away yourself."

Vallek reeled at the reproach, but his sister didn't give him time to respond, turning on her heel to march angrily up to the citadel. He watched her go, fists clenched.

She was right, of course. It was another blow to his pride to admit it.

But the safety of the kingdom couldn't be ignored. And although putting distance between himself and his faeling mate might be frowned upon by others, he thought perhaps a few days apart might be good.

Maybe with a few days' run, he might think of a way to win that trust Asta spoke of. Maybe he could find a way forward that included both unification and his mate.

Not a retreat, then. A strategic withdrawal. To strategize.

<h1 style="text-align:center">12</h1>

It wasn't that Vallek had left that Ravenna minded. He did that often enough. It'd been that he *just left*. Had she been still asleep when he returned to quickly gather a few things for his journey, she'd no doubt he'd have left without saying goodbye at all.

"If I'm not allowed to leave here without your consent, then I don't think you should be leaving without mine," she'd argued, more for the sake of it than anything else.

"The safety of the realm warrants exception," he'd replied as he donned his lighter set of boiled leather armor.

"Oh, well, if we're making exceptions, then mates shouldn't—"

Turning on her quickly, he'd asked, *"So you agree we are mates?"*

Ravenna spluttered. *"I never said we weren't! I said it shouldn't matter."*

It'd been the wrong thing to say, whatever playfulness glittering in his eyes snuffing quicker than a blown-out candle. He finished readying in silence before marching to the door.

"You will remain in my quarters," he announced without looking back. *"I will return anon."*

She was about to call out his hissy-fit, but he didn't give her the chance, slamming the door behind him. Ravenna stomped her foot in frustration, and then scrubbed her face in annoyance at doing something so childish. Fates, she didn't know whether she wanted to throttle him or pet him more. Right now, throttle him.

After the previous night, Ravenna didn't know if it would ever be safe to touch him again.

It wasn't that she hadn't enjoyed their passion. She did.

And it wasn't that she didn't have a little experience already. She did.

It was . . . well, everything. She'd thought herself able to handle her own *azai*. She'd watched him for years, knew enough to suspect he'd be a passionate lover. Knowing something and experiencing it were two very different things, however, and having all of that lust and attention focused on her—and in *anger*—was too much.

It's not supposed to be like that.

Her handful of experiences and years of exploring her own body hadn't prepared her for the onslaught. Of course, she wasn't about to admit that to him. Oh no. Not like this, kept as his prisoner, under threat of an orcess wife.

Ravenna retreated behind her own defiance, a safe place that fit like a well-worn pair of boots. Others may balk at finding solace in mischief and mayhem, but Ravenna found it soothing to look about his quarters and think of ways to make his life difficult. She decided her best course of action was to burn his bed.

She knew of his love for comfort, how on longer trips, his large tent included a plush camp bed. For as rough and rugged as the king could be, he did enjoy his luxuries, too. His bed was a soft target, one she wasn't above threatening, especially since she'd no plans of joining him in it any time soon.

Of course, she'd burn it once he was back. For now, it was all hers.

In the meantime, with little else to do than stew and wait for Brynhíl to check on her, Ravenna soaked in his private bath.

Hot springs could be found all over the mountain, as she understood it, and the restorative mineral water produced in them was renowned across the territories. More than a few intrepid orcs ran thriving businesses bottling the mineral water up for sale, as well as adding it to creams, potions, and tonics.

Although the steam carried a fragrant tang to it, Ravenna still thoroughly enjoyed pulling off her linen robe and sinking up to her chin. The warm water did wonders for the crick in her neck, developed over a night on the sofa.

Alone in the baths, she felt safe enough to unfurl her wings. Even though they folded up into discreet little bundles between her shoulder blades, it'd taken quite a bit of maneuvering to keep them out of sight when Brynhíl helped her bathe the other day. Although Bryn was a kind orcess, and Ravenna as a half-fae was likely expected to have wings like a fae woman, wings were a vulnerability, an easy target for enemies.

That was why they were often only for *azai* to see and touch. And . . . Ravenna's were small. Too small.

Another vulnerability she'd no intention of sharing with her own *azai* any time soon. Not after last night.

Sinking further into the water, Ravenna tried to leave thoughts of that outside the bath.

She'd just gotten relaxed when Oberon decided it was time to chat.

Are you safe, Crow? How are you?

I'm well enough. Still confined to his quarters, even though he's left for some sort of derring do.

The king is away?

That seems to be the plan, she thought grumpily.

Ah, this works in our favor.

What does? she asked suspiciously.

It isn't perfect, but mother has been forming an idea of how to break you out of there.

I see . . .

Do you know an orc that'd make a good hostage?

Ravenna sighed as she dipped below the surface, bubbles cascading around her face.

She would be wrinklier than a walnut by the time she finally made it out of the bath and convinced the herd not to take a hostage to negotiate her surrender to them.

It wasn't until late afternoon that visitors came, and it wasn't Brynhíl. Instead, after a swift knock on the door, making Ravenna jump up from her half-doze on the sofa, Eydis and another orcess entered the suite.

"Good day," Eydis greeted her. "I hope we're not disturbing you."

"Not possible," Ravenna replied, rising to bob her head in deference.

The second orcess smiled as Eydis introduced her. "This is my mate Hilde. She's been anxious to meet you."

"Can you blame me?" said Hilde. "The one who felled Vallek Far-Sight . . . my everlasting respect." She reached out to gently lay her hand on Ravenna's right shoulder, a friendly greeting amongst orcs.

A little shorter and stockier than Eydis, Hilde was nevertheless far more fashionably dressed than her mate. Artfully draped in blue linen robes cinched with a tooled leather belt, she wore sandals laced halfway up her calf. Little fringes of leather decorated her belt and sleeves, some studded with turquoise beads. The same little pops of turquoise could be seen in her many braids, elaborately knotted together atop her head.

Whereas Eydis was all understated elegance, Hilde presented as the height of orcish beauty. Broad shoulders, sharp tusks, and a jet-black mane, she was all powerful lines softened by gold ornamentation. Vallek and Eydis both had blue eyes, though of different hues, fairly rare for orcs. Hilde's were brown, much more common, except that hers were such a light brown they were almost gold, matching the golden clasps in her braids, gold bands around her wrists, and the gold mating torque around her neck.

"I wouldn't go so far as to say he's been felled," laughed Ravenna, "maybe tripped up a little. That's all."

Hilde and Eydis shared a significant look. Taking her hand to pat sympathetically, Hilde said, "Of course, *vini mun,* that's why he's left all of a sudden. Not because he can't make sense of you."

Ravenna's brows rose nearly to her hairline. *Surely not.*

"My brother is many things. Right now, one of those things is stupid." Eydis shrugged. "Males."

"Vallek is one of the best ones, though," Hilde said diplomatically. "He's just out of sorts. The call of the beast can unnerve even the hardest warrior."

"I know him to be a good king," Ravenna replied, "if a bit tyrannical of late."

Hilde and Eydis snickered, nodding in agreement.

"Try to be gentle with him," said Hilde.

"In the meantime . . ." From a deep robe pocket, Eydis produced a familiar leatherbound book. "I believe this is yours."

Ravenna gasped, rushing to reclaim her mother's grimoire. The book almost sang when it touched her skin, and she swore she nearly heard her mother sigh. Giddy with relief, she clutched the grimoire to her chest, defying anyone to take it away again.

"The lord commander is also many things. In this, he was wrong. Please accept my apologies."

"How did you . . .?"

Eydis shrugged. "It wasn't difficult with Ulrich gone."

"She picked the lock," Hilde whispered loudly.

Ravenna's eyes rounded with surprise. "You would take such a risk?"

The orcess snorted. "It's hardly a risk. He hasn't changed the lock in over a decade."

Her mind whirred with the implications, but most important was that the sister of her *azai* had done this for her. Knowing something of the canny orcess, it wasn't without its reasons, but that mattered far less to Ravenna than having the grimoire back.

Ravenna reached to place her hand on Eydis's shoulder. "Thank you, Eydis. This book is precious to me."

Expression gone serious, the orcess nodded in understanding. "I know what it is to only have a few precious things left of a beloved mother. Had they been taken from me, I wouldn't have been half as restrained as you."

Ravenna's restraint had been born from a need to survive, but she suspected Eydis understood that, too. This gesture wouldn't ever be forgotten.

Clapping her hands, Eydis announced, "Now, onto business. I'm afraid this isn't a mere social call."

No, Eydis didn't seem the type to ever make social calls. Information-gathering excursions, yes.

With a fond look at her mate, Eydis explained, "Hilde is the best seamstress in Balmirra and owns one of the most successful workshops in the city. She's come to take your measurements."

Ravenna's brows rose again. She didn't know why she'd let them descend from her hairline in the first place. "Whatever for?"

"An excuse to meet you, for one," said Hilde.

"And for when my brother makes up his mind," added Eydis.

"*And* do you really want to wear that robe around forever?"

Ravenna peered down at herself. She honestly hadn't thought about her attire much. Bryn had provided an extra robe, and it was far more comfortable than her disguise kirtles.

Honestly, she hadn't thought about her attire much at all throughout her life. She and her mother wore practical trou for working, breezy cotton or linen shifts in the summer, and heavier wool skirts in the winter. While her father always provided the best of everything, including silks to line their garments, brocades and fashionable cuts served little purpose in their cottage. The only real nod they made to beautiful clothes were the embroidery they added, something to do during the long winter evenings.

"What else am I supposed to languish in captivity in?" she asked, earning her a round of laughs from the orcesses.

"You'll only have to bear your captivity a little longer, I suspect," said Eydis as she settled down into one of the plush chairs in the den. "Even a king must obey their beast, and his will make him pay for this separation."

Ravenna cared less about his being gone than her being confined, but she kept that to herself. At least for now, she had company.

Hilde ushered her to one of the low tables and helped her step up onto it. It made her only a hair taller than the orcess, but it would have to do.

Pulling a measuring ribbon from her robe pocket, Hilde mimed for Ravenna to hold her arms up parallel to the floor. She did, holding onto the grimoire. It was too soon to let it go again.

"May I?" asked Hilde before coming closer with her ribbon.

Ravenna swallowed hard. Orcs were far more tactile than she was used to. She doubted Hilde ever needed to ask any of her other clients. That she did planted a little seed of fondness in Ravenna's heart.

"Yes. But . . . please don't touch my back."

"All right," the orcess agreed easily. Hilde seemed to think nothing of it, but Ravenna didn't have to look to know Eydis's eyes glinted with interest. There would be nothing getting past her.

"So, Ravenna. Tell me about yourself." Not really a question from Eydis.

Ravenna's gaze fell to Hilde, and the orcess's lips twitched into a grin as she rolled her eyes. "Humor her while I do this, if you please."

Clearing her throat, Ravenna began, "Well, I lived with my mother by the sea . . ."

And so Ravenna spent her afternoons, Eydis and Hilde making a point to visit every day of Vallek's absence. Hilde often brought fabrics for

Ravenna to see and feel, wanting a better sense of what would suit her.

"Your coloring is beautiful," she remarked, "I've so many ideas!"

Something about her fervor, and the stylish way she dressed herself, had Ravenna sweating.

Still, she liked the orcesses very much, and if sampling fabrics and letting Hilde stick pins into prototypes was how she had to spend her time, there were certainly worse things.

Though subtle, the afternoon never went without Eydis fishing for more information. Ravenna revealed enough of what she thought would satisfy Vallek's sister. She didn't think it dangerous to speak of her mother and their cottage, nor the little beach where they fished and looked for sea glass.

These soft interrogations had to be borne, of course, and weren't unexpected. Still, it was a relief when the subject turned to politics.

When Eydis asked what she knew of the conflict between fae and orcs, Ravenna delighted in discussing one of her favorite subjects—history. Much as she might have resented her father's plans, she'd loved nothing more than spending an evening listening to him tell her the many stories of his people. He brought her books of history, rhetoric, philosophy, and mathematics. He taught her languages and swordplay.

In everything he did, Maxim ensured that Ravenna knew about the world she'd one day be thrown into. Staying with her mother for decades by the sea meant that she didn't truly understand the world—she quickly found that out when she snuck into a certain chieftain's camp—but still, her father had done everything in his power to arm her.

Eydis too had a love of history, and it was a treat to compare the histories they knew from a different perspective. With only an occasional good-humored eye roll, Hilde listened on as afternoons were spent debating important decisions and turning points, their discussions often continuing over dinners.

Eydis seemed pleased with Ravenna's knowledge, especially over internal orcish politics.

"Well, I have been paying attention," she delighted in informing her. "Not just sitting around waiting to have visions."

"Indeed. And what say you about the marriage question?"

Hilde snorted over her chickpea and goat meat pie. "Is that what they're calling it? The *marriage question?*"

"Yes," Eydis sighed. "Hardly original."

Ravenna pushed the seasoned carrots and chickpeas around her plate. "I don't have an unbiased opinion."

"I should hope not. Neither do I." Eydis popped a spoonful of pie into her mouth, waiting for Ravenna's answer.

"It seems . . . short-sighted to agree to an Innrini bride," she said finally.

"Why do you say that?"

"It will bring Hrothgar onside, yes, but it will also invite him into Vallek's circle. He will be *family*. He'll try to influence Balmirra through his daughter or niece. Vallek will never be rid of him. Such influence may very well ostracize other chieftains like Kennum, who will certainly be offended that one of his own daughters wasn't chosen instead."

Sitting back in her seat, Eydis swirled her goblet of wine with a satisfied grin. "Very good. We'll make a politician of you yet."

Ravenna bit back her satisfaction. It shouldn't please her so much to have impressed Eydis, but here she was.

"Well then, you little tyrants, what's the answer instead?" asked Hilde.

Eydis grunted unhappily. "Now that's the question."

Ravenna's satisfaction fizzled when she realized even Eydis didn't have an answer to this mating mess.

She knew she couldn't be Vallek's mate, not in truth. Being a true mate to him would mean abandoning her plans, everything she'd worked for to avenge her parents. Taking a half-fae queen would mean forsaking his own plans and everything he'd worked for to unify the orcish territories.

It was and would always be impossible. A cruel joke by the fates.

There was no use mourning what would never be, nor missing someone she would never truly have.

She didn't consider it a mistake that she never saw visions of herself beyond her campaign of vengeance. Whatever her fate, it was tied with Amaranthe's. Her future wasn't hers to give.

Stubborn as he might be, not even a king could change fate.

On the fourth day of her solitude, she received her visit far earlier in the day—and this time it was Asta rather than Eydis.

Vallek's younger sister breezed into the suite, light on her feet despite hauling an enormous basket. Even set on the ground, it rose nearly to her hip, with a lid almost as wide as Ravenna's wingspan.

"Good morning, *tristah*," she chirped.

"Good morning," Ravenna replied, hiding her smile at being called *little sister*.

"I've been talking with Hilde, and we had an idea. I know you've been cooped up in here, so . . ." Asta gestured at the enormous basket.

Ravenna scowled. "No."

"But it's perfect! You'll fit just fine."

"It's a laundry basket."

"Yes. That's why no one will suspect." Asta winked. "Go put on your human disguise."

It was ridiculous, but Ravenna still found herself eyeing the basket. She would indeed fit. Rather comfortably, actually.

The truth was, apart from her visits with Eydis and Hilde, she was breathtakingly bored. Cooped up was an understatement. She'd scream if she embroidered anything else, and she'd already reread her mother's grimoire twice.

There were only so many baths and naps she could take. And sleeping in Vallek's big bed, the silk bedding saturated in his scent, only made it worse.

Her desire for him had been bad enough but manageable when

she was hidden in her disguise. Now though, having been recognized and acknowledged by his beast, her needs were growing more acute. More than once, she'd come awake from a hazy dream of him, her hand caught between her legs.

She refused to touch herself in his bed, and after that disastrous night of angry passion, she didn't dare do it elsewhere, either. The temptation was too great. Given the chance, she'd roll herself up in his sheets and never stop. Not until he returned and she begged him to make the aching stop.

So, no, she dared not even start for fear of never stopping.

She wouldn't give him the satisfaction of thinking she spent her time longing for him.

A day outside could help. She could truly stretch her legs. Get a little sunshine. Perhaps even visit the herd and quell their more murderous plots to take the city and overthrow its government in her name.

"It's your choice," Asta said, far less subtle than her sister would be, "if you really want to spend another day in here . . ."

"*Fine,*" Ravenna relented. "But if anyone asks, this was your doing."

Asta hooted with laughter as Ravenna ran to put on her human disguise.

In no time at all, she was huddled in the basket, wearing a plain brown kirtle as well as her cloak. Asta piled more linens on top of her, giving the appearance of true laundry. The air was oppressively hot within the basket, and when Asta picked it up to begin walking, a moment of seasickness accosted Ravenna's stomach as she swayed.

Her attack of nerves didn't help as the door opened and they walked past the guards. With a friendly word from Asta, they closed the door, not even asking to see inside the basket or check that Ravenna was still within the suite.

The thrill of getting out was tempered only by her swelling nausea. There was nothing to really see in the basket, the weave too tight to spy out of, and so Ravenna closed her eyes and listened as Asta strode down through the citadel.

They crossed paths with dozens of orcs, many of whom called out greetings to Asta that she returned. Still, the orcess's pace never slowed, and no one ever stopped to peer inside the basket.

Ravenna could hardly believe her luck, and it was downright shocking when Asta finally came to a stop and put down the basket. Cool air smacked Ravenna's face as the orcess lifted the layers of fabric off her.

"Welcome to freedom, *tristah!*" Asta whispered.

Poking her head out, Ravenna took the hand Asta offered and quickly clambered out of the basket in her human face.

Asta peered down at her false face, releasing a low whistle. "It's uncanny. I can see you under there in a way. But you look every bit the human."

"I've gotten a lot of practice." Looking around, Ravenna realized they were standing in a quiet part of the citadel, near where the laundry did truly get done. A small door in the curtain wall would lead down a set of narrow steps onto a side street below.

Replacing the lid on the basket, Asta said, "Meet me back here before sundown and I'll take you back up."

"I will."

"And don't even think of leaving the city. Ulrich's warned the garrison to keep an eye out for you, particularly at the gates." Pointing a big green finger in Ravenna's face, she warned, "Don't make me regret this, *tristah.*"

"I won't. I promise."

Vallek hadn't pushed his men so hard in a long while. The berserkers were too well trained to complain, but Mattias insisted they rest rather than making the last push to Toksfinge that second evening.

From one rise over, they could just spot the seaside town. Nothing seemed amiss; no houses destroyed or ablaze, no townsfolk fleeing south. About two leagues northwest, bobbing in the shallow waters of the bay, was a fae ship. All elegant lines, its white sail was stowed, and the chain of an anchor glinted in the late-afternoon sun.

Without an obvious threat to meet, Vallek agreed. His warriors were given their rest while Ulrich and two volunteers were sent ahead to Toksfinge to procure more information.

They returned in time for the evening meal, bringing with them strange tidings.

"The town elders welcome you, my king," Ulrich reported. "They are anxious to be rid of the fae interlopers. When they first arrived, the fae captain demanded to speak with the highest ranking representative they could find."

"So there's been no violence?" Vallek asked. *Strange.*

"Not yet. Although, they have chased any fishing boat trying to sail the bay back into town. They refuse to leave until they speak with someone."

"Well, then. I suppose it's good we've arrived to hear what they have to say."

Vallek lay down that night with uneasiness as a bedfellow. It was more than just the uncomfortable ground beneath his head—much as he enjoyed his comforts, he could run rough with his berserkers if needed. No, he spent most of the night trying to divine the stars.

What could the fae want? It wasn't unprecedented for them to send a delegation to Balmirra or even Kaldebrak when they truly wanted something.

Holding a village hostage was just a petty play at power. Their queen was known to enjoy such games, flexing her might.

And Vallek had literally come running. At their behest, it would seem to them.

Should've asked her what they wanted. If he'd thought about this for half a moment, he might've done the smarter thing and asked his own mate gifted with foresight if she had any information to elucidate the strangeness.

Vallek knew better than to rely solely on Ravenna's visions, of course. He'd been building his unification far longer than he'd known her, even as a soothsayer. Still, a wise king was one who went into every situation with as much information as possible. Kings who ran headlong into the unknown didn't long hold their thrones.

There was nothing for it now but to arrive tomorrow rested and sharp.

At least, that was the smart thing. His unhappy beast had far different ideas.

Its plan was to sink the fae ship and run home as fast as possible. Back to *her.*

For more sneers and nonanswers.

His beast sighed at the thought, smitten. The pathetic thing.

Every step away from her had brought a fresh wave of agony. His body tore itself apart with wanting to turn back. The ache was worse than recovering from a broken limb, the itch was worse than the reddest rash. His need for her bristled under his skin, frustrating him that the bond had already begun to take root. No matter that they'd only really spent a few days in each other's company and most of it had been arguing.

Even memories of having her in his arms, his hand clutching her cunt, were tainted by her reaction. The most natural thing in the world—bringing his own mate pleasure—felt wrong. He hated that most of all.

Between the beast in his chest and the fae camping along his bay, Vallek doubted he'd get any sleep that night.

His beast, monstrously unhappy with him, agreed.

It didn't take long for the berserkers to sense his foul mood the next day. Even Ulrich gave up trying to coax him into conversation. Vallek didn't want to hear it. *Get this done and get home.*

The troops rallied early, ready to march not long after dawn. As they descended the slope toward the shoreline, Vallek split his forces, sending half to form a perimeter around Toksfinge while the others followed him to confront the fae camp.

Pebbles ground beneath their heavy feet, and Vallek watched as a half-dozen fae rose from logs they'd set around a central fire. He pulled Hormhím free of his belt, holding the axe loose but ready in his grip.

The fae fell fluidly into formation, fanning out behind a tall male who took the lead. Hair the color of starlight, he was formidable but would've been more so had he any meat on his bones. Concave cheeks and sunken sockets gave the impression of a walking corpse. Black veins were just visible beneath his thin, gray-white skin.

The fae's leader stared at Vallek with irises of a dull gold, set within eerie black sclera. His lips were tinged blue and ringed in a line of black, and it was a ghoulish sight to see them lift into something between a smirk and a smile.

Vallek stepped forward with just Ulrich and Mattias at his side. A show they were willing to talk—and that they weren't afraid to meet six fae in battle just the three of them.

"Has someone important come to greet us finally?" the fae asked in accented orcish.

"Mind your tone," Vallek warned in perfect faethling. "You speak to a king."

To his credit, the fae warrior's brows lifted in surprise. Glancing over Vallek's shoulder at the neat columns of berserkers, all armed and armored, the ball of the fae's throat bobbed as he swallowed hard.

The fae bowed his head—not much, just enough to show respect—and the others repeated his gesture.

"Forgive my impudence," said the fae. "We come not as enemies but friends."

"I will be the one who decides that," Vallek replied, switching back to his native tongue.

"We have been sent by our queen, Amaranthe the Pure, to warn you. A dangerous criminal is believed to be in your territories."

"Indeed. And what has he done?"

"*She* has committed treason and sown sedition. She's a halfling mongrel, born of a human whore. Our queen seeks to bring her to justice, and should you help her in this, she is willing to renegotiate the terms of the Treaty of Spearhead."

Shit.

Vallek heard Ulrich's sharp intake. Such an offer was more than tempting—the treaty, signed by Amaranthe with the Balmirran chief some two-hundred years ago, created the current although tenuous borders between the faelands and orcish territories. One town along the northern border, Kavala, had been designated as a trading post between the two peoples, but otherwise, contact was limited.

To avoid losing more warriors, the previous chief had agreed to pay hefty taxes on any orcish ships caught sailing on the northern side of the bay, as well as those coming in and out of the estuary to the sea, bound for Balmirra or Kaldebrak. Great shipments of iron and copper were sent to Kavala for the price of a few bolts of silk—less trade and more tribute.

Although not exactly burdensome given the wealth of minerals and iron ore within the Griegens, the treaty had always been unpopular. To do away with it, to keep their iron or trade it for far more, was a prospect no king would turn away from.

"Your queen must want her badly."

"Indeed she does. This halfling is dangerous." Raising his voice, the fae added, "To the one who turns her in—be they fae, orc, human, or otherwise—Queen Amaranthe will reward them with their weight in gold."

Vallek bit down on the growl building within his chest. By the All-Mother, what had his hellion gotten herself into?

Perhaps it's not her. There had to be more than one halfling fae woman in the world.

But what were the odds that one would be just where the Fae Queen thought she was?

Shit.

"What makes you think she's in my lands?"

"Extensive searches have been carried out in the north. She isn't there. That leaves the south."

It was flimsy reasoning by Vallek's estimation, but that mattered much less when he knew such a creature was lounging this very moment in his quarters, no doubt plotting some sort of mischief. The thought of Ravenna only set his beast to growling more fiercely.

Take them, rip them, destroy them.

Even if she wasn't the one Queen Amaranthe sought, these fae were still a danger to his mate.

Starting a war would endanger her even more, however.

The fae leader extended his arm to indicate the wider Dyfan Bay. "We ask permission to sail your waters, to warn your good people of the danger. And the reward."

"No."

The denial came swifter than an arrow, stunning the fae as surely as a true attack.

Ulrich shifted behind him, his displeasure pressing against Vallek's back.

"*I* will inform my people. You will return to yours, as per the terms of the treaty." Just as orcs weren't to be in the northern bay—at least not without paying taxes—so too were fae meant to avoid the southern waters.

The fae's lips thinned. "I see. The Queen would prefer it if all orcs were looking for the halfling."

"And I would prefer it if the Queen didn't let dangerous criminals escape into my lands."

Offended, the fae warriors scowled, looking between themselves. They wouldn't do anything, not with the numbers as they were, but Vallek still eyed them warily.

"I grant you safe passage across the bay. You may tell your queen that her warning has been heeded."

The fae tried a little more cajoling, promising more riches, more towns open to trade, but Vallek held. When they finally realized they would get nothing more from him, the fae leader snorted.

"Very well. Thank you for your time, orc king."

He merely nodded, not rising to their bait. If they truly didn't know his name, then they were poorly trained emissaries. If they thought slights would get them what promises hadn't, then they were stupid emissaries.

Two fae kept their attention on Vallek as the others gathered their things. Then, as a unit, the fae trudged into the water to board their ship.

Vallek stood silent watch to ensure the threat left his shores.

He would leave a contingent behind to make safe the village and ease the minds of the town elders. A scouting team would be sent along the coast to watch the ship and confirm that they sailed back to the faelands. The rest would run with him back to Balmirra once they lost sight of the ship.

All-Mother, who is it my beast has chosen?

Ulrich came to stand beside him, his gaze contemplative as he watched the fae make ready their ship. Vallek knew what Ulrich thought, and his beast began to growl seeing his own second considering the fae's offer.

"My king—"

"*Silence,*" Vallek hissed. His beast roared in his ears, and he was sure it showed in the furious look he threw Ulrich. "You will say *nothing.*"

Ulrich's mouth fell open, a frown darkening his brow. Vallek had never spoken at him in anger before. Perhaps later he would feel remorse for treating his oldest friend so poorly, but right now, he cared far more about the possible threat to his faeling mate.

His second's eyes flitted past him, to the fae wading around their boat.

"Look at them again and I will have your eyes," Vallek growled. "Speak her name to them and I'll have your tongue."

Ulrich and Mattias looked at him like he'd lost his mind, and perhaps he had. Snapping and snarling, he *felt* unhinged, the need to return to his mate, to protect her with the strength of his own arm, a need more acute than taking his next breath.

"It could be *her,*" Ulrich whispered urgently.

Vallek peeled back his upper lip. "So what if it is? The fae are *enemies,* as you always claim."

Ulrich soured. "Then what does that make her?"

"My *mate.*" Vallek's growl was so deep, it nearly garbled the words, but Ulrich heard. "A threat to her is a threat to me. Do you understand?"

When his second didn't immediately answer, Vallek lashed quicker than a snake to grab hold of the gorget round his neck. With one move, he could snap the medal from Ulrich's chest. Take away his position.

"Do you *understand,* lord commander?"

"Yes," he hissed, a deep anger burning in his gaze.

A hand at his shoulder finally made Vallek relent, and when he stepped back, Mattias put himself between them.

"They no doubt aren't to be trusted," Mattias placated. "But perhaps I should know what the hells is going on?"

14

The return run to Balmirra was merciless. Although Vallek didn't keep up the blistering pace for the whole of it, they ran without stopping through the night. His own legs screamed in agony, but he didn't listen. Not when all he could hear was the incessant rumble of his beast, goading him to push on.

It was finally Mattias, ever mindful, who argued for a rest. Vallek allowed it, sensible at least that not all of his berserkers had a damned beast whining for their unclaimed mate—but because of the latter, he refused to stop himself. Mattias stayed behind with the main contingent to rest while Vallek ran, Ulrich and a few undaunted guards right behind him.

That suited Vallek just fine. He couldn't have Ulrich running back the other way to the fae.

It was an uncharitable thought, one he never would've dreamed of having about his oldest friend a few days ago.

But everything had changed.

Whether Ulrich liked it or not, whether Vallek himself was ready, the beast had chosen Ravenna. There was no denying it, no stopping it; they had to manage.

For Vallek, that meant taking Asta's advice and working harder to prove to his faeling that he was to be trusted with her every secret. Then he would find out just *what in all the hells* she'd gotten herself mixed up in. Once he'd filled his senses with her scent, he intended to ask her just that.

He got his opportunity sooner than he expected.

The points of the citadel rose above the craggy horizon, spurring Vallek on. He'd long since reached that disembodied mindset that any warrior had to achieve—else running became a true torture. Disengaged from his body, his mind focused on the approaching city.

All looked well, and his gaze trained on the citadel. *I'm coming for you, sprite.*

His beast paced agitatedly in his chest, the need to see and hold her overwhelming. So much so, he swore he scented her on the wind, a teasing note of jasmine and clove.

One of his warriors broke out of formation to trot alongside him. Raising his arm, he pointed at the southern edifice of the curtain wall. "My king, is there not something upon the wall?"

Vallek's stomach dropped to his tired feet. A glance at the wall confirmed there was indeed something about halfway up the wall. Whatever it was, it wore blue fabric that flapped in the slight summer breeze of the early afternoon.

Drawing a deeper breath, he realized in horror, it wasn't his imagination. Her scent truly carried on the wind.

All-Mother, take me now. What had he done to deserve this?

"Continue to the city," Vallek barked as he prepared to break off from the group.

"You cannot go alone!" Ulrich argued.

"Continue on," was all Vallek said in reply, gritting his tusks as he left the flat path to cut across the scrubby, craggy hills toward the southern wall.

A glance behind him confirmed his men continued on as he'd ordered, although Ulrich lagged behind, an unhappy frown darkening his face.

Huffing, Vallek pressed on. This was between him and a certain hellion.

Rounding the wall, more than one green face appeared over the crenellated ramparts, surprised to see their king jogging the perimeter on his own. They called out to him, asking whether he needed aid, but Vallek waved them at ease.

Her scent grew ever stronger, so much so that even with her cloak and human face, as well as being a good twenty feet still up the wall, he knew for certain he looked upon his very own mate. Scaling the curtain wall.

Vallek finally came to a stop directly below her. Panting hard, drenched in sweat, he planted his fists on his hips and stared up in disbelief at the slim figure currently picking her way down the curtain wall. The afternoon sun glinted off the little hooks she used to dig into crevices within the mortar and stones, and it seemed not even his arrival nor the calls of the curious garrison had broken her concentration.

He didn't know whether to be amused or furious, impressed or frustrated. A bit of each, he supposed. Not only had she managed to slip out of the citadel, she'd also found a way past the other walls to climb down the outer wall. Perhaps he should thank her for finding such a breach in security.

Not immediately, of course. Oh no. He was far too furious for that.

She was so high up. She could fall!

She was trying to escape him!

When he finally caught his breath, he sucked in a lungful of air to bellow, "*What in the gods' name are you doing?*"

Ravenna gasped, pushing herself against the wall when she nearly lost her grip. Clutching her hooks, she peeked over her shoulder down at him.

Her face fell.

"Oh. You're back."

Vallek bit down so hard, his jaw creaked. "I'm back."

Considering him a moment, she added, "This isn't as bad as it looks."

"Well, that's a relief. Because it *looks like* you're defying my orders to stay in the citadel. It *looks like* you're escaping my city."

"Yes. And it's not *one* of those things."

Vallek's eye twitched. Literally twitched involuntarily. "I'm tired from running all this way to return home to you. Only to find you dangling from the wall."

"I'm hardly *dangling*—"

"Explain. In small words."

She squinted down at him in an almost-glare. "I needed to leave the city. Just for today. I meant to return before sundown."

"And why would you *need* to leave?"

"To visit friends."

Vallek rubbed his eyes with thumb and finger, trying in vain not to curse the beast and gods that saddled him with this vexing creature. She was so small, miniscule compared to an orc—how then was she able to make so much trouble?

"And these friends are . . .?" He pointed a finger in warning. "Don't lie to me."

She pouted. "My friends are . . . of the four-legged variety."

All he could do was blink up at her. She was risking breaking her neck so she could go pet some onagers? The hearty mountain donkeys were all over the southern Griegens, and orcs often domesticated them as pack animals when far more agreeable takin goats were unavailable.

Honestly, his little hellion would fit right into a herd of onagers, come to think of it.

"And visiting your friends was important enough to defy me and risk your neck?"

"Well, I have sugar cubes for them, you see. Their favorite. I also haven't visited in a while, since your *loyal* lord commander decided I needed to be watched."

Ulrich was right in that—but watched for an entirely different reason.

Letting loose the longest, most exasperated sigh of his life, Vallek lifted his arms. "Come down now and we'll discuss this further."

He very much didn't like the way she squinted at him, assessing. "I'm not sure I should." Her gaze lifted to the top of the wall, only to find several curious faces peering down at them.

"Either you come down to me or I come up to you. Which will it be?"

Muttering unladylike curses under her breath, she chose the more dignified route of coming down to him. He watched anxiously as she descended, deliberately picking the safest footholds. Vallek wouldn't have been surprised if she was stalling for time, going as slowly as possible, but he didn't mind. More than anything, he needed her safe.

Better yet, safe and in his arms.

He got his desire the moment her legs were within reach. Grabbing hold of her calves, he said, "Now let go."

There was a moment's hesitation, Ravenna looking down to check the distance, before she huffed and pulled her hooks out of the wall. Falling backwards, she landed with an *oomph* in his arms.

From the wall above, the handful of guards watching on clapped and cheered.

Vallek bit back his grin. "Back to your posts!"

Deftly snagging her little hooks, he pocketed them as he held her aloft in one arm.

"You can put me down now."

"Oh, no," he laughed merrily and perhaps a bit madly. "I won't be doing that."

Her eyes went wide in that false human face when she realized— with one swift toss, he threw her over his shoulder.

"I can walk," she grumbled as he began to jog for the nearest gate.

"Yes, but your legs are small and this is faster." And he wasn't sure he trusted her to her own devices. Not yet. Not until he had her somewhere safe and secure that smelled of them both.

Guards at the southern gate greeted him, already anticipating his need for discretion. One female warrior held open the door to the gatehouse for him, and with a nod of thanks, Vallek slipped inside.

Up through the gatehouse they went, catching an inner rampart. They climbed and climbed, taking a roundabout, quiet path up to the citadel. Although it spared having to carry her through the city, he'd no doubt news of this incident would spread like wildfire. Guards were notorious gossips, and the night's entertainment in all the alehouses and pubs would likely be how their king plucked his human soothsayer off the curtain wall. Still, the fewer who actually saw her with their own eyes for now, the better.

Not just because he had an undoubtedly impatient Hrothgar still waiting for an answer.

His mate was as yet unclaimed. The bond not fully formed. Until it was, he would guard her jealously, even the sight of her. Even after the bond was set, he might never want any other to look upon her.

As he carried his feisty faeling mate through the city defenses, he thought he understood why the dragons hoarded their mates away. Covetous to the point of violence, dragons were known to disappear into their caves for years, not reemerging until a strong bond had been formed. Orc-kin too had once spirited away their mates, hiding them from jealous eyes until the bond took root. Such practices were considered old-fashioned, even overbearing by modern orcish sensibilities. However, with his mate's slight weight upon his shoulder, her lithe hands alternatively trying to untie Hormhím from his belt and digging into his sides to, he assumed, find where he was ticklish, he could understand the strategy and the jealousy.

With his deep knowledge of his city, Vallek managed to get them inside the citadel without being spotted by more than a few guards. The warren of passages, corridors, ramparts, and stairwells all eventually led him into the servants' quarters below his own. It was perhaps another weak point in security to discuss with Mattias.

Vallek nodded to the workers he surprised, keeping up his quick pace. They watched him pass with rounded eyes, although he spotted Brynhíl hiding a laugh behind her hand.

"My king," she greeted.

"Bryn. Please have an early dinner sent up."

At the orcess's name, two hands splayed on his back, and Ravenna pushed up so she could see. "Bryn! Please find Captain Asta and tell her not to worry about the laundry."

Vallek sighed. Code if he ever heard it. What were she and his younger sister up to? Leave it to Asta to help his defiant mate . . . well, defy him.

"Of course," agreed Bryn, her voice shaking with laughter.

Peals of giggling followed them further into the citadel.

Vallek's boots pounded the steps up to his quarters. The two guards outside the doors jumped to attention at the sight of him—and then their eyes went wide in horror to see the conspicuous bundle over his shoulder.

"My king . . ." one choked out.

"We'll discuss this later," Vallek said without stopping.

Throwing open the door, he proceeded inside as the guards hurried to close it behind him.

Vallek didn't stop until he stood in the center of the hall. Only then did he finally lower her from his shoulder.

She fell back a few steps, straightening out her cloak and cowl. She also made a show of rubbing at her sore middle. By the time she looked up at him, wearing her own face, she'd rediscovered her scowl.

Even that was a welcome sight to him after days apart.

Taking her by the shoulders, he hauled her close. "*Never* do that again," he insisted. "You could have been injured!"

"There'd be no need to if I wasn't confined," she grumbled.

"It's for your safety. All of it, everything I do, it's to keep you safe." That was the truth of it, if not the whole. Just like a greedy dragon, he'd every intention of hoarding his sharp-tongued mate.

The dubious arch of her brow told him exactly what she thought of his sentiment.

His hands slid up the curves of her shoulders to her neck, and he couldn't help running his thumbs over the silk of her cheeks. Gods, she was so soft. A joy to touch. In the silence that befell them, Vallek indulged in her scent and feel.

For the first time in days, his beast settled. The wily thing wouldn't truly be content until she was bedded and bonded to him, but for now, this was enough.

Drawing deep of her scent, Vallek let his head fall to hers. With their difference in height, it wasn't overly comfortable on his tired back, but that didn't matter. He needed the connection, and for now, she seemed—if not amenable then at least not actively pushing him away.

"I must apologize, *skala*. What we did that night—I regret nothing except that it was done with anger, and that I offended you. That wasn't my intention."

Her face sobered, those violet eyes sharpening. "It wasn't very flattering to be touched like that right after telling me you intend to take an orcess to wife."

Vallek groaned. "I know. I regret that, too." Straightening, he held one of her hands to his chest, over his heart so she could feel it beating. "I didn't mean it, not in truth."

Dark brows rising, she asked, "You won't take a wife?"

If he didn't know better, he'd think she held her breath in anticipation of his answer.

"No. Not when I already have a beautiful mate."

Although apparently unmoved by his flattery, she did nod. "All right. What does this mean, then?"

"It means," he sighed, "that we have much to discuss." Although he'd take no pleasure in it, he had to tell her at least some of the news from Toksfinge. If only to try figuring out if she could be the halfling Amaranthe searched for. No matter the answer, he needed to know.

Leaning down once more to nuzzle her fragrant hair, Vallek said softly, "Let me wash the journey off me, and then we'll talk."

When Vallek returned from the bath a little while later, washed, steaming, and clad in a comfortable pair of loose linen breeches, the late-afternoon sun slanted into the rooms in heavy beams of yellow light. The summer day was warm, but not unbearably so, and he noticed that several windows had been opened to catch the wayward breeze.

Padding into the den, he found Ravenna, also changed from her adventure. He stopped to take in the sight of her. Out of her drab human dress, she wore something between a robe and a gown, all draping layers. The pale pink fabric was cinched at her waist by a belt studded with semiprecious gems, the flowing material hinting at her curves and the long lengths of her legs. Sleeveless, the gown left her supple lilac arms bare, and she'd unbound her long hair from its plait, letting it fall down her back in heavy waves.

He purred before he even knew it. The vision she made was one of a queen at rest.

Hilde had obviously been visiting while he was away. She'd a penchant for garments like this and had been slowly bending the fashion of the Balmirran court to her will. Although Eydis was currently the highest ranking orcess at court, she'd little interest in fashions—much to Hilde's dismay—so it was Lady Silvia, who clung to power of any kind, setting the court's tastes. If he wasn't mistaken, Hilde might have finally found her muse.

His beast raised its jealous head. Ravenna was perhaps *too* alluring for anyone else to see her like this. The softness and easy lines spoke to a more domestic, private garment. He could allow that. He liked her in it very much.

He told her as much.

Her cheeks darkened to a dusky lavender. "Thank you."

A blush from her. How charming.

Vallek was aware of the way she watched him as he poured them both a goblet of wine. It was still early in the day yet for it, but he thought they both deserved it as they awaited their dinner. He could use the fortification for the conversation ahead, too.

Still, his mate's wary gaze only reminded him of Asta's words. *You must reassure her.*

Glancing at how she was again seated at the far window, Vallek decided he must try. If nothing else, days apart had proven to him that such distance couldn't be tolerated again. If he was ever to gain that last ground between them, he had to change his strategy.

Vallek fetched the *talfon* board and set, placing it on the dining table and then the second goblet on the other side.

"Will you join me?" he asked, settling in his usual seat.

She looked between him and the board, her gaze inscrutable, before rising to join him. Vallek's chest swelled with the little triumph, although he hid his grin behind his hand as he opened the box of pieces and pushed it toward her.

"You give up first choice?" she asked.

"For you, yes. And this time, you mustn't just let me win."

Her lips pursed to fight off her grin. "I don't know what you mean."

"Mm. You must adjust your strategy now. I'm no longer your king."

"No?" she said without looking up from her pieces. She'd chosen his preferred black set.

"No," he agreed. "I mean to be your mate." Reaching across the space between them, he picked up her hand to hold in his own.

"Are you sure that's wise?" Her voice fell to a whisper.

"Not at all. Yet . . . I wouldn't change it."

That finally drew her gaze, and she looked upon him in surprise.

"All I've done is complicate your life," she said.

"You've also made me happy." Lifting her hand, he kissed the back, sure to rub her skin with a tusk. "And vexed me to no end." He would take a lifetime of vexing, though, if it meant having her.

His beast was still thinking for him in many regards when it came to Ravenna, yes, but even the more reluctant parts of him had to admit—they were well suited in many ways. He wanted her, and he wanted to get to know her. He wanted the chance.

He couldn't say what that would mean for his kingdom and unification. No doubt more challenges. But he'd met great challenges before. He'd do so again, especially if that was the price he must pay to have her.

Nothing could be settled yet. There were too many moving pieces. Their bond was still new and unformed. Hrothgar was still awaiting an answer. Ulrich still had his suspicions, and the fae's eye was turned toward them. All challenges that perhaps would've been easy to solve by doing away with her.

Yet, even in the early days as they were, doing away with Ravenna would be to cut out a part of himself. A vital part.

He couldn't do that. He couldn't give her up.

Vallek would find a way to be with her.

If it meant sitting alone on his throne, so be it. If it meant fae taxes and Ulrich's anger and outmaneuvering Hrothgar, so be it.

He'd never backed down from a challenge, and he'd no intention to start now. Not when there was everything to gain.

He hesitated telling her all this, though. Something lingered in her gaze as she looked upon him. It was more than just uncertainty. He saw real fear in her eyes, and he wanted to conquer it. There was *nothing* in this world for her to fear. He wouldn't allow it.

You must reassure her.

"Whatever your fears, *skala,* I would meet them. Tell me your reservations."

Ravenna slowly shook her dark head back and forth. "It's . . . I fear I'll only bring you pain."

Vallek rumbled unhappily. "I'm willing to take the risk."

"What if I'm not?"

"Then I will prove to you, every day until you are sure, that it isn't a risk at all." Vallek leaned forward, resting his elbows on his knees so that he could hold both her hands in his. "I will treat with you, *skala.* I mean to be your mate, not your king. So, I won't keep you confined to these rooms."

Her rosebud mouth fell open in shock. "I can leave?"

"No," he grated, working to keep down the growl in his voice. "You will remain with me. And for your safety, for now, you will don your human face when you leave these quarters. But . . . yes, you may leave during the day. Under guard."

She sat rigidly in her chair for a long moment, lips pursed and delicate brows creased. "And what do you want in return?"

Vallek laughed despite himself. *Clever thing.*

"I would have the truth from you. Always."

She clearly didn't like that answer, pulling her hands from his to continue setting up the *talfon* board. "I don't think I can promise that."

"I will earn your secrets. For now, I will be content with an answer so long as it's the truth." With the box of pieces returned to him, he chose the pink quartz set, the one she preferred to play with. "I must have as much information as possible to keep you safe."

She glanced at him from the corner of her eye. "What happened on your journey?"

Gods, she truly missed nothing. Eydis was right, she'd be a formidable politician if given half the chance.

Keeping his body loose and tone light, he told her of the fae ship and what they sought. He recounted the many promises made by Amaranthe through her envoys for the capture of the halfling criminal.

She gave nothing away as he spoke, making her first move on the board.

"Is it you she seeks?"

Ravenna didn't answer immediately, her violet gaze faraway although she stared at his unmoving hand. "I'm not a criminal," was her reply. "I've never met the Fae Queen, and I haven't lived in the faelands since I was a small child."

Vallek nodded, sensing there was far more to her answer. While it may be the truth, that wasn't the whole of it. But that would do, for now. Soon, he would have her trust and her secrets.

Observing how her body had gone stiff, Vallek said, "Amaranthe is no friend of Balmirra or any orc. Perhaps the enemy of my enemy is an ally."

If she was the spy Ulrich thought her to be, Vallek would turn her allegiances. If she was the halfling Amaranthe sought, he'd hide her, protect her. It wasn't just good politics—Ravenna was *his*.

His mate still gave nothing away in her expression, but that was all right. Let her sit with his insinuated promise. When the time was right, she would come to him.

In the meantime, "Can you tell me what you know of the faelands?"

He gambled that this would be a safe enough topic, and he was rewarded when she began to speak at length on the history and politics of the faelands. Vallek listened intently, making his opening move. Ravenna rebutted with her own advance as she explained how the fae weren't unlike a hive, with a Queen at their center. The hub of many spokes, the Queen's line was ancient and powerful, but even she was meant to fade and abdicate.

Except, Amaranthe didn't. Centuries ago, rather than sail to the Twins, a set of islands off the western coast of the faelands, and take the stone sleep, consigning herself and her vast magic back to the earth, Amaranthe had defied fate and nature. She slaughtered her daughters, her sisters, even her nieces, all so no one could replace her. The faelands and its magic needed a center, and as the only one able to act as that conduit, Amaranthe kept her throne.

It exacerbated an already growing problem for the fae. They'd long since begun to rely too much on their magic. They gave up food and drink, sustaining themselves only on magic. They withered, their blood turning black.

Vallek realized with amazement that this was why the fae looked so . . . skeletal. They were literally starving themselves of life.

"You don't forgo food," he noted, capturing one of her pieces.

"I don't. I'm only half fae, though." She explained how her father, in discovering his *azai,* his fated one, in a human, had also redis-covered living without relying solely on magic. "Taking her blood, he was able to eat again." Her smile was soft when she added, "She brought him back to life."

A purr punched through his chest. "The fae bite their mates?"

Ravenna's eyes flicked up to meet his. Her pupils dilated as she gazed at him, those plush lips parting to reveal the very tip of her pink tongue.

"They do."

Vibrating in his seat, Vallek leaned forward to tell her, "I'll wear your bite proudly, *skala.*"

His cock kicked in his breeches when her gaze fell to his throat. "Will you bite back?" she asked, voice dropping to a husky whisper.

"Anything you want, for however long. Say it and it's yours."

Her lips twitched up into the smallest, most tantalizing grin. He *ached* to taste it.

She glanced back at the board, and that grin widened. Moving her most important piece, she declared, *"Groff mi tal." I've won.*

Startled, he looked at the board, too. And indeed, she'd led him deftly into a trap, her pieces expertly arrayed in a pincer movement to prevent escape.

Vallek had lost. He'd never been so pleased.

Booming with laughter, Vallek slapped his knee. "I knew it."

Ravenna couldn't hide her pleased smile, even if she did demurely lift her goblet to her lips to sip.

"Another round," he insisted, downing the last of his own wine. Invigorated by his loss as well as his gains, he dared another bargain. "If I win, you will sleep in my bed with me. No more arguments."

Ravenna snorted. "What will I get if I win?"

"Then *I* will sleep in my bed with *you.*"

"Hm. Damned if I do, damned if I don't." She softened her jab with a wink.

Grinning like a fool, Vallek purred, "We'll be damned together."

15

Ravenna woke to the scent, sound, and weight of her orcish *azai*. Although she hadn't fallen asleep tucked against his massive chest, it didn't completely surprise her to find she'd been reeled across the bed in the night.

After spending a pleasant evening playing *talfon* and making deals, she'd consented to sleep in the bed with him. On her own side. His easy agreement had been suspicious, and as Ravenna slowly came awake to the burning warmth of his bare chest at her back and the heavy weight of his arm thrown across her waist, she began to suspect he'd never meant to let her stay all the way on her side.

So comfortable, though, it was hard to muster any true misgivings. In fact, her instincts, the ones that told her to curl up against her big, strong mate and never let go, were more than content. She might just start to purr like he did. Her instincts were proving to be little hussies for Vallek.

Her soppy heart didn't help matters. She woke that morning to a new reality. Concessions had been made last night, and while her movements were still restricted, he'd made many promises. That he wouldn't take an orcess for a wife. That he meant to be with her.

It all still sounded outlandish to everything but that soppy heart of hers. As a king in a tenuous political situation, he'd no business making her such promises. But he did. And she hoarded them close.

Ravenna knew better than to put much stock in promises and hopes. Promises rarely lasted, and hope could be misleading. Even devastating.

That didn't stop the softer parts of her from hoping, though. She *longed* for the things he'd promised. When he wasn't being obtuse, her handsome orc could be quite charming. It was more than her instincts that drew her to him—for the first time in days, she'd sat in the company of the man she'd come to admire from years of friendly talk and good humor.

The Vallek of before, the one who didn't know her true face, was in some odd way her friend. And she'd missed that friend these past days, just as much as her magic had missed her *azai* while he was away. To have him back soothed and pleased her in a way nothing else had.

None of that meant she could trust him with her plans. If he knew she meant to cut out Amaranthe's heart herself, he'd lock her away forever.

But . . . perhaps she could trust him with a few things.

Perhaps, just perhaps, she could attain her vengeance even faster by his side. In his bed.

The thought was an insidious little thread tugging at her vulnerable heart. Her need for him, to be with and claim her *azai,* could become strong enough to cloud her judgement. It was her own instinct to have him, to give herself to him, that whispered foolish hopes in her ear.

That path likely led to ruin, but oh, what a temptation ruin could be.

A gusty breath ruffled the hair near her temple before the big arm across her flexed and tightened, bringing her even closer to Vallek's now purring chest. The ridges of his nose and tusks pressed against her head in a gentle nuzzling.

"I can *hear* you thinking, *skala*," he rumbled in a deliciously low, sleepy voice. "It's far too early for any of that."

"What should I be doing, then?"

He didn't take her bait, although his chest shook with amusement. They both knew exactly what.

Nuzzling her hair, Vallek sighed, "This is just the way I wish to wake from now on."

"That wasn't part of our negotiations."

"I'm making an amendment."

"On what grounds?"

"That I'm king and I like holding you."

Well, both of those points were hard to argue with. A desperately pleased grin twitched on her lips despite herself.

Perhaps he was right—at least on this. It was too early to think.

Instead, for the first time in a long while, Ravenna allowed herself to just *feel*.

She let her body ease back into his, curling against him like a happy cat. Running her fingers along his arm, she traced the thick sinews and tendons up and down his green forearm, delighted when gooseflesh followed in her wake.

They lay in the soft quiet of dawn together, movements small and sensuous. The arm he'd laid beneath her had tangled in her long hair, and he played with the ends between his fingers. She continued to pet him, indulging in all his textures and marveling at how he was softness stretched over such strength.

It wasn't long before Ravenna felt a certain new heat pressing against the curve of her backside.

Vallek was a big man, and proportional. Although she'd only spied his manhood a few times, including when he slipped into bed last night—naked—she knew it to be formidable. Her handful of experiences with human fishermen paled in comparison to him, and while their difference in size—only accentuated by how he absolutely surrounded her with his body as they lay together—should have concerned her, even frightened her, she felt neither.

No, as she began to move her hips back and forth in the smallest movements, all Ravenna felt was a thrilling anticipation.

It probably wasn't wise to tease him. And her pride remained bruised from their first encounter. Yet, she couldn't help herself. Desire flowed thicker than syrup through her veins, an ancient and powerful lust compelling her to keep going.

Besides, she wasn't thinking. Only feeling.

His large hand rose from the bed to settle on her hip, stilling her.

"I can be as soft and gentle as you need, *skala*. But don't start what you cannot finish."

He might not mean it as a challenge, but Ravenna couldn't help hearing one. Body flushed at the low rumble of his voice at her ear, she began to rock again. She worked to help his cock find the cleft between the cheeks of her backside, gratified to feel how he began to easily slide against the loose fabric of her filmy nightgown.

His purr deepened into something of a growl, but still he didn't move.

Using a little of her magic, Ravenna pressed against the small of his back, drawing him even closer and urging him to move.

A hot exhale buffeted her cheek as he leaned over her. Even in the colorless light of dawn, his eyes captured her with their blue intensity, searing her.

"Can I touch you?" he ground out, voice gone thick.

"Yes." Fates, yes. She might combust if he didn't.

He found his purr again, and somehow she thought it sounded like praise. His hand at her hip made quick work of rucking up her nightgown, exposing her legs to the cool morning air. His palm spanned her thigh as his head dropped so he could bury his face in the curve of her shoulder.

Reaching back to dig her fingers into his thick mane, Ravenna met his hungry lips when they fell upon hers. He devoured her with his kiss, tusks pressing into her cheeks as his tongue teased and coaxed.

He overwhelmed her, dominating all her senses, but this wasn't like last time. Even in their haze of lust, everything felt different. Softer, gentler. Urgent but not frenzied. As though they could and meant to take their time with each other.

This was how it should've been.

Touching for the sake of it. To learn every texture and contour.

Her nails dug into his scalp when his searching fingers found her weeping cunt. He rumbled against her lips to find her already anticipating him, and he took his time running his fingertips through her slick in light, teasing touches. By the time he finally reached her clitoris, Ravenna shook with need.

"So warm and wet for me," he purred.

Pressure gathered between her thighs, and when he moved to part her legs, she followed him willingly, desperately.

She gasped to feel the burning heat of his cock slide along her cunt.

"Vallek—" she choked.

"I know, *skala*. Soon. With practice."

His hips began to rock gently, shuttling his cock in a maddening rhythm between her legs. On every thrust, his cockhead teased the underside of her clitoris, a spark of pleasure so sharp, she bit her lip to the point of pain.

Even with his cock moving against her, his fingers found the entrance of her cunt. He teased her there, circling, circling before finally pushing inside. A mewling sound escaped her throat at his invasion, her cunt clasping his finger in a greedy hold.

"That's it, sprite. Take what you need."

Slowly but steadily he pushed inside to the last knuckle. Ravenna lashed her hips against his, needing more friction, more everything—if only to alleviate the pressure building inside. There was little to do but hold onto his mane in this position, but she was desperate to render him as needy as her.

Her magic pooled at his hipbone before sliding down between

their bodies. Its ephemeral warmth gathered along the underside of his cock and whispered against his heavy bollocks, a kiss of phantom touch and pressure.

Vallek grunted, hips surging forward. "*Fuck,*" he cursed, "you're a menace."

Ravenna smiled in vicious delight, baring her fangs at the far side of the room.

He dropped his head to claim that smile, and she met his greedy mouth with her own. She couldn't help moaning into his as he began to work a second finger inside her.

"Relax for me. Let me make it good."

A pinch before a fullness so wide, she could hardly comprehend. Then he spread the two fingers apart inside her and Ravenna was lost.

Body gone rigid, she came and came, throbbing around his fingers. His cock made sloppy sounds as it slid against her, every bump against her clitoris sending a fresh shock of pleasure through her over-wrought body.

It was too much. It wasn't enough. It was everything.

Frantically, Ravenna reached down between her legs, feeling how hot and slick he'd made her. Her fingers caught his cockhead on the next stroke, and her small touch was enough. Spurts of pearlescent spend burst on her fingers, and Vallek crushed her to him as his hips battered against her.

She didn't know how long it lasted, only that she never wanted it to end.

Even with his hand between her legs and his spend on her hand, she didn't feel exposed like she had before. Not with how he surrounded her, sharing her breath. When he sought another kiss, she eagerly gave it, nipping his lower lip with her fangs.

She was rewarded with another small spurt into her hand.

"I'm amending the deal again," he panted. "*This* is how I wish to start every day."

Normally, Vallek would relish a meeting such as this. Rather than his Balmirran ministers sitting round the small council chamber's table, today it was Hrothgar and Kennum's representatives sitting across from each other. A handful of Vallek's own people, such as Eydis and Ulrich, also sat round, mostly to ensure he had enough bodies to intervene if any fights broke out.

A tense negotiation, bending politics to his will, was its own kind of delicious thrill. He aimed to solve this matter today, or at least find some kind of agreement for the time being.

Really, anything that got him back to his mate, he might just agree to.

He had to put real effort into paying attention to the proceedings, his mind happily running off to think about Ravenna and her luscious little body and the noises she made and the way her claws scraped his head—if given the chance.

Vallek looked up in time to see Eydis widening her eyes at him significantly. Ah, his input was needed.

"I understand your frustrations," Vallek said, "that is why this meeting was arranged—" by Eydis "—to hear and address your concerns. You have all been exceedingly patient as I deal with other matters, and I extend my thanks."

Kennum's representative Rulf nodded, if not pleased then at least understanding, but Hrothgar maintained his squinting scowl.

"You haven't even met with any of my girls," the old rascal complained.

"Nor have you met the ladies of Kaldebrak," Rulf was quick to add. "I would be more than happy to ask Chieftain Kennum to send them. So you may make an informed decision."

Hrothgar's scowl turned to Rulf, who chose not to even look the chieftain's way. He no doubt still felt the menace radiating off the old orc.

"That hardly seems necessary," Hrothgar grumbled. "Just pick one."

Vallek held up his hands. "Both of your offers are more than generous. I'm sure any of your daughters would make a fine wife and queen."

"Yphella especially," Hrothgar insisted.

"Kennum's daughters are all fine orcesses," Rulf countered. "Any orc would be lucky to have any of them for a wife."

"But they're not here and my girls are. So how committed is Kennum really?"

"Strange that you should come and make this offer only *after* my lord Kennum did?"

Vallek cleared his throat. "There's no need to argue, my lords. I don't intend to leave you in suspense."

If Eydis's report was anything to go by, Hrothgar and his daughters and niece had found every opportunity to try pinning her down in his absence. She'd taken to actively trying to avoid them, spending long hours in his quarters with Hilde and Ravenna.

"Deal with him," Eydis had warned on their way to the meeting, *"or I'll tell your new mate all your dislikes rather than letting her find out herself."*

For fear of what his mischievous mate would do with that information, as well as what Eydis and Ravenna might accomplish together, Vallek agreed. He also wanted unification and peace and his citadel back, et cetera et cetera, of course, but he knew very well to heed a threat from Eydis. They weren't made lightly.

His mind had been many places over the last fortnight, it was true, but it was made at least in this: Ravenna was his mate, and he would have only her.

What that meant, how that looked, he didn't know. For now, he had to buy himself time—and unification, if he could.

Leaning forward, he laid his palms on the table before him. Those gathered hushed, rocking forward themselves to better hear his decision.

Affecting a grave tone, Vallek said, "I wouldn't want to sully the bonds between Kaldebrak and Innrinhom. While Balmirra has long been the seat of our kin, that doesn't make your strongholds and people any less important. To give my favor to one or the other may cause . . . bad feelings."

Several gasps met his statement, and more than a few fists banged on the table. Two of them were Hrothgar's. The orc leapt to his feet, far more spry than his age implied, his scarred face animated with outrage.

Arguments erupted around the table, several others standing with and against Hrothgar. Ulrich jumped to his feet to join the fray, trying to shout everyone down, while Eydis slumped back in her seat and rubbed her temple as she shot him a dark look.

Annoyed, Vallek lifted Hormhím beside him and smacked the blunt head onto the floor. "Enough!"

Hrothgar scowled at him. "What are you getting at, boy? My girls aren't good enough for you?"

Vallek fixed the old chieftain with a cold stare. "Watch your words, old man. Remember to whom you speak."

Hrothgar snorted, his lips pursed sourly, but he retook his seat.

Rulf remained quiet, although his look was no less mutinous. It seemed neither side was pleased with this news.

Vallek had hoped that neither losing to the other would perhaps soften neither winning, but alas, it seemed that wasn't so.

"I don't expect you to leave with nothing," Vallek continued, unsurprised when several ears perked. "Instead of one of your daughters,

I invite both Kaldebrak and Innrinhom to send emissaries to join my council. Your opinions and concerns will be heard without having to part with your kin. I am also proposing stronger trade agreements between our great cities to bring our people together. Let orc-kin grow rich and fat with their good fortune and our alliance."

That garnered murmurs—hopefully a better outcome than shouting.

"My hope is that these emissaries will come together to form a council, one that, amongst other things, will ensure mutual aid across the territories."

His final carrot raised a few thick eyebrows. He wasn't the first Balmirran chieftain to unite the territories into a kingdom. He also wasn't the first to promise mutual aid. For all their shared language and culture, orcs could be a tribal lot. Taking orders from another clan rankled—several had left the territories the last time a Balmirran chieftain tried to rule, creating independent, isolated tribes along the far eastern reaches of orcish lands.

"If we are to survive in this world, orc must protect orc. I pledge now that Balmirra will come to the aid of any who need her. But this isn't enough. The threats beyond our borders are to us all, and therefore we must all meet them. United."

Hrothgar huffed. "You expect me to go to war for Kennum?"

"If war cannot be avoided, then yes. Just as I expect Kennum and Kaldebrak to go to war for the Innrini."

The old chieftain didn't give up his scowl, but Vallek didn't think he imagined that Hrothgar's expression softened infinitesimally with thought.

Rising from his seat, the others scrambled to stand, too.

"Think on it, my lords."

Vallek would have left, anxious to rejoin his mate, had Rulf not asked, "Do you mean to never take a queen, then?"

Ignoring Ulrich's withering glare, Vallek replied, "For now, the throne will remain mine alone." That was all he could promise.

Today, let them chew over the benefits of unification and mutual aid. Tomorrow, get them to swallow a half-fae mate.

That was all well and good to plan; however, Vallek had his doubts by the time he returned to his quarters. If he'd thought unification was difficult, it would likely pale in comparison to then getting his new allies to accept Ravenna as his mate, a half-fae he rejected noble-blooded orcesses for.

Fuck, what a headache.

But when he caught sight of Ravenna hurrying toward him, eager to hear what had happened, he couldn't be too frustrated. She might not know it, none might understand it, but Vallek had an itching suspicion that his faeling would make a mighty ally and protector of the realm. More than just his mate, she would make a formidable queen.

When she was near, he caught her hand and raised it to his lips for a kiss.

"Hello, *skala*."

"How did it go?" she asked, forgoing greetings.

Huffing a laugh, Vallek tucked her hand into the crook of his elbow and led her into the den. As they settled down, Vallek in his usual seat before pulling Ravenna down to tuck into his side, he described the meeting and his proposals.

Her dark brows lifted higher and higher the longer he spoke.

"Do you mean it?" she murmured.

"I give you my word. As a king and as your mate."

"But it would be so much simpler to just . . ." Give her up.

Yes, it would. However, "I've never feared a challenge." Gently, he pushed a lock of her long hair behind the delicate point of her ear. "You are worth it and more, sprite."

She rewarded him with another of those lavender blushes he was coming to love.

"How do you think we should proceed?" Although he would fight the Ever-Father himself for his mate, he realized he didn't have to go at this alone. He wasn't alone in this mating and indeed shouldn't be in their effort to be accepted.

Ravenna seemed surprised by the question. "I haven't had any visions of it," she admitted. "I don't know what the other chieftains will do."

"I meant your opinion, love." While a vision would indeed be handy right about now—he'd need a contingency if Hrothgar refused all offers and terms—it wasn't what he was after from her.

Her blush deepened, as if she hadn't expected him to ask for her input.

The realization shamed him. He couldn't have her thinking he only wanted her for his bed.

That wouldn't do at all.

It might take time and some clever politicking, but Vallek intended to have her in all ways, all throughout his life. That was the way of the mate-bond, and he'd not be denied it just because he sat upon a throne.

After a moment's consideration, Ravenna said, "If either chieftain refuses you, escort them back home. Say it's for their safety and bring a sizeable force. Charm them along the way. When you arrive at Kaldebrak or Innrinhom, stay a while. And when you leave, go to the tribes in the east. Having their loyalty will surely bring Kennum and Hrothgar back to your table."

The breath rushed out of Vallek in awe. She said it so confidently, with a certainty as though it were a vision.

Perhaps it was. A vision of another sort.

Vallek smiled. Pulling her close, he nuzzled her temple. "My clever girl. You'll win me my kingdom yet."

16

That was how Ravenna found herself with far more freedom than she'd ever anticipated. Well, *freedom* might be a strong word. More like, boundaries outside of Vallek's quarters in the citadel.

Somehow, her little scrap of advice had, in the span of three mere days, turned into a full march to Innrinhom. The swiftness with which everything was planned still made her head spin; Eydis truly was a marvel.

Although Hrothgar and Kennum's representatives had begrudgingly agreed to the terms of Vallek's proposal, he still deemed it necessary to accompany the old chieftain back to Innrinhom. *To belabor the point,* as Vallek put it. So on his way with his berserkers to finally bring the eastern tribes to heel, Vallek accompanied Hrothgar's party home.

Well, all but one. Hrothgar had shrewdly chosen Yphella, one of his daughters, to act as his emissary, no doubt in hopes that more time in Balmirra, with Vallek, might persuade him an Innrini queen was actually something to consider.

His other daughter and niece used the opportunity of dining each evening with Vallek to flirt and charm.

Ravenna had been dragged along in her human disguise and knew all of this because she too was part of the royal retinue. More than a few looked askance at the arrangement; the king had never felt the need to bring his soothsayer along before. And that she slept in the royal tent? Very strange.

As they set off that first day, boarding barges to cross over to Lake Lovath's eastern shores, Ulrich had made sure to find a moment to get in close. Holding her back by the arm, he hissed, *"People are talking. Stay away from him. Don't ruin this more than you already have."*

"I want this as much as you do," she'd spat back. She needed the largest orcish army possible to one day march against Amaranthe.

"I seriously doubt that."

Fates, what a prick.

She wanted to say he was the worst thing about this trip, but that wouldn't be true. The worst thing was the blisters. Or maybe it was watching two beautiful orcesses flirt shamelessly with her *azai*. Or maybe it was the daily trudge that had her collapsing whenever they stopped for rest.

It was the blisters. Definitely the blisters.

I could carry you, Oberon offered.

Despite the dangers, he and a few of the younger herd members had decided to follow a safe distance behind the party, should she need aid.

Younger?

Less experienced, she amended.

Indeed. This will be excellent training for the foals. But do try to keep up with the column, we're nearly catching you up.

Easy to say when you have four legs.

Yes, four is far superior. I keep telling you this.

Chatting with Oberon did help a little, as everyone else on the journey was far too busy to take much notice of her. She did her best to keep up, as well as find what plants she could to help make a balm for her sore feet. However, more than once, she fell behind the party and was scolded when someone had to go looking for her.

"You must stay near," Vallek chided her one evening. "Anything could happen on the road. You're small enough that an owl might just swoop down and take you. What would I do then?"

She was far too sore from another day marching and cranky from another evening watching him charm Hrothgar's party to dignify his warning with a response. Hunkering down further into her cot, she did her best to ignore him and go to sleep.

He never liked that, though, and wouldn't stand it for long. Despite that she always drew her little cot away from his palatial camp bed whenever it was set out—there were enough wagging tongues about the two beds being in the same canvas room let alone close by— he always dragged it closer to make one slightly larger bed.

Throwing his heavy arm over her, he pulled her in close. Nuzzling her temple, he murmured, "Promise me, sprite."

"I'm doing my best," she grumped. "As you so like to point out, my legs are short. I don't exactly have a litter to carry me round like Hrothgar." When she felt his intake of breath, she pointed behind her at him. "Don't even think about it. People are already suspicious."

"I'd carry you myself."

Ravenna patted his muscled forearm. She knew he would if she'd let him. The problem was, as his staff, her place was in the middle of the great column they made through the countryside. Certainly not *beside* him. Or on his back.

Throughout the day's march, the column passed her by. First the rest of the staff on the journey—the cooks, smiths, and hunters—then the bulk of the berserkers and the supply animals and their keepers. Even the unruly onagers seemed to laugh at her as they trundled past with their loads.

In the end, it was just such an onager that became her salvation. Her stinky salvation.

As she fell behind the next day, a berserker came jogging from the front lines toward her. It took only a moment to recognize Mattias, the berserker captain.

Nodding in greeting, Ravenna tried not to snap at him when he asked how she was.

"I'll manage," she replied, blinking the dust and sweat from her eyes.

Mattias's lips pursed unhappily between his tusks. "If you'll allow me, *kone* . . ."

Without even having to stop the march, he lifted her onto the back of a lightly outfitted onager. The donkey's long ears flicked back and forth, and Ravenna held perfectly still, watching anxiously with an equally wary Mattias to see if the onager would buck her off. After a mild huff, the beast ruffled his short mane and continued on.

"Try to move with him and maybe give him a treat when we stop to rest," Mattias suggested.

Gritting her teeth, Ravenna only nodded. Her feet nearly sang at the relief, but her back soon went stiff with the unfamiliar gait of the beast. Mattias fell into step beside her, apparently wanting to confirm she wouldn't be thrown from her saddle of jerky sacks.

Even with the din of the column and Mattias walking beside her, Ravenna was aware of the looks and the sniggers. Those berserkers in the back lines craned their heads over their shoulders to get a good look, and the onager keepers hid their laughter behind their hands.

Straightening her back, Ravenna threw a leg over the onager, redistributing her weight and taking a more familiar riding seat.

If the donkey's rude to you, I'll have a word with him tonight, Oberon threatened.

While she appreciated the support, this was one fight she had to win on her own.

The onager was mild-mannered enough, thankfully, and with Mattias glaring at the snickering soldiers, the laughter soon died out.

No matter how she poked and prodded, he wouldn't say in as many words that Vallek had sent him to watch over her. Ravenna wasn't sure whether to be touched or annoyed.

It didn't take much effort to assume that while it was true Vallek didn't want to part with her because of his beast and wanting to be near his own mate, he also wanted to keep an eye on her. The thought rankled like a pebble in her boot, only growing larger the longer they marched.

You try scaling one *wall and suddenly you have to have someone always watching.*

And don't you forget it, Oberon whinnied in glee.

While she appreciated the rest, Ravenna found evenings almost as unbearable as the daytime march. She wanted nothing more than to lay face down on her cot, but instead, as part of Vallek's staff, she sat to the side, quietly eating her meal as Vallek, Ulrich, Hrothgar, and his daughter and niece sat around a low table, eating, drinking, and making merry. Reclined in low, cushioned divans that easily folded up for travel, they enjoyed fine camp fare, as well as mead from Vallek's own stores.

Ravenna tried to keep to herself, shoveling food into her mouth no matter what it was. So long as it was warm and filled her belly, she wasn't choosy.

Still, she couldn't help but glare over the rim of her bowl. It seemed the more charming her mate became, the more irritated she grew.

Were she well-rested and blister-free, she likely would've appreciated what a skilled diplomat her *azai* could be. She knew he was a fearsome warrior, but seeing the way he slowly ingratiated himself to Hrothgar, affable and good-humored, Ravenna saw the other side of his skill. This soft power wove its own magic, and day by day, the old chieftain scowled a little less.

As they trudged through the southeastern Griegens, eventually finding their way on wide forested paths, Hrothgar began sharing stories of his youth, regaling the dinner table with tales of battles with dragons and liaisons with sirens. His daughter and niece, Yngrid and Birgít, tutted and rolled their eyes, no doubt having heard the stories many times, but Vallek and Ulrich laughed uproariously, slapping their knees and toasting Hrothgar's prowess.

It was between these tales that Yngrid or Birgít, whichever had managed to get a spot at Vallek's side that night, would gently touch his hand while leaning over to whisper something in his ear. Vallek smiled, his eyes glittering with interest.

Ravenna glared daggers at the orcesses. She knew very well she had to stay put to pull off the ruse, and it wasn't as though she wished to explain herself or her entanglement with Vallek, but that didn't stop her vicious fae instincts from wanting to claw the eyes out of any female who dared look upon her fine specimen of a mate.

If she didn't know better, she might think he did it to make her jealous. Instead, he reassured her, night after night, that she was sat where she could see him to prove nothing untoward happened with either orcess.

"Although, you could stop staring at them so . . . intensely," he said one night as he pulled her cot and then her to him. "You're beginning to unnerve them."

Ravenna smiled evilly into the darkness. *Good.*

Better that they all fear her a little than laugh at her.

As the mountains gave way to rolling foothills blanketed in forest, Ravenna couldn't figure out whether Mattias was shy or had been given orders not to look her directly in the eye. It'd be just like Vallek to order his captain not to get too friendly with his mate—even while said mate sat every night watching him entertain orcesses vying to be his wife and queen.

The captain was stalwart in his company and his silence. Speaking when spoken to and nothing more, he gave little away. Ravenna had to confirm with Vallek whether the captain knew about their mating, Mattias himself giving no indication. Instead, she had to content herself with his ruggedly handsome profile if not his conversation.

Still, she came to appreciate the quiet support. She even came to like her little onager, whom she called Twitch from how his ears liked to twitch back and forth.

What she didn't enjoy was coming away smelling of Twitch at the end of each day. Placed near the back of the column, she felt like she wore the entire road by the time she slipped into Vallek's tent in the evening.

That day was particularly bad, and Ravenna itched to peel off her cloak as she watched the workers deftly erect the king's tent. It was a cavernous, billowing thing, and seeing it rise and collapse and rise again was truly impressive. The skilled orcs could have it up in no time at all, followed swiftly by the king's foldable traveling furniture.

Ducking and weaving to avoid becoming a nuisance or obstacle, Ravenna dove into the tent as soon as she was able. Padding quickly through the spacious main room, she folded back the flap to the inner bedchamber. His massive camp bed, with its many cushions and pillows and silk sheets, sat ready and waiting. As did her sad little cot in the corner.

She sighed happily when she pulled the cloak from her shoulders.

She almost let her disguise slip, but then heard several orcs come in—carrying something heavy by the sound of it. Ravenna remained still and silent, waiting for them to finish whatever it was they brought.

When Vallek softly called her name, though, she peeked out from behind the flap.

His gaze swung to her immediately, and a grin warmed his face. Fates, she didn't know whether his charming Hrothgar's party was more annoying than how easily he charmed her, too.

Holding out his hand, he drew her out from the back bedroom. With his free hand, he gestured at one of the best sights in the world.

A hipbath, full of warm, steamy water, sat behind a privacy screen against the canvas wall. An audible groan escaped her lips.

Chuckling, Vallek hugged her to his side. "I know how hard the road can be. I've ordered the tent be left empty for an hour so you may enjoy your bath."

She wanted to throw her arms around him and weep with happiness. Instead, she joked, "So you think I smell, too?"

"I know you do," he teased back, noisily nuzzling her head and taking a big whiff.

She huffed in mock outrage as he pushed her toward the bath, giving her backside a gentle smack on her way. Peering over her shoulder, she bit her lip as she looked him over head to toe. Also a bit dusty from the road, he nevertheless looked handsome as ever, and this was the first instance, aside from being in bed, that she'd been alone with him in many days.

"I'm to enjoy this all alone?"

Vallek himself groaned, closing the distance between them. Partially hidden by the screen, he dipped his head to bestow a teasing kiss.

"Don't tempt me, sprite. When we return to Balmirra, you'll do nothing without me."

That should've worried her, but she couldn't feel much of anything over the lust throbbing between her legs.

With one last kiss, Vallek left her to her bath. After waiting a moment to see that she truly had the tent to herself, Ravenna stripped and nearly dove into the bath. Submerging beneath the water, her moan of pleasure bubbled around her.

Scrubbing and soaping, she lathered every inch of skin and hair. By the time the bathwater cooled, she was raw-skinned and utterly delighted. Pulling off one of the bath sheets left hanging over the privacy screen, Ravenna wrapped it round herself before grabbing her grubby traveling clothes and hurrying back into the bedroom.

Although she wanted to chuck the kirtle right into that night's bonfire, she carefully hung it from a peg. The idea of getting back into it tomorrow was loathsome, but at least for tonight, she was clean.

Sitting cross-legged on her bed, she forwent her nightgown for now, instead staying wrapped in the bath sheet as she combed the tangles from her hair.

The quiet tread of footsteps on the carpets laid over the main room perked her ears. She didn't think it'd quite been an hour, but she couldn't blame the others for wanting to get their tasks completed. Still, she begrudgingly reformed her false face.

Although—she looked up in suspicion—it honestly sounded like only one set of footsteps.

The flap of the bedchamber twitched back, and suddenly a scantily clad orcess stood before her. She met Yngrid's startled gaze, watching the orcess's bosom heave with surprise.

"Oh! Uhm . . ."

"Can I help you?"

Yngrid looked around, as if searching for an answer that wasn't that she'd thought Vallek was in here and she meant to seduce him. Ravenna's frown gained in ferocity for every moment the orcess prevaricated.

Clearing her throat, Yngrid finally said, "Where is the king?"

"Not here."

"I can see that." Finally taking a moment to look over the rest of the bedchamber, Yngrid actually stepped further inside, much to Ravenna's chagrin. If the orcess came within grabbing distance, she wasn't responsible for her actions. "He truly does have you sleep beside him."

"He likes to keep me near. In case of visions."

Yngrid nodded. "All right." Sighing, she added, "Men are strange creatures, are they not?"

Ravenna blinked. "I suppose."

Drawing her translucent shawl, a lovely green hemmed in silver thread, higher on her shoulders, Yngrid considered her a moment. Ravenna could appreciate the real intelligence shining in her eyes, even if she wanted to scratch those eyes out.

"I don't suppose you've seen who he'll take as queen?"

Ravenna shook her head. "No, I've never seen it. I don't think he means to take a queen."

"So he says." Considering a moment, Yngrid pulled a dangling gold hoop from her ear before approaching Ravenna's cot. "For your vision. Tell me what you see for me." Placing the earring on the cot, she held out her hand for Ravenna to take.

All Ravenna could do was blink some more, a bit baffled by this turn of events.

"Are you sure?" People often thought they wanted their fortunes told, but that was only if there was something good to tell.

"Quite sure." And she waggled her green fingers to prove it.

Shrugging, Ravenna touched her hand to the noblewoman's, closing her eyes and beckoning forth a vision.

It took a moment, as it often did when she was the one to summon it, rather than the vision choosing its own timing. They were fickle like that, preferring to play by their own rules, but since the magic was still inherent to her, Ravenna maintained at least some control.

—I swear it, father—silver thread binding needles of pine—brought a golden horn to her lips—two baby birds, one flying first from the nest—all my days to my people—

Pulling back from the disparate images and impressions, Ravenna regained her presence in the tent. Her eyes fluttered open to behold an anxious Yngrid, eyes unblinking as she awaited her fortune.

"You will rule," Ravenna told her, "but not Balmirra."

A triumphant smile overtook Yngrid's face, and she clapped her hands together. "Well, that's excellent news!"

"Is it?"

Yngrid nodded excitedly. "No offense, but Balmirra is austere. And drafty. Nothing to the beauty and comforts of Innrinhom."

Ravenna only nodded mildly.

Chuckling to herself, Yngrid patted Ravenna's shoulder. "I like you more and more, *kone*. What a treasure you are! No wonder he keeps you close." Leaning down, she whispered, "Should you ever tire of him, you've always a place at my court." With that and a wink, Yngrid straightened and flounced from the bedchamber.

Ravenna stared after the orcess, bemused.

What just happened? she asked Oberon, relaying the strange exchange.

Diplomacy. I think.

17

It was finally when they reached Innrinhom that Ravenna was able to catch her breath. Vallek didn't plan to stay long, wanting to continue the journey to the eastern tibes so that their return to Balmirra wouldn't be bogged down by autumn rains. Yet, it would've been the epitome of rudeness to refuse the chieftain's offer of hospitality.

"It'll only be for a night," he reassured her early that first morning. As a mark of friendship and trust, he entered Innrinhom to accept Hrothgar's hospitality with a reduced retinue. At least Mattias would be with him.

"I'll be fine," she reassured him right back, finding his fussing rather endearing.

Ravenna kept to his tent and to herself. She'd thought the time alone—including having his big bed all to herself—would feel like a treat, but she quickly grew bored. When she slept alone in the bed, she was more than a little annoyed to find that she already missed his burning heat at her back. She'd slept alone most of her life, but after a mere fortnight of sleeping beside her *azai,* she found herself tossing and turning.

Her only consolation was that he wasn't likely to sleep very well, either. Which meant he'd be awake and aware of any other attempts at seduction.

—white eyelashes fanned upon a pale cheek—saltwater burned her eyes—a scream of anguish—a battle cry—

Ravenna rolled over, woken from her afternoon doze. Fates, that was the third one today, all of the same or similar images. Her power was trying to tell her something, but from the images she saw, she wasn't sure she wanted to listen.

Without much else to do than lay around and relieve her tired feet as she and the rest of the camp awaited Vallek's return—*any time now*—Ravenna attempted to doze, making up for her poor night's sleep. Her visions had other ideas, however, as they so often did. *Impudent little buggers.*

Rubbing her head, she sat up in her *azai*'s bed, feeling . . . melancholy. Fates, did she truly miss him that much? It'd been just over a full day without him, and he wasn't far. She could expect his return at any moment.

Really, she should be enjoying her time alone. She hadn't had much of it on this journey, and safely ensconced in his bedroom, she didn't even bother with her glamour. While she did appreciate the reprieve from her false face, there was no quarter from the boredom. She told herself that the sharp pain in her side from missing Vallek wouldn't be so acute had she anything to do. Even a bit of embroidery. Boredom made everything worse.

She wasn't sure she entirely believed it, though.

Ears trained for any sign of his arrival, she jumped up from the bed when she heard someone rush inside.

"Hurry!" someone said. "They've spotted *unicorns!*"

A gasp met the announcement, and two pairs of feet hurried from the tent.

Ravenna's stomach dropped to her toes, which she quickly shoved into her boots. Hesitating only long enough to don her glamour, she didn't even waste time grabbing her cloak, just went running out of the tent.

No no no no . . .

Obi, where are you? she asked desperately, arms pumping. She followed a curious crowd moving north, heart racing faster than her feet pounded the ground.

Nearby. Why? Is something amiss?

Someone says you've been spotted.

I hardly think—

Oberon!

A handful of berserkers were keeping the curious orcs back, but Ravenna didn't stop. Putting on speed, she used her magic to encourage the warriors' gazes to look elsewhere as she swept past. She couldn't truly make herself invisible, but she could ensure no one was looking for her.

Dry pine needles crunched beneath her boots as she wove between trees, mounting a steep rise. The slope went nearly vertical near the top, forcing her to claw her way up. At the crest, chest heaving, she spotted a small party of orcs just down the other side of the slope, pointing. Following their line of sight, Ravenna could just spy the silvery glint of Oberon's flank.

They're on a ridge! To the south! You have to move!

Are you in danger? Should we—

I'm fine! Just go!

The silver flashed between the tree limbs, like sun glinting on the surface of a lake, and then disappeared into the denser brush.

"They're on the move," said one of the party's hunters.

Ravenna's heart lurched when she saw him draw an arrow from his quiver.

"No!" she cried. Without thought or worry, she slid down the slope, nearly crashing into the hunter. Reaching for his burly arm, she stopped him from nocking the arrow. "You can't!"

The other orcs—two more hunters, three berserkers, and Ulrich—

grumbled unhappily, eyes shifting back to where the unicorns had been in the valley below.

"Those beasts are dangerous, *kone*," said one of the berserkers. "They wouldn't hesitate to attack a stray orc."

"They've moved off," Ravenna argued. "They can't mean us any harm."

"Sentimental fool," Ulrich growled. "Unicorns have slain many kin. They're to be killed on sight."

Glaring up at the lord commander, Ravenna said, "It's bad luck to slay a unicorn."

"Perhaps for *your kind*," Ulrich sneered. "An orc wears their horns as trophies." Nodding at the others, Ulrich said, "Track them."

"No!" *Run fast!*

I won't leave you, Crow.

Oberon, they mean to kill you!

With Ravenna holding onto him, the hunter looked first at her and then his comrades, obviously unsure what to do about the human woman dangling from his arm.

"Unhand him. *Now*," Ulrich warned.

"They aren't a danger!"

"*Kone,* please—" The hunter gripped her arm with his free hand, trying to pull her off.

"You would defend a unicorn?" Another laid a heavy hand on her shoulder.

"She's mad," scoffed another, blocking her in.

"I said unhand him!" Ulrich clapped a heavy hand on her other shoulder, fingers digging below her left clavicle.

"Please don't hurt them!"

"What's the meaning of this?"

Their scuffle stopped, and as one, they all looked up the ridge. At the top stood Vallek, Mattias, and over a dozen berserkers. Rage contorted Vallek's face, his nose wrinkled like a great cat's, his mouth pulled down.

"Unicorns, my king!" Ulrich hurried to explain. He pointed out where they'd been spotted. "Not four-hundred yards from camp."

"Unicorns? This far south?" Mattias said.

But Vallek said nothing, glowering down at the strange tableau they must have made. As if she'd caught fire, the hunters released her.

Ravenna spun around to face up the slope. She met the angry gaze of her *azai,* unsure what he was maddest at. Probably her.

That mattered less to her than Oberon's safety.

Bending, Ravenna knelt on the needles and detritus, folding her hands before her.

"Please," she begged, "please spare them. They've already moved on."

Vallek's eyes rimmed in white to see her kneeling. "Unicorns have long been the enemy of orcs."

"These aren't your enemy."

"How could you know that, foolish woman?" Ulrich demanded. "They aren't pretty ponies, these are warhorses! Bred to hunt and kill orcs!"

"If they meant to hurt you, they would have already," Ravenna spat.

Ulrich huffed, spitting on the ground near where she knelt.

"Enough." Vallek didn't need to raise his voice, the low warning carrying down the slope to them. Ravenna shivered with its impact.

Please, she mouthed to him. Reaching out with her magic, she gently caressed his face before lowering the phantom touch to his chest. Over his heart. *Please. For me.*

An interminable moment passed in which Vallek considered—and gave nothing away. She wasn't sure he would bend, and for a horrible moment, she thought orcish hatred for unicorns might weigh heavier than her word.

Finally, he motioned for her to stand.

She did so cautiously, her knees aching and her lip trembling. She bit it to hide how it quivered. *Please please please.*

"We will respect Hrothgar's lands and let the beasts be," he announced.

"My king . . ."

"Increase patrols around camp and stay vigilant. We start east tomorrow." After issuing his orders, Vallek pinned her with a significant look. *And* you *will explain yourself,* that look said.

Fine. She could tell him about Oberon, she supposed.

But first, it was time to make her grandmare proud.

After a long, *long* night away from his mischievous mate, all Vallek had wanted to do upon returning to camp was find her waiting in a quiet, cool tent. She would open her arms to him, greet him with kisses, and whisper how much she missed him as he eased into the cradle of her body.

Nothing was ever so simple with his sprite, though.

Instead, he came back to word of unicorns and his own mate down on her knees, begging for their lives. Vallek had no intention of starting a feud with a herd of unicorns, especially with a camp full of lives he was responsible for, but he wouldn't soon forget how Ravenna had gotten down on her knees and pleaded.

He hadn't . . . liked it. She didn't belong on her knees.

Seeing her surrounded by males hadn't done much for his mood, either.

All in all, it made for a tense dinner that night.

With Hrothgar and his retinue safely back in their city, there was no longer the need for as much pretense. Both Mattias and Ravenna joined him and Ulrich at the table, although the company didn't make for good conversation.

Ulrich listened attentively to Vallek's account of Innrinhom. He wanted to know everything—the layout of their citadel, the depth of their curtain walls—and Vallek endeavored to tell him. However, his attention never strayed long from his mate.

She still wore her false human face for the benefit of the handful of servants and guards in the tent. She remained quiet throughout the evening, only picking at her meal. Vallek didn't like it. She needed to eat—their journey was far from over and now came the hard part. The eastern tribes would be far less hospitable than Hrothgar.

She didn't seem to pay the conversation much attention, her gaze instead flicking now and again to the bowls on the table. Between her fascination with the bowls of food she wasn't eating and Ulrich doing his best to ignore her very presence at the table, once Vallek concluded his tale of the night in Innrinhom, the conversation lapsed into silence.

Pulling the jar of pickled turnips toward him—a dish only Ulrich enjoyed—the lord commander asked, "And did he say anything about the timber?"

Opening up friendlier relations with Innrinhom and Hrothgar could mean a vast wealth of timber for Balmirra. Although a city of stone, there was plenty they could do with more fine Innrini timber— including building more ships and barges to sail Dyfan Bay.

"Only a mention, but he's interested," Vallek confirmed.

"We'll need to—*hrk*—" Ulrich choked on his words, bending in half and clutching his stomach. "Forgive me, I—*ack*—" Face contorted in a grimace, Ulrich panted as his stomach grumbled and groaned ominously. Sweat broke out across his brow, and his face flushed puce.

He stood so quickly, the table and all the dishes rattled. Still clutching at his middle, Ulrich hurried from the tent, and it wasn't long before they heard the miserable sounds of retching.

"Bad luck," Ravenna muttered, although not quietly, grinning over the rim of her cup.

The servants and few guards looked amongst themselves and murmured.

Frowning, Vallek reached for the jar of turnips to smell.

Ravenna was quicker. "No no," she said almost breezily, snatching the jar away. "It's likely bad."

Vallek didn't think pickled turnips could go bad. He narrowed his eyes at his mate, the most animated she'd been all night.

She wouldn't . . .

Mattias dropped his spoon and leaned back from the table.

"Don't worry, captain," Ravenna chirped, "I like you very much."

Mattias, one of the strongest, bravest orcs Vallek knew, gulped as he gawked at the small woman sitting across from them.

Vallek dropped his face into his palm and sighed.

"The whole camp will be terrified of you by morning," Vallek grumbled later that night as they lay together in his bed.

His annoyance at this bitter enmity between his mate and his lord commander was beginning to chafe. That didn't mean, however, that he didn't want to hold her lithe body close and feel all her delicious curves against him while he scolded her. He *had* been away, after all.

"Good," she said, utterly unrepentant.

Vallek didn't know whether to be proud, aroused, or annoyed. Perhaps a bit of everything.

Smoothing his hand up and down her leg, he rucked her nightgown higher with each pass. One day soon, he would convince her of the needlessness of the garment. He slept naked and so should she. For efficiency, if nothing else.

"What did you do to him?"

"Nothing fatal." The minx smiled when she said it.

Vallek sighed, ruffling her dark hair. "I can't have you poisoning my best men, sprite."

"I didn't poison your best men. I poisoned Ulrich."

"Why do you despise him so?"

"He raided my room, took my mother's grimoire. Tried to strangle—" Her nostrils flared, and she took a moment to regain her composure. "Besides," she eventually continued, "he started it. He's always been against me."

Well, that was true. Ulrich had wanted to leave her where they found her. *We don't need a soothsayer. Your future is clear enough,* he remembered Ulrich saying.

"Ulrich has been my most loyal friend since we were boys," he explained.

"I know. That's why it wasn't fatal." She traced her fingers down the side of his face, her touch featherlight. "He sees what you refuse to—that I threaten, even undermine all that you've worked for."

Vallek tightened his arms around her, not liking that at all. "I liked it better when you disagreed."

"He doesn't want you to throw everything away for me. I don't want that, either."

"I'm hardly throwing everything away," he snorted. "I'm *adjusting.* As anyone would when they'd found their mate."

"Yes, but not just anyone is a king."

"Because I'm king I can't have my way? That hardly seems right."

"It means sacrifice. You've already worked so hard toward unification. You will achieve it, I know you will." She smiled sadly. "I worry our bond would only thwart you."

"Never." Pushing his hand past the hem of her nightgown, he splayed his palm along the warm skin of her lower back. "Perhaps all this time, unification has been for you."

Her lips parted as the breath rushed out of her. "You don't mean that."

"Maybe I do," he said, his mind whirring. "Maybe all this time, I've worked to unify my people so that I could take a faeling mate."

"You don't have to be king to do that," she reminded him.

"Perhaps not. But to keep a hellion like you safe, yes." Nuzzling her hair, he added, "But no more poisoning."

Smoothing her hands over his chest, she told him, "I do nothing unprovoked. I'm small compared to all of you. I can't let *anyone* get away with threatening me."

"*No one* will threaten you," he vowed. His blood rushed with anger just thinking about it.

"Ulrich does every day."

The revelation struck him harder than a blow. He knew Ulrich was determined to separate him from Ravenna, but to *threaten* her, even knowing she was his mate?

A growl built in his chest.

"No, none of that," she whispered, kissing the skin over his heart. "I'm not trying to tattle. I can handle myself. Ulrich is loyal to you and has his use. I can bear that."

His growl didn't quite abate, but he managed to bite it back into a purr for her. It seemed he needed to have a word with his lord commander. While Ulrich had served him loyally for years, that didn't excuse such behavior toward his mate. Ulrich didn't have to like Ravenna, but he did have to respect that she was in Vallek's life now.

"Very well," he said reluctantly.

Quiet overcame them, and if Vallek was a little more selfish, he might have let her continue to pet him softly in the velvety darkness. The night was cool and the tent quiet. It would've been nothing to finally enjoy his mate.

But he made himself say, "Now tell me about the unicorns."

Ravenna pulled a face. "Yes. That." Sucking in a long breath, she explained, "There are currently four unicorns trailing the camp. They come from a larger herd that grazes outside Balmirra."

Vallek's ears rang. So many unicorns so near his city—and *no one* knew?

A choked sound escaped his throat.

"They came with me, you see. To protect me." Vallek listened, stunned and amazed, as she told him of her father's dread-mount Oberon, a silver stallion, and how he and his mother's herd had sworn to protect Ravenna.

She spoke of them with love, her face softening as she described Oberon, Callistix, and the others. She knew all about the herd politics, described the newest foals, and which young mares would soon want to challenge for leadership or leave to form their own herds.

He could only listen in wonder. Many orc-kin had died on the sharp point of a unicorn horn, and his natural aversion to the beasts was there. Still, he couldn't help but admire the loyalty and love shared between Ravenna and her unicorns.

To have traveled so far, to live in unfriendly lands so long, just to keep her safe . . .

He didn't even mind so much when she told him of their plans to besiege Balmirra when Vallek had first confined her to his quarters. While he was mildly horrified to hear it, he could still appreciate their devotion.

Vallek was quickly coming to realize there wasn't a city he wouldn't besiege, an enemy he wouldn't destroy, nor a land he wouldn't conquer for Ravenna.

"I should like to meet them," he found himself saying, "when it's safe."

Her brows arched in surprise before a warm smile broke across her face. "You would?"

"Yes." Drawing her leg over his hip, he said, "I have to thank them for bringing you safely to me."

Her smile grew wry. "Oberon will have many things to say about my safety."

"I look forward to it." And he did. From her explanation, and the way she so desperately begged for their lives, it was clear that these unicorns were Ravenna's kin. It pleased him to know she wasn't alone in the world. That she hadn't just materialized out of the mist one day.

She had shared this truth with him, and he vowed it was to be the first of many. She had a past, his mysterious mate, and he intended to find out every little bit. He would have her secrets, starting with this.

His chest swelled to know that he'd gained some of her trust.

Purr deepening, his hand slid over the plush curve of her backside to delve between her legs. Her sharp inhale had his pupils dilating, and he buried his face against her neck, soaking in her scent as his fingers began to work.

"Now then, I think it's time we get back to practicing, yes?"

18

Although they had to delay another day on account of Ulrich being *indisposed,* the march to the splinter tribes moved through the eastern foothills like the tide, inevitable and indomitable. They made good time, much of which Vallek put down to Ravenna and Ulrich playing nice. Or at least, being kept at opposite ends of the column.

Her point having apparently been made, Ravenna accepted riding near the rear of the column on her assigned onager, Mattias once again watching over her. Vallek would've much preferred to spend the day marching alongside his mate and send Ulrich to the rear. Especially given how foul his mood was after what he and Vallek were calling a bad jar of pickled turnips—although the whole camp soon knew otherwise.

Vallek didn't know whether to be impressed or exasperated with how his whole camp, from warrior to cook, now looked at her askance with real trepidation in their eyes. She wasn't allowed anywhere near the mess tent.

Ravenna . . . it wasn't that she enjoyed the notoriety, but she certainly rode her onager with the poise and regalness of a queen. A smug queen.

A few days of hard marching, however, soon made everyone—not forget, but at least think about other things. The hard days of journeying had their rhythm, and soon all fell into step. Vallek made himself be content with spending his days strategizing while marching, for at least he was holding his mate close in the night.

He kept her back with all the others who weren't warriors, though, when the smoke of the first tribe's camp was spotted on the horizon.

Vallek sent scouts ahead, and when they reported back on size and strength, he deployed his berserkers. As one disciplined unit, they encircled the camp, moving inexorably inward to tighten the knot. When the tribesmen realized what had happened, it was already too late.

One by one, the tribes pledged their allegiance. Surrounded and overwhelmed, they had little choice. Sharp-Tooth, Green-Back, Silver-Tusk, Shorn-Head, and Iron-Chest, they all came to understand that unification with the growing orcish kingdom was in their best interest.

Not every encounter went smoothly. The Green-Back chieftain challenged Vallek to combat. It was a good fight, one that got Vallek's blood pumping, and in the end, he was by rights the new chieftain of the Green-Backs. His first decree was to order the remaining kin to choose a new leader before sending representatives to Balmirra.

Challenging and fighting for leadership of every clan wasn't practical, but it did expedite his demands. It also had the unforeseen benefit of softening his little hellion towards him.

His mate fussed over his minor scrapes from the challenge even more than his healer Fenna did, which pleased him no end. He could very well get used to having Ravenna flutter and fuss, her soft hands searching him all over for any more bumps or bruises. He let her check over the healer's work and even dab on her own salves and tinctures.

"A kiss from you would heal all my hurts," he crooned, trying not to be too obvious about looking down the neckline of her nightgown.

Her rosebud lips pursed in an unimpressed moue. "You're fine."

When she made to stand up, he grabbed her hand, pulling her back down to his side. "No, you must check me over more. I'm bruised and weary from missing you."

"You saw me this morning," she said grumpily.

"Hours and hours ago. Agony to my poor heart."

Ravenna patted his chest. "Your heart is fine."

"A kiss would ensure it."

She squinted at him a long while, but in the blink of an eye, her expression grew sultry. A vixen's smile played at her lips as she gently pushed at his chest. He fell back into the bed willingly, ignorant of his sore body as he watched her climb first onto the bed and then onto him. Straddling his waist, her nightgown pushed up to her hips, she arched one dark brow at him as she ran her hands up and down his chest.

Enchanted, his purr buzzed through him, and his hands slid up her thighs to frame her hips. He hummed with pleasure when she leaned over him, balancing her weight on one hand so she could hover just above him.

"Just one kiss?" she murmured in a dulcet, cock-teasing tone. "I think you will demand far more than that, my king. You're greedy."

"It would depend on the kiss," he mused.

Ravenna hummed in consideration, her long hair falling around them in a dark, fragrant curtain. Intoxicated by her scent and nearness, Vallek's hands began to knead her flesh, urging her silently to come closer, to let him devour her.

"Well, if it would mean the health of the king. Just kisses."

Something niggled in his mind that he should've been worried, but then that lush mouth was on his, and he wasn't thinking anymore beyond that. She kissed him first in gentle little nibbles, teasing touches that were never quite enough. The lightest pressure, the barest taste, and then she was gone, moving to his chin or his tusk before coming back to give him hope again.

Her hands found their way into his hair and traced the tipped edges of his ears. Her fingertips were as light as her kisses, feathery and maddening. No matter how he coaxed, she wouldn't be rushed. Instead, over long, *long* moments of tantalizing agony, she slowly increased the pressure and length of her kisses.

Whenever his hands strayed beyond cupping her pert backside, her magic took hold of his hands to push them back in place. It was vigilant, never letting him stray into the wet heat he could just feel above his lower belly.

Too late he realized she truly meant it. Just kisses.

But oh, her kisses fed his soul. He couldn't feel his stinging cuts or aching bruises. His pride and triumph at conquering another tribe were nothing to the thrill of her lingering kiss.

Gods, why was he here in this wilderness when he could be comfortable in his great bed in Balmirra, locked away with his luscious mate?

Once this was done, once the east was secured, he intended to march straight back to his city and ensconce himself and Ravenna in his quarters for days. There, he would take his due for every teasing kiss, every arched brow and defiant grin. If it wasn't his fingers inside her, then it would be his cock, every day, always, claiming her until their scents mixed and she was convinced of the fact that he'd never part with her.

He endured her play for as long as he was able, meeting her kisses with his own, murmuring promises to her, and trailing his fingers ever closer to the cunt he knew was swollen and soaked for him.

Squeezing her backside, he growled against her lips. "You win, sprite. Now ride my cock before I truly get cross."

Her laugh puffed against his abused lips. Lifting herself up, she bit her bottom lip, keeping his gaze as she deliberately slid down to kneel above his straining cock. A groan tore from the deepest depths of his chest when she lowered herself onto him, cradling the underside of his cock.

"A different kind of kiss," she breathed.

Vallek's hips punched up in a violent roll, a hiss bursting between his gritted teeth. A needy moan caught in her throat, and Ravenna began to move, maddening little rocks of her hips that had him seeing the afterworld and all the ancestors.

With his grip on her hips, he moved her faster, grinding himself up into the seam of her body. She soaked his lap, their bodies making slick, sloppy sounds as she moved faster, faster. Her nails dug into the meat of his chest, and Vallek bared his teeth. *Fuck,* they needed to practice more, for he didn't know how much longer he could bear not being inside her.

She claimed his climax, those infernal little moans and rolling motions sending him careening off a cliff. Throwing his head back, his bellow filled the tent as spurts of spend lashed his belly. The bite of her nails stung, digging in almost enough to draw blood, and he felt her throb against the underside of his cock.

Chest heaving, he watched greedily as she came apart, every muscle tensed. Seeing her lose control, how those violet eyes went hazy with passion, fulfilled something needy inside him, something that was desperate not just to care for his mate but to earn how she looked at him now—like he was the male for her.

Faster than she could react, he tumbled them around, reversing their positions. She gasped up at him from the bed, her violet eyes sparkling as he loomed over her.

Rumbling with a seductive purr, he lowered his head to hers to whisper, "You're right. I'm far too greedy for just one."

The last camp, the most northerly of the eastern tribes, was also one of the most isolated. In the fortnight he and his berserkers had marched up the foothills, he'd heard plenty about the Stone-Skin camp. About their penchant for cruelty and taking human slaves.

It was why he left his mate safe and secure in their camp over a day's journey from the Stone-Skin tribe, making the last push with only his berserkers. It was why they approached in the gloaming, tightening the net as the tribe gathered round their central fire to eat.

And it was why, as he passed between great boulders meant to funnel enemies into an easy kill zone and finally into the camp, he was shocked to find the tribe to be the smallest of them all.

With a flick of his wrist, the net closed.

His berserkers sprang from the shadows, herding the Stone-Skins toward the center of camp, where the bonfire crackled. Shouts rang out through the craggy hills, but before any of the warriors could draw their weapons, his berserkers were there, pushing them between the circles of tents.

"Gather by the fire!" Mattias ordered. "In the name of the king!"

Confusion choked the camp, and wide, fearful eyes flashed in the firelight. Scuffles broke out across the camp, those warriors who could fighting back with bare fists. It was for naught, the battle over before it'd begun. Summarily overwhelmed, the tribesmen were dragged toward the bonfire as more berserkers cleared every tent.

When Vallek passed through his berserkers into the light of the fire, Hormhím ready at his side, startled cries and gasps drowned out the crackling of the great flames. In all, Vallek counted just forty or so kin, at least half orcesses or orclings. They stared at him in horror and fright, an apparition come to slaughter them in the night.

"Who is your chieftain?" Vallek boomed.

An older orc stepped forward, a noticeable limp slowing his stride. "Who are you?"

"Watch how you speak to your king," Ulrich growled.

The older orc looked truly baffled, his graying brows rising in shock. "King?"

"You stand before Vallek Far-Sight, chieftain of Balmirra, king of kin," announced Ulrich. "You will kneel before him and give your loyalty."

"It's time for all eastern tribes to join in allegiance with their kin," said Vallek. "Your fellows have already knelt. They say Krul is chieftain here. Where is he?"

"Died. Years ago," said the older orc. "I'm chieftain here."

By the Ever-Father, these kin truly were isolated. They even spoke with an accent he'd only heard from the very eldest of Balmirrans.

"And you are?"

"Fulk."

"Well, Fulk, you will speak for your tribe and swear fealty to me and the orcish throne."

Careful to not quite sneer, Fulk said, "Never heard of a king of kin."

"Your tribe refused the last one," said Vallek. "That won't be tolerated again."

Hearing the blatant threat, Fulk's gaze flicked down to the great axe Vallek held. "We haven't heard of you, so why should we believe you?"

Hefting Hormhím to rest the top of the shaft on his shoulder, Vallek stepped further into the firelight. The flames caught on Hormhím's dual blades, as well as Vallek's armor, polished to a high shine. He towered above Fulk and the Stone-Skins, and while he wasn't above using the threat of his size, he felt a niggle of pity for them.

Kept away from others, they had become small and scared in their rocky hills.

"You've heard of Balmirra?"

Fulk nodded reluctantly. "Yes."

"You've heard of Kaldebrak, Innrinhom, and Holdur?"

"Yes."

"All the great orcish cities are mine. Their chieftains have sworn fealty to me. The Sharp-Tooths, Green-Backs, and all the other eastern tribes have knelt before me. The Stone-Skins will, too." Closing the distance between him and the older orc, Vallek said, "I have no need of your little camp, Fulk Stone-Skin. Your people are but a handful of kin."

"And yet you're here."

"And yet I'm here." Vallek smiled, all teeth. "Your loyalty won't be for nothing. You join all kin, together, in a nation that will rival any on the continent." Sweeping his gaze across the huddled tribe, he added, "Come out from your hills. Your people will know prosperity they can only dream of."

They didn't need to know his ultimate aim—to eventually join the tribes together into an eastern bastion, a stronghold to guard the east like that of Kaldebrak in the north and Balmirra in the west. He would fortify the east, strengthen its people to stand strong against the Pyrossi incursion. For now, though, he just needed their fealty.

"And if I don't?"

Vallek dropped his smile. "Then all of you will be taken to Balmirra and interned." They were a liability otherwise.

"Bastard!" A blur caught in Vallek's periphery, and he moved backwards in time to avoid the swinging fist of an enraged orc.

Before the attacker could even think about striking again, the berserkers were on him.

The orc, a young, strapping male and the biggest of the Stone-Skins, gave the berserkers a good if untrained fight. All unbridled strength, he could only throw brute force against the berserkers, who soon outwitted and outflanked him.

Together, three berserkers secured the orc's arms, pinning them behind him at a painful angle. A swift kick to the backs of his knees saw him crash to the dirt.

Although caught, the young hunter glared up at Vallek. Interestingly, from just one eye. A crude patch hid the left one, the edges of a jagged scar poking out from the upper and lower rims.

"We'll *never* bow to you," the orc snarled.

"Shut up, Kaldar," Fulk growled.

"We never had a king! We don't need a king!"

"I am the only thing standing between you and the Pyrossi horde, boy. When they sweep through these lands, who else will come to save you?"

"They wouldn't dare."

Vallek snorted. "Of course they would. They already are. And you, the weak underbelly of orc-kin, are their easiest way inside. I won't allow it."

Kaldar swung his angry gaze to Fulk. "Don't you dare fucking do it, uncle. We don't need these fuckers!"

The berserker holding Kaldar's right arm pinched it back tighter, earning a grimace of pain.

Fulk met Vallek's gaze. He sighed. They both knew with Kaldar's words that Vallek would have his way.

Vallek agreed when Fulk said, "He's young and stupid."

That he was.

"But you will be wiser." Lifting Hormhím to point at Kaldar, Vallek warned, "Your fealty for his other eye."

Fulk's lips thinned. The threat was foreseeable, yet the other Stone-Skins gasped in horror. Several cried out for mercy.

"You fucking bastard," Kaldar sneered, only to have his face thrust into the dirt.

Gods, the boy had more bulk than brains.

It wasn't hard to see that Fulk thought something similar as he glanced at his nephew, dejected. There was no way out for this sad little clan. If Fulk wanted all of his tribe to see morning, he'd kneel.

Only a few more moments passed before the older orc sighed again and creakily got on his knees.

"No!" Vehement, muffled denial echoed from the ground, where Kaldar wriggled against the berserkers with their knees in his back.

"I defer to you, Vallek Far-Sight," said Fulk. "The Stone-Skins pledge fealty to Balmirra."

"Wise."

Although he didn't rise, Fulk's gaze lifted to pin Vallek with a grave look. "The Stone-Skins have known many cruel leaders. Don't be the next."

Lowering Hormhím, Vallek nodded solemnly. A reluctant respect for this limping, aged chieftain took hold in his chest. Fulk would bend but not break.

Vallek saw such defiance and strength in Ravenna, too. And he loved her for it.

"You have my word." Reaching down, he offered Fulk his hand. The older orc took it, regaining his feet. And with a wave from Vallek, the berserkers released Kaldar to scramble to his feet. "Teach that one some manners, though."

Fulk snorted. "There's no use." Peering up at Vallek with a shrewd look, he said, "As king, you'll want something we found."

Intrigued, Vallek watched on as Fulk called for another of his hunters to fetch *those irons*.

"Found them on some Pyrrossi soldiers last winter," said Fulk. "Didn't know what to do with them."

The Stone-Skin hunter returned bearing two sets of manacles. He dropped them at Vallek's feet and quickly backed away.

The firelight caught in the dull metal, and at first glance, there didn't seem to be anything remarkable about the irons. Yet, the longer he looked, a sense of foreboding churned up his guts.

"There's something wrong with them," Fulk spat, echoing Vallek's own thought.

He didn't need to touch them to feel the wrongness emanating from them. Something was indeed wrong with the metal. Magic radiated from them, but not in a way he'd ever felt before. It seemed almost . . . greedy. As though it whispered and longed to be clapped onto wrists.

Pyrrossi soldiers with enchanted manacles.

Vallek exchanged looks with Ulrich. *Gods, what now?*

Later that night, so late it was practically tomorrow, Vallek sat with Ulrich in one of the larger Stone-Skin tents. What pertinent bits hadn't been sorted out yet could be done in the morning, when nerves and tempers were a little less frayed. Fulk hadn't seemed enthusiastic about offering up one of his own tents for them, but he did it all the same.

The strange manacles sat in a sack nearby, and it was a relief to have them out of sight. Fulk told them what little he knew, just that Pyrrossi soldiers had been caught with them and he believed there were more out there. It was something to investigate, and Vallek would take them to Ravenna for her opinion on what kind of magic they were spelled with and what this could mean.

For now, though, with berserkers posted as guards outside the tent flaps, Vallek and Ulrich were confident enough to share a celebratory flask of mead to revel in their victory.

Raising it to Ulrich and then to his lips, Vallek said, "To a plan come to fruition."

When he passed the flask back to Ulrich, his second took a long, hearty swing. "To the unification!" he said a little too loudly. Ulrich never could hold his spirits.

Chuckling, Vallek rested his wrist on his bent knee, trying to get as comfortable as possible reclined in a strange tent. While this victory was something to savor, he couldn't help wishing he was back in his own tent, with his mate for company instead. This triumph would be all the sweeter with her in his arms, pretending to be unimpressed, as he stole kisses.

Gods, he was getting to be a soppy bastard.

His beast merely sighed like a forlorn puppy, wondering why they really needed to stay here rather than reunite with Ravenna.

Telling himself to enjoy it, he took in the laughing Ulrich, candescent with their victory. His second's obvious good mood lifted Vallek's. Perhaps it was just the surrealism of so many years and plans finally reaching fulfillment that made him feel apart from the new reality.

Although his alliance with Hrothgar and the fealty of these eastern tribes would all need reinforcing to solidify the way he desired, this very night, the orcs were, if only in name, unified. For the first time in over one-hundred years, Vallek had done something no other chieftain, Balmirran or otherwise, had accomplished.

His kingdom, a new dawn for his people, began this very night.

That truth rang in his ears louder almost than Ulrich's good cheer.

When Ulrich passed the flask back, Vallek found but a sip remaining. That was all right. He enjoyed a cheerful, chuckling Ulrich, for such a thing was so rare these days.

Stronger than the usual fare, the mead Vallek kept in his flask was perfect for the road when he might not get his customary one goblet. Two swigs of the flask was the same as a goblet in Balmirra, and Ulrich's flushed face was proof enough of that.

With his second so jolly, perhaps now was an opportune time to sort out another of his challenges.

"I knew this day would come," Ulrich was saying, "felt it in my heart, I did. Knew since we were boys that we'd do something great."

Vallek grinned fondly to think of those two orclings conscripted into Mordis's army. They had little to live on but hopes and dreams then.

Look at them now. *I hope the old bastard chokes in the afterworld when he finds out.*

"Ravenna knew it would happen," Vallek said. "She saw the tribes coming round."

Ulrich grunted, his cheery face falling. "Easy enough to predict. What other choice did they have?"

Maybe so, but Vallek hadn't put it past any of the tribes to go out with a fight. These kin had valued their independence so much, they left the last orcish kingdom in defiance, eking out a living in these craggy foothills rather than moving forward with the rest of their kind.

Watching Ulrich from the corner of his eye, Vallek asked, "Why do you dislike her so?"

His second grumbled, waving him off. "Let's not talk of her tonight. There's far more important things to speak about."

"No, Ulrich. I want to know."

Although he seemed rather unsteady in his seat, swaying slightly from side to side, Ulrich stilled long enough to glower at Vallek.

"She means nothing good," Ulrich said finally. "She's trouble. And the people will never accept her."

The people, or you?

Twisting the cap onto his flask, Vallek said, "Well, they will have to one day soon. I mean to take her as my wife." She deserved no less. As his mate. As Ravenna.

There was still so much he'd yet to know about her, but this, at least, he was sure of—his beast had chosen well. Perhaps it was political catastrophe, but Vallek doubted he'd ever find anyone more suited to him than his devious, sassy hellion. There was likely something wrong with him that he looked forward to finding how she'd undermine or thwart him next, that he lived for her cutting tongue and sweet bite.

Ulrich reared back, his usual tact dampened by drink. "You ask too much of the kin. Accept a halfling queen? *Never.*"

Pinning his friend with a stare, Vallek replied, "I won't give them a choice."

Not sensing the danger in the calm, serious way he spoke, Ulrich shook his head. "You'll ruin what we just built! Can't you see? She brings nothing but trouble." Waving his arm to gesture vaguely west, he insisted, "Give her to those fae. Reopen the border. The people would love you for it—a peacemaker, a prosperity-bringer. History will remember you as the greatest chieftain the kin have ever known!" Ulrich rocked forward unsteadily, catching himself on Vallek's shoulder. "Don't give it all up for a halfling whore."

Vallek peeled his lip back from his tusks, slashing them through the air in warning. "Watch yourself, my friend."

But Ulrich was too irate, pointing a finger at him accusingly. "You're thinking only with your cock. We're so near the end—you can't just throw this away for a tight cunt."

Vallek's arm sprang forward to fist Ulrich's tunic. "You won't speak of her like that. She's my *mate.*"

The other orc's nostrils flared, a bit of clarity returning to his hazy eyes. "Go back to Hrothgar. Take one of his kin to wife. If you must keep the soothsayer, fine, but do this for our people. Our kingdom. For everything we've worked for."

Vallek bared his teeth. Gods, how had he not noticed how often Ulrich said *our* kingdom, *our* plans, *our* work. Vallek wasn't insensible to all that others had done for him, especially Ulrich, in making this unification into a reality, but he didn't care for the way his friend laid claim to it. Nor how he disregarded and insulted Ravenna.

Ulrich couldn't have done what Vallek did. He didn't challenge Mordis, too scared for his own skin. He didn't woo the politicians and chieftains and rival leaders. Ulrich hadn't the charisma, cleverness, or ambition to be king, let alone bring together all the tribes and clans.

And yet the way he spoke, Vallek might as well be snatching the throne out of Ulrich's hands.

Uncharitable of Vallek to think? Petty? Yes.

But he was tired of Ulrich's wheedling, of his incessant need to have control over everything Vallek did.

It was he who was king. The berserkers knew it. Fulk Stone-Skin and every eastern tribe chieftain knew it. It was time Ulrich knew it, too.

"I will have only her, Ulrich."

"Be sensible! She'll destroy all we've done!"

Jostling Ulrich by the collar, Vallek hissed, "I will make it so. The beast has chosen, and so have I."

Ulrich's eyes darkened, a look of utter betrayal flashing across his face. "You forsake all we've done, all we—"

"I take what is promised by the gods: a life with my mate. You would question your king? The gods themselves?"

Lips thinning between his tusks, Ulrich pulled out of Vallek's grip. "She's enchanted you. Poisoned your mind as she poisoned my body."

He didn't like the look of epiphany that crossed Ulrich's gaze. An unnatural light reflected in his eyes, and Vallek stood to meet it.

"Hear me, Ulrich. I tolerate this insult because you are my friend, but not forever. She will be my wife, and you and all kin will have to make peace with it."

Pushing Ulrich back into his seat and tossing the flask into his lap, Vallek strode from the tent. His mood was foul and he needed air.

If Ulrich couldn't respect his choice, as a king and as a friend, then it was time to consider a new lord commander.

19

Despite all the gains and successes, the homeward-bound march was a far more serious affair. Many days had been spent consolidating the eastern tribes, ensuring each sent representatives back to Balmirra—representatives, *not* hostages, he'd firmly reminded them—and knew the next steps for unification. That had taken longer than intended, so by the time the road home was again underfoot, the late-summer rains threatened.

It made for much more miserable marching, yet Vallek pushed the column hard. Everyone wanted to get home, to share the news of their triumph—and not get caught in the wilderness when the first autumn frosts came. None complained, although evenings were often quiet, his people weary from the road.

Were it just him and his berserkers, they could have reduced their time by running, but with so many camp followers, all they could do was keep a steady walking pace.

That was, until a berserker came trotting up from the back of the column with word from the rear.

"My king," the warrior panted, "Captain Mattias requests the column stop for a few moments for the *kone* to catch up."

Vallek's mindless feet came to an immediate halt. "She's fallen behind?" he growled.

Beside him, Ulrich huffed. Row by row behind him, the column ground to a halt.

"It seems so, my king."

Lifting his head to try peering over the column, he couldn't see the rear. Knowing that Ravenna was out of sight, had fallen behind in the vast wilderness, had his beast pawing at his chest cavity.

"Go back to Mattias, have him bring her to me."

"Yes, my king." The warrior bobbed his head and then was off, boots splashing in the little puddles gathering from the day's rain.

It'd stopped for the moment, but the humid air made breathing laborious and stuck hair to skulls. There was a modicum of relief away from the trees, and they followed a well-worn path leading through the foothills and deeper into the mountains.

The region was known for its crags and crevasses. Like cracks in dry, overspread clay, deep gouges crisscrossed the gray stone, forming a network of dangerous sheer drops. A breeze wafted up from the deep gray canyon to their left, sounding not unlike the howl of a forlorn wolf. The gorge was so deep and the air so humid, that a thick layer of mist gathered far below, obscuring the stone floor of the great cut in the earth.

There was a majesty to this landscape, rugged and untamed. The only real trace of orcs or any others was the path leading the way safely through it. Enough souls had lost their lives to the mountain's sinister smiles that everyone knew to stick to the path.

Throwing back his oilskin hood, Vallek squinted at the overcast sky. The monochrome gray that had brought the rain was beginning to break up into great, puffy pillars. Thunderstorms came from clouds like that.

"We wouldn't stop for a tired warrior," grumbled Ulrich. "Nor any of your staff. We shouldn't stop for her."

"And yet we have," Vallek sneered, his mood matching the foul weather.

His berserkers wouldn't have spoken a word either way, accustomed to the harsh realities of serving their king, but Vallek didn't think he mistook the glints of relief in their eyes when he announced, "Enough for today. Make camp! Let's get out of the weather."

A hum of activity began as word was passed back and the column began looking for the least water-logged patches of rock. Hunters and woodsmen broke off from the column to begin gathering game and timber, and more than a few berserkers stretched out their arms and backs.

With the growing commotion, no one but Vallek heard Ulrich growl, "Weak from the rain, are you? Or is it her that makes you weak?"

An answering growl grew in Vallek's chest. "I've warned you, Ulrich."

His second snorted. "You've never called for camp so early before. We could make another five leagues before dark. If it weren't for her."

Surging forward, Vallek put his face in Ulrich's, making their tusks *clack* together. "Everyone's tired of the rain, and I'm tired of you. Be *silent*."

Ulrich's face somehow soured even more, and Vallek turned away so he didn't have to see it. His old friend had been nigh insufferable since the Stone-Skin camp. Rather than heed his warning, Ulrich found every opportunity to malign Ravenna or question Vallek about her. No one else would have dared such insubordination, and Vallek had long since begun wondering why he bore it.

It was as if Ulrich sensed that when they returned to Balmirra, everything would change. Vallek couldn't quite say how yet, but he knew at least that after consulting with Eydis, plans would be put in motion to introduce Ravenna to the court. Wearing her own face. Ulrich, canny as he could be, no doubt sensed this and rallied for one more campaign.

It would be his last.

Although Ulrich had served him ably, Vallek couldn't have someone so opposed to his mate so close. When they returned to Balmirra, he would inform Ulrich of his dismissal. Vallek only delayed now out of an abundance of caution. Perhaps before, he might not have suspected his oldest friend capable of anything against him, but the sheer hatred in Ulrich's gaze whenever he looked upon Ravenna meant that Vallek wouldn't risk inciting him against her more. Not until he could sequester her away somewhere completely safe.

He was conferring with one of his seneschals about the placement of his tent, Ulrich hovering nearby like a gloomy shadow, by the time Mattias came jogging up the length of the column, a glamoured Ravenna in his arms.

Wisely, he put her down to walk the last distance between them.

The bite of Vallek's unease softened just a little at the sight of her.

Only to snap down hard again when he saw how she limped. Hurrying to her, he held out his arms, taking her slight weight. He drew her into the safety of his body, not caring that his people watched on, pretending they didn't but certainly interested.

"Wandering off again, *skala?*" he chided gently.

"Twitch went lame this morning, and I didn't want to burden another onager since it was raining," she explained. Using her grip on his arm for balance, she lifted one foot to begin pulling it out of her boot. "I didn't get *that* far behind. Mattias could see me the whole time."

Over her head, his gaze flicked up to confirm it with his captain. Mattias nodded solemnly.

A little noise of pain drew his attention back to her, and he saw how red and raw her heels were, a bright blister oozing midway up.

Vallek groaned. "You promised me you were all right to walk."

"I am," she insisted. "Hold this." Pulling a little pot from her cloak pocket, she handed it to him then twisted off the lid. Gathering a dollop of salve, she applied it liberally to her abused heel. "There," she said through her wince, "I should be fine until we make camp."

"I've already called for it. We make camp here."

Her shoulders slumped. "Thank fates." Blowing out a breath, she grinned cheekily up at him. "I'm ready to see the end of today."

He couldn't help the plaintive note in the low purr rumbling in his chest. "I won't allow you to hurt yourself further."

"I have to walk, Vallek," she reminded him quietly.

"No. I will carry you until your feet heal."

Her lips twitched with wanting to grin, but she bit it back, shaking her head. "You can't do that. You know how it will look."

"I don't care." Sinking to one knee before her, he lifted her hand from his forearm to his shoulder then her bare foot from the ground to his bent knee.

Ravenna's eyes went round as she watched him dab more of the salve onto her foot. Nails digging into the leather on his shoulder, she whispered urgently, "They're watching."

"Let them," he replied, keeping her gaze as he checked the rest of her foot and ankle to assure himself she wasn't injured any worse.

Her lips parted on a gasp when he bent to kiss the top of her little foot. There. Let them see. Every orc would know who she was soon enough—why not start with those in the column. These were supposed to be his most loyal warriors and staff.

She was his mate, and it was his right to care for her. Had he been anyone else, had they known who she was to him, no one would question it. He refused to accept his own mating being any different. He'd waited decades for her, for the chance to cherish and care for his woman, and by the Ever-Father, he would have it.

He expected the murmurs—but not the savage, sudden growl behind him.

"*No!*"

Vallek was violently pushed aside, landing in a puddle.

Ripped away from him, Ravenna gasped, her yelp cut off as a hand closed around her throat.

He threw himself back up to his feet, a raging roar erupting from the depths of his chest.

"ULRICH!"

Vallek surged forward, frantic to reclaim his mate, desperate to rend Ulrich's head from his body.

"Stop!" Ulrich snarled. Lifting Ravenna by the throat, he shook her viciously as her toes scrabbled. "Show them! Reveal your true face!"

Vallek's heart stopped as Ulrich backed toward the sheer drop of the canyon, his look malicious and wild. He whipped his tusks down, gashing along Ravenna's shoulder and ripping the fabric of her blue cloak until it fell in a heap at their feet.

She gurgled, wriggling in midair, hands clawing at the fist that held her. Tears seeped from her eyes, gone violet in the struggle.

With a gasp, the last of her glamour fell, revealing her true face.

"*Fae!*"

"She's a fae!"

Shouts rang out from the column, and Vallek felt his berserkers push forward, their anger and confusion a writhing thing at his back.

He hardly heard or cared, his hand going to Hormhím's hilt.

Ulrich sneered, lifting Ravenna higher. "Behold, the fae spy! She's infiltrated our ranks, enchanted our king!"

"Back, stay back!" Mattias shouted.

"Release her!" Vallek demanded, voice nearly lost to his growl. "And I'll make your death swift."

"Do you hear him?" Ulrich laughed madly. "He threatens *me,* his oldest friend. He's been poisoned, *spelled!*"

"Put. Her. Down." Vallek pulled Hormhím free of his belt, and the noise behind him gathered.

Ulrich tracked the movement, how Vallek edged ever closer. He was close enough to see the fanatic glint in Ulrich's eyes and even worse, the terrified gleam in Ravenna's.

Get her. Destroy the threat. Kill him.

Terror and betrayal whirled inside him, but his anger burned so brightly, it was cold. Calculating. It cleared his mind of all else; all other loyalties died, all other priorities were forgotten.

Nothing mattered but freeing her.

Ulrich stumbled forward, his leg bending at an odd angle. He grunted in pain, sweat beading down his face.

Her magic.

Yes, skala, kill him.

Snarling, Ulrich staggered back, dragging Ravenna with him, and only regained his balance at the edge of the cliff. Chest heaving, he glowered at her as he moved her over the open maw of the gorge.

No!

"Witch," Ulrich wheezed.

Ravenna bared her fangs at him, legs wheeling, and something sprang from her back. Iridescent purple membrane unfurled from her shoulders and began beating at the air.

With Ulrich's gaze on her, Vallek moved.

Faster than a snake striking, Ulrich flung Ravenna off the cliff.

Her scream echoed through the humid air, bouncing off the inside of Vallek's skull.

NO!

"My king, you're free of—"

Hormhím's blade smashed into Ulrich's face, cleaving it in two. Hot blood spurted across Vallek's chest as Ulrich's body teetered backwards, his ruined head leaking brain and blood. Unseeing eyes gaped at him, hands grasping and spasming in the last throes of desperation.

The force of the blow knocked Ulrich off the cliff, and he fell backwards into the mist below.

"Ravenna!"

Hefting Hormhím, Vallek leapt after her.

Mate mate mate don't die don't be dead mate—

20

She fell.

Hard.

Her poor wings fluttered madly to break the fall, but it was just too much.

Ravenna hurtled down into the deep gorge, the layer of mist passing over her like a veil. A sudden, cool shock of air that had her dreading—*I've died.*

Her own scream echoed in her ears, dulled only by the furious buzz of her wings. She instinctively threw out her arms, magic gathering in her palms.

From one blink to the next, the stony ground raced up to meet her. Her magic bounded off the ground, buoying her at the last moment. Her whole body groaned with the change in momentum, and she went careening to the side, rolling through the air until the ground caught her.

The breath punched from her lungs, and starbursts dominated her vision. She could do nothing but spread her mouth wide in agony as she felt one of the delicate bones in her right lower wing break. Her right wrist sizzled with pain, and her ribs creaked ominously.

Don't break don't break don't—

—the sea rose up to meet her—salt burned her eyes—one more punch—an agonized howl on the wind—

She skidded to a stop on her side, cheek and shoulder oozing blood from her myriad of scrapes. Ravenna coughed and gasped, desperate for air, but her lungs refused to expand.

For a long, horrible moment, she could do nothing but lay still and shiver, body frozen in shock.

A wave of nausea crashed against her stomach. She'd *fallen.*

That bastard *threw her off a cliff!*

It was her outrage that warmed her blood enough to finally begin moving. So, so carefully, she rotated her ankles then twitched her knees. She'd just gotten to her hip when—

A great *whoosh* and then not far away, a body smashed into the stone. Loose gravel leapt into the air with the impact, and blood splattered across the canyon floor.

Ravenna screamed though she hadn't any air to, fresh horror biting down on her like the maw of some wild beast. The body lay in a horrible lump of broken flesh, blood leaking from a wicked wound cleaving the head in two.

One eye stared at her from the ruined face.

Ulrich.

But he'd—

"Ravenna!"

She gasped, her soul and magic reaching out through the mist to him. Her fingers scrabbled desperately in the dirt and gravel, the will to push herself up there but not the strength. Wilted wings collapsing against her back and her right side smarting with agony, it was all she could do to push herself onto her left elbow.

"Vallek!" she cried hoarsely, barely a whisper. Voice raw from her screams, her throat burned as she tried again and again, calling his name.

Perhaps the mist played tricks on her. It blocked out the meager afternoon light, constricting the canyon floor in a preternatural gloom. The air was heavy with moisture, every breath a fight to take into her battered chest. Sweat and moisture ran down her face to join her tears, stinging every cut and scrape they found.

His call grew louder.

At first, she didn't believe what she saw.

Sparks burst from the rock face of the cliff behind Vallek as he scaled the slope, using Hormhím's blade to catch crevices and slow his descent. As deftly as a takin, he maneuvered his big body ever downward, great legs pumping to keep his balance.

Her mouth fell open, an unintelligible, desperate sort of sound all she could manage.

He's coming for me.

Fat tears rolled down her ripped face, a frantic need to get to him overwhelming her. Through the pain, she tried to lift herself to her feet.

"Vallek!" *He's coming, he's coming for me.* "Vallek!"

"Ravenna!" His voice cracked with relief, his mighty chest heaving. "Stay there!"

Her sobs grew harsher, her body shaking with panic and shock, and she pulled herself along the ground, needing to get to him even a moment sooner.

Hormhím screamed hideously along the stone, more sparks flying from the blade only for the mist to snuff. When Vallek neared the ground, he bound from the rock face onto the canyon floor, casting down his axe as he ran for her.

Falling to his knees beside her, Vallek gathered her into his arms.

Ravenna crumpled against his chest, her sobs uncontrollable and unstoppable. She blubbered his name, her fingers kneading at his tunic. The pain was sharp, but she didn't care. She wanted to crawl inside him, where she knew it was safe. Somewhere dark and warm, where no one meant her harm, no one cared who she was.

"I have you," he murmured, "I have you, sprite."

When the rain resumed, Vallek gingerly carried her down the length of the gorge in search of shelter. Ravenna did her best not to whine or wince whenever her battered body was jostled, but her *azai* quickly caught onto just how injured she was.

Picking up his pace, he soon found something of a cave. Really, it was a glorified depression in the rock face, but with a large boulder shielding one side of the opening and about two body lengths of depth, she was dry at least when he gently set her down. He left her a dagger from his belt, hefting the half-ruined Hormhím onto his shoulder to search for firewood.

He returned soon with an armful of scrub and twigs, his expression dismayed to find her completely unmoved.

Ravenna watched through heavy lids as he went through the motions of starting a small fire. It sputtered and spat, reluctant to catch fire in the damp air. Finally though, as in all things, Vallek bent the scrub and sparks to his will, coaxing a meager flame from the gnarled branches.

Sitting back on his heels, he glared at the fire, apparently displeased with its small size. "I'll find more wood."

"Don't trouble yourself," she said through chattering teeth, "I'm not c-cold."

Peering at her over his shoulder, his lips thinned between his tusks. He sat down before her, one large hand reaching out to cup the less bloodied side of her face.

A low, unhappy rumble vibrated in his chest. "You're cold as ice."

"It's the s-s-shock." Although knowing that didn't seem to make her shaking stop.

"Will you let me look?"

She wasn't enthusiastic about being touched, every part of her feeling like an exposed nerve, but she jerkily nodded.

Moving in closer, Vallek started with her wrist. Holding it so gently in his big hand, she nearly began crying again, she watched as he delicately probed the bones of her wrist. The joint had already swollen and was red, but she agreed with him when he muttered, "I don't think it's broken. Not badly, anyway."

She sat against the cave wall in still silence, tracking him as he assessed her injuries. He filled her vision, lending her just enough calm to begin pushing her magic toward those injuries.

Her father had always warned her about using magic to sustain herself. Healing oneself with it, consuming it rather than food or drink, relying on it rather than sight or hearing—it bred an unhealthy reliance. One the fae had suffered from for centuries. Maxim himself hadn't realized his unnatural state until he took a human *azai,* Aine's blood helping him return to the way he always should have been.

"Use it wisely. Just in emergencies," he'd always counseled her.

If this wasn't an emergency, she didn't know what was. If she moved in a slightly wrong way, which was any way, the stab of pain in her ribs had her worried she might pass out.

The invisible threads of her magic wrapped round her middle, supporting her as it sank into her skin. The relief was immediate, dulling the pain enough to be bearable.

Marking her little sigh of relief, Vallek's intense blue gaze flicked up to hers. Then to the collection of jagged scrapes on the left side of her face. She wondered if it looked like she'd been clawed by some wicked beast as much as it felt.

"I have nothing to cleanse the wounds with," he said, his tone regretful. "I have nothing at all . . ."

"It's all right. I'm using my magic."

His brows rose. "You can do that?"

"To an extent. Never had this bad . . ." She grimaced. "It would be quicker if I was full fae."

As it was, it took all her concentration and magic to begin knitting her ribs back together. Her mind shied away from looking too long at the breaks—three ribs were broken. That's all she needed to know. Her magic would handle the rest.

"Ravenna . . ." An agonized look passed over his face, and his hand hovered over her, as if he didn't know where it would be safe to lay it. "I'm sorry. So, so sorry."

Fresh tears stung her eyes. A part of her wanted to be angry—what was he thinking, openly treating her like his mate in front of everyone? What did he think Ulrich would do? Just because he was king didn't mean everyone would agree with him, even those closest to him.

But as she watched him, saw the look of desolation in his eyes, Ravenna realized he knew. It was a discovery that cost him in blood and regret, and his shame emanated from him as surely as his body heat. Heavy lines underscored his eyes and bracketed his mouth, and she hated the sight of them.

She was too tired to be truly angry, and, as she sat still while her magic worked, Ravenna couldn't help feeling that what really mattered was, "You came for me."

"Always." Leaning over her, he cupped the side of her head. "I will *always* come for you."

Ravenna tried to swallow past her dry throat and only remembered at the last moment not to nod in acknowledgement and irritate her head.

His thumb passed gently over her unbroken cheek, his gaze forlorn as he watched the small movement. "I can't do much for you like this, but . . . can I hold you?"

She wanted to say yes, but the idea of being moved filled her with dread.

"I'm told the purring of a mate is soothing. Even healing."

"All right," she found herself saying. It was less for herself and more for him.

That's what she told herself, anyway.

His relief was palpable, and he took infinite care lifting her to set on his lap. Propped on her better side against her *azai*'s chest rather than with her back to the cave was an immediate improvement, and she couldn't help how she sighed and melted into his warmth.

That purr hummed against her, and fates if it wasn't soothing. The tension in her shoulders loosened a little, and Ravenna's heavy eyes fluttered shut.

"When were you going to tell me about your wings?" he asked softly.

Never. "Eventually." She wished she could fold them up against her back as she usually held them, but with one definitely broken, there was nothing for it right now. Her wing had to wait its turn. Until then, she sat exposed, the delicate iridescent purple membranes out for all to see.

His curious gaze weighed as heavily on them as his hand on her knee.

"They're beautiful, sprite. Why do you hide them?"

"They're vulnerable. Only for mates," she muttered.

"Then I intend to see them much more."

Already back to issuing demands.

"We'll see," was all she could think to say before sleep dragged her down into its embrace.

She woke sometime later to a darkened, cooler cave. The rain hadn't abated with the night, and she couldn't help a shiver in her still-damp clothes. Although, the tremors had seemed to stop.

Tipping back her head enough to see Vallek's face, she found him staring silently into the darkness. Following his line of sight, she found that with the light from their little fire, the lump that had once been Ulrich could just be seen. A formless, shadowy lump, it was a dark omen against the rain-spattered ground.

She averted her gaze, not wanting to think any more about him.

Although unsure whether it was the utter exhaustion or the bond to her *azai* or just her imagination, Ravenna thought she could hear how the heart beneath her cheek was breaking.

"Rest," he murmured. "They'll find us by morning."

Nuzzling against the patch of exposed skin at his throat, Ravenna sighed. "Your heart is heavy."

Vallek's exhale ruffled the hair at her crown. "I killed my friend."

It was a brutally simple statement, but four words carried enough weight that Ravenna could almost see it pressing on his shoulders.

"You did."

He didn't look at her, but the arms he had banded loosely around her tightened. Ravenna winced, not quite in pain, and he immediately relaxed his grip.

"I've known him since we were orclings. We served together, fought together. I considered him my brother. He stood beside me when no one else would."

Ravenna listened quietly, easily imagining the person Ulrich had been. She could see youthful Vallek and Ulrich, cocksure and angry, ready to remake the world.

What they had accomplished was nothing short of astounding. But somewhere along the way, something darker had developed inside Ulrich. She'd never questioned his loyalty to Vallek. If anything, his devotion was fanatical. He guarded Vallek almost jealously, blind to how his king and friend had changed, too.

"I'll admit—I won't mourn him nor miss him. But it brings me no pleasure to see how heavily it weighs on your heart."

"Going soft on me, sprite?"

"Hardly. But I have a heart, cold and dark as it may be."

They lapsed back into silence, Vallek's gaze never wavering from the motionless form of Ulrich. More than once, she thought to ask him why, but as the night lengthened, she began to suspect he watched over his lord commander as much as he did her. If nothing else, no scavengers would pick at Ulrich tonight.

It was a long while before Vallek spoke again, and the words he did finally say made Ravenna's cold, dark heart ache. "I regret having to kill him—but I don't regret that I did. Does that make sense?"

"Yes." It did. And it shouldn't have pleased her so much, but it did, too.

Perhaps it was ugly of her to be happy that Vallek would kill for her—even his own friend and second. Perhaps it wasn't right to be pleased he'd choose her over all others. Especially when she herself had avoided their mating and been begrudging all along the way.

She never wanted to have the choice put to him, but now that it'd come to pass, she couldn't help the prideful pleasure tucked beneath her heart.

He came for her. He defended her. He killed for her.

Fates, how could she deny him now?

As if he could read her thoughts, Vallek said, "You'll have your way, *skala*."

That cold, dark heart of hers dropped to the cave floor. "What do you mean?" she asked through cold lips.

After all this, was his heart so heavy he meant to give her up?

Her denial was ferocious and desperate, her fingers digging into the material of his tunic.

But before she could argue, he continued. "You are my mate, and I will take you for my wife. And my queen. There's no other way."

Ravenna blinked out into the rainy night, not sure if she'd heard him right.

"I don't want to be queen," she blurted. "I've never wanted any of this."

When he might have grumbled or argued, Vallek instead purred louder. He ran a hand gently down the length of her tangled hair, kissing the top of her head before telling her, "And that is why you'll be a queen for the ages."

"*No.* I won't. I can't."

Her heart, still on the floor, fluttered with dread. Fates, it was one thing to be his mate, a carefully guarded secret. Perhaps she could have gotten used to the arrangement, helping him from the shadows as she had before but also sharing his bed and private life.

But to place her beside him on the throne? To declare *her*—a fae-human halfling—queen of orcs? Preposterous. Impossible.

"You can and you will," he said, still in that gentle tone that she was beginning to find infuriating. "The gods don't make mistakes."

Ravenna laid her palm on his forehead to check for a temperature. "Did you hit your head coming down the cliff?"

Vallek snorted, taking her hand in his and kissing it. "No. I'm thinking quite clearly. Perhaps for the first time in months."

"I don't—"

"Is it that you don't want me, sprite?"

Ravenna choked on whatever she'd been about to say. She tilted her head back again to glare at him. "You know that's not it."

Although it didn't reach his eyes, his smug grin was still insuffer-able. "Then we will be as all other mates. I will take you to wife. I cannot give up my throne and the unification of my people. But I cannot give you up, either. So you will just have to be my queen."

All she could do was splutter and stare in horror at his wild jumps in logic. Denial clamored up her throat, but nothing more than sounds of shock came out. No true words or arguments came to her, nothing to truly make him see the sheer audacity and risk of such a thing. All she could offer was wordless, vague concern that doing this would lead to his ruin.

Just as Ulrich said.

Taking advantage of her speechlessness, Vallek pressed, "I'll make you a deal, *skala,* as you're so fond of them."

"I'm *not*—" They had made *one* and suddenly now *this* was how their mating worked and *he* was the one always making deals and *changing* them and—

"Do this for me, stand beside me, and I will aid you in whatever scheme it is you play at."

Ravenna's mouth ran dry. "What?" *How does he know?*

That little grin fell away from his face, and he regarded her seriously when he said, "I know you have plans for something. I'm not a fool—a soothsayer falling into my lap isn't coincidence. You have many secrets, and I intend to know all of them."

"Vallek . . ." Despite her pain, she tried to squirm out of his lap, but he held her fast.

"I won't pry. Not yet. But when the time comes, you will tell me your secrets and your plan. You will ask for my help." Leaning down, he touched his nose to hers, taking up all her senses when he said, "And I will give it. If you become my queen."

The breath rushed out of Ravenna in a hiss. She wanted to curl up on herself, hide away from that penetrating lapis-lazuli gaze. He knew too much. Saw too much.

It was like he peered inside her, even in the dim light of their little fire, and saw everything. She shrank away—what was there to see but an angry, hurting little girl out for revenge. He wouldn't find the queen he wanted. She was nothing but a shut-in, sequestered away for all her life by the sea with her gentle mother.

She was nothing grand, nothing special. A halfling of two worlds who belonged in neither. Her visions were more of a burden than a gift.

She brought him nothing but her anger and her plotting. She meant to use him and his people. He was a fool for wanting to put someone like her on the throne beside him. A stupid, cocksure, handsome, noble fool.

Mistaking her silence, Vallek added, "I swear to you, I will keep you safe. And the safest place is beside me."

He couldn't promise that—he was willfully ignorant at best, raving mad at worst to think it. But then, she couldn't make him promises, either. Not if she meant to have her vengeance.

And she did. She would. Nothing mattered more than that.

But . . . what if with this agreement, she could secure the army she so needed? If it meant getting that and her revenge, would it be so terrible to stand beside him? To have and claim him as hers while she could?

Everything inside her, from magic to heart to mind, was fiercely pleased with the idea of claiming him. That he would be unequivocally hers for as long as she had left. No more marriages of alliance, no more flirting courtiers. Orcs respected matings, and in their eyes, while they may not like or accept her, they would at least recognize that he was bound to her.

He was a fool for offering her such power—was she a fool too for taking it? Or would she be more of a fool to reject it?

Her desire for him and need for revenge tumbled inside her, a violent clash that split her priorities in two. The turmoil of her indecision ached more than her ribs, leaving Ravenna breathless.

Closing the last little bit of distance between them, Vallek's breath fanned against her lips. "Be my mate. Please."

Fates. He was as ruthless as he was dear.

He kissed her gently, lips moving in a light, tender touch that ignited her black, black heart.

Vallek said he couldn't give up his throne nor her.

As his gentleness seared her, making her magic sing, Ravenna realized—she couldn't give up her revenge nor him.

He wanted both.

So did she.

Another way they were well suited.

She knew better than to believe she could truly have both. Life was never that simple, fates never that kind. They were both fools, it seemed. She would just have to hope that the consequences didn't rain ruin upon all orc-kin.

"Yes," she breathed against his lips. "Yes."

21

Ravenna didn't know how she would ever go to sleep again, her mind turning over everything he'd said and she agreed to. Although neither of them moved much at all, her world had utterly changed that night.

Yet, her frayed nerves and exhaustion eventually overcame her again. When her eyes next opened, predawn light filtered into the shallow cave. The air was cool and damp, heavy with the crisp smell of petrichor. The rain had finally ceased, leaving behind soggy gravel and little puddles that reflected a sky still saturated in twilight colors.

A little cold, Ravenna tucked herself tighter to Vallek's chest as she assessed how far her magic had gotten. It still enveloped her ribs, working away at knitting each back together, but she could at least breathe a little easier. Her cuts and scrapes had scabbed over, good enough for now.

It was her poor broken wing that hurt the most.

Vallek carefully ran his big hand up and down her arm, infusing her with his warmth. "How are you feeling?"

"Pulverized," she muttered.

"Not many could have survived such a fall." Understandable—the canyon wall was probably a thousand feet high. She didn't miss the pride in his voice, and maybe when she was a little more healed and well-rested, she'd appreciate that more. For now, she was tired, hurting, and hungry.

At least she was comfortable. She had her big, stubborn mate to thank for that.

The scent of petrichor mixed with his own musk, a heady combination. She nuzzled her cheek against his chest, her eyes slipping shut again.

A shiver ran through her when she felt the tip of one finger trace the bone of her upper right wing.

Instinctively, she began drawing them back against her, the delicate membrane folding intricately into smaller and smaller sections. But when it came time for her right bottom wing to fold, a stab of pain had her baring her teeth. Her other three wings unfurled again as she broke out into a cold sweat.

She could force the other three into place on her back, but it would be uncomfortable without the fourth. They were meant to fold together, creating a neat little bundle at the center of her back. The bones bent at the joints, forming a little protective shell on top of the more vulnerable membrane.

Vallek made a plaintive noise, his purr growing in volume. "I would set it, but I think you'd better wait for the healer."

She nodded, fighting back a wave of nausea. Ravenna loathed the idea of letting someone touch her wings—it was difficult even to let Vallek see them, let alone a healer manipulate them. But she would need the bone reset before healing began, even with her magic.

When the pain and nausea subsided, Ravenna slumped back against Vallek's chest. He gathered her close again, running his hand gently through her hair.

"Your wings are beautiful," he murmured.

"They're *small*," she grumbled.

"Are they?" She felt him cock his head to take a better look. Ravenna fought her instinct to try folding them away again.

"Yes. Too small to fly."

"Well, they were enough to break your fall. For that, they are my favorite."

It was an absolutely ridiculous thing to say, and the sudden smile it brought her was just as ridiculous.

"Is it all right to touch them?" he asked, even as his fingertips began to trace the upper bone again.

"Gently," she murmured. "And just the top." She might crawl right out of her skin if he touched the membrane. Incredibly sensitive, the membranes were meant to sense the most minute shifts in air pressure, as well as traces of magic. Even now, just having them unfolded and exposed to the morning air, was far more sensation than she was used to.

But before his fingers could move far along the curve of the bone, Vallek's head rose abruptly, gaze fixing down the gorge.

Ravenna heard what he had a moment later—calls for Vallek echoing down the stone walls.

"They've found us," he sighed. She couldn't quite tell if he was relieved or disappointed.

There was no time to ponder, though, Vallek swiftly standing up with her in his arms. She fisted his tunic, throwing her arm around his neck. After kicking dirt onto the dying fire, Vallek walked out from the shelter of the cave.

"Here!" he called, great voice booming down the length of the gorge.

The small party of orcs cried out with relief, hustling toward them. They skirted the mangled body of Ulrich, their gazes quickly averting from the gory scene.

In their lead was Mattias, a welcome sight, and he was the first to reach them.

"Thank the gods," he panted, "we worried you both were lost."

"I'm far harder to kill than that," Vallek said. "Thankfully, so is my mate."

Mattias turned to regard Ravenna, his expression softening. "I'm glad to see you, my lady."

She nodded, emotion clogging her throat. "Thank you, captain." It was a relief to not see anger or blame darkening his eyes. It wasn't outlandish to think that she would be blamed for Ulrich's demise, especially by any who agreed with his opposition to Vallek taking her as a mate.

Ravenna had grown to like the quiet, steadfast captain.

She gratefully took the waterskin Mattias offered, guzzling down gulps of the best water she'd ever tasted. When her thirst was quenched, she held the skin up for Vallek to drink. It was ridiculous how mesmerizing he could be as he drank, the ball of his throat bobbing with every swallow.

Her bite would look perfect right at the base.

Fates, even injured, her mating instinct hadn't suffered from the fall, it seemed.

"Lady Ravenna needs a healer. And Commander Ulrich must be . . . " A tendon ticked in his cheek. "He is to be treated with respect."

"Of course, my king," said Mattias with a nod. Efficient as always, he waved at two of the warriors who carried the deconstructed parts of a stretcher. Together they strode for Ulrich's remains, starting the grisly task of collecting what was left to bear back to camp.

"And here is the healer." Mattias waved forward a smaller orcess, her graying mane plaited and bound up into a tight knot at the top of her head. Ravenna vaguely recognized her from not only the camp but within the citadel, too. Fenna was one of Vallek's personal healers, and Ravenna had studiously avoided the orcess all her years in Balmirra.

"Let's take a look, dearie."

The orcess wasted no time inspecting Ravenna's injured wrist, her hands dry and warm. She went about her assessment without blinking an eye that it was a half-fae she looked over, nor that the king himself refused to put her down.

"I can stand," Ravenna told him. At least, she thought she could.

"You're missing a shoe, love," he told her gently.

Oh. That's right.

It wasn't that she disliked being carried—it just felt awkward being the only one not standing in a group of big, burly orcs. Like she was little. Fragile. She contented herself that there would be time yet to seem big and strong before them. For now, it was all right that her strong *azai* carried her.

Fenna was exceedingly gentle, softly explaining what she meant to do before doing it. After a few pokes and prods, she declared Ravenna's wrist badly sprained but not broken. She marveled at how far along her ribs were in healing, pleased with their progress. "Now that's a useful trick." Winking, she moved on to the wing.

Ravenna gritted her teeth, forcing her wings to stay still. She hated how everyone looked at them, eyes wide with interest. Fenna was at least extremely careful, touching the wing as little as possible while she inspected the break.

"Never worked on a wing like this before. You suppose it's similar to a bird's wing?"

She swallowed hard. "Somewhat. The bone is hollow like a bird's. But there's one more joint."

"Fascinating!" Fenna leaned in closer. "And they fold up along your back otherwise?"

"Yes."

"Like a beetle. Will wonders never cease."

Ravenna chewed her cheek, not loving the comparison but unable to argue with it, either.

Pulling a little stoppered bottle from the small pack belted round her waist, Fenna handed it to her. "For the pain."

She sniffed the contents, catching notes of willow bark and poppy milk. She took the barest sip, not wanting to be too foggy—and knowing it was likely mixed with orcs twice her size in mind.

"All right, one, two, three—"

The flash of pain burst brightly across all Ravenna's senses, her body contracting in Vallek's arms. He held her fast, a frantic note to his purr, as she shuddered and groaned through the burning pain.

The worst of it was over within a few moments, the bone reset, and her magic flowed down from her chest to her wing to take over the healing. Still, she was left with an aching pain all along her back.

"One more sip, dearie. At least to get you back to camp."

She did before stoppering the bottle and handing it back.

"Very good. How're you feeling now?"

"I'll live."

Fenna smiled. "Excellent. Just what I like to hear."

A reluctant grin touched Ravenna's lips.

"Thank you, Fenna," said Vallek.

"It's an honor, my king." She squinted up at him, shrewd eyes searching him for injury. "You don't look too badly off."

"Hormhím took the worst of it."

Nodding in approval, the healer assessed Ravenna once more before declaring that she was stable enough to travel back to camp.

In the time Fenna attended to her, the warriors had secured Ulrich's remains, and so, as the sun rose over the gorge, they set out.

Between her tiredness, the poppy milk, and her own magic, Ravenna floated in her mate's arms, barely feeling the sway of his gait. Resting her head on his shoulder, she let herself be carried along, worries left behind in that shallow cave.

The worries found her again by the time they reached camp. It took several hours of walking and a precarious climb up the cliff face—split between natural outcroppings and a series of ropes—to finally reach the column. Vallek, Ravenna, Fenna, and a few warriors went on ahead as Mattias and the rest hoisted up Ulrich's body.

Her heart had only just returned to a normal pace after the terror of scaling the cliff—or, rather, clinging to Vallek as he scaled it—when the column came into view. They were soon noticed, and a great cheer went up from the orcs, relieved to see their king.

Even as he nodded and thanked his people, Vallek caught how her face flicked between her own and her disguise. It was a reflex, her nerves telling her to hide away. She tucked her wings as tightly as she could to her back even unfolded, hoping her long hair hid them.

"You must show them your true face now, sprite."

That's what terrified her.

Fingers dug into his tunic, Ravenna sat stiffly in his arms as they walked along the column. More than a few cheers died when the orcs realized Vallek carried her, their shock evident. Those in the back of the column had likely only heard rumors about what happened yesterday, too far away to have seen for themselves.

She had to wonder what was said, how outlandish the story had become.

Her nerves strung tighter and tighter the further they went. Every eye followed her, boring into her skin to ascertain just who it was the king had jumped off a cliff for. By the time they reached the head of the column, she was no longer stiff but squirming, trying but failing to contain her unease.

Vallek strode confidently on, determined to make a clear statement. Turning to face his berserkers and staff, their curiosity and eagerness potent, he took a running start to bound up a tall boulder, gaining height. Ravenna bit down on her squeak of alarm, holding on tight as he came to the top of the rock. From their height, his voice boomed across the landscape.

"My good people, you have the good fortune of being the first to meet my mate."

Shocked murmurs met his declaration, and he let them permeate before continuing.

"She is Lady Ravenna of the north. You have known her as the *kone,* and she has counseled me wisely these years. You behold her now as she truly is—half-fae and my mate."

More murmurs, and the full weight of the column's attention turned upon her.

She wanted to shrink. To wither away and hide.

But she couldn't now.

Her world was different. *She* was different. Today, she had to start standing beside her *azai.*

That was the deal.

Although she still kept her wings down, she threw back her shoulders, sitting as regally as she could in his arms. Meeting each stare she came across, she stared down the column of orcs, willing them to at least listen.

"My beast knew her the moment I saw her true face. She has claimed my heart and soul, as is any mate's right. Any who would dispute this may join Commander Ulrich."

No murmurs to that, but quite a few of the orcs looked amongst themselves, worry marring their faces.

"I will fight and kill for my mate. Just as any of you would do. She now shares my bed and my life—and upon our return, she will share my throne, too."

Ravenna worked to keep her face rigid, holding onto a confident placidity despite wanting to wince. She couldn't tell how the crowd would go, their silence growing ominous.

"I am your king—but this means nothing without your support. Do I have it?" His question was met with that dreadful silence, and she couldn't help the way her heart sank to her toes.

"*Do I have it?*" he cried.

At first, nothing. But then, something incredible happened.

One by one, one after the other, row by row, the orcs knelt. A wave rippled back through the column, heads bowing as they bent to one knee. Arms crossed over chests to hold right fists over hearts, showing their allegiance.

"King Vallek!" they shouted. "Hail Vallek Far-Sight!"

Vallek bared his teeth in a ferocious smile, and with only a wink as warning, he lifted her high above his head.

"Your queen!" he proclaimed. "Queen Ravenna!"

A cheer broke across the column, the orcs jumping up to stamp their feet and beat their fists on their chests. It deafened her, a resounding din that shook the very ground.

"Queen Ravenna!" they cried, clapping and hooting.

They shouted congratulations, they shouted their names.

She stared out at the sea of tusked faces, not sure if she could believe it.

Ravenna dropped back down into his arms with an *oof*, leaving her heart somewhere up above his head.

That head dropped down to claim a big, overblown kiss that got the column cheering even louder.

When he pulled back, it was with a smug little grin. She met it with a scowl.

As the cheers continued to ring, filling every gorge and ravine for leagues, Ravenna poked Vallek's chest and whispered, "If I'm going to be queen, then from now on, we *discuss* things like this *beforehand.* Yes?"

Vallek grinned down at her, breezily agreeing. "Of course, *skala.*" Of course, because he'd already gotten what he wanted. Ravenna rolled her eyes. Fine. Starting now.

An idea came to her then, making her lips curl with evil delight.

Well, starting in a moment.

Oberon, are you near enough to make a dramatic entrance?

Yes, but you have much explaining to do.

Oh, she was sure. She'd told Oberon the rudiments of what happened, and while he'd wanted to charge in to help last night, she'd warned against it. The orcs would be especially wary without their king, and Vallek was wound tight as an orc defending his mate.

Now, though, she welcomed Oberon's help.

When the cheers finally began to abate, Vallek called, "Let us leave this place. Move out!"

His order sent the camp into a frenzy of activity. More quietly to her, he said, "I don't want to linger in this place. We won't travel far, though, and I will carry you."

"That won't be necessary."

His brows arched in surprise, but before he could say anything, gasps rang out from the back of the column.

"*Unicorns!*"

Vallek's gaze lifted to see Oberon charging up the line, the three younger unicorns close behind him. Her *azai* sighed mightily.

This time, it was her who grinned and him who scowled.

Vallek jumped down from their perch in time to meet Oberon. The gray unicorn pawed the earth, horn bobbing through the air.

"Another lift, if you please, mate."

Vallek huffed a laugh, doing as she asked and boosting her onto Oberon's back.

She'd just gotten her seat when the unicorn warned, *Hold onto me.*

Ravenna threw her hands into his mane and leaned forward as Oberon reared onto his hind legs, letting loose a thunderous whinny. His front hooves punched the air, and his horn glittered in the sunlight.

It was a dazzling sight, she was sure, but it was a relief when he came back to standing.

"This is Oberon," she announced to the stunned orcs. "He is my guardian and means you no harm."

That remains to be seen.

Please behave. This is all very new to me.

Is that an order from the queen? He snorted a horsey laugh. *Now, tell me all about these scrapes and who I need to stab.*

They indeed didn't travel far that day, not by their usual standards, but the landscape was different when afternoon found them, and that was good enough for Vallek. He called for a halt, and as the camp began to spring up around him, he helped his weary mate down from her lofty perch.

The unicorn stallion watched him, his head turned round to pierce Vallek with an eerie liquid amber gaze. He chuffed, tapping Vallek on the shoulder with his horn.

Vallek held perfectly still, ancient instincts to protect his vulnerable bits against that wicked horn riding him hard. Unfazed was his little hellion, though, who merely patted his chest.

"Oberon says I'm your problem for the night."

He blinked, looking back and forth between his sleepy mate and the unicorn, who Vallek couldn't help feeling was expecting something from him.

"You can . . . talk with him?"

"Unfortunately." She tapped her temple. "In here. Thanks to the bond he forged with my father." A thought seemed to come to her. "There's a chance you might start to hear him, too, actually."

Vallek's face paled at the prospect, which only made her snort with giggles. She immediately regretted it, hugging her ribs, but couldn't seem to stop laughing.

Oberon dipped his big head, nipping at her with his lips. They seemed to tease each other, and through the affectionate display,

Vallek craned his head this way and that to avoid getting an eye taken out by the waving horn.

"Stop making me laugh," she groaned.

It was a surreal scene, but Vallek decided to be charmed by it. The love between Ravenna and her father's mount was obvious. That the stallion had not only followed her deep into orcish territory but actually went east and back again to watch over her . . . Vallek had only the greatest respect for that.

"Thank you for her," he told the stallion.

Oberon lifted his head again, piercing Vallek with the full intensity of his unnatural gaze. The stallion regarded him seriously for a long moment, taking Vallek's measure. To have such a dangerous, ancient being look him over from head to toe had a shudder following in its wake.

Ravenna suddenly let out an exasperated puff of air. Apparently, there was something of an argument going on between the two.

"What does he say?"

Grumbling under her breath, she finally admitted, "I told you so."

Neighing merrily, Oberon shook out his long mane, the color of starlight. Dipping his head, he pawed the earth again before turning and leading the other unicorns back into the forest.

Vallek watched them go, utterly baffled.

"You'll get used to him," Ravenna said, easy as could be.

He gave her a horrified look, mostly to make her laugh again, but he'd be a liar if he said he wasn't at least mildly perturbed by the notion.

Having a faeling mate would come with many challenges. He just hadn't imagined one of them being making nice with unicorns.

He wasn't alone in feeling a bit more at ease with the unicorns gone, those of his staff nearby noticeably relaxing as they went through the familiar motions of building camp.

When his tent was erected, he called for a divan to be set out for Ravenna. He placed her upon the cushions gently and turned her over to Fenna's continued care. Vallek lingered, loath to let her out of his sight, but Fenna eventually shooed him away.

"You go do your work and I'll do mine. She'll be right as rain in no time."

He might not have believed it had anyone else said it, but Fenna had taken care of him and his sisters for decades. An old friend of their long-departed mother, Fenna watched over them with the domineering care of a mother hen, and despite her advancing age, never missed the chance to travel with an official royal party.

"Keeps the old bones moving," she liked to say.

Content that his mate would be well cared for and was as comfortable as he could make her, he indeed went out to see to anything he could find to do. Mostly, though, walking amongst his people, he took the opportunity to gauge their moods. Able to speak more privately to him, he knew his berserkers at least wouldn't be too shy to tell him their real feelings.

A few avoided his gaze or merely nodded, but no more than he was expecting. Several reached to take his hand, congratulating him. Others stopped him to ask if Ravenna truly was the human soothsayer they'd become accustomed to.

The first true hostility he met was from the handful of representatives from the eastern tribes. One from the Iron-Chest tribe scowled sourly, demanding, "What does this mean?"

"That she will be your queen."

The orc's upper lip curled. "First a king and now a faeling queen? What is the world coming to?"

Stepping up into the other orc's space, Vallek smiled maliciously. "A new age," he said before moving on.

Resentment from the eastern tribes was expected. Many would no doubt look for ways to renege or escape. For now, Vallek just had to get them back to Balmirra. Install Ravenna on the throne. The rest would work itself out.

He could almost hear Eydis's snort of derision. No, it wouldn't be that simple, of course. He expected opposition. But he trusted almost everyone in this party, and they had to start somewhere.

Eventually, Vallek found his way to the back of the column. There, he helped Mattias requisition several crates to form a makeshift coffin. Already bundled tightly in canvas, Ulrich was sealed inside, prepared for the journey ahead. They would deliver him to his sister's house, and he would be buried with the honors befitting a lord commander.

His heart hurt thinking about taking Ulrich home like this.

It didn't have to come to this.

No, but it had. Ulrich had made his choice and so had Vallek.

He missed his friend, but honestly . . . he missed the friend he'd known as a youth. The one who stood beside him in battle, drank with him at bonfires, and plotted with him in those first years of being chieftain. They had been almost of one mind then, so alike.

Vallek mourned the friendship that had died along the way. He didn't know when or where it had happened, only that their paths diverged somewhere. He regretted that it took him so long to realize it, and that the consequences had spilled blood.

He would never apologize for defending his mate, though.

Laying a hand on the nailed coffin lid, Vallek sighed. "Safe journey, my friend." He hoped in the afterworld, Ulrich finally knew peace.

Much later, he lay comfortably in his camp bed, watching lazily as his beautiful mate brushed out her long hair. Upon returning to his tent that evening, he was pleased to find Ravenna far improved. Bathed and bandaged, salve coated her scrapes, and her wrist was splinted. Dressed in her nightgown, they made a simple affair of dinner before climbing into bed for an early night.

After her second grumble of frustration, the splint making the otherwise simple task difficult, Vallek sat up. Plucking the brush from her hand, he positioned himself behind her.

"Allow me." Filling his hand with the dark cascade of her hair was pure sensorial pleasure, the soft silk overspilling his palm like water slipping through his fingers. His purr deepened as he began to brush, mesmerized by the way the low light of the lamps seemed to be absorbed by the darkness of her hair.

She peered at him over her shoulder curiously. "You don't have to."

"I want to." Very much. He might want to every night, actually.

Falling back into silence, Vallek enjoyed himself immensely, the gentle strokes methodical and soothing. He loosened tangles and coaxed out snarls gently, brushing out her glorious locks to a high shine. He didn't know he could so thoroughly enjoy something so domestic, something other than *talfon,* at least, but this simple act of caring for Ravenna quickly became something he could see himself doing again and again.

Lifting the heavy mass of it, he carefully laid most of her hair over her right shoulder. It left much of her back exposed, the loose neckline of her nightgown allowing her wings to lay down the length of her back. Unable to resist, Vallek bent to kiss the space between her wings and shoulders.

He tasted the shudder on her skin and kissed her one more time before straightening.

A wobbly breath escaped her. Looking forward, at the tent wall, Ravenna whispered, "I'm not ready to be a queen."

Vallek hummed with understanding. Setting aside the brush, he coaxed her down onto her good side facing him. He suspected she wouldn't want her back against his front with her wings exposed, but this was better. Vallek gathered her hands in his and held her gaze when he said, "I wasn't ready to become chieftain. I was angry. There wasn't a plan. I just had to do it."

"This is different," she insisted. "And I fear . . . your people will hate you for it."

He feared that, too, but that fear did them no good. They had to have faith that his people were as good and kind as he believed them to be. But, more importantly, Vallek was confident he'd do everything within his power and strength to secure her place beside him.

And it wasn't just because she was his mate. No, in the time he'd known Ravenna, both with her true face and in her disguise, he'd come to admire his little hellion. There was a fire inside her, a clever, capable mind that matched his own. He could see it clearly now, how she would be a queen they wrote sagas about. She would bring peoples together, unite realms.

Now, he just needed others to see it, too. Including her.

"It won't be easy," he admitted. "But the gods don't make mistakes. We were brought together for a reason."

If anything, her expression only grew more troubled. It was obvious to him that something ate her inside. He'd hoped she would tell him when he called her bluff last night, but she was cagey, his mate. She gave nothing away easily.

Perhaps he was mad, but he was beginning to crave the challenge.

Still, he didn't like seeing the unhappiness in her eyes. Whatever it was she kept from him, it was a heavy weight to bear.

"I don't need your gift to see that we are meant for each other. We will rule this new kingdom together." Moving down the pillows to tuck his face close to hers, he said, "You do the kingdom a great service staying beside me, for I don't know what I'd be willing to do to keep you, sprite." He grinned sadly. "It terrifies me to think . . . there's nothing I wouldn't do."

"It scares me, too," she whispered. "I shouldn't do this. I should run as far away from you as I can get."

His purr stuttered into a growl at the thought, but then again, he didn't hate the idea of a chase. There was no question he'd catch her. She wouldn't escape him.

She traced his face with her fingertips. "But I can't. I can't leave you. No matter that I know I should."

The need to ask, to push was a living thing inside him. Yet he slayed it, wrestling it back into the depths of his heart. Her eyes glistened with unshed tears, and he knew with a conviction that should have worried him that her tears could easily slay the rest of him. He was no match against them.

"One day, you will tell me, *skala*. When that day comes, know that I will love you then as much as I do now."

Her lips parted on a shuddering breath, more tears gathering. He was about to start panicking when she closed the breath of distance between them, capturing his mouth in a wet, fierce kiss.

He wanted to devour her, press her into the bed and soothe the lingering terror of almost losing her. His body ached to claim her, to strengthen the bond blooming between them. Yet he held back, dreading the thought of disturbing her bandages or bringing more tears.

When he finally sank inside her for the first time, it would be in his bed in Balmirra. She would be healed and healthy and ready for him, dripping with her need.

Vallek purred against her lips, heart full of hopes and aches. Gods, she made happiness painful and sorrow bittersweet. She shifted the axis of his world, and he knew then, as clearly as he did his name and his mission, that he would do anything for her. Remake the world. Bend the other realms to his will. If he had to conquer the faelands themselves to make her safe, he would do it. Gladly.

She didn't give him the words back, but that was all right. When he earned them, it would be all the sweeter for the challenge.

Still, she sent a thrill of vicious pleasure careening through him with a little growl against his tusks. "There's no one for you but me," she said, her ferocity pleasing him to the most primal depths of his soul.

Chuckling, he nuzzled his nose against hers. "It'd be more romantic to say, 'there's no one for me but you.'"

"I'm not being romantic. I'm making a threat."

"Ah. My mistake."

Gods, how was it that her threats kept making him painfully hard.

Perhaps he really was mad. If so, this was the sweetest madness, and he embraced it.

For Vallek was lost to his faeling mate. There was no hope for him now.

Their course was set, their path laid. Now all that was left was to walk it. And he would, with Ravenna beside him.

They would leave the world remade in their wake.

22

They parted ways with Oberon and his charges on the eastern shores of Lake Lovath. Ravenna bid them farewell with promises to visit soon and tell Callistix all about her adventures, as well as bring Vallek to formally meet her and the herd.

Ravenna tried not to snicker at the look of concern on Vallek's face when she informed him.

"Aren't mares known for being even more vicious?"

"Yes, and for good reason. Callistix has led the herd for centuries. You two will get along royally."

She chuckled at her own joke despite his pout. Ravenna took his hand and squeezed in recompense.

"Don't worry. I won't let them bully you. Much."

"This is revenge for my sisters, isn't it?"

"Maybe a little."

They shared a laugh this time, and Ravenna found herself looking forward to being with Eydis and Asta again. She'd actually missed them—just a little—on this journey, and they weren't a small part of why, when the spires of the city rose from the horizon, a few of the knots in her stomach loosened.

The remaining march back to Balmirra had been far less eventful—and far more pleasant with her getting to ride Oberon most days. Her magic did its work, healing her battered body so that only the most stubborn bruises and cuts were still visible. Her ribs and wing still ached, but she could at least fold her wings against her back again for longer and longer periods.

Twitch the onager didn't seem to miss her, while Oberon enjoyed making a show of whenever she mounted or dismounted. He'd also come to relish racing Vallek. On straightaways and in mountain meadows, her mate and Oberon raced the wind—and each other. An odd sort of friendship bloomed within the competition, one which she would've found endearing had she not had to serve as an intermediary between them, with herself as a common topic.

Over the last six days of travel, the party of orcs had quickly grown accustomed to her now staying beside the king, wearing her true face. While not all were happy about the new arrangement, they appeared to begrudgingly accept it.

That was good enough. At least for now.

It was strange. Whenever she noticed a lingering wary gaze, a new determination grew inside her. It took a few days to describe it to herself, but eventually Ravenna found that she . . . wanted their approval. She cared what these orcs, those closest and most loyal to Vallek, thought of her.

The sensation was a new one. Isolated in the seaside cottage with her mother, there were never many people she had to impress. By the time she was an adolescent, they'd stopped visiting Aine's remaining family, and she hadn't seen Maxim's Illyinia kin since she was small. Once in a while, they traveled to the nearby fishing village, Ravenna disguising herself with glamour to appear as Aine's full-human daughter. The fishermen and their families were hearty, no-nonsense people who rarely thought about the recluse and her strange daughter.

Now, though, she wanted to make a good impression. More

than that, she wanted their respect—not just as the king's mate but as Ravenna. It wouldn't happen immediately, of course, and she intended to earn that respect. Yet the realization that she wanted to endeavor at all still surprised her.

As the barges ferrying them across Lake Lovath neared Balmirra, the port walls extending into the crystalline water spread wide in welcome, Ravenna once again slipped the glamour over her face. She and Vallek had agreed that until an official announcement was prepared, she would maintain her *kone* disguise outside of his quarters in the citadel. Those in the party had been told last night to keep their silence until the announcement was made.

The thought of the announcement had another nervous knot in her gut pulling tight. She didn't know what form the announcement would take, nor how it would be received, and the unknown left her feeling more unsteady than she did on the lake waters.

Vallek had made plenty of assurances, but there was only so much he could truly promise. Still, his confidence didn't waver, and so neither did Ravenna.

The king's return to Balmirra was met with the usual enthusiastic fanfare. The barges pulled up to the dock to the roaring applause of hundreds. Orcs lined the streets and leaned out windows to get a look at their triumphant king. As their party disembarked and began the climb up to the citadel, criers were sent ahead, announcing the news that the eastern tribes had pledged fealty to Vallek Far-Sight.

On one of the switchback turns of the main promenade, Ravenna spied down from her place near the front of the column to see the group of eastern tribesmen, kept in the center of the party and bracketed by berserkers three deep. To a one, their heads turned like an owl's, their eyes just as wide as they gaped at the majesty of Balmirra.

What an experience it must have been, to go from the small encampments in the eastern foothills to the splendor of this ancient stronghold. She could sympathize.

The climb up to the citadel, marching in procession as they were, took the better part of two hours. Ravenna was determined to do it unaided, just like everyone else, even though her thighs were positively burning by the time the citadel's curtain wall rose around them. *Thank fates.*

More than a little sweaty under the cowl of her cloak—which Mattias had kept safe for her after Ulrich ripped it off—Ravenna hid beneath its shadow. As the party spilled into the courtyard, finding relief in the shadow of the citadel as they greeted friends and kin, she slipped to the front of the column.

She watched with no small amount of pride as Vallek ascended the stairs of the basilica, turning on the top step to face the party. Pulling Hormhím from his belt, he lifted it high above his head to another bout of applause and whoops. Berserkers beat their breastplates and staff stomped their feet in a loud show of support.

"My people! We return united!"

Cheers echoed through the courtyard, surely down into the city below.

"This day is yours. So is my gratitude. You have helped forge this kingdom, *your* kingdom. To peace!"

"To peace!" they cried.

"Rest, celebrate, and know that the histories will always remember your strength."

The courtyard burst with applause and good will. Eventually, the neat column broke up into smaller groups, warriors seeking their barracks, others returning home, some staff heading up into the citadel, and others leading the eastern tribesmen into the basilica.

A touch on her shoulder had Ravenna turning to behold Asta, beaming down at her.

"Welcome home, *tristah!*"

Despite the glamour, Asta threw her muscled arms around Ravenna in a crushing embrace.

"Hello, Asta," she wheezed.

"You're a sight for sore eyes. It's been so *boring* with both you and *breddah* gone."

Ravenna snorted a laugh. Yes, they had been well into their own melodrama when they left for the east.

After finally releasing her, Asta took Ravenna by the shoulder to lead away. "C'mon, let's get you off those weary feet."

Once they were safely inside the cool walls of the citadel, deep within Vallek's private wing, Ravenna let the glamour fall.

Asta hissed through her tusks to see the fading bruises. "All-Mother, what a prick. Honestly, it's about time Vallek dealt with that bastard."

Ravenna only nodded diplomatically, not quite wanting to admit that although the sight of Ulrich's smashed body would haunt her, she wasn't at all sorry about it. She doubted most orcesses would bat an eye at their mate cleaving a head in two for them, though.

They entered the king's quarters to find Brynhíl awaiting them. The older orcess smiled fondly, hurrying to take Ravenna by the shoulders for inspection. She tutted over the almost-healed bruises and scrapes.

Gaze flicking over Ravenna's head, Bryn scolded, "You were meant to take care of her."

Ravenna looked over her shoulder to see Vallek walking through the threshold, Eydis and Hilde close behind.

Rather than a quip or imperious promise in answer, Vallek's face fell with shame. "I know. It won't happen again."

"I hope you killed whoever did this."

"Yes."

"Good boy." Patting Ravenna's unhurt cheek, Bryn said, "Now, tell me all about why it looks like you broke a fall with your face."

After changing out of their dusty clothes, Ravenna and Vallek recounted the tale as crates of his things were brought back and unpacked. A light meal of breads, cheeses, salted meat, and grapes and apricots was brought up from the kitchens, the six of them gathering in the comfortable den to talk.

"We'll need to have the announcement soon. Three days at the maximum," said Eydis as she contemplated an apricot. "I have the utmost faith that your people will try to keep it quiet. However, back from an exciting journey, some won't be able to resist spreading news."

"It needs to be formal, official," said Vallek. "The whole Balmirran court and all the representatives gathered to hear."

"We have to expect dissent—possibly from the other chieftains," said Eydis.

"The whole garrison can be deployed throughout the city to manage any riots," added Asta.

The fruit and cheese already in Ravenna's stomach churned ominously. She didn't think her unease showed on her face, but when she met Hilde's gaze, the orcess leaned forward, clapping her hands together.

"Yes, yes, but most importantly, *the gown*." Pointing at Ravenna, she waggled her brows as she said, "You're mine for a few days, my queen."

"That sounds ominous," Ravenna teased, but she was grateful for the distraction.

Hilde waved her hand in an unconcerned gesture. "The gown will be the single most important statement you can make. You'll enter the basilica—first they'll see a fae, and then the gown."

"*Your* gown," Eydis teased.

"Yes, my gown." A greedy gleam in her eye, she told Ravenna, "I'll come back first thing tomorrow with some fabrics."

Ravenna forced a smile. The thought of a formal gown, one to reveal her to all of Balmirra, didn't fill her with enthusiasm—at least not as much as it did Hilde. Still, it would serve as a decent distraction. Keeping her hands busy would hopefully keep her mind from wandering. Toward those possible riots.

Taking Vallek's hand, she asked, "Are we sure such a big event is wise? Might a more controlled release not be wiser?"

"Unfortunately, we're beyond that," said Eydis. "Over a hundred kin who know about your true identity are now loose. Some will keep their promise. Others will no doubt become loose-lipped. To get as ahead of it as we can, I think we do this in one fell swoop."

Scowling at her mate, Hilde squeezed Eydis's thigh. "What Eydis means to say is, you're too wonderful a secret to hide."

Eydis and Ravenna both pulled a face as Vallek and Asta snickered.

Hiding her amusement more diplomatically behind her hand, Bryn reassured them, "The kin are loyal. They may be shocked by this, but they'll take it in stride. This isn't the first mating between an orc and otherly—even a fae."

"No, but it'll be the first chieftain, the first king," said Eydis.

"I hope for their loyalty, but we'll watch for those who may feel as Ulrich did," Vallek said. Wrapping his arm around Ravenna to tuck her tightly to his side, he told Asta, "I want her own guards assigned to her. Have them sent by morning."

"I'll choose them myself," Asta agreed.

Breaking another apricot in two and giving half to Hilde, Eydis said, "Three days will mean some attend the announcement already suspecting something."

"There are plenty already talking about the king's human soothsayer," Bryn said.

Vallek nodded. "Yes. So this event will set our narrative."

"It should be enough to get my people in place," said Eydis.

"Your people?" asked Ravenna.

A sly smile curled Eydis's lips. "Hasn't he told you yet? I'm Balmirra's spymaster."

Ravenna's brows rose, but after a moment to think on it, no, that wasn't really surprising. "That would explain a lot."

Asta snorted. "Ulrich thought he, as lord commander, was spymaster, but really, it's always been Eydis."

Looking more than a little proud of herself, Eydis brushed nonexistent lint from her robes. "I live to serve the king."

Vallek barked a laugh. "No, you're just nosy."

"That, too."

Ravenna held up a finger. "Forgive me, I'm a novice at espionage. How does the announcement help your spies?"

"Don't be modest, you infiltrated the orc king's court very adeptly," said Eydis with a wink.

Vallek threw her a sour look, but Ravenna just shrugged. "I'm sure only because you let me."

"Well, that's true. Although, we never found much about you at all." Eydis's gaze was meaningful, and Ravenna had no doubt the orcess would love to peel her away to reveal all her secrets, just as she did the apricot, but Ravenna was harder than that. She didn't know if she would even tell Vallek, and she foresaw few scenarios where she admitted anything to Eydis before Vallek.

Less because he was her mate and more because Eydis was far scarier.

"But to answer your question, this will provide an excellent opportunity to plug a known leak."

Asta groaned. "Don't let her go on about the leak again."

"She needs to know," Eydis argued. "We believe there is at least one member of staff currently selling information north. Definitely to an Eirean margrave, possibly even to the fae."

"It might help explain why they think their criminal is in our lands," said Vallek. He didn't look at Ravenna when he said it—in fact, no one looked at her at all—but the implication still sat with them in the den.

"Ulrich claimed he had leads on who it might be. I have my doubts." Eydis shrugged. "His actions the past few months have been . . . questionable."

Snapping her fingers, Asta sat up straight. "That reminds me. We need a new lord commander."

Bryn threw her hands up. "I'm going to bed."

"The sun isn't even down," said Hilde.

"Yes, but you young people are exhausting!"

They laughed and bid her farewell, but Bryn's departure didn't deter Asta from the question. Ravenna almost wanted to follow Bryn—it'd been a long day, and it seemed all the decisions were being made this evening.

"The post can go unfilled for a while. It's not like Ulrich was at his best lately." Asta chewed on a hunk of cheese before adding, "But the whole situation will be best managed with a new lord commander."

"Indeed." Vallek turned to look at Eydis. He opened his mouth, but before he could say it, Hilde got bodily between him and his sister.

"*No.* I already hardly see her as it is, she won't be taking another position."

Eydis chuckled as Vallek swung his gaze over to Asta.

She shook her head furiously. "Not interested."

"It would take time away from fucking her way through the barracks," Eydis teased.

"*Exactly.* Plus—paperwork." Asta pulled a face.

"There's Captain Mattias," said Ravenna.

"He would be a solid choice," agreed Vallek. "He's loyal, and that's just who I need around us. Especially now."

"I'm not sure Mattias is devious enough," observed Hilde.

"Yes, he's tragically noble," added Eydis.

When Vallek's gaze fell on Ravenna, she met it with a scowl. "Careful," she said, "I might become offended."

"I hardly think it's an insult to call you devious." Toying with a lock of her hair, Vallek said, "We will need to find you duties as queen. To keep you occupied."

The others giggled as Ravenna pinched his side mercilessly.

"I *do* think you'd be an effective lord commander," he insisted, trying to both squash her to his side and avoid her pinches.

"Seconded," declared Eydis.

Ravenna flushed. The vote of confidence meant a great deal coming from Eydis.

Noticing the change in her, Vallek laughed. "You trust her opinion more than mine?"

"Yes. You're biased."

Hilde and Asta hooted with laughter, and Vallek grinned fondly.

"That I am." Leaning down to kiss her temple, he gently suggested, "Think on it?"

"All right." Although, when she did think about it in the moment, one thing did come to mind. "I'd like to take part in discussion with the eastern tribesmen, though, whatever I decide."

Vallek's heavy brows lifted. "Oh?"

Nodding, Ravenna explained, "I too am a newcomer to Balmirra."

He beamed with pride, making her flush again.

"My queen," he praised. "You will be one for the ages."

When Hilde arrived the next morning, buried beneath armfuls of supplies to beset his mate with options, Vallek took his leave. Although there was much to prepare for his introduction of Ravenna to all of Balmirra, there was one task that had to be done first.

Vallek had to bury his past before he looked to his future.

He met Mattias and a handful of his berserkers near the barracks, Ulrich's pitch-sealed coffin covered in a burgundy shroud. Atop it lay the chains of office he wore and the signet ring he used. With a Balmirran rock Mattias handed him, Vallek struck each, breaking the chain and ring.

The ruined regalia glittered uselessly in the morning sun, the sight of it curdling Vallek's stomach. Although hidden beneath the shroud, the coffin's telling shape was a haunting reminder of that day—and how little Vallek wished to perform these last rites.

It shouldn't have been like this.

But it was.

And he'd vowed, as not just a chieftain but a king, to fulfill all rites. He occupied his throne in celebration and in mourning, in victory and in uncertainty.

Vallek nodded to his warriors, and as one, they lifted the poles attached to the side of the coffin, bearing the former lord commander on their shoulders for his last journey.

He led them in a small, somber procession from the citadel. Those up and about early enough stopped what they were doing, watching on in solemn silence as they passed.

Down through the city they went to the house of Ulrich's sister Uma. She lived with her mate and aunt, the last of Ulrich's kin. As far as Vallek knew, Ulrich had grown estranged from his kin as his duties increased. It'd been many years since Vallek himself had seen Uma.

Still, when he knocked upon her door, he immediately recognized her when she opened it. Although bearing a few more lines and gray hairs, she shared Ulrich's serious mien. Uma took in the sight of the king with little expression, her gaze eventually flicking behind him, to the shrouded coffin.

She didn't seem surprised to see any of it.

Calling over her shoulder for their aunt, Tylda, she said nothing to Vallek until joined by the older orcess.

"Ulrich's finally come home," said Uma.

Vallek bent to kneel on their threshold. He swept his hand through the dirt on their stoop, and despite the distressed noises the orcesses made, he smeared the grime across his forehead.

An ancient act of shame, of contrition.

"Please," he said. "Forgive me."

Ravenna hadn't quite realized what all designing and constructing this special new gown would entail. Hilde arrived early, as promised, and they spent the better part of the morning debating fabrics and fits.

Over breakfast, a more traditional orcish silhouette was rejected. Even in a few of Asta's old garments from when she was an adolescent, the thick, stiff pieces overwhelmed Ravenna's lither frame. It was a relief to shrug off the heavy leathers and brocade.

Instead, they focused on the duality of light fabric and precise construction.

By lunchtime, they had sketches and a plan.

Ravenna spent most of the afternoon standing on the low table, pulled out from the den into the central hall to give Hilde room to maneuver. It took hours, but eventually, with just pins and fabric, the shape of a gown began to appear from the chaos.

Even when she held pins between her teeth, Hilde was all friendly chatter, telling Ravenna about her shop, the recent city gossip, and Eydis's plans. "At least I have you for a few days," she sighed. "Eydis is having a little too much fun laying all her plots and traps."

That was certainly what it sounded like when Bryn checked in later, recounting all the commotion going on below. The citadel was a hive of activity, everyone executing their part to ensure everything went perfectly. It was surreal to hear that so many were doing so much; up in the king's quarters, she and Hilde didn't hear anything as they pinned and planned.

As dinnertime approached, Ravenna's enthusiasm began to flag. Hilde, however, remained energetic, excited by the prospect of creating an entire wardrobe for Ravenna. Based around their ideas of duality and combination, Hilde envisioned dozens of gowns with the structure and stiff lines favored by orcish fashions mixed with the flowing fabrics and draping lengths more common in human and fae garments. She spoke of different colors for different seasons, the symbolism of possible beadwork and embroidery, as she turned Ravenna about, wielding her pins.

While Ravenna appreciated her enthusiasm, the thought of conveying so much with just her clothes had those knots in her guts tightening.

And she was growing tired and hungry. And honestly a bit dizzy from all the turning.

Still, she tried to be gentle when she reminded Hilde, "I'm not a doll, Hilde."

The orcess blushed. "No, you're not. You're a muse. The one I've been waiting for."

With a flourish, Hilde spread the layered skirts around her, the silky fabric kissing Ravenna's legs like cool water. Hilde stepped back to angle a long mirror so Ravenna could see herself.

Her lips parted in surprise. She knew this was what they'd been designing all day, but to see it . . .

Burgundy silk cascaded down her body like wine pouring from a bottle. The bodice sat snugly to her torso, pinned into a diamond pattern with ribbons marking where more rigid boning would be encased in gold to act as stays and structure. Billowing sleeves artfully draped from the outer curve of her shoulders, gathered with glittering ruby buttons at her wrists. The skirts flowed from her hips in gleaming waves, the first layer of burgundy ending around her knees, with a second beneath of a slightly darker red, then another, and another, with the final layer frothing past her feet a blood-red crimson.

Hilde leaned to the side to grin at Ravenna in the mirror. "Good, yes?"

"Very good," she breathed. "Hilde, this is . . ." Ravenna blinked hard, refusing the prickling in her eyes. "This is the most beautiful thing I've ever seen."

Hilde tutted. "It's not even finished. But I'm always ready for praise."

Reaching out a shy hand, she laid it on Hilde's shoulder. "Thank you."

The orcess winked. "Say nothing of it. You are kin now." Turning to make a few minor adjustments, Hilde told her, "I know it's a lot of fuss, but it's necessary. Not to be dour, but you have one chance to win the hearts of Balmirra. Let's stack the odds in your favor."

Ravenna laughed, wiping away tears that definitely weren't there. "At least if they don't approve of me, they can't say anything against my gown."

"Precisely. We'll make them all mad with envy."

She held still as Hilde finished up marking where the intended embellishments—beads, crystals, gold thread—would go.

"If you come back tomorrow, I'd like to help with the embroidering. I'm handy with a needle."

Hilde beamed. "Excellent! We'll gossip, and the gown will be done in no time."

Ravenna highly doubted that, as the work needed to complete the gown was far beyond just the two of them, but she very much liked the thought of contributing. It felt right to sew some of herself into a garment meant for such an important day.

Hilde was gathering her things when Vallek finally returned.

He looked tired, his face creased with worry. Still, he approached Ravenna where she stood on the table, still waiting for Hilde to help her out of the gown without disturbing any pins.

His purr vibrated along his lips as he swooped in for a kiss. They were nearly the same height like that, giving Ravenna a clear view of the dark smudge across his forehead.

"How did it go?" she asked softly.

"I have atoned, and they gave their forgiveness," he said.

Ravenna lay her hand on his chest. "I hope your heart is a little less heavy."

"It is. Though, I will carry his weight a while yet."

"That you carry any at all means you have a heart."

Her mother sometimes mused that that was the burden of having a heart—it could be filled by so much yet broken by much more. When Ravenna was little, Aine once described heartache by pointing out the moss growing on a boulder.

"The moss grows how it will. It can cover the boulder. But the rock beneath remains strong."

Ravenna's heart bore no moss for Ulrich, but it did to see her *azai* grieve.

Lifting her hand to his mouth, he kissed the back. "I must bathe. I'll join you after."

She watched him go, wishing she could take a little of his burden away.

As Hilde helped gingerly pull off the dress, she was good enough to explain the rituals around atonement. Tied into funerary rites, it involved seeking forgiveness from the closest kin, as well as ritual cleansing after laying the deceased to rest. She described the labyrinthine crypts deep within the mountain, where Ulrich had no doubt been placed with his ancestors.

"It's good then that they gave their forgiveness," Ravenna said.

"They wouldn't deny Vallek."

"Because he's king?"

"Yes. But also because of why he did it. They will have known Vallek wouldn't do such a thing unless faced with no other choice."

Carefully laying out the gown on one of the sofas in the den, Hilde kissed Ravenna's cheeks before bidding her farewell. "Rest those fingers! We'll put them through their paces tomorrow!"

Alone finally, Ravenna cracked her neck and stretched her back. Then, she turned to the narrow stairwell that led down to Vallek's private baths. She couldn't help him in his ritual cleansing, but she could at least be of some comfort.

23

Ravenna woke to the sound of trumpets. At first, she couldn't quite believe the day was here—nor that she'd fallen asleep at all. Such a feat felt impossible last night, no matter how many orgasms her *azai* was determined to give her with his fingers and tongue.

She let out a long exhale, not quite sure if she was ready for it to be the day. Planning was one thing. Sewing a gown was one thing. Standing before hundreds of orc-kin claiming to be their queen was another.

Vallek's big body stretched behind her, and the arm he had flung over her waist flexed, tucking her neatly to his front.

"Good morning, my queen," he rumbled sleepily. "Are you ready for today?"

"I don't know," she whispered.

"I'm ready enough for the both of us." Pushing up onto his elbow, he pressed tender kisses to her cheek and temple.

Ravenna tried to let his warmth and affection soak into her skin, but her nerves were strung too tightly.

"Will I really be queen," she murmured, "just because you say it's so?"

"Yes. That's one of the perks of being king, love."

She huffed a solitary laugh, despite herself. Another kiss was pressed into her cheek, and against her skin, he whispered, "Until you can believe in yourself, believe in me. Today will be a triumph."

Triumph sounded a little too grand. Ravenna just hoped for *not a disaster*.

Reaching back to caress his face, she told him softly, "I do believe in you, *azai*." She'd witnessed his reign for too long to undercut everything he was capable of. If he wanted her as queen, then so it would be.

He purred happily. "Then there's nothing to fear."

There absolutely was, but she kept that to herself. It was a daunting bargain she'd struck, and now that it was time to uphold her end, her fears and doubts lay with them in their bed. It wasn't him but she herself Ravenna worried about.

An obnoxiously loud knock sounded at the front door to his quarters, and a moment later, Asta's voice boomed down the hall. "Wake up! It's time!"

Vallek's purr turned into a growl, and he buried his face in her hair. "Unfortunately, there's but one thing more powerful than even a king, and it's the schedule he must keep."

Soon, there was hardly any time or space for her worries. Asta, Eydis, Hilde, and Brynhíl arrived with the force of a summer thunderstorm, dividing and conquering to help ready Ravenna and Vallek.

Asta and Bryn got to work dressing Vallek in his ceremonial regalia while Hilde recruited Eydis to help Ravenna into her gown and all the finery they had chosen. Ravenna suspected she'd need to avoid direct sunlight to keep from blinding any observers, so intensely did she gleam and glitter.

It took over an hour, but by the end of it, she was dripping in gold and jewels. Gold leaf was even applied to her fingernails, and Hilde delighted in applying a thin cream infused with crushed pearls and gold. The resulting effect made Ravenna's skin shimmer almost like a full-fae woman.

As Hilde brushed her hair, though, a question Ravenna had been dreading did come up.

"What about these wings I keep hearing about?" Hilde asked.

"I say have them out," said Eydis. "It will leave an even stronger impression."

"I hear fae wings are iridescent—they'll shine beautifully in the light of the basilica."

"Wings stay hidden," Ravenna insisted. When she saw Hilde beginning to pout in the mirror, she said more firmly, "They stay hidden. They're only for mates and family to see."

Hilde winked. "Well, then, I expect to see them very soon. I'll need to find fabrics to complement their color."

Eydis and Ravenna shared a grin. "She's incorrigible," said Eydis.

Once her hair was brushed to a high shine, Hilde helped her turn to face the long mirror. Ravenna hardly recognized herself.

The gown flowed down her body like liquid flame, glittering gold catching the light. The whole effect made her look alight, a fire sparking to life. The stiff bodice gleamed with gold thread, the intersections of the diamond pattern interspersed with fire opals. With their embroidery and beadwork, the skirts weren't any lighter, patterns of stars, birds, and roses cascading down the length and gathering along the hems.

Rings glinted on almost all of her fingers, thin, delicate chains of gold were looped around her neck, and rubies the size of grapes dangled from her ears. Eydis added little braids to her hair, as well as pins studded with garnets, while Hilde applied rouge to her lips and a little more of the pearlescent cream to her cheeks and browbones.

It was overwhelming, and Ravenna could easily have been lost under all the finery. Except . . . the choice of the sparkles helped make her own skin shine as brightly as the gold and jewels. With a dollop of hair oil, her tresses shone, tamed into soft waves the likes of which she'd never managed on her own.

Ravenna looked at herself in the mirror and . . . smiled.

"There she is," murmured Hilde.

Her smile grew even wider. Looking between Hilde and Eydis, hearing Asta and Bryn's chatter with Vallek in the other room, Ravenna's heart was full. Too full for so many worries to live.

For the first time, Ravenna had friends. Well, two-legged friends, anyway.

"Thank you for this." She didn't know what else to say, how else to convey her gratitude. How could she be terrified under all her finery? It would protect her, like armor.

Eydis grinned. "You'll make us proud, *tristah*."

Hilde and Eydis looked up at movement, and Ravenna turned to behold Vallek. He strode from the bedchamber, somehow looming larger in his regalia.

Ravenna's breath caught in her throat. He was magnificent.

Adorned in a ruby tunic with golden thread, Vallek wore a gorget studded with rubies just below his throat, etched with the symbols of Balmirra. Ceremonial robes draped from his shoulders, denoting his rank as chieftain, gathered at his wrists by gold bands. Fine leather trou and boots polished to a high shine clad his legs. A belt spanned his thick waist, the elaborate steel buckle so bright it nearly shone like silver. Everywhere little details gleamed in the morning light—gold-threaded embroidering on his collar, iron epaulets at his shoulder, gold hoops in his ears, and rubies in his hair.

He looked for all the world a king, and most importantly, he wore the regalia with all the confidence as though he'd been born to it. That confidence buoyed her spirits.

Such a man wasn't to be defied. Such a man commanded kingdoms with an iron will.

A lascivious smile spread between his tusks, also capped in gold. "Look at you, love. My queen." He offered his hand to help her carefully step down from the low table.

Her steps made no sound in the cushioned, pearl-studded slippers as she was pulled into the curve of his body. Vallek dipped down to nuzzle her—

"Don't you *dare* smudge or wrinkle anything!" Hilde screeched.

Vallek's sigh buffeted Ravenna's cheek instead of his kiss. He chuckled before pressing a kiss to her forehead.

"You are a woman who deserves the world placed at her feet. Today, I intend to do it."

"I don't want the world. Just you."

Eyes glittering, Vallek raised her hand to his lips to kiss her palm. "Come, then, my queen. Let me show the people my good fortune."

Vallek offered his arm, and together, they strode down the hall to the doors, the orcesses chattering behind them. The doors opened, the guards on either side bowing low, and then down the stairs they went, headed for Ninevar's Basilica.

Ravenna was quickly breathless, and not just from their steady pace and her heavy regalia.

This is it. It's happening. She wasn't sure how her parents would feel about all this, but at least they'd sought to prepare her as best they could.

Stealing a glance at the handsome profile of her *azai*, Ravenna smiled to herself. They would've liked Vallek. And not just because he meant to bend an entire kingdom to his will for her.

A familiar nudge pressed against her mind as they walked, Oberon seeking a word.

Good luck today, Crow. I know you will make us proud.

Thank you, Obi. For everything.

Anything for my favorite foal. Oh, and mother says to bite anyone who looks at you too long. To assert dominance.

Vallek stood alone before his throne, staring down the hundreds, if not thousands of kin packed within the high walls of the basilica. Horns trumpeted the beginning of the event, and bodies pressed forward, the central aisle of open space collapsing as kin stepped forward, all wanting the best view of whatever it was to be announced.

Looking out at all the curious faces, Vallek ensured every guard was in position. From her place to his left, Asta winked beneath the brim of her helm. On his right, Eydis nodded from her usual place to the side of the dais.

Excitement prowled inside him, barely caged within his ribs. Perhaps another chieftain, one more careful, might dread what was about to happen, but Vallek could hardly wait.

Just wait until they see.

She would be a secret no longer.

Although orc-kin were jealous over their mates, he would have to share her with the people. At least a little. It seemed a small price to pay. Soon, in mere moments, they too would see what he saw, know what he knew.

Together, he and his faeling were destined for greatness.

Raising his open hand above his head, the horns blew a final time, bringing forth a buzzing silence. Every orc-kin within the basilica leaned forward, eager to hear the news.

Vallek Far-Sight wasn't one to stand on ceremony, even for official duties. But here he stood, every inch of him clad in the regalia of his forebearers.

This announcement was important.

Indeed, he didn't want to look like he didn't belong beside his magnificent new queen.

"My good people!" he proclaimed, voice booming across the basilica.

As one, the court took a breath and held it.

"Thank you for coming today. It is with great pleasure that I announce to you—I have chosen my bride, your queen."

Murmurs darted amongst the crowd, but to a one, they stared up at him, breath bated.

"She is Lady Ravenna Broch, and she is my mate." Sweeping his arm to the side, the crowd's gaze followed.

Trumpets and flutes played a celebratory tune, and from the small door leading back into his personal wing, beneath burgundy banners and golden flags, came Ravenna. She stepped forth into the light of the basilica, a vision in red and gold. She seemed to catch flame the further she came, the late-morning sun sparkling against her skin and jewels.

Hair rippling behind her, she descended the shallow steps to him. Holding her skirts with all the grace of a trained courtly lady, her little slippers peeked beneath the hem. She took measured, graceful steps, and the closer she drew, the harder Vallek's heart beat in his chest.

Pride lanced him through, and when he offered her his hand, he nearly shuddered to feel her cool hand slip into his.

Drawing her closer, he smiled down at her.

He could see the nervousness gathered at the corners of her mouth, but she stared up at him, her jaw set in that defiant little way she had.

My brave girl.

Together, they turned to face the shocked court. Scores of wide eyes stared back at them, and more than a few mouths dangled open.

Offering Ravenna's hand a small squeeze of support, he told the orc-kin gathered and all the world, "The beast has chosen a mate, and your king his queen."

His declaration was met with only silence, although this one seemed far cooler than the one of a few moments ago. The eager anticipation had bled from the crowd; now, many seemed confused, baffled even. But not angry. Vallek would take it.

He heard Ravenna take a deep breath, and beside him, she made the vows they had practiced over the past three days.

"I, Ravenna Broch, swear loyalty to the throne of Balmirra, the kin of Balmirra, and the heart of Vallek Far-Sight. The protection of the realm shall be my sworn duty, and service to its people my honor. I am Ravenna Broch, mate to Vallek Far-Sight, and it will be my honor to be your queen."

Two heads shorter than all the orcs, lilac skin stark against his green hide, she stood tall, making her declaration proudly, loud enough for every ancient stone of the basilica to hear.

Gods, he loved this woman. He might demand she say all this for him again, in the privacy of their bed later tonight.

Her declaration was met with more silence. It seemed he had truly shocked them.

"Some of you may already know Lady Ravenna as the *kone* in my service. She has aided me these past years in bringing prosperity and unification to our kingdom. With her beside me, Balmirra will lead the way into our new age." Gesturing for Eydis to step forward with the box she bore, Vallek said, "It is a gift to have found my mate and an honor to be claimed by her."

Opening the box, Eydis offered Ravenna the gold torque laid on a bed of velvet inside. It was a piece he'd had designed well over a decade ago, in anticipation of finding his mate. Years had gone by without cause to wear it, and it'd been at least seven since Vallek had last opened the box.

The smooth surface of the torque gleamed brightly, a large ruby inset on either end winking up from the velvet. Ravenna lifted it from the box, Eydis backing away to leave the two of them atop the dais.

When Ravenna looked up at him again, a genuine smile wreathed her lips. He relished the covetous glint in her eyes—it pleased her to claim him before everyone.

I'm yours, he mouthed to her.

She lifted onto her toes as he bent to meet her—

"This is a farce!"

The crowd gasped and muttered, backing away from the orc who'd spoken. It was Grogar, an impetuous young orc of noble blood. He'd become the scion of his house far too young, and he was far too proud of the wealth and prestige his family—not him—had accumulated.

Vallek turned to curl his lip at the impudent whelp when another stepped forward.

"Is it true she's *fae?*" demanded Lady Silvia.

More gasps from the kin, outraged this time.

"I am half-fae," Ravenna admitted, "but have never been loyal to the faelands."

"You would make us kneel to a halfling? A *fae?*" Grogar spat.

"Yes," Vallek growled. "You will kneel before my mate, your queen."

Grogar shook his head. "I will not. I challenge for the right to be chieftain."

A few kin shouted their support, bringing a smug grin to Grogar's face.

Vallek exchanged looks with Eydis over his faeling's head. So this was to be his game. Grogar wasn't the only young paladin looking to reap the reward of Vallek's work, but he seemed to be the bravest. Or stupidest.

At least, until three more stepped forward, all throwing their names out in challenge.

Even one of the eastern tribesmen, a representative from the Iron-Chests, stepped forward. "The eastern clans recognize no king. We won't be forced to kneel to a faeling queen, either."

And another handful of orcs stepped forward, declaring much the same.

Vallek counted a dozen challengers. Not bad. He honestly expected more.

"Very well," Vallek declared, his answering smile all teeth.

He moved to begin unbuttoning his fine tunic, but Ravenna's nails dug into his forearm. "Vallek . . ." she murmured, her pulse visibly beating at her throat.

"Stay here," he whispered. "This won't take long."

She met his bravado with lips thinned in concern. Vallek kissed her forehead, sliding his arms out of the tunic and robes. Laying them across the throne, he hefted Hormhím from its place beside the great seat.

"I accept your challenge," Vallek proclaimed as he descended the dais steps. "All of them. And when I win, all of you—every single one—will kneel and pledge your fealty. To me, and to my faeling queen."

With a wave from Vallek, a guard strode across the basilica to offer Grogar his axe. The crowd pushed back toward the great red limestone columns, creating an oval of cleared space for the challenge. The other eleven upstarts gathered behind Grogar, some of them beginning to look anxious now that the protection of the crowd had fallen away.

When another guard offered Vallek his axe, he declined.

Grogar's brow twitched, and Vallek smiled viciously. He didn't need a fresh axe to defeat this whelp, he could do it with one blade ground nearly to the poll.

Vallek had defeated his share of challenges in his time, most of them in the early years of his reign. It'd been some years now since the last, but these weren't unexpected. Like all the rest, he would win.

He'd won against Mordis for the sake of his sisters.

He'd defeated all the later challengers for the sake of the kingdom he wished to build.

Today, he would win for his mate.

Mattias stepped forward to ensure they were both ready—and that the rules of the challenge would be kept. No other weapon. No outside help. The life of the defeated was decided by the victor.

His beast howling inside him, Vallek charged.

Their axes met in a spark of ringing metal, reflected in Grogar's glare. The whelp had lost his bluster, the seriousness of his challenge finally seeming to dawn on him. A bead of sweat ran down the side of his face as he put his weight and strength behind throwing off Vallek's attack.

Vallek snorted, thrashing his tusks at Grogar's face. The younger orc snarled, rage contorting his face.

Finally, Vallek decided to stop playing with him.

Adding more of his brute strength, he nearly bent Grogar backwards. The other orc's legs shook with the effort of not falling to his knees beneath the onslaught of weight. Lips peeled back in a grimace of exertion, Grogar roared before jerking backwards, out from under Vallek and Hormhím.

He danced backward, trying to get some space to launch his own attack, but Vallek was there, bringing Hormhím down with a force that nearly cracked the handle of Grogar's axe. He just caught Hormhím with the toe of his blade, arms shaking like mountain aspens in a gale.

With a heave, Vallek freed Hormhím, wheeling the axe behind him in an arc before battering Grogar's middle with the blunt head of the handle. The younger orc sputtered, the air knocked out of him as he stumbled backwards. Another blow from Hormhím's blade sent Grogar's axe spinning out of his hand, onlookers scattering out of the way.

It took one kick to send Grogar to the ground. Planting his boot on the orc's chest, Vallek leveled his blade on Grogar's throat.

The paladin stared up at him in utter shock, breath coming in stuttering pants.

Vallek stood above the whelp for a good long moment, letting him really think about his choice, before finally *tsking*.

"Mercy," he sighed. "And be grateful for it."

Stepping back, he allowed Grogar's friends to help him up. They hustled him away, back into the safety of the crowd.

With the toe of his boot, Vallek flipped the other axe toward the group of waiting challengers—interestingly smaller already. "Next."

One after another, they met the same fate. Flat on their backs, Hormhím pressed to their throat or gut. Some gave him a more spirited challenge than others, particularly the Iron-Chest warrior. Their duel truly got Vallek's blood burning, and they danced across the basilica for the better part of ten minutes, exchanging furious blows. It was the eastern tribesman who managed to nick Vallek's cheek, sending blood dribbling down his neck to wet his collar.

Vallek merely grinned ferociously, his beast thrilling at the challenge. He relished the burn in his muscles and the look of awe in every orc.

By the time it came to the last challenger, whose only hope was that Vallek would be tired enough to finally defeat, it was clear to everyone else that it was Vallek Far-Sight who would win.

He was victor today.

He was king.

In the end, he spared seven lives, the others rescinding their challenge and melting back into the crowd.

"Mercy," Vallek said for the final time.

The orc scrambled to his feet, hurrying back into the crowd.

Alone in the cleared space, Vallek turned round in a circle twice. "Are there any others? Or is this matter settled?"

The gathered orc-kin rumbled and murmured, but Vallek had no fear. All orcs respected the challenge and its outcome. If he was wrong, if the gods disagreed with him, then it was he who'd be laid flat on his back.

Turning, he strode across the basilica, ascending the dais again. Ravenna watched him come, her lips twitching with a relieved grin.

He grinned cockily back, his blood still hot, and it was only because of the thousand pairs of eyes on them that he didn't take her on his throne right that moment. Flushed with victory, heady with triumph, Vallek knelt down onto one knee before his faeling.

Her touch feather-light, Ravenna clasped the torque round his neck. The weight of the gold settled on him, a mark that he was claimed.

His beast sat back, pleased. Her claim was there for all to see. Indisputable.

Her cool hand touched his face, and he felt the gentle swipe of her thumb over his cut. Her magic tingled along his cheek, and his breath hissed between his tusks to feel the pinch of his skin closing shut again.

The crowd surged forward toward the dais, trying to get a closer look at how the king was healed. Sounds of wonder echoed through the basilica, followed by a few cheers when, after lifting his chin with a finger, Ravenna bent to kiss him.

"Stay here," she whispered against his lips.

His good mood faltered. *What?*

Turning to face the court, Ravenna announced, "I know this is a shock to many of you. If your objection is with me, then I will earn the right to be your queen. Who would challenge me?"

She truly had surprised them. Astonishment rendered the usually boisterous orcs silent again, many of them blinking back at her offer with bemusement.

Ravenna stood firm. If the chieftain, the king, could be challenged, then let her be, too.

She would be queen not just because Vallek said so, but because she won it.

Perhaps she was overconfident, even mad. Perhaps she was feeling a little bloodthirsty after watching her mate's magnificent display of physical prowess. Perhaps her fae instinct was desperate not just to claim him with a bit of gold but to defeat any foolish enough to think he belonged to anyone but her. Perhaps she was tired of living in the shadow of others.

Perhaps it was a bit of everything.

After a prolonged moment of disbelief amongst the crowd, someone did step forward.

She recognized the orcess—Yphella Long-Tusk, daughter of Hrothgar, who stayed behind in Balmirra to act as the Innrini representative. Unsurprising that she would try one last time to claim the hand of the king—and the throne.

Unfortunately for her, both were Ravenna's.

"I will challenge," said Yphella.

Nodding her acknowledgement, Ravenna descended the dais to meet her opponent. She thought she heard Hilde's squeak of concern—probably for the gown—when another guard stepped forward to offer his axe.

Ravenna took it, straining under the heft. A few nervous laughs burst from the crowd as they backed away to give the two space.

As Yphella hefted her own axe over her shoulder, she looked upon Ravenna with pity. "Don't mistake foolishness for bravery, faeling."

"Mind your axe, and I will mind mine."

Shrugging, Yphella smirked.

Mattias again came to stand between them, ensuring their readiness. "Are you sure, my lady?" he whispered.

"Yes. Thank you."

Obviously unhappy but unable to stop her, Mattias nodded curtly before stepping back.

Yphella regarded her curiously, waiting to see if Ravenna would make the first move. When she didn't, Yphella charged.

The axe in her hands careened to the ground, followed by Yphella. She landed hard on her side, her right arm pinned. Ravenna tightened her magic around the orcess's arm, making sure she felt the pull on her wrist.

Yphella struggled to regain her feet, but it was no use. The most Ravenna allowed was for her to climb to her knees. No matter how she tried, she couldn't free her arm, Ravenna holding fast with her magic.

The orcess grunted and struggled, panic beginning to glint in her eyes as Ravenna walked toward her.

Arms shaking with the effort to hold the weapon, she rested the axeblade on Yphella's shoulder. "Mercy," she said.

Yphella stared up at her in amazement as the crowd gasped and murmured around them.

Ravenna held perfectly still, waiting to see what the orcess would do. Few reacted well to defeat, even worse to humiliation. But she needed this, needed all these big, strong orcs to understand that not only would she stand beside Vallek, she would defend him and herself. That she wasn't an ornament or oddity.

To her own shock, Yphella threw her head back and laughed. "Well met, faeling," the orcess chuckled. "I should have known."

Pulling back, Ravenna set down her axe before letting Yphella's clatter to the ground. Then she let her magic fall away from the orcess.

She offered her hand.

Yphella took it with a grin, clasping it tight as she stood. Eyes twinkling, the orcess said, "It's a good reminder for us all—never underestimate an opponent. Even a small one."

Ravenna grinned. "The small ones tend to bite the hardest."

"Indeed."

Yphella stood beside Ravenna, waiting for any other challengers, but it seemed the crowd had had their fill of fighting.

Ravenna met their curious gazes, more hopeful now than she had been when she first entered the basilica. She found less suspicion and shock—even a little, dare she hope, respect? She knew it would take more than this little display to win them over, but it was a start at least.

When no others stepped forward, Ravenna left Yphella to retake the dais.

As she approached, colorful light from the great stained glass window set behind the throne bathed her in its warmth. Her mate cut an imposing shadow through the light, splitting it with the wide span of his shoulders. Even through the glare, she could see and feel how he smiled at her, his gaze full of pride.

Ravenna smiled back, glowing. In the light of Ninevar's Basilica, for the first time in a very long while, Ravenna knew she was *seen*.

With a little roll of her shoulders, she unfurled her wings.

Gasps resounded through the basilica as her wings caught the light. She felt the warmth spread through the delicate membranes, casting colorful fractals on the steps behind her. Fluttering her wings, she let them sparkle in the light.

Ravenna took the hand Vallek held out for her, joining him again before the throne. Bathed in light, he claimed a searing kiss, tusks pressing into her cheeks.

To echoing applause, he turned them to face the crowd, his hand at her waist drawing her into his side. "Your queen!"

24

By the time all the challenges were met, the declarations made, and the great feast eaten, the court seemed far more amenable to their king taking a faeling queen. At least, they were too full or drunk to care anymore about it that night.

The feast began at luncheon but lasted well into the night, turning into a customary orcish celebration. Lots of rowdy songs, lots of raucous dancing, and lots of boastful bets. Vallek sat at table on the dais with his mate, presiding over it all with amusement—and a modicum of relief.

He'd known the day would end well for them, but finally seeing it come to fruition with minimal bloodshed was something to savor.

As they feasted, criers throughout the city announced the news to the people. Balmirrans everywhere were invited to celebrate with their king in finding his mate, offered as many tankards of mead and wine as they wished from Vallek's own stores. Alcohol and good cheer flowed through Balmirra, and by the evening, Vallek's heart and stomach were overfull.

A great cheer rang out when he finally stood from the table. Not bothering with more speeches, he thanked them again and bid all goodnight. Vallek led Ravenna from the dais to thunderous applause and well-meaning jeers, a few of which had the both of them giggling by the time they made it through the doorway into his personal wing.

Safe within the cool, abandoned corridors, they took the chance to meander lazily, working off their dinner. Alone together—with their guards, of course—Vallek covered the hand she had tucked at his elbow with his own.

"You were magnificent, sprite."

Even in the dimness of the corridor, he could spy how she flushed with pleasure at his praise. "So were you. I only had the one challenger."

"One was all you needed. And all I could bear. Promise me, no more brawls in the basilica."

Ravenna snorted. "I can't make that promise, and neither can you!"

Well, that was probably true, given the boisterous nature of orckin. Still, "Then at least promise me you'll make your best effort."

"Fine," she laughed, "if you promise the same."

"It may surprise you, but I prefer feasting to fighting."

"It doesn't surprise me, no. But you still haven't promised."

"I haven't. And," he leaned down so only she could, ostensibly, hear him—his guards were far too well trained to react either way—whisper, "neither did I specify what kind of feasting."

Ravenna came to a halt in the middle of the corridor. "That might be the worst innuendo I ever heard."

Affecting offense, Vallek laid his hand over his chest. "Innuendo? Never." Her only warning was his sly grin, and then he was lifting her in his arms, resuming their path back to their quarters.

Rather than get comfortable in his hold, Ravenna pushed away from his chest until her arms were nearly straight. "Don't you dare throw me over your shoulder in this gown," she warned with a scowl. "I'm far too full."

Vallek's booming laughter echoed down the corridors, lasting all the way back to their private rooms.

They left the guards at the door, and after kicking it closed, they were finally, blessedly alone.

Although nearly the entire citadel was down in the basilica celebrating, the sconces had been lit, offering a warm wash of light to the central hall. After setting Ravenna down, he marveled at how she glittered in the soft light. She was all the colors of sunset, but his favorite was the lavender flush in her cheeks.

Leaning down, Vallek kissed both of them.

"You held your own today. My formidable mate. No one will dare question your place beside me."

"I doubt that, but . . . thank you." She grinned up at him, her hands coming to lay on his chest.

"Soon, we will get you a crown. And your own throne."

"Until then I . . . what, sit on your lap?"

Her laugh fell away when she realized that yes, that had been his plan. The idea of presiding over his court, his beautiful mate spread over his lap, the folds of her gown spilling across their legs onto the dais, was one he immediately wanted a reality.

Running her hands up and down the material of his tunic, she asked, "Do you intend to merely make declarations, or will you really take me as your wife?"

He sensed her playfulness, suspected she flirted, but this was too important an answer to be flippant. "I will take you in all ways, sprite. Today was nothing to the wedding we'll have. The whole kingdom will come to pay homage to you."

"That's then," she said, sultry eyes snaring his attention as she closed the last distance between them. Her lithe body pressed to his, she pouted, "What about tonight? Will you finally make me your mate?"

A violent purr rattled his chest, and his hands moved from delicately tracing her shoulder blades to grabbing her waist.

"You know I won't deny you, sprite. We *have* been practicing."

Her violet eyes, dark and sparkling like amethysts, pulled him down to her. Their lips met in a sensual slide, a soft kiss that teased and tested.

"I suppose we can wait a little longer," said the minx, "if you aren't ready."

Vallek nearly choked. "Were I any readier, I might perish."

Her brows lifted in two twin arcs. "What a good king you've been, sacrificing for everyone else."

A grin spread past his tusks, and with a little flex of his arms, he lifted her onto the low table still set in the hallway. Moving her by the hips, he turned her to begin the grueling process of loosening the crisscrossing laces that scored the back of the gown. As intricate as a sailor's knot and as supportive as scaffolding, he wasn't surprised when they mounted a worthy defense against his trembling fingers.

Working to keep his purr from growing into a growl, Vallek said, "I *will* have you bare. But we keep the jewelry."

"Just so long as I get to undress you next. And you keep the torque."

He winked at her in the mirror. "You won't find me without it again, love. Your claim stays there." Finally, the keystone knot gave way, allowing Vallek to slide his greedy hands inside the fabric. "Although, I wouldn't be opposed to more claims."

Surprise colored her ethereal face in the lantern light as the gown went slack. "You'll . . . let me bite you?"

"I will insist."

The weight of the gown made pulling it from her body simple, and Vallek caught the exquisite garment, careful to lay it across a chair after Ravenna gracefully stepped out of the pool of fabric. He knew better than to incite Hilde's wrath.

Clad in only a thin linen shift, the dark silhouette of her body hid just beneath the nearly transparent fabric. Her arms came to lay on his shoulders when he returned to her, but she didn't give him the kiss he sought.

"Now you."

Impatient, Vallek toed off his boots as Ravenna tackled the row of gold buttons at his front. When the sides of the tunic parted, he shrugged it off with his robes, and his undershirt and trou quickly followed.

Some of the play left her face when he took hold of the hem of her shift. She watched him carefully, almost . . . cautiously. He'd seen her naked many times by now, had had his fingers and tongue deep inside her, but tonight . . . tonight, none of that mattered. They stood together at the beginning, and that deserved gentle reverence.

Slowly, Vallek pulled the shift up over her head. Gods, it nearly pained him how beautiful she was.

Her hair fell around her shoulders, mantling her in soft darkness. High points on her body still glimmered with whatever Hilde had applied, the jewels and gold she wore sparkled almost as brightly as she, and best of all, her pert little nipples, dusky lilac and berry-sweet, awaited him eagerly.

Finally, he took his mate in his arms, skin to skin. Her softness burned him, the silky suppleness of her body molding perfectly to his harder bulk. Gods, morning had been too long ago.

Vallek dipped his head, claiming one pouting nipple. He rolled it with his tongue along a tusk, delighting in how she gasped and squirmed in his arms.

"Vallek . . ." she murmured, nails digging into his scalp.

There was nothing in this world better than his mate clawing at him while he pleased her. Nothing.

But if there was, he intended to find out tonight.

Sucking gently, it took only slight pressure from his palm at her lower back for her to throw her legs around his waist. He carried her like that to their bed, placing her on the cool sheets with all the veneration of a supplicant come to worship at the altar.

Though he was loath to leave her, he had to see. Rising onto his hands, he stared greedily down at the vision she made.

Dark hair spread behind her, her limbs lay lax on the bed, ready, welcome. She seemed to glow—whether it was the cream or her magic or something else, he didn't know. Only that he'd never seen anything so lovely.

"Nothing could have prepared me for you, sprite," he breathed.

Her lips parted, though she said nothing. Raw emotion shone in her eyes, even a hint of sadness.

He wouldn't have it.

Ducking to claim her lips again, he filled her mind with only him. He overwhelmed her senses, demanded all her attention. Giving her some of his weight, he lay above her, pressing her into the bed as his tongue plundered the hot well of her mouth. He drank her down, every moan and mewl and sigh, until he was sure she would think of nothing but him.

Hungrily, he began trailing kisses down the center of her body; her chin, her throat, her sternum. He made a necessary detour at her breasts, lavishing each with attention, not satisfied until both nipples were erect and swollen. He only replaced his tongue with a hand when she began to squirm beneath him. Plumping her breast in his hand, he slotted her nipple between two fingers as he squeezed the tender flesh.

She parted her legs for him as he approached, and he purred with praise. "My good girl," he rumbled, burying his nose where her scent was richest.

Setting his lips against her sensitive clitoris, he deepened his purr, letting her feel the vibrations. Ravenna gasped, the fingers carding through his mane turning to talons. She held him there between her thighs, directing him with greedy rolls of her hips and presses of her palms.

He spent long moments lapping at her, enjoying every reaction as he ran his tongue from cunt to clitoris. She wept for him, slick glistening along her rosy flesh and running down her thighs.

A feast fit for a king.

Pinning her hips with a heavy arm, he set his thumb to circling her clitoris as his tongue delved down to indulge. He rimmed her entrance before pushing inside, curling his tongue against her trembling inner wall.

Ravenna thrashed on the bed, chest heaving, the golden chains round her neck, some as fine as thread, tangling in her midnight hair.

One of her heels dug into the dip between his shoulders, and Vallek, wise to her tells, withdrew his tongue. She whined and growled at him, only to gasp his name as he pushed first one and then two fingers inside.

"That's it, love. Come on my hand and then we'll see about my cock."

She might have barked something at him, but the words morphed into a long moan of abandon. Her body tensed, her tight cunt contracting around his fingers. Gently, he pushed his fingers apart, a little more with every pulse, readying her as much as he could.

The moment before climax, he worked a third finger inside, stretching her. Ravenna whined and mewled, brows snapped together in a rictus of pleasure. As reward, he set his tongue along the other side of her clitoris, sweeping around the base.

With a choked gasp, she came apart. Her cunt milked his fingers, as if to draw him further in, wringing every scrap of pleasure she could as he held them still inside her. Vallek greedily sucked and kissed her clitoris, prolonging the pleasure for as long as he could.

When she collapsed back on the bed, body limp, he purred with satisfaction. Kissing the delicate skin of her inner thigh, he began to move his fingers again, little movements that kept her flesh sensitized and her body prepared.

He straightened from his kneel before the bed, climbing in beside her. Laid out comfortably on his side, he arranged her how he wished, petting her as she came down from the precipice. His cock throbbed angrily at her hip, but he could ignore it for now; the sight she made, all flushed and dazed with swollen lips, was too delicious to miss.

Soon. Finally. We'll have our mate.

Vallek was as surprised as he was delighted when she turned to face him. He expected more kisses, perhaps soft whispers across the pillows, but instead, she used her hands to gently urge him onto his back. He watched with intense interest as she sat up over him, those dark brows arching again in a sultry expression.

"Shall we see about your cock?" she said.

Before he could answer, he felt the warm press of her magic slither over him. It bound him to the bed in an invisible hold, ephemeral cuffs at his shins, wrists, and neck. He could wiggle a little, and he suspected if he really tried, he could break free, but otherwise, he was laid out before her, a helpless offering.

His cock pulsed painfully, a little spend leaking from the head onto his belly. Gods, he'd never found being kept immobile alluring before, but everything Ravenna did seemed to please him, even those parts he knew nothing about.

Her magic spread like a blanket across the rest of his body, up his legs, across his arms, down his chest. Everywhere but his cock. That she claimed for herself, her hand smoothing up and down the underside before taking him in a firm grip. Her magic was impossibly soft, even where it held him down at the limbs and neck, caressing his skin, swirling over his nipples, even kissing his lips, for she couldn't reach both his cock and mouth at once.

Her rhythm was purposeful and maddening, almost as much as the little grin she wore. Pressed to his side, her breasts mashed into his abdomen, he could feel the erect points of her nipples, a distracting layer of sensation. Sometimes she lifted up to trace her nipples across his skin, making them both gasp; others, she leaned down to press fluttering kisses to his abdomen, making the muscles jump beneath her lips.

Always her hand moved, lubricated by the spend leaking from his swollen cockhead. The fat veins lining the shaft pulsed and throbbed, his cock nearly moving of its own accord whenever she loosened or changed her grip.

He bared his teeth at the ceiling when her magic gathered below her hand, pooling in a slight, warm weight along his bollocks. She juxtaposed the soft caress with a firm twist of her wrist at his cockhead.

Orgasm gathered at his lower back, but Vallek fought against it valiantly.

"Inside you," he growled, "*I need inside you, skala.*"

"I think maybe we should take the edge off," she teased, neither hurrying her movements nor giving him any quarter.

He snarled, testing his restraints. Her magic held, telling him silently that she wished to play longer.

Slumping back onto the bed, Vallek resigned himself to his fate. His hellion wished to play, and he was nothing if not her servant. Whatever the reason, for now, she found flirtation and playfulness preferable to the more intense moments they'd shared. While she might be ready for his cock, he thought perhaps she wasn't prepared for the more intimate connection to be had in sex.

She wanted dirty talk and praise, not I love you's.

That was all right. For now. He'd have both, in the end. And sooner rather than later, if he had his way. Which he usually did and would in this.

And so Vallek submitted to her attentions, dutifully coming all over her hand and his belly when he could bear it no longer. She demanded all that he could give her, hand keeping up the pace along his soaked, sticky shaft.

When he thought the climax had begun to release its grip on him, she surged up his body to sink her fangs into the meat of his left pectoral, just over where his heart pumped wildly. With a grunting yelp, he came again, lashing her hip and flank with more pearlescent spend.

Body rigid in his surprise and rapture, he shuttled his cock through her hand, pumping furiously. Air kissed every tooth, his lips peeled back in a grimace of ecstasy as she pulled her fangs from his flesh and swirled her tongue across the little punctures.

When she lifted her head to grin at him, a dribble of blood escaped the corner of her mouth. She caught it with her tongue before drawing her spend-soaked fingers into her mouth, licking each clean.

Vallek growled, his hunger unabated. He tested his bonds again but found them still in place. Gods, he couldn't take much more. He needed to be inside her, to pound her tight cunt and kiss the smug grin off her face.

Ravenna threw a leg over his waist, her warm, wet cunt teasing his abdomen as she leaned down to kiss him. He tasted himself on her lips, his spend and blood mixing with her own essence to drive him nearer to frenzy.

If she wasn't careful, she'd incite his rutting instinct.

He'd thought to be a bit more civilized their first time, but his hellion enjoyed flirting with danger.

She pulled away, no matter how his lips clung to hers, smiling down at his torment before sliding off the bed. Flouncing over to the linen cupboard, she pulled out a cloth to clean him up. Her swipes over his belly were prolonged and meant to tease, and she was careful to leave his cock, still at half-mast for her, glistening.

When next she met his gaze, Vallek matched her arrogant grin. Nodding at the sideboard, he told her, "Top drawer, on the right, there's a glass bottle. Bring it here."

She lifted one brow at being bossed about, but his patience was wearing thin.

Ravenna opened the drawer and pulled out the bottle, holding up the clear liquid to the dim light. Carrying it back with her, she set it on his abdomen before climbing onto the bed.

He needed to have stairs made for her. All the better for her to walk right into their bed and sit on his waiting cock.

Pulling out the glass stopper, she held the bottle to her nose to smell. A knowing smile curled her lips.

"Vallek Far-Sight indeed," she quipped.

She poured a generous dollop into her palm before setting the bottle on the side table. Taking his swollen shaft in her hand, she spread the syrupy liquid up and down. Warm tingling followed in her wake, the lubricant stimulating every nerve ending.

Vallek tested his bonds again and found them looser, perhaps because she was distracted by how, in just a few strokes, his cock stood erect in her hand again, gleaming in the low light. Lifting a hand finally, the rest of his bonds fell away.

He pushed himself higher on the bed, head resting comfortably on the pillows. Catching her knee, he drew her up with him as he took hold of the base of his cock.

"You'll set the pace, love, but let me touch you at least."

Biting her lip, she nodded before again throwing her leg over his hips. Hands spread for balance on his lower abdomen, her curtain of dark hair fell around them as she looked down to watch her hips descend.

Vallek held his breath—and his cock still as she came to him. He couldn't help his hiss of pleasure when her cunt kissed his cockhead, and his purr dropped into a growl as he watched her slowly take him.

After a deep breath, Ravenna lowered her hips, and the head slid inside her.

"Ooh," she moaned, fingers digging into his skin.

She took a moment to adjust, her teeth sunk into her lower lip, before resuming her descent. Vallek moved his hand away to hold her hips, watching rapturously. It was like a dream, seeing himself slowly disappear inside her.

She took little breaks, her breath beginning to come in heavier pants. Rubbing at her thighs and hips, he praised, "My formidable mate. You take me so well."

Ravenna only huffed, perhaps a laugh, before starting again. She lifted up a little before falling back down, and he felt how she pulsed. Vallek's throat ran dry as she slowly, steadily consumed him. He was lost to her snug heat, her cunt holding him tighter than a fist.

By the time she seated him fully inside her, her chest expanded with panting heaves. She quivered under his hands, and Vallek was no better, quaking with the need to hold her hips to his as he shoved up in greedy strokes.

He held still only through force of will, gaze riveted on how her cunt stretched wide to take him. Her clitoris peeked along his root, pressed between them. Gods, it seemed impossible that she should be able to take him, his mind not quite able to comprehend the sight. Yet, between their slick and spend, the lubricant, and the magic he felt caressing where they joined, she'd taken him.

Holding her by the hips, he stretched his thumb to find her little bud of nerves. She jerked with his touch, her head tossing back and forth. He couldn't tell if she meant for him to stop or if it felt too good and kept his touches light.

Ravenna shuddered above him, her cunt clasping him tight in a small orgasm.

Vallek purred. "Take what you need, love. Take it all."

"So full," she choked. "It's . . ."

Vallek held onto the last scraps of his sanity as she began to move in tiny little rolls of her hips. He had to hold on—he had to be gentle. A good mate. He could give her this time, even as he careened closer to a rut.

At least, he thought he could.

He became less sure with every passing moment and jerk of her hips.

She'd just found something of a rhythm when she lifted a few inches up onto her knees—and fell back down with a wet *slap*. A feral sound hummed in her throat, and she did it again, bouncing on his lap.

Vallek smiled viciously. "That's it, sprite. Take me. Take your pleasure."

Holding her steady, he watched her begin to move in earnest. Her slick flowed between them, stimulated by her thrusts and the lubricant. Her movements made sloppy, wet sounds as she gained momentum, and Vallek saw stars when she twisted her hips on her next downstroke.

Need her need her need . . .

Vallek thrust up to meet her, a roar gathering in his throat. She clutched him tight, soaking him in her slick as she bounced and rolled her hips. She kept the pace as long as she could, and when he felt her beginning to fade, he lifted her by the waist, bringing her down again and again and again onto his waiting cock.

He reached up inside her, fused them together. He claimed her. He came home.

He didn't know when he'd begun coming, only that he went mindless with need. His thrusts grew jerky and desperate, unintelligible sounds echoing through the bedchamber.

Vallek sat up, changing the angle and crushing her to his chest as he came apart. Hips smacking, he filled her with spend, his pleasure ruthless. He chased it down as surely as the rut chased him.

He couldn't stop it.

As his last thrusts pulsed through her, he laid her down on her back, watching as she came down from her own pleasure. Her cunt throbbed around him, milking his cock for more.

You'll have it. Anything you want.

Ravenna moaned as he slid his cock free. Spend gushed from her pulsing cunt, and Vallek had the novel thought of pushing his fingers inside, ensuring nothing escaped. He wanted her full, saturated in his scent, thoroughly claimed.

"Are you all right?" he managed to bite out.

Ravenna nodded, her expression still dazed from their lovemaking. Her eyes fell to his cock, still hard and bobbing against his belly.

A mewling sound escaped her lips—greedy, and perhaps a little trepidatious.

Oh, she should be.

"You've lived amongst kin long enough to know about ruts, yes?"

Her eyes went wide. Licking her lips, which only incited a frenetic purr in his chest, she whispered, "Yes. You're . . .?"

"Oh yes, sprite. I thought I could resist it, but who could resist your teasing?" He swooped down to claim a brutal kiss, closing his hand around her throat to keep her just where he wanted. "You know what it means?"

"Why don't you explain it to me."

His huff fluttered the fine hairs around her face. "It means you're mine. And—" Without warning, he dug his hand under her hip to flip her to her front. She landed with a little *oof*, her luscious backside bouncing. Vallek purred, filling his hands with the soft flesh before pushing her legs wide. She'd just gotten her hands under her when she gasped as his cock teased her cunt before pushing deep inside in a single thrust. "—it means I'll be inside you more often than not. Are you ready?"

Her answer was to bury her face in the bedding as he began to move, their flesh meeting in loud slaps. She arched her back, allowing him even deeper, and he purred his praise.

"That's good, just like that, sprite."

Covering her with his bigger body, he leaned over to take her throat in his hand again. He lifted her chin to meet his kiss, his tongue keeping counterpoint to his thrusting hips. She moaned and mewled into his mouth, driving him higher, wilder.

"If it's not my cock, it will be my fingers or my tongue," he growled against her lips. "For days and days and days, you'll be full of me. That's rut."

Ravenna shuddered beneath him. "Fates. *Fuck.*"

His next thrust was brutal, his bollocks drawing tight to hear her swear. Straightening, he held her by the hips, his big hands spanning her waist, and pulled her back to meet every stroke. He greedily watched her backside bounce against him, the dimples just above the plush flesh teasing him.

A glimmer of iridescence caught his eye, and his attention snagged on the little bundles of her folded wings. It was hard to believe he hadn't noticed them before, but tucked so tightly to her skin, they hardly made a ridge against her back. But as he thrust, connecting them deeper and deeper with every stroke, he saw how the intricate folds began to break.

"Show me your pretty wings," he demanded.

Ravenna turned her head to stare back at him, her lips swollen and her gaze unfocused. For a moment, he wasn't sure she'd do as he said, but then, one by one, her wings unfurled. He watched in awe as they seemed to unspool, each intricate fold undone to make room for the next. It took only a moment, and then the translucent purple membranes fluttered at her back, catching the light.

"Fuck," he cursed. "You're beautiful. Too fucking beautiful."

He shoved inside her, finesse gone. Balancing on one hand, he ran the tip of a finger along the lower rim of a wing, feeling just how delicate the structure was.

Ravenna shuddered and moaned, pushing back into his hips with abandon. The wings buzzed softly under his hand, little vibrations that harmonized into an otherworldly hum.

Vallek smiled wickedly. *They're sensitive.*

Oh, there was no hope for his little mate now. He would take no mercy on her. He had her now, and as he came, pouring himself inside her, he knew it was only a matter of time before he claimed all her secrets.

25

Ravenna wasn't sure she'd ever spent a happier handful of days. There had certainly been happy days with her mother, but there was always a wistfulness, waiting for her father to return.

There was nothing quite like holing up with her *azai,* though. To be the sole focus of a man like Vallek Far-Sight could be daunting, intense, but always rewarding.

Although she'd spent much time with him by now, never had it been in this way for so long. Vallek of the evenings, the relaxed man who slowly sipped his mead and relished a game of *talfon,* was the man she spent the next three days with.

Of all the Valleks she'd come to know—king, warrior, brother, politician, *azai,* lover, friend—this was her favorite.

He always carried himself with an easy confidence that lent itself to good humor and teasing. He spoke openly of anything and nothing, happy to answer her questions, comfortable spinning tales and visions of his own. Affable, charming, and tender, Ravenna found this Vallek the most dangerous of all.

It was clear why so many adored him. She already did, and if she wasn't careful, she'd careen down the slippery slope she already traversed to fall madly in love with him.

There was nothing novel about loving one's *azai,* of course. She'd even rationalized to herself that it would benefit her plans to have his love and give her own in return. None of that lessened her terror, though. Even though she predicted the softest of landings, letting herself fall at all was its own risk.

For years, she bore her cold, dark heart by keeping it closed. She lived for her revenge, for the moment when she fulfilled the vision that had ruined her life and ended her parents'.

If she loved Vallek, she would be living for him, too.

And that was the nature of vengeance—it could have no bedfellow. A split heart, divided priorities, would gain her nothing and neither.

Such thoughts were cold comfort and far less attractive than indulging in long, sumptuous days with her mate. Who could resist late mornings, lying in bed whispering across pillows? Who would deny themselves luxurious baths that went on so long, they both wrinkled? Who could walk away from cozy evenings feeding each other the choicest bits over a lively game of *talfon?*

No one, and certainly not Ravenna.

She was weak. She feared she always had been.

Vallek was her ultimate prize and her greatest weakness. The softest part of her withered heart. Which was ridiculous given his bulk and strength, but the thought of anything happening to him, of bringing suffering to his door because of her . . . it was too much to bear.

And so she indulged, ignoring the little sparks of worry, denying them air to ignite.

She was selfish. Greedy. She took a mate's due, and the more she did, the more pleased her *azai* became. Pleasing him was fast becoming her greatest goal, and that, too, was terrifying. For she knew, one day, that would come to an abrupt and painful end.

Of course, their lazy days came only after a full day of fucking. He hadn't exaggerated his rut. She spent that first night with his cock inside her more often than not. Her cunt ached from overuse, but whenever he pulled away, it ached more for his return.

When she truly did need a moment to catch her breath, she delighted in using her magic and mouth on him. It was particularly fun to make him decide which he preferred; his lips mashed between his tusks, obviously not wanting to answer incorrectly and miss out on her magic or mouth again.

In a single journey of the sun, from setting to rising and setting again, she felt as though she made up for all her lost time and experience. He took her in all ways imaginable, and then many more she'd never thought of. Her hair and the bedding were hopelessly tangled by the time his rut finally released him.

He was infinitely gentle with her sore body, carrying her down to the baths as the bedding was stripped and changed and food brought in. He washed her sticky inner thighs with reverential strokes, nuzzling against her belly as he cleaned her up. Holding her in the water, they both relaxed in the warm baths, letting their muscles unwind.

A meal of finger foods followed, as well as a nap. He let her rest, never allowing her feet to touch the floor. If they wished to sit in the den, he carried her. If they wished to lay in the bed, he carried her there, too. The only place she refused his company was the garderobe, although he tried to carry her there more than once.

They hardly bothered with clothes, for what was the point. If it wasn't being ripped away for better access during sex, it was being pushed down or out of the way to allow skin-to-skin contact. The more of it Ravenna had, the more she wanted. Even those handful of moments alone in the garderobe started to become unbearable.

The bond was taking hold. Formed over their weeks together, it was rapidly strengthening. Ravenna swore it was becoming tangible, a link between them that hooked round her heart and his. It pulled taut whenever they physically parted, urging them back together.

And so, there was little reason to spend any real time out of his arms. They played *talfon* with her in his lap, the board balanced on hers. They washed each other in the baths, arms always intertwined. They slept in a tangle of limbs, pressed together from chest to toes.

They hardly saw anyone else—mostly Brynhíl in passing. It was a strange sort of fantasy, a dream they lived, just the two of them. For three days, nothing of the world outside their quarters existed; everything that mattered was right there, in her arms. Mates, *azai*. Those three days were perfect.

By the fourth, Ravenna was accustomed to the overwhelming sensation of her mate filling her to the brim. He pushed inside, his pace steady but merciless. Morning light backlit him in a white-gold glow, the wide cut of his shoulders an impressive silhouette.

She bit her lip, head and shoulders moving restlessly on the pillow as she watched him disappear inside her. Soon, her backside came to rest on his thighs, and she crossed her ankles at the small of his back.

He was so deep like this, as if he could reach inside her and carve out his own place. Pushing out all her troubles, leaving room for only him.

A moan of pleasure hummed in her throat at the delicious pressure. Even seeing how he spread her obscenely wide, it was almost incomprehensible how he managed to fit inside her. Yet, her body welcomed him more easily every time; he satisfied an ache he created, offering the relief only a mate could provide.

"Show me your pretty breasts," he rumbled, hips beginning to move.

Plumping each in her hands, she cupped the undersides. They bounced against her palms as he began to move in earnest, and he didn't have to prompt her to thumb and pinch her pouting nipples.

That earned her a purr of approval. "Just like that, show me."

Pleasure cascaded through her in a surge of bright bursts, her body oversensitive already. The cool morning air along her skin, the soft give of the pillow under her head, the slide of the silky sheets at her back, every sensation combined with the pinch of her fingers and the excruciating bliss of his cock filling her to overwhelm her in the best way. Every scent, every touch was heightened—it was like being drunk, but on him.

From his place knelt at the center of the bed, he levered her by the hips, pulling her down to meet his increasingly brutal thrusts. His pace quickened, every stroke leaving her begging for another—yet, she hadn't the time to get the words out, for he was there again, pushing inside, hitting every nerve and sensitive spot inside her.

So deep, so full, it didn't take her long to climb her peak. After days of this, she was primed to take him and his pleasure. Hers came quickly, as though at his command rather than hers. He could conjure it with just a few words and touches, his own kind of magic.

"Let me see you, *skala*. Come for me."

She knew better than to deny him—or herself.

Her body clenched, gripping him tight as the pressure in her low belly unspooled. Throwing her head back on the pillow, Ravenna gasped, body rolling through an exquisite orgasm.

Some of their lovemaking was fierce, brutal. Other times, he was all gentleness and prolonged gratification. This climax bubbled and fizzed in her blood, a sweet indulgence that was as honeyed as it was rich. The pleasure sparkled more brilliantly than all the jewels she'd worn the other night, and as she felt her *azai* fill her with his own orgasm, she stared up at him in awe. He took up her sight, blocking out the light. Her world was only him.

When he'd wrung every bit of pleasure he could from her, he fell to his hands, claiming her mouth in a searing kiss. Purring, he eventually slumped to his side, taking her with him. With a hand behind her knee, he lifted her leg to rest over his hip, keeping him snuggly inside her.

Ravenna sighed happily. "Good morning, my king."

"Good morning, sprite." Smiling, he claimed another kiss. And another. Then another, and soon enough, they were kissing in earnest, her hands buried in his mane, his hands running up and down her back.

His cock had just begun to throb inside her again when a heavy knocking came at the door to their quarters.

Grumbling, Vallek pulled back just enough to whisper, "Ignore them and they might go away."

His hopes were immediately quashed when the sound of the door opening greeted them. It didn't sound as though anyone entered, merely poked their head inside.

"Are you both decent?" came Eydis's voice.

"If it's not food, then no!"

"It's your loving older sister, whom you respect and adore very much!"

Vallek snorted. "I haven't such a sister."

After the swish of robes, the door closed behind an apparently determined Eydis. "Either you come out with clothes on or I come in and we all suffer the consequences."

Ravenna giggled while Vallek rolled his eyes.

"It *has* been three days," she reminded him gently.

"Who is king of this mountain?" he grumbled.

With a few more kisses in apology, they finally rose from their bed. Hastily cleaned and clothed, they joined Eydis in the den.

"Good to see you both," she teased, a fond smile adorning her lips. "I bring congratulations from the family and most of the court."

"Which could've been a note under the door."

Ravenna elbowed her grumpy *azai*.

Eydis merely rolled her eyes. "Breakfast is coming soon, so spare me the worst of your growling until you've eaten."

"If you didn't bring breakfast, what did you come with?"

"News, of course." With a flourish of her robes, she took her usual seat, announcing that this wouldn't be a quick visit.

Vallek sighed mightily, slumping into his own customary place and pulling Ravenna down with him onto his lap. She easily found a comfortable position as he laced his fingers together at her hip. It was effortless, the way they came together, folding their bodies to align. It actually made Eydis smile.

"While I respect the desire to sequester away until the bond is finished with you, I need you both to show your faces."

"The people understand what new mates do," Vallek said.

"Yes, but you aren't just anyone. While there's generally been good feelings toward your announcement, there are still whispers abounding throughout the city."

"What do they say?" asked Ravenna, although she could guess.

"They wonder if this is a true mating or a stunt of some sort. They speculate who this mysterious half-fae woman is, where she came from. And my favorite, whether she's enchanted the king." Eydis snorted. "That's a favorite in the pubs, too. The speculation is quite breathtaking."

"And so we should . . . do what? To prove it to them," Ravenna said.

The orcess smiled, although it was one of her more unnerving smiles, the one that made Ravenna think she already had many plots and schemes in mind.

"You will charm them. You will go out and be visible and let the people see you. Hold hands, kiss, whatever feels right."

"This is how she won Hilde, you know," Vallek told Ravenna gravely, "with all the romance."

"I've got more romance in my little finger than you do in your whole body," Eydis said breezily. "I just save it for when it counts."

Ravenna shared a look with her mate, biting her lips to hold in her giggle.

"They just need you to be present," Eydis insisted. "The enemy of curiosity is banality—make the reality of your mating commonplace. Begin your normal duties again, and the people will quickly settle."

It was a simple enough plan, even if it did incite those riotous butterflies in Ravenna's stomach again. *Normal duties* were still an uncharted realm for her.

"Very well," Vallek sighed. "We'll greet the court today, feast in the basilica, and hold open grievances tomorrow. I will hold a council meeting with the ministers the day after, which Ravenna will attend. See that a chair is placed for her."

"Consider it done."

"In exchange—" Vallek grinned evilly at his sister "—I want you to begin planning the wedding. I want it to be a lavish affair, Eydis. Something to remember. Every chieftain and paladin is required to attend."

His sister looked less than pleased. "That will take time, *breddah*. I'll of course begin planning, but it may be wiser to look to—"

"No, we start now. Ravenna will be queen, with a crown and throne. She will have the authority to issue edicts. But until we are officially wed, there will be lingering doubts."

Eydis threw up her hands. "Fine! I'll make a list of required guests. In the meantime—" she pointed toward the archway that led down to the baths "—clean yourselves up. Everyone already knows what you've been doing."

That was how Vallek found himself walking with his mate out onto the citadel's ramparts, waving for the gathered crowd. He didn't know how Eydis had rallied so many to see them on such short notice, but thousands of happy, cheering orc-kin gathered in the streets below, waving burgundy banners and throwing *vinya* petals.

It filled his heart with pride to see his people, out in vast numbers to cry their support. He took just as much pleasure in presenting his beautiful faeling to them. The crowd's cheers grew louder as she stepped from the protection of his side, letting the late-morning light hit her.

Ravenna dazzled, gleaming and sparkling from head to toe. Today's concoction by Hilde was a plum-colored gown, with more flow and drape than the last, embroidered with *vinya* blooms. It emphasized the lilac hue of her skin, once again covered in that cream that gave her the iridescence of an opal just pulled from the ground.

When she raised her hand to wave, the gathered orc-kin gasped and sighed, no doubt in awe of her beauty. A smile touched her lips to feel the tide of well-wishes surging past the curtain wall. The nerves from a few moments before, when he'd whispered reassurances, eased from her tense shoulders.

A purr building in his chest, Vallek stepped up beside his queen, taking her by the waist to tuck into his side and raising his other arm to wave. The cheers redoubled, the air scented with sweet blooms and happiness.

"They love you," Ravenna said.

"They do, and I'm grateful for it. They will come to love you, too."

She didn't agree, but she also didn't deny it, either. She would see. Just give her a little time, and Vallek knew she would win over the people of Balmirra—and then every orc throughout the kingdom. He couldn't wait to show her off to other courts, too; the stratified, patriarchal Pyrrossi would be apoplectic.

He meant to name Ravenna as lady commander of Balmirra once she had a few more administrative duties to cut her fangs on, such as attending council meetings with him and overseeing negotiations with the eastern tribesmen. He'd no doubt that once she found her footing, she would fly.

"My good people," Vallek boomed across the city, "it is my greatest pleasure to introduce to you, your queen. Ravenna Broch!"

Wild clapping followed his declaration, and more flowers were flung into the air. Hundreds of kin stomped their feet in celebration, a deafening clamor that shook the mountain.

Vallek kept his speech short and similar to what he'd told the court. They cheered and clapped at the right moments, but everyone was far more interested to see what the new queen would say.

When Vallek applied gentle pressure to the small of her back, alerting her it was time, Ravenna peeked up at him. He nodded, offering his silent support.

Gathering a big breath in her chest, Ravenna said, "Thank you for your warm reception. I vow to be a queen worthy of you—and your noble king."

It was just enough, the crowd falling into fits of applause. They whooped and shouted their approval when Vallek bent to gently kiss her. Ravenna cupped his face in her little hand, playing her part perfectly.

"Just a little more," he whispered against her lips before deepening his kiss.

His affection went on a little long, perhaps, but he was hardly past a rut and his mate was temptation personified. He'd had her naked and beneath him, thrusting inside her warm body just that morning, but something about standing there with her, hidden beneath their finery, thousands of eyes upon them, had him lusting all the more for her.

He released her finally with more than a little reluctance, although he kept her hand as they began walking along the wall again. It took them the better part of an hour to make it round the outer circumference of the citadel's wall, stopping every few paces to wave and thank the people.

By the time they finally took the winding stairwell within the eastern tower back down into the inner courtyard, the noonday sun hung high over the city. They emerged from the gatehouse to yet more applause, this time from a smaller crowd of the city's preeminent denizens—orcs that represented the city elders, the various mining outfits, all the craft guilds, merchant unions, representatives from the hospitals, scholariums, and orphanages, and many more.

Ravenna met each with an open, charming manner. She stood beside him, receiving each orc's well-wishes and taking pains to ask names and roles. She expressed interest in everything, promising to visit this trade hall and that hospital.

Watching her, seeing how the city's denizens went away from their meeting her with nods and smiles, only grew his pride. Enough that it soothed his otherwise jealous beast, which hadn't stopped pacing agitatedly inside him when he saw just how many others looked upon her.

He knew this would be the reality of their mating—if she was to be his queen and stand beside him, it meant sharing her. Perhaps it would get easier in time; although, he thought he could be forgiven for the niggle of jealousy he harbored, what with their bond still solidifying.

Yes, after this, the thing to do would be to get her straight back in bed.

That tempting thought saw him through that long afternoon. He and Ravenna did as Eydis wanted, standing prettily for others to admire, accepting their well-wishes, and listening to their suggestions and concerns. It was one of the more grueling activities a chieftain or king could do, not unlike running a political gauntlet, but with his lovely mate beside him, it wasn't so bad.

It was when the crowd of denizens had begun to thin that Vallek started trying to catch Eydis's eye. Ravenna carried herself bravely, but she was flagging. It was time for a late luncheon and to get her out of the afternoon sun.

He'd just begun to lead her through the pockets of kin, all carrying complimentary goblets of wine or mead, when Mattias wove his way through the crowd to intercept them.

Bowing, he said quietly, "My king, my queen, there's something that needs your attention."

Vallek exchanged looks with Ravenna. His serious captain wouldn't draw them away from such an important function for nothing, and so they followed him from the throngs into a quieter corner of the courtyard. It was at least shadier here, the coolness a welcome relief.

Waiting for them were a handful of warriors, dusty and sweaty from the road. The style of gorget hanging round their necks identified them as soldiers who patrolled the borders. It was a fairly new practice, each contingent leaving a fortnight after the other so that aid was never far behind if needed. When a contingent returned, they rested for a fortnight before heading out again.

These warriors looked fresh from the road, their faces lined in grime and concern. The three of them, all with the rank of captain, bowed to him and Ravenna.

"My king," said one, "and queen," he added quickly, "we found these on a group of Pyrrossi soldiers on the southern border."

Dread gripped Vallek's innards in a cold fist, and before another warrior tipped a burlap sack upside down, he knew what would spill forth.

A half-dozen sets of manacles clattered to the cobblestones.

Ravenna's nails dug into his forearm, and he heard her sharp inhale.

With everything that had happened since, the manacles that Fulk Stone-Skin had handed over had escaped Vallek's attention. He'd known investigations would need to be carried out, but with even more of these strange manacles staring up at him now, that became a priority.

Just as the ones in the Stone-Skin camp had, these manacles gleamed dully in the late-afternoon light. At first glance, there was nothing remarkable about them. Still, the longer he looked, an eerie sense of menace emanated from the metal—yet, he had the strange desire to touch them.

Before he could stop her, Ravenna knelt to do just that. She touched the chain of one with her fingertips, and her body immediately shuddered and her eyes went blank.

Vallek lifted her back up by the elbow, drawing her protectively into his side. He watched with worry as she remained dazed. *A vision.*

The warriors shifted from foot to foot nervously, glancing between him and Ravenna.

It was long moments before she came back to him, longer than he'd ever witnessed her visions taking. He ran his hand up and down her back, soothing himself as much as her.

Ravenna's look was troubled when she finally came back to him, creases underscoring her eyes.

"They're definitely spelled," she confirmed.

Fuck.

26

—arms spread wide—manacles at either wrist—a citadel gone to ruins—apple blossom petals crushed underfoot—blood spilled down Vallek's chest—

Ravenna's skin was cold and clammy when she came back to herself in the middle of the corridor.

Damn. It was the third time in as many days that she'd had that same vision. Ever since touching those strange manacles, the same series of images had assailed her.

"My queen?" One of her six personal guards stepped forward, his concern pulling the corners of his mouth down past his tusks.

It was still so strange having six hulking warriors shadow her every move outside of the quarters she shared with Vallek. It was hard to overcome the sense that she was being followed—because she was. Her father had taught her to be wary, to constantly check over her shoulder. For their size, her guards were all light-footed and discreet, yet old habits clung to her nearly as well as the orcs did.

These visions—or, more accurately, this *one* vision, over and over—had rattled her.

She couldn't get the image of Vallek in chains, beaten and bloodied, out of her mind. It unnerved her so much, she hadn't admitted to him what she'd seen, for fear that saying it aloud would make it all the more possible.

Her visions always came true, one way or another. She knew that. But Ravenna refused to accept this one.

Mouth gone dry, she had to wet her lips to reply, "I'm all right. Just a vision." She attempted to smile, to alleviate their concern, but this only seemed to alarm them more.

Ravenna resumed walking, thinking the best thing for them all was to continue on.

She was due to attend her first council meeting with Vallek, and she didn't want to be late.

As they walked, Ravenna pressed the heel of her palm into her stomach, willing her nerves to settle. She'd hardly slept the previous night, kept awake by all the ways she could embarrass herself and Vallek. She knew the ministers' names and faces but little about their natures; they were all eminent orcs, most of them paladins, many elders. They were meant to be a moderating voice for the chieftain or monarch, and even Vallek admitted he didn't know how favorably they would look upon Ravenna.

The visions and her nerves meant that she was in no mood to be stopped on her way.

Nevertheless, when Lady Silvia, at the head of her own group of retainers and guards, rounded the next corner, Ravenna found herself stopped.

Despite her forbidding glare and not acknowledging Lady Silvia's half-hearted nod of greeting, the orcess put herself bodily in Ravenna's way. Stopping short, Ravenna lifted her chin and her glare up to meet the orcess's saccharine smile.

"Good day," said Lady Silvia.

"Good day."

"You seem to be in quite the rush," Silvia noted. "No doubt on royal business." Her retinue tittered behind her, as if the idea of Ravenna attending to important matters was laughable.

"I am indeed. If you would move—"

The orcess did, sidestepping Ravenna to run a curious finger down her shoulder. With her back partly exposed by the swooping neckline of her gown, Ravenna felt the dulled point of Silvia's claw trail along her skin.

"It's too much to believe that you manage to hide those wings away. We've been debating since the king announced your existence whether it was a trick or not. Settle a bet, would you?"

Ravenna felt her guards move in closer, knew that with one word, they would surround her, cutting off Silvia's loathsome touch. If she ordered it, they might even detain or harm the orcess on Ravenna's command. It was probably a bit evil to take pleasure in that knowledge, that she could have Lady Silvia thrown from the nearest window with a mere wave of her hand, but Ravenna withheld her baser inclinations.

For now, at least.

Besides, she couldn't be seen as weak and reliant on her guards to defend her.

She motioned for the guards to halt, and they did, although she could still sense their concern pressing against her back.

"My wings are real, and they're certainly not for you."

Lady Silvia blinked. "I beg your pardon?"

"I am your queen, not a pet monkey to poke and prod."

The orcess smiled maliciously. "And yet you are hardly bigger than one."

Ravenna rolled her eyes. If Lady Silvia would resort to teasing her size, then Ravenna would play just as dirty. She had places to be.

Her magic wrapped round the orcess's wrist. "You don't touch me." With a forceful yank, she jerked Silvia down by the hand. Forced to her knee, Silvia struggled to pull her hand up from where it was mashed to the flagstones. Her retinue gasped and whispered, looking amongst themselves to find if anyone knew what to do.

Silvia sputtered, eyes gone wide in horror as she struggled. "You're mad!"

"I'm your queen," Ravenna corrected, taking the opportunity to smile maliciously herself. "Chosen by your king. He had every opportunity, every chance to choose you, Silvia. Even just to take you to bed. And he didn't."

The orcess stopped struggling long enough for a dawning anger to overtake her face. "You dare—"

"When he first saw my true face, he threw me over his shoulder and claimed me. *I* am his choice, Silvia. You will respect it, or I will tell you in great detail everything in your life that will come to pass." The orcess paled to a sickly green, and Ravenna nodded. "No surprises, no questions, just the dreadful knowledge of what's to come and being unable to stop it. It's a horrible fate, Lady Silvia. Don't bring it upon yourself."

Without giving her the chance to respond, Ravenna stepped around the orcess, continuing down the corridor. The sound of Silvia struggling to stand and her retinue arguing amongst themselves followed her, and it wasn't until she rounded the corner that she released her magic.

Ravenna didn't miss the quiet huff of amusement and twitching grins from her guards, and while she wanted to take pleasure in the little victory, it ended up feeling as cheap as Silvia's accusation of false wings. Compared to the unsettling vision she kept having, the orcess hardly mattered at all.

Ravenna continued her path down the corridor, her worries dogging her steps. *What do they mean?* She'd never let herself ponder her visions too much—looking at them too closely yielded no more answers. They would come to pass, one way or another, whether she wished it or not. Yet, these past few days, it was difficult not to worry herself sick over this particular vision.

She'd never seen something like it, her own *azai* in danger. Ravenna refused to stand for it—but without more information, she didn't know how to thwart it. She had to keep him safe—but how?

After the interlude in the corridor, it was both a relief and surprise for Ravenna to find that the council had little interest in questioning Vallek on his choice of mate and queen. Whether it was because they liked and supported Vallek or were already accustomed to his unprecedented decisions, she couldn't say.

Several of the ministers, including those for tax and mining, were especially quiet, offering lukewarm congratulations at best. Ravenna would accept that over outright hostility any day. Their reticence was something to note and tackle later—which was what she conveyed and agreed to in a quick, silent conversation of looks between her, Vallek, and Eydis.

All sat round an oblong table; a high-backed chair had been added for Ravenna. Vallek's seat had been slightly shifted to the left, creating room for her close to the head of the table. She sat quietly in her chair, feet dangling off the ground thanks to the seat cushion. Although she was still far shorter than everyone else gathered, she could at least comfortably lay her arms on the tabletop without looking like a child.

Not that she'd dare touch the tabletop. Not with those manacles laid at the center.

After a few introductory words about Ravenna and receiving the ministers' congratulations, Vallek opened the meeting—beginning with the most important matter.

Between those brought in by the patrol and those taken from the Stone-Skin camp, over a dozen spelled manacles sat there. Although benign looking enough, an aura of malevolence seeped from the iron. Ravenna hated even looking at them, fearing it would bring on another vision, worse than the one that already plagued her.

Rising from his seat, the scholar minister bowed to Vallek. Head of the many learned, scholarly orc-kin of Balmirra, the scholar minister oversaw the largest library and records archive in the city, as well as the administration of the three scholariums. Vallek had charged him with investigating the manacles, both in the records and scientifically.

Tall even for an orc, the scholar minister kept his mane cut short and his ears and tusks capped. Silver streaked his mane, and his expression was grave as he said, "My king, my queen, further study will be required, particularly in the archives, as nothing mentioning such items has yet been discovered. However, we did test the manacles' function and properties." The scholar nodded at the pile of manacles. "From what we can deduce, they are meant to negate the magic of the wearer."

An uneasy rumble went through the council, and Ravenna felt more than a few pairs of eyes land on her.

Negate magic . . .

The thought made her queasy.

Magic was inherent to all folk except humans. Although fae were the only folk left who could harness it, magic was what gave orcs their strength, sirens their songs, harpies their flight, and manticores and dragons their bestial forms. To strip them of such an integral, intrinsic part of themselves . . .

Who would create such a thing?

"The humans are getting devious," grumbled the trade minister.

"They couldn't have done it on their own," said Vallek. A glance at her *azai* saw him wearing one of the most terrifying expressions she'd ever seen. If he could set fire to those manacles with his gaze, they'd be congealed slag by now.

"Twice now, Pyrrossi soldiers were found with these irons," argued the minister of coin.

"Who would be fool enough to help them?" asked the minister of beasts.

Amaranthe. That hideous hag was conniving enough. She likely thought that even with such a weapon, the humans were still no match for the fae and so it was shrewd to send the Pyrrossi off to weaken other folk for her. Except, Ravenna didn't know if she could believe Amaranthe would ever agree to work with humans—even in something that might benefit the faelands.

There was Araxos, the *anax* of the Droplets. Although he'd seized power over ten years ago, he was still fighting vicious rebellions against his numerous half-siblings. He was known to be as cunning as he was cruel, but with his attention turned toward his islands and own family, few other folk had had much to do with the dragons since his father reigned.

And, of course, there was every likelihood that a rogue actor could have colluded with the Pyrrossi. Their emperor had a far reach and deep coffers, more than enough to sway any mercenary looking to make a new life—or escape the notoriously brutal dungeon complex beneath the palace at Lycea.

Really, there were almost too many suspects.

Even more worrying was what the Pyrrossi meant to do with these irons. Given their merciless conquest of the human territories to the south, as well as the homelands of the manticores along the Irynian Delta, and their current incursions along orcish borders, it wasn't hard to guess.

Leveling his piercing gaze on Eydis, Vallek said, "I want our spies to find who the Pyrrossi are working with." To the borders minister, he ordered, "Send out messengers to every patrol currently out. I want all orc-kin looking for any more irons."

"What shall we do with these?" asked the grains minister, nodding at the manacles.

"Melt them down," the tax minister growled. "Destroy them."

"No."

Everyone looked up at Ravenna, perhaps surprised to finally hear her speak.

The tax minister scoffed. "I'd think you'd want them destroyed most of all, my queen."

"I don't like them, it's true. I shudder just looking at them. But they could be useful." Nodding at the scholar minister, she said, "We must study them more to figure out how they were made."

The scholar nodded, a little relieved if she wasn't mistaken. No doubt he and his colleagues wished to investigate the strange irons more.

"Something so dangerous should be destroyed," the mining minister argued.

"We don't know what will happen to the entrapped magic if they're thrown into the forge," Ravenna reasoned. "And, from what we know, it was common soldiers who had these irons. That would imply they are plentiful enough to issue down the ranks."

Several ministers lifted their brows, apparently not having considered this.

Reaching to lay his hand over hers, folded tightly in her lap, Vallek offered his quiet support. "They are more useful to us intact. For now, at least," he said. "Study what we have. Confiscate the rest. Hunt down whoever's doing this."

It was a solid plan, one that had everyone eventually nodding in agreement.

Still, Ravenna unclenched her fingers to hold onto Vallek's hand. The reassuring warmth of his fingers got her through the rest of the meeting, as her attention kept straying to the manacles.

She sensed their malice, and yet, it was as though they commanded their own sort of orbit, luring her in. It was a strange sort of trap, the irons neither aesthetic nor valuable, yet the power of the magic imbued within them was enough to draw one in.

If she held Vallek's hand, she couldn't reach across to touch one.

She didn't *want* to touch them, not really. She didn't want another vision. Not when she wanted so desperately to forget the last one.

And yet, as surely as a siren's song, the manacles echoed in her mind. They were important somehow, an enigma sent to tempt and entrap. For now, all she could do was hold onto her *azai*. She needed more answers, for she refused to allow her vision to come to pass.

27

—tears fell from white lashes—arms spread wide—blood dripping beneath the irons—saltwater burned her eyes—

Ravenna plunged through the dark corridor, the walls around her contracting but the hall going on and on. There was only one way, forward, and she ran as fast as she could, her wings beating her back to give her more speed. Run, urged her father's voice, run, my raven. She ran and ran, yet the door that sat ajar at the end of the corridor never came nearer—

—a throne of white oak, singed at the top—waves churning and battering the rocks below—They are with you, Crow. Always—

Throwing herself at the door, Ravenna tumbled through into the cozy parlor of her mother's cottage. The faint sound of waves crashed in the distance, and gray light eked in through the windows, illuminating Aine where she sat on the deep, cushioned window seat.

"Maman," Ravenna choked on the word.

—Your father was right—unicorns screamed, their horns tipped in blood—don't, sprite—there are no dreams in the deep sleep—then why do I see—

Crumpling before her mother, Ravenna's face was wet with tears when

Aine leaned down to gently cup her cheek. Her mother's smile was sweet but distorted, not quite right, as though Ravenna couldn't quite remember her exact appearance.

"My love, why have you abandoned us?"

Ravenna's heart lurched. "I haven't! Maman, I swear—"

"But you have. Your father and I gave our lives for yours. Will you not avenge us?"

"I will! I promise!"

—but don't you see, it's all folly—throwing your life away—ask me as a queen would—saltwater burned her eyes—

Ravenna gasped, forcing herself awake.

The night was quiet and still, a stark juxtaposition to her racing heart. When she shifted her head on the pillow, her hair stuck to her neck with cold sweat.

She blinked through the darkness and haze, her stomach threatening revolt. Fates, her dreams had never bled into visions like that. She couldn't discern what was imagined and what was real, what was prophecy and what was fear.

Days of that one vision, of her worries over the manacles and their strange pull, had upended her mind's peace. They were never far from her thoughts, and although she threw herself into any and all distractions—working with carpenters to design her throne, meeting with the eastern tribesmen to begin negotiations, riding Vallek's thick cock until her body gave out—they always found her.

Like touching the tip of the tongue to a sore tooth, she couldn't help it. The dread, although unpleasant, was easy to sink into.

Despite the heat emanating from her sleeping *azai* at her back, a shiver ran down her spine. The blankets were suddenly too much, the air in the bedchamber too stuffy.

Using her magic, she gently lifted Vallek's heavy arm just enough to roll out from under its weight. She kept it gently suspended there, not wanting to wake him.

He would ask her what troubled her. He would try to comfort her.

Either might break her then; she couldn't bear the thought of his gentleness. Not with the phantom of her mother's voice echoing in her ear.

As she silently slid her hands through the arm slits of her blue cloak, she slowly lowered his arm back to the bed. After a moment to confirm he wouldn't wake, Ravenna tip-toed from the chamber and down the hall.

There was the den, the baths, but she sought refuge in none of their rooms. Instead, as quietly as she could, she slipped from their quarters entirely, the silent eyes of the night guards following her.

The flagstones were cold beneath her bare feet, but Ravenna hardly cared. Her heart raced, urging her faster. She shivered at the cold night air against her clammy skin, her dampened hair sticking to her back and wing bundles.

By the time she found her way out to the curtain wall, she was almost sure she'd be sick.

Gulping fresh air, Ravenna clung to a stone crenellation, the night breeze biting. Autumn was coming, a telling chill caught in the breeze, but Ravenna couldn't bear to go back inside. Not to her sleeping mate, who loved her, who bent a kingdom to his will for her.

Fates, how could she not love him for it? Everything he'd done, everything he was . . .

Ravenna loved her mate, so deeply it hurt. And that was terrifying.

She wasn't supposed to love him—not when it made everything far more painful. How could she love him, be his mate, be his queen—when it meant giving up her vengeance? The vision of her mother haunted her, the distorted face a ghoulish reminder of her vow.

Playing at being his queen and mate, she'd let herself stray from what she'd vowed to do. Her parents' sacrifice wouldn't be in vain—Amaranthe had to fall.

But that, too, was terrifying. How could she seek her revenge—when it meant giving him up, or worse, endangering him? She couldn't. To forsake him, their bond, now would be akin to ripping out her own heart.

Vallek would never allow her to march into the faelands to confront Amaranthe alone. He would forbid her from going—or march beside her. Ravenna couldn't stomach the thought of something happening to him now. His people needed him. She needed him to live.

Under the cold moon, there was no hope, no way forward. How could she walk two paths?

Her mind too full, she wrapped her arms around herself and wandered further out along the rampart.

Maman, maman, her heart cried. *You abandoned me first.*

Vallek wasn't sure what awoke him in the middle of the night, only that he lay alone in their bed. His senses roused to alertness within a single blink, and he reached across the bed to feel how her place had almost gone cold.

"Ravenna?" he called softly.

Nothing.

Throwing back the blankets, Vallek went searching for her, calling Ravenna's name but finding her nowhere. Not even down in the baths.

Unease gathered in the pit of his stomach, and he quickly threw on a loose pair of linen breeches.

Opening the door to his quarters revealed one of the two guards missing. The remaining one bowed her head.

"Where is she?" Vallek asked.

"If you will follow me . . ."

The guard led him down the stairwell and past several turns before pointing him on to another night watch. One after another, they pointed his way, leading him swiftly out to the ramparts of the curtain wall.

The wind bit at his exposed chest as he stepped out into the night. Another guard nodded silently before pointing further along the wall. There, her hair streaking behind her like a banner, stood his mate.

His heart ached to see how little she looked against the thick crenellations of the rampart. His beast paced uneasily inside him, sensing something was wrong. She'd never left their bed before.

His unease only grew as he made his way to her. She'd been troubled of late. Assailed by visions that she wouldn't explain, the manacles especially had upset her. Although she did her best to hide her worries, Vallek wasn't blind to the dark circles growing beneath her eyes.

He'd thought perhaps it was from all the new burdens placed upon her narrow shoulders. There was far more to being queen than glittering gowns, and she'd met it all bravely, yet he couldn't fault anyone for buckling under the strain. He well remembered his first days upon the throne, how he'd spent sleepless nights crushed by the weight of his decisions.

Guilt tugged at his throat. He'd asked so much of her in so little time. In just a few days, with just a few words, he'd changed her reality. Vallek regretted none of it, he would have her beside him, but as he approached her there on the curtain wall, he couldn't help his worry that she'd been pushed too far.

She had to sense him; he came to a halt only a breath away. Yet, her eyes remained fixed on the dark horizon, her black hair rippling around her in soft waves. Her arms were clutched round her torso, but far tighter than just for warmth; it was as though she needed to hold onto herself, to wrap herself up to keep steady.

Vallek considered his words carefully, tossing several platitudes aside. Finally, he settled on asking so, so gently, "Why are you out here, love?"

It took her a while to answer, so long, he wasn't sure she would.

Eventually, she murmured, "Bad dreams."

"Visions?" The idea that she'd had a vision worrying enough to send her fleeing out into the cold had dread coiling in his gut.

"Some of them."

The vague answer came through stiff lips. She was determined to be a mystic it seemed, her attention still far away.

Easing a little closer, Vallek chanced setting his hand to the small of her back. She was cool to the touch, her cloak unbound and loose about her shoulders.

His beast gnashed its teeth, anxious to comfort her, to make it all better. He didn't even know what was wrong, but his overwhelming instinct was to fix whatever it was that troubled her so.

If he could crush whatever brought that haunted look to her eye with his fists, eviscerate it with Hormhím, or squash it beneath his boot, he would. However, as with many things about his often enigmatic faeling mate, he feared her troubles weren't something to be smashed or pummeled or pulverized.

Politics had taught him that problems that could be solved with brute force were far easier to handle. The strength of his arm hadn't been in question since he was a youngling. Matters of the mind and heart, though—those took far more finesse and fortitude.

He counted himself a decent politician—nothing to Eydis, of course—but as he stood on that curtain wall, a cold wind at his back, Vallek doubted himself. It wasn't something he'd had the luxury of doing in years. Yet in a moment so critical, when he sensed his next steps would be paramount, the ground he stood upon seemed shaky.

There was a brittleness to her, fragile as glass. He feared the wrong words, the wrong move, would cause a break.

He couldn't do nothing, though.

He saw her suffering and had to make it go away, however much he could.

"Tell me how to help you, love," he begged.

A tear slid down her pale cheek, but she didn't move to wipe it away. Everything inside him told Vallek to gather her close, to hide her with his bigger body from the evils of the world. He could protect her, keep her safe. His hand itched to wipe the tears for her, but he dared not move.

"I see their faces, and I—I know I've failed them," she whispered.

Suddenly, she turned her head to look at him, the movement so unexpected, his stomach dropped. Moonlight glittered in her glassy eyes, and the breath hissed out of his lungs to see how close to the brink she stood. Not just on that wall with him, but within her own mind.

"Ravenna," he groaned her name, "please." He didn't know what he asked for exactly, only that he begged for her.

Those haunting eyes of hers were strangely cold as she told him, "My parents died for me. To keep me safe. I saw them in my dream."

Vallek nodded slowly. He'd guessed something tragic in her past; she never spoke of living family. The few things she'd said were of a childhood spent hidden away with her human mother—she hardly ever spoke of her fae father.

It was a morsel of information that left Vallek hungry for more. That was just like her, to reveal a little but keep back the most. He sensed far more to the story, but again, he dared not push.

"Such a sacrifice would leave its mark on anyone," he told her gently. His own parents had died fairly young, his father in battle, in service to Mordis in one of his petty feuds, and his mother just a year after. Already weakened from the loss of her mate, his mother was easy prey for the sweating sickness that swept across Balmirra. Were it not for Eydis holding the remains of their family together, fate would have been far less kind to Vallek.

His parents' deaths had felt senseless, useless. As an angry youth, he'd often lashed out in his pain. How could he swallow his grief and loss when it was so meaningless. His father had been sent to his death for nothing, eventually taking his mate with him and leaving his younglings orphans.

That had left its own kind of scar, although he knew it to be different from the one his mate clearly bore. From just her few words, her parents seemed to have died for completely the opposite. Their deaths meant something. *Sacrifice.*

As the cold wind stung his cheek, Vallek realized what a burden such deaths would be.

Lips drawn thin, Ravenna shook her head. "They died for me. For *nothing.*"

"No," he breathed. "They died protecting what they loved most. It is an honorable death."

More tears spilled from her eyes in earnest now, alarming Vallek. Gods, he was making a mess of this.

"I didn't want their deaths," she said through bared teeth. "I wanted them to live."

"I'm sure, love. Such a choice wouldn't have been easy. But you mattered enough to them for it to be worth the sacrifice."

"But I'm not," she whispered, breaking his heart. "I'm *not.*"

"You *are,*" he growled, voice gruffer than he meant it to be. "You are worth every sacrifice. I would give my life for yours, love. Happily."

It was the wrong thing to say.

Her eyes grew wild. A horrified gasp split her mouth wide, and she turned to clutch at his forearms, her nails digging into his skin.

"You *won't.* Promise me you won't!"

Her demand scored his soul, ripping across his very being like the sharpest of claws. He couldn't promise her that, for it went against everything he was, everything he felt for her.

"*Vallek—*"

"I can't promise you, for I know it to be true. I would die for you, sprite. It would be my honor."

A wail escaped her lips, a wordless sound of anguish that pierced his heart and resolve. Tears streamed down her face, and when her arms slumped to hang limply at her sides, Vallek put aside his stubbornness.

There was no need to argue.

He didn't need to die for her tonight. He'd much rather live for her—and give her what comfort he could.

When he stepped closer to take her into his arms, she threw herself against his chest. Burying her face between his pectorals, her sobs came hard and merciless, wracking her small frame. Vallek wrapped his arms around her, his soul finding a little peace to have her where she belonged, even as she wetted his skin with her tears.

He didn't know what was wrong, but he stood in silence anyway, purring a soothing cadence.

Her cries were broken only by sobs of, "You can't, you can't." Vallek held his tongue, not wishing to upset her more.

Sheltering her from the wind, he nuzzled her hair as he purred. Vallek held her for long moments, willing her to take his strength, his assurance. Anything at all she needed, he would give. She had but to ask.

"I love you, sprite," he murmured at her temple. "That is why I would lay down my life for yours. Your parents loved you, too, I'm sure. You are alive and well, and so you cannot have failed them."

"I saw you—" she choked on a sob "—I *saw you*—in chains."

His blood ran cold at her garbled words, be he didn't dare let on, didn't let his purr grow into a growl nor immediately deny that he, Vallek Far-Sight, would never be held in irons.

Somehow, he held her even tighter. Gods, were some of these tears for him?

He wouldn't allow it.

"In your vision, was I dead?"

"N-no . . ."

"Then don't waste your tears on me, love. No chains can hold me."

It was too much to hope that his confidence and poor attempt at humor would dry her tears, of course. Still, he grimaced when her sobs redoubled, shaking her body more than his purrs shook his.

"I can't bear it," she whispered. "I can't let you die for me, too."

"I'm hard to kill," he promised, "and I've far too much to live for. A kingdom to oversee. A mate to keep out of mischief."

She sniffled against his chest, a far better sound than a sob. Cradling the back of her head in his hand, keeping her secure to him, he rocked them gently.

"I swear to you, before I do any dying, I will live a long, happy life for you." He'd accept nothing less than decades with his fierce faeling. He meant to see this kingdom they stood at the creation of flourish. When it was time to leave it all behind for the afterworld, he'd do so old, fat, and happy. With her at his side.

She said nothing to that, but her sobs did seem to be reaching their end. He couldn't help the inkling he had that, as much as her parents and her vision were on her mind, so too was whatever secret scheme she kept from him. It was clear that her own fears and burdens had sent her fleeing out into the night. So much weighed on her mind . . . yet she still wouldn't tell him.

His frustration could wait, though. As could her answers. He'd waited this long for them; he could wait a little longer yet.

Tonight, he would hold her. Tonight, he would gain a little more of her trust.

Until he had her full trust, Vallek would shelter her from the cold and dry her tears. It was a mate's due, after all, to have the bad days with the good. Being king meant not only having a beautiful queen on his arm but carrying his queen when she needed succor.

"Come inside," he gently pressed.

She offered only a single nod, but Vallek took his chance. Sweeping her up off the cold stones, he held her high on his chest and turned to head back into the citadel.

Ravenna drew her arms around his neck, burying her face in the crook there.

That's it, sprite. I have you.

He swiftly carried her inside, out of the wind, and back to the quiet safety of their bed. The watchful eyes of the guards followed them, their heads bowing to their king and queen as he and Ravenna passed.

It was a relief to enclose her away with him in their quarters. Placing her in the bed, he climbed in right behind her, throwing the blankets over them, even their heads.

In the warm cocoon, she curled herself into his front, her head tucked under his chin.

Vallek forwent words, keeping to a soft, steady purr. Arms secured around his mate again, he would keep watch over her tonight. No more visions, no more tears—he would see to that.

<h1 style="text-align:center">28</h1>

Sleep eluded Vallek that night and for much of the three nights afterwards. He stayed awake into the longest, darkest hours, watching over his sleeping mate to ensure that should a nightmare find her again, he was there to banish it.

It was a small price to pay for the wellbeing of his queen, although he wasn't convinced it actually helped her much. His frustration mounted alongside his exhaustion as the days passed, but he wasn't to be defeated.

Although he was adamant she take time to rest and get her mind straight, Ravenna refused. She claimed she liked the distraction, and Vallek was loath to deny her. She was patient through the final touches and installation of her own throne, a beautifully crafted piece that announced to all that Balmirra had the most skilled carpenters. As big as his, it'd been stained almost black to hide that the arms and seat were masterfully angled to ensure she wasn't dwarfed by the chair.

A cushion gave her a little more height and some comfort, which she needed when she insisted on attending the seasonal petitions. Most legal matters were handled by Balmirra's robust network of local courts, magistrates, and justiciars, but since the time of the ancestors, any citizen of the city could bring their matter before the chieftain. Vallek kept this honored tradition, and at the beginning of each new season, he heard those petitions and grievances that had risen through the system.

It always proved to be a long day, one that required patience and stamina. Matters that had reached all the way to him were often prickly, and his judgement was final. To his immense pride, Ravenna sat regally in her new throne, listening carefully and offering thoughtful advice. Honestly, it pleased him to find she could be as ruthless, if not more so than him when it came to these petitions, for Vallek didn't suffer fools.

These traditions were important for both the chieftain and the people, and they had to be taken seriously.

He wasn't the only one who threw off all his finery at the end of that day. Ravenna hastily unhooked her many earrings and lifted the coronet from her head before using her mother's grimoire to mix a simple remedy for headaches. She shared with Vallek, and the two of them sat in exhausted, companionable silence for the rest of that evening.

He'd hoped, with how tired she was and how distracted, that her visions would cease. But as they turned down the blankets to get into bed, her eyes went distant, her shoulders stiff. When she returned to him, her lips had thinned and she wouldn't meet his gaze.

He tried every trick he knew to help her rest. He purred for hours to soothe her, rubbed her shoulders and legs, stayed up late whispering across pillows with her, suggested sleeping draughts and reading and long bouts of *talfon*, licked and fingered and thrust inside her cunt until she was exhausted of pleasure, but nothing seemed to help in the end.

"There's just much on my mind, is all," she told him one morning, her smile achingly sad. "I'm sure I just have to get used to it."

It was true that taking on the burdens of a kingdom came lightly only to those who didn't care about the people and proper management, and despite how aloof or sarcastic Ravenna could be, no one could accuse her of not caring. If anything, she cared too much.

Gathering her up in his arms, he bent to kiss her cheek. "You have a soft heart, love."

"I absolutely don't," she scoffed.

"You do. You're soft and generous and kind and ever so adorable."

"How dare you?" she laughed. "I'm dangerous. Ruthless. Not to be trifled with!"

"That, too."

He glutted on her giggling, relieved to see her smile turn genuine. Moments like these reassured him that all would be well. She just needed time to find her footing. Every day would be easier than the last, and one day soon, he'd see her emerge the fully fledged queen he knew she would become.

Her happiness bubbled inside him, his beast content for the first time in days.

When Eydis walked into the den to join them a moment later, a grave look on her face, he almost barked at her to get out.

But Ravenna had seen. "What is it?" she asked, all the play falling from her face.

Vallek scowled at his sister, who deftly ignored it.

"A spy has been apprehended on the Spearhead. He meant to sail to the faelands with information."

A growl punched up Vallek's throat, his annoyance with Eydis eclipsed by his rage at the traitor. Sellswords were vermin, but to sell secrets? To endanger Vallek's mate?

Unacceptable.

"Gather the court and bring him before me," he growled.

Vallek had insisted, more vociferously this time, that Ravenna need not attend this. His anger was vicious, and this part of kingship was ugly, if necessary. It wasn't a part of him he wished for her to see.

But, ever stubborn, she accompanied him to the basilica and took her throne. "It wouldn't do to be absent now," she reasoned. "It would show weakness."

While that may have been true, it didn't lessen his desire to hide her away from this. Petitions and politics and feasts were one thing—meting out justice to traitors was another. Threats to her couldn't stand, and he had no qualms over spilling blood to prevent them, but that didn't mean he wished for her to see it.

Curious murmurs echoed from the court, no one sure why they had all been summoned. The king had been gathering his court much more often than usual, and so they no doubt expected another unprecedented announcement.

However, the whispers abruptly ceased when the prisoner was led in.

With hands shackled before him and a thick iron collar circling his throat, the spy was led forth into the center of the basilica. The guards held him by flexible staffs inset on the collar. When they stood before Vallek and Ravenna and the traitor wouldn't kneel, pressure was exerted on the staffs, bending the orc to his knees with a grimace.

Upper lip peeling back, Vallek bared the full lengths of his tusks at the traitor. He recognized the orc, a berserker. One of his own most trusted warriors.

Although he'd needed reminding of the warrior's name, Byrk, the male not having distinguished himself within his service, to know that one of his own elite warriors was the culprit struck deeply. He could rationalize, even expect betrayal from an ambitious paladin or even just a disaffected orc looking to make a sack of coin.

But his own berserker?

Unforgivable.

If he couldn't trust his best warriors to keep him, but more importantly his mate, safe, who could he trust?

The question soured his stomach. In that moment, he hated this orc. For betraying him. For endangering Ravenna. For undermining his trust. Every warrior, from seasoned berserker to fresh recruit, would need to be investigated again. There was never just one spy—they coiled together like snakes for warmth, hiding in shadow.

A single orc had made the whole of Vallek's city unsafe for him and his mate. Such treachery had to be dealt with swiftly and brutally.

Rising from his seat, Vallek took hold of the newly repaired Hormhím before descending the dais steps.

Mattias met him at the basilica floor, the captain's disgust for Byrk Broad-Back pulling down the edges of his mouth. Bowing his head in shame, he handed over the gorget that had once hung from Byrk's neck, a sign of his status as the king's warrior.

Vallek folded and crushed the soft gold in his fist, letting the mangled gorget clatter to the flagstones.

"Byrk, you have been brought before your king, accused of the crime of treason for selling secrets. How do you answer this charge?"

The orc snorted. "Guilty."

The court gasped, whispers rebounding between the red limestone columns.

There was no reason to lie; he'd been caught in the act, followed to a remote beach on the Spearhead where he'd meant to meet a small boat of fae scouts. Eydis's people had given her their sworn testimony, and a raid of Byrk's home had revealed a stash of fae silver.

His betrayal had gone on long before Ravenna was revealed as Vallek's mate, but the timing of his most recent journey to the Spearhead was telling. Different friends and kin had differing stories on where he was, none of them matching and none the truth.

Ever efficient, Eydis had laid out the evidence before him. Allowing Vallek to render an equally efficient verdict.

Pulling a small sack from his pocket, Vallek strode to where Byrk knelt.

"You would betray your oaths, your honor, for a few fae coins?" Lifting the sack, he upended its contents onto the ground. A dozen silver coins *clinked* onto the floor. "Are you really so cheap?"

Byrk's nostrils flared. "It's nothing personal, my king. A man has to make a living."

Vallek slashed his tusks through the air. His men were generously paid, and what was more, enjoyed the highest reputation within Balmirra.

A reputation now tarnished by one orc.

The flippant excuse didn't ring true, but honestly, the real reason for his betrayal didn't matter.

Hormhím nearly vibrated in his hand, thirsty for blood.

"You are a traitor to your kind and your king. The only sentence to give you is death."

The guards braced themselves as Vallek closed the distance.

He'd heard that humans preferred beheadings for their executions, but orcs found this far too messy and imprecise. Deaths in one blow were honorable, and if a chieftain was to sentence death, it was he who would carry it out. It was a mark of honor, of strength.

Hefting Hormhím onto his shoulder, Vallek waited for Byrk to bow his head. Most did.

However, the disgraced warrior kept Vallek's gaze, defying him one last time.

If Byrk thought this would unnerve or sway Vallek, he was sorely mistaken. His swift, honorable death was for the benefit of Ravenna. Had Vallek gotten his way, Byrk's death would have been slow, agonizing, his blood painting the curtain wall of the citadel for a fortnight.

Cold rage coiled round his heart, Vallek smirked down at the traitor, relishing when fear passed over his eyes.

I am Vallek Far-Sight, king of kin, mate of Ravenna. And today, I am your death.

In one heavy blow, Vallek brought Hormhím down in a wide arc. The blade caught Byrk's face, splitting his head in two.

It took only a blink, a moment, and the traitor was dead, his blood and brains soaking the basilica floor.

The corpse slumped forward, lifelessly crumpling into a heap.

When Vallek pulled Hormhím back from the traitor's head, blood and viscera streamed down the blade. Running the flat of the axehead on his palm, he smeared the blood across his hand, raising it for all to see.

"So is the fate of any who would betray their kind and their king!" he roared. "We are one kin, one kind, and we are stronger together. His treachery isn't just against me but us all."

The court looked on with wide eyes, only a brave few daring to look at the pitiful sight of Byrk. An array of expressions met his declaration, from grim understanding to nervous respect to poorly disguised disgust. He could handle them all—he would convince those who doubted.

What he wouldn't stand, though, was betrayal.

That thought stuck starkly in his mind, even as his blood ran hot from the violence.

It clanged like a solitary bell in his mind when a reckless fool stepped forward and said—

"So we aren't to speak to the fae, but it's all right to fuck them?"

The basilica went utterly, preternaturally quiet.

Vallek slowly turned on his heel to face the accusation.

Grogar met his cold stare with an impetuous false bravado. Looking down his nose at Vallek, the stupid young paladin took another step forward. "How can you say we're one kin when the whore beside you has no orcish blood at all?"

The fool was goading him. Vallek knew it. The court knew it.

Even his beast knew it.

But that day, Vallek hadn't just brought Hormhím with him. He'd brought his days of concern over Ravenna, compounded now with new fears over keeping her safe within his own citadel. He was tired, angry, and his sympathy only extended so far.

A flash of his tusks was Grogar's only warning.

Vallek flung Hormhím at the paladin, end over end, aiming for Grogar's head, just as he had for Byrk's.

The court hardly had time to gasp as Hormhím *whooshed* through the air.

They gasped again when the axe stopped in midair, the blade suspended a mere inch from Grogar's nose.

The paladin let out a choking sort of cry, his trembling knees buckling as he fell back into the crowd.

Hormhím shuddered before floating back to hang in the air before Vallek, waiting for him to retake the hilt.

Before he could, Ravenna entered his vision.

"There's been enough blood for one day, my love," she told him gently.

Vallek reached to take Hormhím, feeling her magic fall away from the axe once he had hold of it. Frustrated bloodlust, fears over her, and a sharp lust to see her wielding her magic were a potent mix inside him.

He felt his pupils dilate as he watched her come round to stand on his other side.

Looking out at the gathered crowd, Ravenna spoke in a clear, calm voice. "I may be part fae, but I was raised as a human. I've spent more time amongst you than I have my father's people. I have no love nor loyalty to the Fae Queen." Wrapping her hand around Vallek's arm, she said, "My love and loyalty belong to Vallek Far-Sight, your king, and therefore, to you."

Vallek's attention narrowed to only her. It wasn't how he'd expected to get the words, and he'd certainly ask for them again later, in private, but his chest swelled with a painful, overwhelming pride. Gods, she was something to behold.

"The word of the queen," Vallek announced, although he couldn't tear his gaze away from his magnificent mate. "Let all here remember it—and her mercy."

29

Later, so much later that it was only Ravenna, Vallek, and their guards remaining in the basilica, she stood from her throne and climbed into her *azai*'s lap. His warmth and arms immediately surrounded her, tucking her to his chest as they found a familiar position. Her tired back melted into his big body, letting him take her weight.

Fates, what a day.

It wasn't that she thought being his mate and queen would be easy—but she couldn't have anticipated how it was one damn thing after another. She supposed she should've expected this; not only was Vallek in the middle of forging a new kingdom, his taking her as his mate was, at least for orc chieftains, unprecedented.

Although, she doubted the life of a monarch, especially one as active as Vallek wanted to be, was ever truly peaceful. There would likely be lulls to look forward to, but if it wasn't one thing, it was something else.

It was a reality she had to get used to.

The past few days had proved to her that while Vallek would do all he could to ease her burdens, she couldn't rely on her previous coping techniques. She couldn't run away and seclude herself. There would be no more long stretches of days by herself, with only her thoughts for company.

She wasn't the halfling girl in that seaside cottage anymore.

Ravenna wasn't sure what she was. Oh, to be sure, she knew what Vallek would tell her. She was his mate and queen of orc-kin. Perhaps that was true, but it didn't feel as true as the halfling girl by the sea.

And perhaps, watching Vallek split open the head of a traitor, she could understand why.

At the heart of their mating, their friendship, their very acquaintance, was a betrayal. A lie by omission.

Although the spy's body had long since been taken away and the blood mopped up from the flagstones, Ravenna could still see the shadows of that gory pool. She didn't regret witnessing the execution, nor bear any sympathy towards the traitor—yet, in her darkened mood, she couldn't help a shudder.

Vallek's arms tightened around her. "Are you cold?"

"No, just tired." She was, in fact, so warm and cozy in his arms that she was loath to move, even back to their rooms to undress. Her ears ached from all the earrings, and her shoulders complained from all the stiff posture, but for the moment, she was far too comfortable to get up.

"I regret you had to see that," he rumbled, "but you handled it impressively."

Ravenna lifted her head to better see him. He offered a conciliatory grin that didn't reach his eyes. Oh, her poor *azai* was hurting. He might have said she had a soft, vulnerable heart, but, really, it was his that was softest.

Laying her hand over that vulnerable muscle, she whispered, "I'm sorry you had to do it at all. It can't have been easy."

"Yes and no. Eliminating a threat, especially to you, is as easy as breathing. It's the thoughts afterwards that are harder to bear."

"I can understand that." Her life these last few days had been dominated by such thoughts. "You did what had to be done, and you prove your conviction by being the one to carry out the sentence."

He rumbled with perhaps agreement, perhaps placation. "Let's just hope this is the last execution for a while."

Ravenna nodded, her insides twisting. He looked tired, too, the weight of the execution heaviest now, in the hours just afterwards. It troubled her to see his conscience gnawing at him, but, then, would she love him so much if it didn't? For as big and brutal as he could be, Vallek Far-Sight could never be accused of not caring.

How anyone could doubt him, *betray* him . . .

Burying his face in her hair, Vallek sighed. "Tell me again, sprite."

"Tell you what?" she asked, although her stomach flipped with anticipation.

"Tell me who has your love and loyalty."

Ravenna flushed. Fates, she hadn't quite meant to admit her feelings like that, in front of the whole court, *before* telling Vallek. Her instinct was to tease, to say, *The people, of course, just like I said,* but another peek at his handsome face told her now wasn't the moment for banter.

He was hurting and needed the words.

"You do," she said softly, nuzzling his nose with hers.

A sumptuous purr hummed beneath her hands on his chest. "Again."

Setting her lips at his ear so only he could hear, she whispered, "I love you, Vallek."

His purr deepened as he lifted her a little higher in his arms. Burying his face in the crook of her shoulder, he kissed her bare skin and rubbed his tusks along her clavicle.

"The gods have blessed me with you," he murmured. "Tested me, too."

Ravenna tried to grin at his good humor but couldn't manage. Her own regrets and fears ate her inside, his gentleness and affection only feeding them.

Her stomach threatened revolt when he said, "You have my heart, sprite. I love you so much, it sometimes feels too great to bear."

Tears escaped her eyes, and no matter how quickly she blinked and tried to hide them, Vallek soon smelled the salt. Straightening, he frowned to see her upset. His purr took on a plaintive note, his big hand cupping her cheek to wipe away the tears.

"Why do you cry?" he asked, concern burgeoning in his eyes. "Please don't cry."

Ravenna shook her head; she couldn't help it. Everything was coming out of her, she could feel it.

She stood upon a precipice, teetering on the edge. She would fall in just a moment, she knew it, couldn't bear to be torn in two anymore.

But the thought of losing him, of being cast aside, hurt more than anything. She clung to that precipice with her fingers and toes for fear of being parted from her *azai. I can't lose him. I can't I can't.*

This was why she'd not wanted to love him in the first place. Why she had wasted three years in her disguise. The moment she'd dreaded since she first walked into his tent had come. Her shame pressed at the small of her back, urging her forward, off the edge. For all she'd fought it, belayed it, tried to avoid it, there was nothing for it now.

She couldn't walk two paths. She couldn't be the halfling girl and the faeling queen.

After this moment, she feared she'd be neither.

Don't leave me, too.

Clutching at the embroidered collar of his tunic, she could hear the desperation in her voice when she said, "Remember you love me. Remember that when—" She choked on more tears, and Vallek's expression grew alarmed.

Taking her face between both big hands, he held her steady. "Breathe, sprite. Whatever it is, it's all right."

"But it's not, it's not," she sobbed. "I'm not who you think."

She grasped at his wrists, holding him to her, so he had to nod at the guards to send them away. They filed out, no doubt taking up positions just on the other side of the thresholds, but within a few moments, they were as alone in the basilica as they ever could be.

"I know who you are," he said slowly, "but why don't you tell me yourself."

Through gasps and sobs, she finally admitted, "I'm a liar. I've lied to you, Vallek. I've *used* you."

He regarded her seriously for a moment. "I'd be more surprised if you hadn't, love. I never once thought you joined my staff for altruistic reasons."

"But it's more than that." She'd been naïve to think that when she made her deal with him, dirty and bloodied in that shallow cave, she could have it both ways. She made that deal thinking it justified her capitulation. The simple truth was, she wanted him, wanted to be his mate. She still did. Perhaps more than she wanted her revenge. "Everything I've done, it's been to strengthen your position as king, so that one day, the orcs would be strong enough to attack the faelands."

If possible, his expression became even more grave. Ravenna kneaded his tunic, desperate for him to say something.

He kept his silence, though, waiting for more truth.

"My parents died protecting me. They were slain by Amaranthe herself, refusing to give me up to her."

"Why?" he asked, ominously quiet.

"Because of my gift. Seers are rare, even within the fae. And—" she gulped down air "—I saw her downfall. I was only a child. No one should have believed me, but the vision spread through the faelands."

"Would killing you thwart your vision?"

"No. I don't know." She shook her head until she was dizzy. "I haven't cared. Since they were slain, all I've wanted, all I've worked for is vengeance."

"You want to kill the Fae Queen."

"Yes."

"The one who slaughtered her own family and has ruled for twelve-hundred years."

"Yes." Sensing he meant to speak more, dreading what he'd say, she hurriedly added, "I've seen her fall. I know it will happen. I know I can make it happen." Ravenna clutched his tunic so tight, her knuckles went white. "She killed my parents, Vallek. She destroyed my whole world. She has to pay for that. I have to make her pay for that."

"With an orcish army."

"Yes. No. Not anymore. I don't know. But I have to do this."

Her stomach clenched as she watched him nod slowly.

"I understand," he said. "We will—"

"No!" she gasped. "I can't bear to risk your life, too."

He frowned at her wording, no doubt catching that *too*. Before he could question it, she said, "It's not fair of me—it's not right or fair—but in the end, I wanted to be your mate. At least while I could."

His nostrils flared with alarm, but Ravenna smothered it with a kiss.

"I've had visions of Amaranthe's defeat, but never anything beyond. I don't know what will happen afterwards, if I'll . . ." *If I'll survive to come home to you.*

"You mean to die with her," he growled.

"Maybe. I haven't seen another way."

"You've always known . . . that you would leave me."

The truth spoken aloud struck deeper than any wound. Her face crumpled with sobs, and it was a few moments before she could speak again.

"I didn't want to. I *don't* want to. But I have to do this. They're my *parents*. They gave everything . . ." Wiping at her face, she said, "I kept away as long as I could. I thought to protect us both, but . . ." Nothing had quite gone to plan.

He was silent for long enough that she thought she might be sick. His grip remained tight, and she wasn't immediately cast away from him, but Ravenna couldn't read his hard face.

She wanted his forgiveness—but also his anger. She'd used him, betrayed his trust, undermined the sanctity of matehood, a thing held sacrosanct for both orcs and fae.

I'm nothing but an angry, orphaned halfling girl. She didn't know why she thought to ever be more. She'd known her fate since she was a little girl, predicting the downfall of a queen. There would be no escaping it. The more she tried, the more people she hurt, and she couldn't hurt him, not anymore, not—

"Is there anything else?"

Ravenna gasped and held her breath. His words and expression were serious but not angry. Those lapis-lazuli eyes assessed her, looking inside her for more revelations.

"No," she whispered through numb lips.

So stunned was she by his sudden grin that she didn't believe what she saw. Lifting one brow cockily, he nodded at her.

"Very well. Remember what I promised, sprite. You've upheld your end of the bargain."

Ravenna's heart lurched painfully in her chest. "No, Vallek, I can't—"

"You can. It is a mate's due." Nuzzling her cheek, he said, "You've told me your scheme. Now ask for my aid like the queen you are."

She reared back, not understanding, not believing. "You can't mean . . ."

He nodded at the empty space before the dais. "Ask."

Her poor heart didn't know whether to beat right out of her chest or stop altogether. Her fingers spasmed in the abused fabric of his tunic, holding onto him as if he was the last harbor against a storm of insanity.

He waited patiently, helping her stand and find her balance. Ravenna's tears dried as she descended the steps in a daze, her mind buzzing with a new reality she couldn't quite accept yet.

When she turned to face the throne, she looked up to find the imperious orc king staring down at her. Legs spread, hands gripping the curved ends of the armrests, he was every inch the conquering warrior and anointed monarch.

He was magnificent, and he was her mate.

Bowing her head, Ravenna said, "I come humbly before you, King Vallek, to seek your aid against a shared enemy. Amaranthe of the fae is a tyrant and a threat. I beseech your help in defeating her."

"Intriguing. And what will I receive in return?"

Ravenna's lips twitched with a grin. "My eternal thanks. And my love."

Vallek rumbled with interest, leaning forward in his throne. He held out a hand, which Ravenna gracefully ascended the steps again to take. Drawing her forward, Vallek kissed the back of her hand.

"Now ask me as a mate would."

She couldn't stop the grin this time. Fates, this man. How could he so easily wring out her heart and fill it, too?

Holding onto his hand, she knelt between his spread legs. His pupils dilated as he watched her, a vein visibly pulsing in his neck.

"Will you help me, my love?"

Bending down to share breath, he murmured, "Your enemies are mine. And you know how I feel about threats to you. Consider it done."

More tears threatened, a bewildering mixture of relief and jubilation and dread, but Ravenna held them back with sheer will.

"You mean that?"

"I do." One side of his mouth lifted in a cocksure grin. "It will be my pleasure to bring you her head."

That dread inside her only deepened, but she didn't correct him. Not yet. There was too much to be grateful for. If he meant to help her, there would be time to find a way that would involve the least amount of risk to him. He was what was most important to Ravenna and the orc-kin.

After a gentle tug on her hand, Ravenna regained her feet. Vallek spun her round before pulling her into his lap, her back to his chest. His fingers curled loosely around her neck to hold her just so as his other hand began rucking up her skirts.

His lips buzzed along her cheek, his purr a warm comfort at her back. Ravenna gasped then bit her lip to feel his touch slide up her inner thigh.

"We'll do this together," he said, fingers working their own magic.

The idea of letting him touch her like this, so exposed and open to the great basilica, even empty, should have horrified her. Instead, when his fingers found their way past the gusset of her underthings, she was already wet for him. He rumbled with approval, fingers beginning to play in her slick.

With the hand round her throat, he gently pulled her back into the curve of his body. She rested her head on the meat of his pectoral, letting him have his way with her. She was, after all, eternally grateful and more than willing to show it.

Reaching back, she found the shell of his ear and began to delicately trace the whorls and ridges, earning another rumble.

He began to strum her clitoris with his thumb, making her squirm on his lap. Should anyone walk in, it'd be obvious what they were up to, even with his hand almost hidden by the hem of her gown. Although no one would, a thrill zipped up Ravenna's spine at the thought of someone seeing them.

Let them see. Let them witness how a halfling claims a king.

His fingers strayed from her throat to delve below the neckline of her gown. He pushed it down until her left breast burst free, his greedy hand claiming the giving flesh. He plumped her breast and pinched her nipple as he rolled her clitoris beneath the pad of his finger—an onslaught of sensation that sent her overwrought mind into sweet oblivion.

"Whatever visions you may or may not have, I know this to be true: You will survive, sprite. I demand it. I demand all of your years, for they are mine by right."

Ravenna could only gasp and moan as his hands worked her body masterfully. He'd been a devoted study to her pleasure, and by now, he knew just what she liked. How to build her up quickly and how to prolong her anticipation. He played with her, and she knew his game, knew that in this, they would both win.

"I have my own vision, you see. Together, we'll build this kingdom and rule it. We will see many harvests, and we will have many good decades."

"Maybe more," she gasped, mind already full of his vision when he pushed two fingers inside her. "Fae blood and magic." She needed to explain it to him in full, how her own human mother was almost three hundred before she bore Ravenna, but she couldn't form the words.

Vallek understood enough, purring with pleasure. "Excellent. We will lead this kingdom into a new age, and when the land is safe and secure and the people are finally sick of us, we'll choose our favorite child and leave it to them. Then we'll go off and have our own new adventures."

He supported her weight with one hand as he loosened his trou. Ravenna greedily reached for him, moving her skirts aside until she could feel the searing press of his cock along her flesh. She shuddered with an agonizing pleasure as she began to feed him into her body.

"Can you see my vision, sprite?" he asked, gone breathless as he stretched her wide.

Ravenna could only moan, his cock reaching so damn deep inside her, she couldn't feel where she stopped and he began.

"I'll give you her head, and you will give me all your years."

Bracing a hand on the armrest, Ravenna held onto his neck with the other as he bounced her on his lap. His cock shuttled in and out of her, the wet slap of their bodies echoing across the vast basilica. Her knees shook on either side of his legs, barely able to hold herself upright under his onslaught.

"Promise me," he growled against her cheek.

"Yes!" she cried. "Yes!"

He could have it all, everything she was and would be. It was a small price to pay.

"My good mate. Hold onto me."

That was all the warning she got before he took hold of both her hips and began thrusting up in brutal strokes, holding her steady to meet every single one. She could do nothing but take his lust as he used her body; every time he pulled away, she ached for his return.

"Harder," she moaned, head lolling from side to side on his chest.

"*Fuck.*" Fingers dug in so deep they'd leave bruises, he thrust her hips down as he rammed himself up. The force of his strokes rattled her teeth, and Ravenna dug her nails into wood and flesh as she came violently apart.

Body gone stiff in a rictus of pleasure, her hips rolled and rolled, chasing down her orgasm. Arms banded around her, securing her to his chest, he roared into the empty space, the basilica echoing with his triumph.

He pumped inside her, filling her with spend. She overflowed with him but greedily wanted more, her muscles milking his cock, eager to wring every bit of pleasure from him.

"Everything, sprite," he growled at her ear.

"Everything," she promised.

30

Ravenna slept better than she had in a fortnight. Although she and Vallek were both early risers normally, they stayed abed long into the morning. It was Brynhíl bustling in with their breakfast who finally roused them out of bed, tutting as she stoked the fireplaces.

"The king and queen lazing about after the ninth bell—whoever heard of such a thing."

"We are known to throw precedence to the wind," Ravenna quipped as she spread butter across a roll of warm bread.

Bryn chuckled before bidding them farewell.

When they were alone again, Ravenna chewed on her question alongside her roll. It was a long few moments before she managed to ask him what had been on her mind since waking.

"Are you sure?"

Vallek's eyes flicked up to meet hers. Without hesitation, he nodded. "Yes. It will benefit the kingdom, and if it makes you safer and happier, then it is well worth it."

Ravenna tried to smile, tried to be relieved, but she'd spent too long in the shadow of Amaranthe to let a few promises vanquish all her fears. Even promises from her *azai*.

"I don't want anything to happen to you. You're far more important than me."

Vallek's brows crashed down his face in a forbidding frown. "You will never say that again, sprite."

"But it's true. You mean far more to many more people. Me included."

He huffed as he split and cored a pear. Handing her a piece, he said, "Nothing will happen to me."

"You can't promise that. My vision . . ." Although she'd managed to go a day without seeing it, the images were still seared into her mind.

"Have you seen me dead?"

"No." Thank fates. She'd have fled far and fast from him if so, to ensure the vision never came true. "I haven't seen anything after her fall."

"Have you seen everything that has ever happened to you?"

Ravenna frowned. "Well, no . . ."

That cocksure grin she loved and loathed twitched on either side of his tusks. Leaning forward in his seat, he caught her lips in a pear-flavored kiss. "Did you see that in a vision?"

"No," she grumbled.

He kissed her again, this time his free hand cupping her breast over her nightgown.

"Or this?"

"No, but I could've predicted it."

"Not the same," he said with a wink. "If you haven't seen it, then there is every chance we succeed. We just have to be clever about it."

Leaning back in his seat, he looked far too sure of himself. Between that and the easy, confident way he peeled and cut up an apple, his big hands moving dexterously with the small paring knife, she couldn't decide if she wanted to tear her hair out, cover him in kisses, or wallow in relief.

She *wanted* it to be that simple. If there was anyone who could deliver her the opportunity for revenge, it was Vallek. She'd known that for years already. But to have him onside—*knowingly*—had something very, very dangerous blooming inside her.

Hope.

The first test of that hope came not long after, when Asta, Eydis, and Hilde arrived.

"You wanted to speak with us?" said Eydis, taking her usual seat in the den.

With all of them gathered round, and her hand held firmly in Vallek's, Ravenna admitted much of what she'd told him the previous night. The orcesses listened without interruption—knowing the three of them as she did, Ravenna wasn't sure whether this was heartening.

When Ravenna finished, her tale was met with complete silence. It was an awful moment.

Hilde broke it first, a smug little grin between her tusks. "I knew you were up to something. Didn't I say that, Eydis? 'That woman is up to something.'"

"You did," Eydis agreed absently, the cogs of her brilliant mind clearly turning.

Ravenna couldn't hold her sharp, assessing gaze for long.

"I asked you here to help plan," Vallek said. "I mean to kill the Fae Queen."

His declaration was met with an even longer, even more ominous silence.

"Is that . . . wise?" Asta asked, looking between Vallek and Eydis.

"It's not," Eydis said slowly, without inflection. She was clearly still pondering, a little crease visible between her furrowed brows.

Vallek held up his hands. "Maybe not, but it must happen. She's obviously hunting Ravenna, and sooner or later, she'll find out where she is."

"You can't just go around killing other monarchs," argued Asta. "That would lead to war. Unless you already mean to march on the faelands with an army."

"It's not my preferred strategy, but I will defend what's mine."

"With an unprovoked attack?"

"*Preemptive* attack, yes."

"And what if that invites, say, the Pyrrossi emperor to *preemptively* attack you?"

Vallek grumbled, conceding the point.

"I will do it." Everyone turned surprised looks onto Ravenna. She nodded, insisting, "This is my revenge. I'm grateful for aid, but Asta's right, Vallek can't be the one to slay her. I will. Honor demands it."

Vallek's expression darkened. "I won't allow you to be so close to danger."

"Then we don't do this at all," Ravenna shot back. "I won't allow you to fight in my place."

"What do you think, Eydis?" asked Hilde.

Her question diffused a bit of the tension growing between Ravenna and Vallek, although she knew they were far from finished. She could already tell from the stubborn set of her mate's jaw that this would be the point where he dug in his heels.

All looked to Eydis, strangely quiet so far through their discussions. The orcess leaned forward to balance her elbows on her knees, her mien still pensive.

"I think it's not the wisest course of action, and we can't control nor foresee all the ramifications. You know I don't like loose ends. However . . ." She scrubbed her hands over her face. "There is some mad logic to it."

"You're not serious," Asta scoffed.

"Maybe—I haven't totally made up my mind. But if Vallek is right, if Amaranthe truly is hunting Ravenna, it's only a matter of time before she learns Balmirra has hidden and aided her. If the tales of her are true, we can expect a swift, brutal response."

"The tales are true," Ravenna confirmed.

Eydis nodded gravely. "We found one spy but there must be others. I have my people following leads, but it's possible one may slip our net. And then, of course, news will spread. It will be slower, but, eventually, the whole continent will know the orc king took a faeling mate. We therefore have a limited window of opportunity."

"It will be the only time we wield the element of surprise," Vallek agreed.

"Risky as it is, we may have no other choice," said Eydis. "If we wish to decide the rules of the engagement, we'll have to strike first."

"Be that as it may," argued Asta, "that doesn't mean an attack on the faelands will succeed. Even crossing the water west of the Spearhead will mean at least two days of marching. You could attack from the sea, but they say Fallorian is set high on a cliff. There's no way to maintain the surprise, not once you touch foot in the faelands."

"So then we draw her away," said Ravenna. She met Eydis's steely gaze when it cut to her. "She's already sent scouts to ask about an escaped criminal. Tell her you have them. Use me as bait."

Eydis's eyes glittered. "As a fellow monarch, Vallek would be within his rights to request a parley," she said over Vallek's growing unhappy growl. "We say it's important enough that the king comes himself but can only deliver his news to the Queen herself."

"Would she fall for it?" asked Hilde.

"Maybe not a few centuries ago," Ravenna said, "but she's grown evermore spiteful and paranoid. If she thinks Vallek means to hand me over, there's a good chance she'd come herself."

Eydis grinned viciously. "There's a spit of land at the mouth of Dyfan Bay. Where the Treaty of Spearhead was signed. We draw her there with the promise of neutral territory."

"No army, no war," said Ravenna. "An ambush."

"It could work," Vallek grumbled, "if she takes the bait. But—" he lifted their clasped hands to hold over his heart "—I don't like it. It's too much risk to you."

"It has to be me," she reminded him gently. Ravenna leaned over to kiss his chest, right where the fresh scar of her first bite was. "You'll be there to keep me out of mischief."

He grunted, drawing his arm around her to tuck her tightly to his side. "I would prefer you stay safely here and let me bring you her head."

"I know. But Asta's right, you can't be the one to kill her."

"I will do whatever I must to keep you safe," he growled.

Ravenna held his serious gaze, knowing that they wouldn't agree, at least not that morning. For now, that was all right. There was still time to plan and plot—and convince him.

Never had the chance to fulfill her vow for vengeance felt closer, her blood running hot with fresh hope. She wouldn't let anyone take that from her, not even her *azai*.

"There are many fae who despise Amaranthe. With her gone, the faelands may finally know peace," she told them. "We can send word to my father's friend Allarion. He brought me to safety after my parents were killed. I know he went north, to Eirea, to try to find refuge."

Vallek nodded. "Messengers can be sent. Kennum has a growing partnership with one of their cities."

"Dundúran," provided Eydis.

"Yes, that's it. He can facilitate contact."

Eydis clapped her hands, looking a little too gleeful about the prospect of assassinating the Fae Queen. "Let us lay our trap and lead her into it."

If nothing else, Eydis loved a good plot.

Hilde just sighed

31

For all the excitement of planning their next moves, once they were put into motion, there was little to do but wait and see. Messengers were sent to Fallorian and Kaldebrak, and Ravenna had to stop herself from looking out on the horizon any time she passed a window, to see if she could spot their return with news.

After the first fortnight, the messengers sent to Kaldebrak returned with confirmation that Kennum would send word north in search of Allarion to pass on Ravenna's handwritten and sealed missive. While there was some small relief that her note, written in a cryptic form of ancient faethling even a fae scholar would have trouble deciphering, continued on its journey, Kaldebrak was the last known waypoint. They wouldn't know when the message reached Dundúran, nor how long it might take to pass on from there.

The weeks bled into one another, and to keep from going mad with waiting, Ravenna decided she had to find other ways to prepare.

Vallek worked closely with his berserkers, checking over every member with Mattias to root out any more traitors. Thankfully, none were found, and the unit began to heal together through training, overcoming the shame of a traitor in their midst.

If he could train, so would she.

However, Ravenna knew how he felt about her being the one to ambush Amaranthe. They still hadn't come to an agreement on what the attack would look like.

And so it was to Asta she went instead, finding her one morning in the courtyard outside the garrison barracks. "Train with me? And teach me to fight like an orc."

The orcess tipped back her head and laughed from her belly upon hearing Ravenna's request. "You are bold, *tristah*. I'm glad you aren't my enemy."

"Worse. I'm family." It was the first time she'd quipped about it, and her belly flipped with nerves as the words hung there between them.

Asta huffed a laugh. "That you are. All right then, let's see what you can do."

Ravenna followed the orcess through the courtyard and around the barracks to the back training yard. It was thankfully almost empty, most of the guards having already completed their training and headed inside for breakfast.

As Asta rummaged through a barrel full of wooden swords, Ravenna asked, "Are you doing this to help me or annoy Vallek?"

"Why can't it be both?" the orcess snickered. "Besides, we all know, even Vallek, that you will be the one to deliver the killing blow. Keeping it between fae." She threw Ravenna a wink over her shoulder. "Now, what are you already comfortable with?"

A bit more rummaging procured a practice sword with the right amount of heft for Ravenna. It was one more commonly used by young, untrained recruits, half the size of normal orcish swords. She also pulled out a wooden dirk; a standard small dagger for an orc but for her, a longer weapon almost half the length of her sword.

Asta's brows rose in interest. "The dual-handed style, hmm? I'm intrigued." Pulling out a serviceable common sword for herself, Asta led her to the center of the training yard. "All right, show me what you know—"

Ravenna's sword smacked against Asta's, thrown up just in time. The orcess grunted, dancing backwards, and Ravenna followed, pressing her advantage of surprise.

Her father had spent long years training her in the art of swords and daggers. It was an ancient way of fighting, preferred more by the common fae fighter than the elegant fencing practiced by the noble sword masters. It took considerable concentration, training, and daring—dirks were meant to get in close and stab.

Asta guffawed before getting her feet under her. In a moment, she'd stabilized herself to counter Ravenna's onslaught. The orcess used her superior strength, sending Ravenna skipping backwards.

Retaking her stance, Ravenna braced as Asta rushed her.

Back and forth they danced across the training yard, kicking up dust. Asta was a better and bigger fighter, but Ravenna was fast. And mean. She didn't hesitate raking the dull blade of her dirk across Asta's calf when she had the chance, a blow that would've severed the tendons in her heel had they fought with real blades.

Still, that was the worst strike she landed against her opponent. Asta came at her with all her strength, pushing Ravenna back. She had to use both sword and dirk to catch Asta's downward stroke. Her arms shook under the strain of keeping the sword at bay—just for Asta to punch her in the undefended gut.

—white eyelashes—a white unicorn with violet eyes and a lilac horn—a stream burbled through the meadow—fire crackled across her eyes—

Ravenna went sprawling back into the dirt. She suspected that had hardly been a tap from the strong orcess, but still, it rendered her splayed on the ground.

When she finally got some air back in her lungs, Ravenna chuckled as she wiped at her grimy brow. A great shadow fell over her, Asta's hand appearing near her face.

She took it, letting the orcess heft her back to her feet in one pull.

"Let's not tell Vallek about that one, yes?"

"Definitely not." Shaking off more dust, she said, "Well, can I be taught to fight dirty?"

"Of course. You've already got impressive skill. Although, it's not fighting *dirty*." Asta winked. "It's fighting *smart*."

Oberon didn't much care that she was getting beaten to a pulp every day by Asta, he still insisted on seeing her in person once every three days. He wasn't keen on the plan for vengeance, even scowling at Vallek for a whole afternoon when he learned the orc had promised Ravenna the Fae Queen's head.

You're supposed to keep her alive, Oberon grumbled his displeasure with Vallek, *not support her ridiculous plans.*

Wanting to avenge them isn't ridiculous, she told him for the thousandth time.

Oberon stamped his front right hoof. *It is when you go off and get yourself killed.*

I'm not going to do that. I'll have Vallek with me, and two hundred of his best warriors.

Oberon huffed in his horsey way, thick lips flapping. *You're young. You haven't seen what she's truly capable of.*

No? She killed my parents, Obi. She tortured—the thought caught with a sob in her throat—*maman.*

That's the least of what she'll do if she gets her hands on you.

Vallek had only grown more concerned as the silence stretched for him, watching their wordless argument. Eventually, they just had to leave their argument there, at an impasse.

Ravenna hated being at odds with the two most important males in her life—Oberon over seeking revenge at all, Vallek over who would deliver the killing blow—but just like with the waiting, she had to learn to bear it.

She hoped, when they returned three days later, that Oberon would at least be a little more reasonable.

Instead, he changed tactics.

Is the bond formed with him? he projected loudly at both Ravenna and Vallek. *I need to speak with this one directly.*

Vallek nearly tripped, his wide gaze fixing on the unicorn with alarm. "That voice . . ."

Ravenna sighed. "It seems you can hear him now thanks to the bond."

If she wasn't mistaken, Vallek seemed to turn a little greener as the realization sunk in. Oberon hardly gave him time to adjust to the idea, launching into a thorough lecture about why Ravenna's need for revenge was ill-advised and dangerous, complete with hoof stomps and mane tosses.

Ravenna took no pity on either of them, crossing her arms and watching the foals rather than acknowledge Vallek's sidelong looks pleading for help.

Their dozen guards stood a respectful distance away, fanned out to cover more ground. This just meant more obstacles for the foals, weaving between the silent orcs, in their new game. At least one foal attempted to provoke a guard into dueling with her while another had his muzzle buried in a guard's pack searching for snacks.

The mares looked on, obviously amused by the orcs' discomfort and happy to have someone else entertaining their young. That they allowed the little ones anywhere close to the guards spoke to how much they trusted Ravenna's word that the orcs meant none of them harm.

The guards went to pains to prove it, none of them wanting a protective unicorn mare bearing down on them.

And another thing—

Vallek threw up his hands. "I understand your concerns, *vini mun.* They are mine as well. I have every intention of keeping her alive. I'll protect her with my life."

Ravenna cast him a sour look, but Oberon bobbed his head, apparently pleased to hear it.

I understand you orcs are fierce about protecting your mates.

"We are. There's nothing more precious."

Oberon couldn't help a sidelong, patronizing wink at Ravenna hearing Vallek call her *precious*.

She stuck out her tongue and rolled her eyes, looking away again. The foals were far more amusing than her nanny goat and mate anyway.

Oberon listened as Vallek explained the sacred bond between mates, that when it was formed, it was the strongest magic in this realm. Smoothly, he transitioned into describing their plan for ambushing Amaranthe, and Ravenna tried not to scowl at how well his politician's silver tongue worked on Oberon.

It wasn't long before the infernal pony was nodding along as if he *liked* the plan.

"And why are you considering it when *he* tells you?" she grumbled. "Just because he's a male too doesn't mean—"

Because you *aren't capable of objectivity,* Oberon replied primly.

"Neither is he!" she spluttered. "He's my *azai!*"

Yes, but he can look at this rationally, unlike you. Or at least, his sister can. I should like to meet this Eydis.

Oh, fates, no. The two of them together would be far too cunning and insufferable to bear.

A warm puff of breath on her head had Ravenna looking up to find Callistix hovering over her shoulder.

Don't pout. It isn't becoming of a queen.

Yes, grandmare.

Good. Now, I wish to speak to this young man of yours.

A strange choking sound escaped Vallek's throat. "I can hear her, too. Why can I hear her?"

Reaching up to pat Callistix's neck, she explained, "Well, as a mare, and a powerful one at that, Callistix can talk to anyone she wishes with enough concentration."

Ha, it hardly takes any effort. What takes a little concentration is scrambling up a mind.

Vallek turned his horrified gaze to Ravenna, obviously unsure if he should dare laugh at Callistix's joke or take it as a threat. Ravenna just shrugged, for it was honestly both.

I wish to parley, leader to leader, Callistix announced.

Swallowing hard, Vallek nodded. "Of course."

Since we will be staying close to our darling girl, I want protections for us. I know our kinds haven't always gotten along, but unicorns can be the bigger animal. Shaking out her mane, she added, *I won't stab you if you don't stab me. Or make her cry.*

Vallek considered his words carefully. "It will take time to overcome the centuries of enmity, but I can promise an edict securing your herd's safety. May it lead to peace between our kinds."

That will do. As a sign of our new friendship, I will accept three crates of sugar cubes each fortnight.

Ravenna nearly choked on her laugh. "*Three,* grandmare?"

You're right, that's a pittance. Four then.

Vallek cleared his throat, again unsure whether to laugh or weep. "I believe that can be arranged."

You believe? You're a powerful king, are you not? Or has my darling grand-foal spoken too highly of you?

For the first time ever to Ravenna's knowledge, Vallek flushed.

"I will see to it myself," he wisely amended.

Very good. In exchange, I promise we won't besiege your fine city. At least when it isn't mating season. I can't make any promises for mating season. You know how young ones get when the blood runs hot.

Vallek attempted to smile, but it was the stiffest, most uncomfortable expression she'd ever seen him wear. Ravenna had to hide her snorts of laughter behind her hand.

"We're agreed," he forced himself to say.

Excellent. Now, then, Crow, tell me your plan again and how many stallions I should send north.

"North?" asked Ravenna.

Yes. I will send a few ahead, to seek out news and spread the word amongst the herds. Perhaps we'll have a bit of luck and discover the where-abouts of Bellarand the Black. Flicking her tail across her flanks, Callistix said, *There is little love amongst the herds for Amaranthe. When she falls, we'll be ready.*

Vallek wanted to let himself ride the current of normalcy that over-took their lives. With their plans laid and messengers sent, there was nothing else to do but get on with the business of everyday exis-tence. He trained with his men in the mornings, took luncheon with his mate before attending meetings together all afternoon, then spent quiet evenings with her and sometimes his sisters.

It was all a pleasant lull, a glimpse at what life could truly be like.

Vallek relished it. Exerting himself in the training pits brought sat-isfaction, but so too did seeing all the political maneuvers he and Eydis had worked over a decade toward coming to fruition. One by one, all the chieftains sent their congratulations on his mating and confirmed they would attend the wedding. Even irascible Hrothgar sent a two-line note.

Ravenna dedicated herself to talks with the eastern tribes, and slowly, over days of negotiating and building a rapport, she was mak-ing progress. Vallek could have strode into the room and made his demands, yes, but Ravenna's slower, more diplomatic approach would lead to a stronger construction in the end. The eastern representa-tives respected that she too was an outsider to Balmirra and understood what it was to live an isolated life. Vallek had no doubt a ratified agreement would be ready for his signature soon, allowing him to start building up defenses in the east.

Every day, Vallek ruled alongside his magnificent mate, and every day, he grew even prouder of her. Day by day, she was winning over the people with her patience and good humor. He'd even begun to suspect they liked that she was a little strange and looked forward to what off-hand thing she'd do or say next.

Every night, he slept with his mate in his arms after long bouts of lovemaking. They fell together into sleep with bodies spent from pleasure, whispering sweet nothings across the pillows. In those nights, he memorized the texture of her hair and the hundreds of hues in her eyes. Everything was precious to him, and he gorged on every little detail that made up Ravenna.

There were times it felt too good—that it couldn't be so true to the legends and stories about perfectly suited mates. Even with their disagreements, Vallek went to sleep each night a hair happier than he had the night before, then woke every day the happiest he'd ever been.

Even so, it wasn't a surprise when all of it proved to be an illusion. They had existed on borrowed peace, for messengers eventually returned with news.

Vallek almost wished he could send them away again.

But it was far too late for that.

Gathered in the small council chamber, he, Ravenna, and Eydis met with the three messengers sent to the border with the proposal for Amaranthe.

He didn't need the sealed parchment, nor the emissary's message, to know that this pleasant little life he and his mate were building now had to end. Or at least, sacrificed for a time.

Eydis broke the seal, eyes quickly passing over the missive.

Looking up, she gravely nodded. "She'll meet with you."

32

From her higher vantage atop the basilica steps, Ravenna watched as three pairs of spelled manacles, bundled safely in layers of cloth and tied up in a discreet sack, were loaded into one of the side baskets of a waiting takin. It wasn't a vision that compelled her to take them along but instinct. Perhaps, if their first plan of a dirk to Amaranthe's heart didn't come to pass, the manacles could be of use.

As Ravenna slipped her leather gloves on, she felt a gentle movement of air beside her. Looking up, she beheld Eydis grinning kindly down at her.

"Good luck, *tristah*. I fear you'll need it."

"Thank you, Eydis. For everything."

"Don't thank me yet. And don't say it like you aren't coming back."

Ravenna smiled stiffly. She hadn't let herself dwell on her lack of visions past Amaranthe's fall. Oh, she still had plenty of visions, but they were the same strange, unsettling images again and again. White lashes. A white unicorn. Amaranthe falling. The burn of saltwater in her eyes. Vallek in irons . . .

Stomach clenching, she pushed those thoughts aside. Today wasn't the day for worries.

No, today was a show of confidence and strength.

Although the berserkers knew only that they headed for the western coast—the rest of the populace told simply that they went to negotiate with the fae—it was clear that this was no normal mission. Even when escorting Hrothgar's party back to Innrinhom, there hadn't been so much fanfare.

Atop their usual armor, all the berserkers wore burgundy surcoats with golden trim and the crossed axe emblem of Vallek Far-Sight. Every other warrior at the edge of the column, alternating rows, held a banner that flapped in the gentle autumn breeze. Even the takin and onagers were swathed in burgundy cloth, their halters and bridles inlaid with golden axes.

At the far side of the courtyard stood Vallek, resplendent in his regalia. He too wore a long surcoat, trimmed in gold. A heavy gold gorget hung round his neck, the leather strap hidden by his mating torque, and a circlet of gold sat round his head, a ruby as large as an egg inset at the center. Ears and tusks capped in gold, with a dozen hoops dangling from his ears, and Hormhím strapped to his wide leather belt, he was every inch the conquering king.

Ravenna herself wore similar attire, Hilde delighting in playing with the form of the surcoat to make something for her. And it wasn't just Hilde and her seamstresses working long hours to prepare—the smiths and tanners were set to work on creating a suit of light, flexible leather armor for Ravenna, plated strategically in steel.

It was perhaps the most comfortable thing Ravenna had ever worn. So many brilliant craftspeople had poured hours and hours of work into her kit, from her leather boots, cuisse-plated trou, fitted silk gambeson, etched leather-and-plate greaves, her own gorget with a unicorn engraved on its face, as well as her own circlet with a matching ruby. The craftspeople had thought of everything, even hidden slits at the back to allow her wings through, if needed.

She didn't plan on getting thrown off a cliff this time, though. Of course, she hadn't planned on it the first time, either. So better to be prepared.

Ravenna and Eydis watched as Asta bounded up the steps. She, too, was outfitted in finery, a golden armband on her right bicep denoting her rank as the king's sister. Vallek had asked her to personally guard Ravenna and help her with whatever she might need to prepare for the ambush.

Winking beneath the visor of her helm, she asked, "Ready?"

"No, but let's go, all the same." Turning to Eydis, Ravenna said, "Until we see each other again, *tristah*."

In a rare show of affection, Eydis wrapped her up in a fierce embrace. "It'll be so quiet without all of you."

When Eydis released Ravenna, Asta leaned in to peck her sister's cheek. "Will you miss me too, *tristah?*"

"Just barely." Eydis kissed both her cheeks. Squeezing Asta's shoulders, Eydis commanded, "Run swift, be safe, return soon."

"If you insist."

With final farewells, Ravenna and Asta descended into the courtyard to take their places at the front of the column.

Nerves fluttered in Ravenna's belly at the sight they made. Warriors bobbed their heads in respect as she walked up the line, some greeting her, *my queen, my lady, Your Majesty*. Ravenna returned their greetings, still not quite sure if this was real.

Her plans to move against Amaranthe had been barely more than ideas for so long. Even with Vallek's help, with messengers sent, there wasn't truly anything for her to *do* to further the plan. Now, though . . . Now, it was the beginning of the end.

What would that little halfling girl, hidden away by the sea with her mother, think of all this? Striding down the line of warriors, crown atop her head, Ravenna looked like the warrior queen she might have read about with her mother in one of their storybooks.

It was surreal. Unbelievable. And yet, as she made the front of the column, it was she who took the offered hand of the king. It was she who received his kiss to the back of her hand and his rumbled, "My queen."

It was more than her warrior's attire that matched his. It was more than the crown on her head and the emblems emblazoned across her chest.

Today, for the first time, Ravenna felt at the beginning of something great. Like running down a hill, legs wheeling to keep upright, she sped onwards, careening toward destiny.

Are you ready, Crow?

Ravenna turned to behold Oberon and smiled to see what a striking figure he made.

The night before, he and three other unicorns had been quietly let inside the city via the western gate and led up to the citadel. He refused to be left behind on this, insisting he carry her.

We've gone this far together, Crow, he'd reasoned. *Let us finish it together, too.*

He and the other unicorns had deigned to wear caparisons, the burgundy silk and golden thread announcing their allegiance with Ravenna and Vallek.

How handsome you are! she gushed.

Oberon vainly shook his mane. *I know. It's a good color for me.*

Reaching up to pet his velveteen muzzle, Ravenna said, *Thank you, Obi. For this and for always taking care of me. Even when I didn't want to listen.*

You are my herd and my foal, Crow. I would go with you to the ends of the world.

Ravenna quickly wiped at the tear that escaped. *You're a sentimental nanny goat.*

And you are an impetuous foal. Now, get on, and let's go impress these orcs.

It was Vallek himself who cupped his hands, offering Ravenna a leg up onto Oberon's back. A cheer rose from the berserkers to see her mounted, and with a shy smile, she waved back. For his part, Oberon preened, making sure the light hit his horn at a good angle.

Raising his fist in the air, Vallek called, "Form up!"

In a wave of synchronized skill, every berserker found their place and stood at attention.

On Vallek's right, Mattias raised a horn to his lips and blew. The call to move out ran down the line, and as one, the column swayed forward before the din of two-hundred sets of marching feet shook the cobblestones.

Ravenna waved and blew a kiss back at the basilica for Eydis and Hilde before turning forward to meet the cheering crowd.

Sitting tall astride Oberon, Ravenna kept pace alongside Vallek as they marched through the citadel gates out onto the main promenade of Balmirra. Flowers rained on them, littering their path. Petals were crushed underfoot, adding a sweet scent to the air.

Down they went through the city, applause and well-wishes following them as they made the switchbacks to the lower levels of Balmirra. They passed neither square nor street that wasn't lined with orcs to see them off, calling out goodbyes and wishes for them to return soon.

And it wasn't all for Vallek. She heard her name called, her title, too, and even cries for every warrior to protect her well.

Her heart ached to hear and feel their concern.

They were good people, the Balmirrans. When she and Vallek returned, she intended to do right by them. To put her past behind her and be the best of queens. For them.

First, she just had to slay a bad queen.

Oberon nickered. *I suppose, if we have to go through with this foolishness, it's better to do it with a small army of orcs.*

It is indeed.

She still couldn't quite believe it, but as the western gate opened for them, revealing the great scrubby expanse and serpentine path that awaited them, her heart began to thud.

Vallek put on speed, and together, they led the column through the gate at a charge. The berserkers roared behind them, the city cheered, and a blue autumn sky opened wide before them.

And so the end began

33

Vallek lingered in that space between sleep and wakefulness, not quite ready to open his eyes. He could just hear the growing bustle of a camp coming awake outside the tent, but nothing too noisy and they were well ahead of the breakfast bell.

Plenty of time.

Except . . .

Vallek frowned when he realized there was nothing beneath his arm but bedding. Finally peeling an eye open, he let out a long sigh to find himself alone in their bed. Her spot beside him was cold, indicating his mischief-maker had long since slipped away.

Not only did that mean he'd have to wait to delight in her warm little body until this evening, but he likely now needed to extricate her from whatever scheme she'd gotten herself into. Of course, if he was lucky, she was merely up and about with the unicorns or even chatting at—*at* not *with*—Mattias, but experience told him Ravenna's penchant for mischief was too great to hope for such banality.

With another sigh, Vallek rose from the warm, cozy bed and stretched out his back. Three days of marching had seen them departing the southern Griegens for the colorful swathe of the coastal foothills. The rolling hills were blanketed by thick forests, many of the trees wearing their autumn colors. The forest was sweet with the smell of decaying leaves, sometimes obscuring the path that led from the mountains out to the coast.

When Vallek stepped from the tent, he found camp a bit soggy from an overnight bout of rain. Morning mist clung to the hills, shrouding them in a damp cloak that moved heavily through the nostrils. His fellow early risers were bundled in cowls and scarves, huddling near stoked fires.

He never liked fog. It was the perfect place to suffer an ambush. The coastal hills were notorious for their soupy mornings, and if Vallek could've made Amaranthe's meeting date by following the coast of Dyfan Bay, he would have. Instead, to make the Fae Queen's meeting, just four days hence, on time, their party had to cut through the sparsely populated hills. And the fog.

Looking around, Vallek found Asta in the crowd but no Ravenna.

Keeping an eye out for his mate, should she materialize from the mist like the mysterious creature she was, Vallek approached his sister.

Asta nodded in greeting, offering him a bowl of breakfast mash.

Shaking his head to decline, he asked, "Where's Ravenna?"

Asta's eyes went wide before they slid away from him. "Uhmm . . ."

"Never mind. Keep mine warm."

Shrugging further into his fur-lined cloak, Vallek allowed his instinct to lead him. There were far too many smells in camp to track her by scent, but his instinct proved correct when he spotted one of her guards hovering near the west side of camp.

Bowing her head in deference, the guard pointed him onwards.

Through the brush he went, following a newly made path. Every so often, he came upon another guard, who pointed him on his way to the next.

He'd walked nearly half a league and was thoroughly bewildered by the time he came to the sixth guard. The orc nodded in the direction of a bramble of blackberry bushes. There, along the lower branches, was the unmistakable silvery tail of Oberon.

Well, at least she'd taken guards and unicorns with her.

Rounding the blackberry bush, Vallek beheld one of the stranger sights he'd ever seen.

Ravenna lay on her belly fully dressed in her leathers, although no surcoat, instead covered in her blue cloak. She had a set of manacles in one hand and what looked to be a small club in the other. Oberon lay on his own belly beside her, his long head stretched out low to conceal him behind the bush. Although, the last few inches of his wicked horn rose above the leaves.

"What is it exactly you're doing?" he asked.

He expected a laugh or a flush of embarrassment—not for both Ravenna and Oberon to swing mighty glares at him.

"*Shh!*" she hissed. "Get down."

Bemused, Vallek sank to the ground, sitting with his legs crossed in front of him.

"And the reason we're sitting in brambles is . . .?"

"A vision," she whispered, "and be quiet, we don't want to scare them away."

"Who?"

"I don't know."

"Ah ha."

We've been out here for over an hour waiting, Oberon pouted.

The vision didn't show when I needed to be here, just that I did, she grumbled.

I'm perfectly content to wait. It's just the others are getting bored and asking when something will happen.

Well, tell the others that I don't know. And to be patient.

Oberon let loose a quiet whicker, catching Vallek's eye. *Foals can be difficult to love sometimes.*

You'll get breakfast soon enough.

The unicorn huffed and grumbled but fell quiet. It was probably for the best that she had the unicorns away from the mess tent for a while. Three days in and the cooks were already complaining to him that the unicorns were bullying their way into the carrots and apples.

Vallek itched to ask more questions, and to fill his gurgling stomach with breakfast, but he found himself rooted to the spot. To anyone else, it might look as though Ravenna and Oberon hunted, laying in wait for a deer or boar to pass by. It couldn't be so simple, not with her, although she seemed unwilling or unable to elaborate.

So Vallek stayed where he was, shifting a little to get a better view of what Ravenna watched.

Past the brambles sat a burbling little stream of crystalline mountain water. Snaking along the floor of a small valley between hills, blackberry bushes lined one side while on the other sat a small meadow. Tall grasses and mossy boulders decorated the clearing, and as Vallek watched, a handful of birds swooped down from the trees to root around for grubs in the dirt.

It was an idyllic scene, although he suspected Ravenna wasn't here to enjoy it. A little frown of determination creased her brow, and she sat there perfectly still and silent, her focus entirely on that clearing. She only looked away to scowl at him when his stomach rumbled.

Although hungry, his curiosity won out. He stayed sitting there long past his feet going numb and having to change position. Gods, he hadn't laid out in the wilderness on a hunt in ages—and now he remembered why.

At first, he thought the flicker of movement on the far side of the clearing to be a figment of his wishful thinking. He wanted breakfast and to stretch his legs and get the day's march going.

He told himself the large shadow that passed between the trees had to be an illusion, a trick of the lingering fog. Maybe even just more birds.

But then the shadow grew.

He heard Ravenna's sharp inhale as an extraordinary sight emerged from the trees.

Through the clearing, to the stream, came an ethereally beautiful white unicorn. With dark amethyst eyes and a lilac-colored horn, she was like nothing Vallek had ever seen. In the shafts of diffused light filtering in through the mist, the unicorn seemed to glow.

Even more remarkable was her rider.

Down from the unicorn's bare back slid a fae woman. Her long white hair had been bound behind her pointed ears, falling between the folded sets of stained-glass wings. Beneath her simple tunic and trou, her dusky lilac skin gleamed opalescent, the glitter of the stream catching along her skin.

Vallek's stomach clenched. This had to be who—

Now!

A moment after Ravenna's command, Oberon and the other three unicorns burst from the bushes, encircling the white unicorn and fae woman. The trap sprung, and Ravenna was right behind them, wielding the manacles.

In a burst of speed, she flung herself across the stream, tackling the fae woman to the ground. Utterly shocked, all Vallek could do in the moment was stand and watch the . . . scene unfolding.

—white lashes—lilac horn—burbling stream—the spelled manacles in her hands—

In the span of a moment, it all made sense to her. Why her vision had woken her so early that morning it was still night. They had led her here, to this moment, this stream, so that she might find this woman.

Ravenna didn't think anymore—she moved.

Leaping from her hiding spot, she ran at the fae, barreling into her. Wrapping her arms around the woman's arms and wings, she took them to the ground, using her momentum and surprise.

The white unicorn screamed in outrage, trying to defend her rider, but Oberon and the other unicorns were there, blocking her from stopping it. The *knock* of horns and *slap* of angry hooves filled Ravenna's ears as she tussled with the fae woman, working to get on top.

The woman was thin but deceptively strong. Magic buffeted Ravenna's side, trying to knock her away, but she held her ground, countering with her own magic. Wriggling like a fish, the woman fought like a wildcat, all scratching claws and flashing fangs.

Ravenna let loose her wings, using their flapping to provide more force and momentum in keeping the fae down. The sight stunned the woman momentarily, her eyes, so dark blue they were nearly black, flicking over Ravenna's shoulder.

Getting her hands round the woman's arm, she clamped the first manacle around her slim wrist. A shudder passed down the woman's body, and Ravenna hurried to seal the irons shut. She had only moments—she could hold her own for a while, but her magic would eventually fold to that of a royal fae's.

When the second manacle *clicked* shut, Ravenna blew out a breath of relief.

The woman groaned beneath her, shuddering again as the fight went out of her.

"What have you done?" she growled.

"They're spelled," Ravenna answered in faethling. "They negate the wearer's magic."

Rising to her knees, Ravenna clambered off the fae woman to sit in the dirt beside her. It was the first chance she had to truly look at her.

Despite the tattered homespun clothes, there was no mistaking a fae woman of the royal bloodline. The silvery white hair, the wings the color of a starry night sky, and her dark eyes—she was just as Maxim had described the royal family. The only difference was, her cheeks held a glow of warmth. Her blood was obviously a healthy red, not the inky black of a fae subsisting only on magic.

Behind them, the white unicorn screamed again. She fought ferociously to make a break for her rider, but Oberon and his stallions handled her masterfully. Blocking and rebuffing her with their necks, they got her turned around before she could make it far.

"Don't hurt her," the fae demanded.

"They won't. Just tell her to stop fighting."

The fae woman turned an icy glare on Ravenna. "Who *the fuck* are you?"

"I'm queen of these lands."

The woman snorted in derision. "That's impossible. These are orcish lands."

Oh, she had quite the story to tell her. But first, "And which are you? A niece or a daughter?"

The fae lost what little color she had left in her face, those indigo eyes fixing on Ravenna with a terror so potent, Ravenna herself felt it skitter down her back.

"I don't know what you mean."

"No need to be coy. I know you're of royal blood." Her father had told her of Amaranthe's most wicked deed—almost five-hundred years ago, refusing to give up power, she slaughtered her sisters, daughters, and nieces. The fae needed a hub for their magic, a Queen to rule the hive, but such power corroded. It was the fate of every Queen, when her time came, to sail to the Twins and take the eternal sleep, returning her soul and her magic to the earth and the goddesses.

Without a successor, the fae had no choice but to suffer Amaranthe. The cycle didn't renew, and the corrosive magic seeped across the faelands.

Except, Ravenna was looking at a successor. A possible new Queen.

From her white lashes and brows to the indigo iridescence of her wings, this fae was exactly as her father and all her books described the royal line. The stories told of how the palace at Fallorian had once been full of white-haired sisters, daughters, and nieces, all more beautiful than the last. They helped channel the magic, strengthening the borders and the bond with the land.

Fates, it just couldn't be so simple. Suspicion raised her hackles; this smacked too much of destiny or divinity. There were forces at work far more powerful than her, Vallek, or a royal fae.

"How did you escape?" Ravenna asked. She must have been quite young at the time of the slaughter, for she still carried a youthful look to her that most fae maintained in their first millennium.

Her question was met with a fiercely suspicious glare.

"There's no use denying it. I know who you are, even if not your name. The fates set our paths to collide this day." Quickly, she explained her visions and how she'd been led to this time and place. Unfortunately, the longer she spoke, the more horrified the fae woman seemed to be.

"But why . . ." The woman shook her head. "It's impossible."

"I've learned it's better to let the fates guide you than rail against them. That way leads to madness."

The fae woman shot her a look that said she clearly thought Ravenna was already far down that path.

She shrugged. "My name is Ravenna Broch-Illyinia. And you are?"

The woman frowned. "You're only half fae?"

"Yes, my father was Maxim Illyinia." Grinning wryly, she teased, "Have you not seen a fae in so long you couldn't tell the difference?" Although Ravenna might seem utterly fae-like to the orcs, full fae would notice her dissimilarity immediately—shorter ears, small wings, and unruly magic.

The woman's lips went tight.

Ravenna's stomach dropped. Fates, had she truly been on her own for that long? To be sure, she would've had to flee the faelands to avoid the slaughter of her kin. Had she been in the wilderness all this time? Alone?

Her stomach did another uncomfortable flip. Fates, she knew what it was to flee and hide, but she'd never truly been alone.

Lost in her contemplation, Ravenna didn't notice until Vallek's footsteps were quite near that he approached. Standing on the other side of the stream, he loomed above them, his arms crossed over his expansive chest. He raised one brow when Ravenna met his gaze, obviously expecting a thorough explanation.

The fae barked a humorless laugh. "So you'll what—sell me to this brute?" She jutted her chin at Vallek.

"Of course not. He's my *azai*." She scowled at the fae woman. "So don't look too long at him."

"*He* also speaks faethling," Vallek grumbled. "And outlawed the selling of people long ago." He turned a thunderous, annoyed frown on Ravenna. "What *in all the hells* is going on?"

Finally retaking her feet, Ravenna brushed off the worst of the dirt from her cloak. "This is—well, she won't tell me her name. But she's the next Fae Queen."

"*What?*" the fae sputtered.

Vallek, too, looked alarmed. Gaze bouncing between the two women, his face finally sank into his hand. Rubbing the bridge of his nose as if a headache gathered there, he muttered in orcish, "Just how many fucking fae fugitives are there in my land that I don't know about?"

"That you *don't* know about? I can't say. But we are likely the most important—and the most wanted by Amaranthe."

Vallek's scowl clearly communicated how unimpressed he was with her answer.

"You're mated to an orc, you have visions . . ." The fae woman slumped back into the grass. "Fates, just take me."

"Not yet. I need you." Kneeling down beside the woman, Ravenna said, "I mean to kill Amaranthe. It's where we're headed now, to meet her. Come with me, and I'll help make you Queen. You can renew the cycle."

"No, thank you."

"You can help me kill her."

"Still no."

"Don't you hate her?"

"*Of course* I hate her. The bitch killed my mother."

Ah, a niece then.

Ravenna's smile was all teeth. "She killed my mother, too."

The fae woman met Ravenna's gaze, her expression losing some of its annoyance. She searched Ravenna's face for a long while. Even with the manacles suppressing her magic, Ravenna could feel its immense power writhing just beneath the woman's skin. They might hold her for a time, but Ravenna suspected no manacles, spelled or otherwise, could contain her forever. A royal fae's magic was vast, too much to suppress, even with spelled irons.

Which meant she needed to get the fae onside before those manacles wore out.

Reaching down, she took the woman's elbow to help her stand.

—red wings blocked out the sun—flames danced along her legs—liquid gold dripped down a gaping maw—

When she returned to herself, it was to find the woman, still in the motion of standing, staring up at her as if she'd just said something outlandish.

"What was . . . I felt . . . ?"

"Strange," Ravenna breathed. "Your future is set in flames."

The woman nearly tumbled back over. "And that's not worrying to you?"

"No. Why would it be?"

"It isn't exactly a rousing vision for my future, is it?"

"It could be metaphoric," she said with a shrug.

"You're mad."

"I'm *motivated*." With the woman standing, Ravenna unpinned her cloak from her shoulders and threw it over the fae's. Lifting the hood, she made sure the woman's white hair and face were well hidden. "I'll explain everything, but—" she looked to Vallek for confirmation "—we need to get moving."

He nodded. "We do." Looking between them again, he offered his hand to help them jump across the stream. "Please forgive my mate, she is . . . unique. I promise you will come to no harm from either of us or anyone in my command."

The woman frowned at the hand Vallek offered. "And why should I believe any of that?"

"It's the promise of a king," he said.

The defiance faltered in her eyes. "The land whispers . . . you're Vallek Far-Sight?"

"I am. And she is Ravenna, my mate. So, strange as her word is, it's that of a queen."

The fae looked like she might faint from shock as her gaze bounced between Vallek and Ravenna. "This is madness," she muttered, head shaking beneath the hood.

"This is politics," Ravenna corrected. She gently laid a hand on the woman's shoulder. "What's your name?"

The woman chewed her cheek for a long moment, and Ravenna was almost convinced she'd refuse to give her name again.

But finally, she whispered, "Leita."

The name meant nothing to Ravenna—if her father had known of Leita, he hadn't named her.

Patting Leita's shoulder, Ravenna said, "And your mount?"

Leita turned to look behind her, where the unicorns were in something of a standoff. The mare's chest heaved for breath as she took a moment to think, but the fury hadn't left her eyes. She would continue fighting until she got to Leita or she was dead.

"Thalia."

Turning to the unicorns, Ravenna called, "Thalia!" The mare's ears swiveled at the sound of her name. "I mean neither you nor your rider any harm. But she must come with us. You're welcome to follow us and join the herd."

The last thing the camp needed was an irate mare stampeding through it.

She's very angry, Crow, Oberon warned. *She's got some very rude things to say about you.*

She expected nothing less from an incensed unicorn mare. There was a reason mares were considered too wild and ill-tempered to be taken as dread-mounts.

We'll walk back to camp. Bring her with you and work some of your charms.

Even I may not have enough charm to bring her round.

That wasn't heartening, but they'd just have to make do.

Taking Leita's elbow again, Ravenna accepted Vallek's hand. Together, they hopped to the other side of the stream.

After a few steps, though, Leita came to a halt.

"I don't want to be Queen," she told Ravenna solemnly.

"I'm sorry, Leita, but I don't care. Amaranthe must be destroyed." Gripping the fae's elbow tight, she leaned in close to say, "Help me kill her, and I'll free you."

Leita shook her head sadly. "To be consumed by the faelands. There are worse imprisonments than these irons."

Ravenna's blasted heart ached suspiciously, but she wouldn't allow herself to have sympathy. The truth of the matter was, "Something more powerful than either of us has ensured our paths crossed. It's too late now to turn back."

The cycle must renew. And Amaranthe must fall.

34

Vallek didn't end up liking the plan, but it was all far too late now. Standing on a serpentine sandbar in the middle of the narrow mouth of Dyfan Bay, orcish territories behind him and the faelands just yonder, he watched as a dozen fae ships bobbed in the shallows. His own ships, ordered west from the Spearhead to meet them here, had been beached behind him. They were still manned should anything happen, but the majority of his berserkers waited in formation.

Somewhere amongst them stood Asta, guarding the reticent Leita. Disguised and glamoured, the fae woman was still shackled; in the four days since her capture, Leita still hadn't come round to Ravenna's plan. Not for lack of trying, of course. His mate wheedled, cajoled, coaxed, and threatened, anything to bring the fae heir onside.

He bore a sliver of sympathy for the woman; it was clear she wanted nothing to do with Amaranthe and the faelands—and she couldn't be faulted for that. From the scraps Ravenna had been able to glean from Leita's sparse answers, she'd been alone for almost five-hundred years, wandering the wilderness with her unicorn.

Still, Vallek wasn't above using her as bait. She was here to entice

Amaranthe, for while disguised and glamoured, her magic would still be on the wind. It would serve as a distraction from Ravenna's own magic, distinct, she said, from a full fae's and noticeable to them. Even if their senses would be somewhat dulled away from the faelands.

While that may have all been true, Vallek still wasn't sure he supported Ravenna's final plan.

Before assuming her guard of Leita, Asta had taken a small raft, just her and Ravenna. She helped Ravenna hide somewhere on the sandbar before rowing back. Alone.

Not even Vallek knew where she hid. *"It's better that way,"* Ravenna had reasoned. *"You can't give anything away if you don't know."*

He was man enough to admit that he found the insinuation that he'd give away her location offensive—and that his annoyance with her was really an easier emotion to have than this worry.

Plans were all well and good until they went to shit in the face of the enemy.

And what a face it was.

Vallek had never seen the Fae Queen in person, just likenesses in statues and stories. From Ravenna's warnings, he knew that the face she wore was false, a glamour just like the one his mate had used to pass as human.

Still, even knowing that, he wasn't prepared for the sight of the Fae Queen gliding across the sand to meet him. Unbound hair streamed behind her in soft white ringlets, nearly touching her bare feet. Robes of the palest blue velvet and silk hung from slender shoulders, accentuating a supple figure. Hands as pale and delicate as roosting doves were folded demurely before her, shell-pink nails elongated into elegant claws. With her long, graceful neck, winging brows, and small mouth, she resembled an exotic songbird. Her robes rippled behind her, and her iridescent wings gleamed opalescent in the late-morning light.

Her beauty was ethereal and terrible—and devious. Although not a fae, Vallek could sense the power radiating from Amaranthe as she stepped across the sand, hardly leaving footprints behind her. She was small, pale, and utterly deadly. Her form as beautiful as the finest blade and just as lethal.

Indeed, for all her beauty, the effect was marred somewhat by her forbidding expression.

She came to a halt about two body lengths' away, two warriors on either side of her. Vallek nodded in greeting as Mattias, on his right, bowed his head lower.

None of the fae moved. The warriors stood silent sentinel, their dark eyes trained forward. Vallek was unsettled by their statuesque posture, as though they were drones, merely awaiting command.

"Your Majesty," Vallek said in faethling. "Thank you for meeting me."

"The faelands suffer without their Queen, so we must keep this brief." Her gaze, dark as the night sky with indigo irises and black sclera, flicked past him to assess his forces.

"I wouldn't make such a request were it not important." Using the excuse to look at Mattias, Vallek scanned the sandbar for any sign of his mate. There were a handful of barnacle-clad boulders and a shelf of long-dead coral for cover, but none seemed deep or wide enough to make an effective hiding spot.

He had to trust she would strike when the moment was right. They'd spent hours going over the plan, how Vallek would do his best to lure Amaranthe as far from her warriors as he could. Distract her with promises, get her attention focused entirely on the chance at capturing Ravenna or Leita, and in that moment when she thought she would triumph, snatch it all away.

The plan had a certain poetry to it, at least in theory, but standing there with his boots in the sand, across from the frigid stare of the Fae Queen, Vallek could only pray that his mate's instinct and aim were true.

"In the summer, you sent messengers to a coastal village. To warn of a half-fae criminal."

Those dark eyes flashed with interest, and if Vallek wasn't mistaken, her expression bordered on smug. The message Eydis drafted to lure the fae here hadn't outright stated that they had more than possible information on whoever Amaranthe hunted, but the Fae Queen had to have suspected. Otherwise, she wouldn't have come herself.

Had Vallek sought someone so dangerous, so prized, he'd have come himself, too.

That he'd not only agreed to but followed through in bringing his own mate right to the being that wanted her dead hadn't escaped him. He'd lain awake for long hours the night before, pondering this very conundrum.

"I did," Amaranthe confirmed. Her gaze again skittered across the lines of berserkers. "Passing along fair warning seemed the neighborly thing to do."

"Indeed. However, it does make me wonder about the safety of our borders and whether or not a . . . renegotiation of them might be in order."

One of her brows ticked up infinitesimally. "And undermine centuries of precedent and good will? I think not."

"With so many renegade fae in my territories, I hope you will reconsider. I too have a kingdom and people to make safe."

That arched brow lost a bit of its imperiousness as she searched Vallek's face. He held perfectly still when he felt tendrils of magic begin slithering up his legs.

Clearing his throat, he adjusted his weight, sending the tendrils fleeing.

"You have her?" Amaranthe breathed.

"I didn't say that."

"You haven't said much at all. I haven't the time nor patience for games, Orc King."

"But you are so wise and long of years," countered Vallek, flashing her a roguish grin. "I took your warning to heart and have scoured my lands for such a criminal. I didn't find one matching your messengers' description. The one I have is fair . . . like you."

The air around them went totally, utterly still. The waves ceased to rise, the breeze ceased to blow. Seabirds hung in midair, and the sand made no crunch beneath his boot when he shifted.

"Impossible." Her voice came from far away, terrible and deep. "You lie."

"Lying wouldn't be neighborly," he said. "I swear upon my honor that I speak true."

"Bring her to me."

Vallek nodded easily, stepping to the side to sweep his arm to indicate behind him. "Follow me to my camp, and I will give her over to your custody."

"No. Bring her here."

"I'm sure you'll understand why I cannot do that. Not until we've worked out some neighborly assurances."

His easy smile was met with a vicious snarl. Lips peeling back from her pearly fangs, Amaranthe hissed, "You will surrender her to me, orc. *Now.*"

"Of course. She is yours—in my camp."

"Do you think I'm stupid?" she sneered.

"No one who has sat upon their throne as long as you could be stupid."

"Perhaps you haven't sat upon yours long enough." Taking one threatening step forward, the Fae Queen commanded in that terrible voice, "You play with powers your mortal mind cannot comprehend. Produce her now, or I summon the tides to drown you all."

Vallek raised his open hands. Fuck, he hadn't wanted to dangle Leita so close to the shark's mouth, but—

Sand burst into the still air, a boulder springing to life. From one blink to the next, it wasn't rock but fabric, blue fabric, flapping behind a furious, determined faeling.

Ravenna took a running leap, dirk aimed for Amaranthe's heart.

Magic wrapped around Vallek's ankles, pulling his feet out from under him. He crashed to the ground on his back, just in time to watch an invisible blow of magic catch Ravenna's middle. A gurgling wheeze punched from her lungs, and she was thrown backwards, dirk skidding through the sand.

"*Traitors!*" Amaranthe screeched.

"NOW!" Vallek cried.

Mattias leapt forward to defend him, and his berserkers let loose a fierce battle cry. The sand under Vallek's back trembled as he slid Hormhím free of his belt.

He hadn't wanted to do this the hard way, but now there was no choice.

Kicking his legs free, he took the hand Mattias offered him, bounding up. Fae warriors rushed up the sandbar, coalescing around Amaranthe, as his berserkers came charging up behind him.

A dark blur leapt through the air again, Ravenna renewing her attack. Vallek's heart jumped into his throat as he watched her fall upon the wall of armor and flesh guarding the Fae Queen. She dove at them in a fury, fangs flashing.

Vallek gripped Hormhím tight and charged forward.

Smaller but swifter, Ravenna darted between the warriors, faster than the flash of a blade. From her belt she pulled a pair of irons, and for a moment, Vallek's hope soared as he watched her go for Amaranthe's arm.

Ravenna took a blow, Amaranthe's claws raking down her chest, but she pushed on, desperate to get the manacle around the Fae Queen's wrist.

A horrid screech rent the air, followed by a percussive wave of magic. The force of it brought Vallek to his knees.

Grasping Ravenna's arm, Amaranthe tightened her grip until the irons fell away.

Ravenna made a distressed sound, one that called to Vallek's beast.

Mate, get to my mate.

Surging up from the sand, Vallek swung Hormhím at the tangle of fae. At least three swords rose to catch the axeblade, arms straining under the weight of Vallek's attack. He pushed forward, using his superior size and weight, frantic now to grab his mate and retreat.

Nothing mattered except getting her out alive.

The sound of clashing bodies met his ears, his berserkers throwing themselves into the fray.

"Vallek!" he heard Mattias call, but it was too late.

Fae warriors surrounded him, encircling him, Ravenna, and Amaranthe. His mate wouldn't give up, clawing at Amaranthe's face like a wildcat, even as the Fae Queen bent her other arm back to the point of breaking.

Gone to her rage, she didn't respond when Vallek shouted her name.

"To the king!"

"Secure the king!"

His berserkers slammed against the forming wall of fae, but despite their speed and force, the line held.

Vallek swung Hormhím, throwing back the three fae and dodging the blow of a fourth. The warriors circled him like lions waiting to pounce, but Vallek only bared his tusks.

They came at him in a coordinated rush, forcing him to swing Hormhím as fast as he could just to keep them back. He dodged and danced across the sand, catching any fae he met with his axe, buying what time he could.

The next time he spun, he found himself facing Ravenna and Amaranthe, locked in their own strange duel. Lashes of magic whipped the sand, the two women struggling over the manacles. One of Amaranthe's hands clutched his mate's arm, her claws sunk into the meat of her bicep.

Red trickled into Vallek's vision as drops of his mate's blood trickled onto the sand.

Vallek roared, throwing himself forward. The sting of a blow landed across his back, but he hardly felt it.

His legs pumped, getting him closer. Fae leapt onto his back, held onto his arms, but still he ran, desperate to get to her.

He'd almost made it when finally, six fae brought him down. Knees buckling, Hormhím went flying from his hand.

"Enough." The Fae Queen snarled, catching Ravenna by the throat and tossing her back.

His mate landed in a heap before him, blood soaking her sleeve.

As fae closed in around them, Ravenna's wide, horrified eyes snapped to his.

We've failed.

"Take them!" Amaranthe cried.

No.

With his berserker strength, Vallek seized Ravenna by the waist. Throwing off some of the bodies holding him down, he got two running steps before tossing her through the air—across the fae line and to his own warriors.

"*Vallek!*"

"Fall back!" he bellowed. "*Fall back!*"

A hiss pierced his ear as more fae swarmed him. The *snick* of irons locking shut hit him next. Cold burned up his arm, suddenly weak and lethargic. The fight in him stuttered, the red bleeding from his vision.

He wrestled with five, six, seven, many fae. They held him down as the second manacle was clasped round his wrist.

Nausea rolled over him, the enchanted metal sucking at his strength. He bared his tusks, refusing to be beaten, but his chest could hardly draw breath under the weight of all the fae.

"To the ships. Bring him!" commanded the Fae Queen.

His vision swam as he was dragged through the sand.

He knew he should be concerned, but his mind couldn't quite manage it through the haze.

She's safe. That's all that matters.

With the last of his strength, he cried one last time, "FALL BACK!"

35

"NO! No, turn back, we have to go *back!* Vallek!"

Ravenna threw herself against the carved stempost of the boat, meaning to jump into the churning shallow waters. A big hand caught the back of her cuirass, pulling her down into the footwell in front of the first oarsman seat. She landed hard on her backside but was up again in a moment, pulling herself upright by the hull rail. She would have thrown herself overboard had the hand not pulled her back again.

Asta's heavy booted foot landed on Ravenna's chest to keep her there.

"Stay down," the orcess growled at her. Bloodied and sweaty, her strong arms flexed as she kept time with the other rowers, her face set grimly.

"We have to go back!" Ravenna cried. Wriggling under Asta's foot, she clawed and fought to get free, desperate to go back. To help him. "We can't leave him! We can't—we can't—can't—"

She just managed to peek over the hull rail. Across the narrow mouth of the strait, the sails of Amaranthe's ships caught the breeze, the fae fleet fleeing quickly northward toward Fallorian. At least six orcish ships—sleek longships that cut through the water—were in pursuit. Their ships chased Amaranthe like some pod of marine predators, but that wasn't enough—Ravenna needed to be with them, to chase the hag down herself. She had to get her mate, she had to fix this.

"Asta—!"

"No." The orcess snarled at her, something she'd never done before. Tusks bared in a grimace of pain, she said, "I promised him. Don't make this any harder."

She didn't think it possible, but Ravenna's heart ached even fiercer at the sight of Asta's pain.

Tears streamed down Ravenna's face, although she was too numb and frantic to sob. She refused to stay put, to let herself be carried to safety when her mate was in enemy hands. Because of her.

Searching wildly for any way out, any way to get Asta to turn the boat around, her gaze fell on Leita.

Curled up in the next footwell over, she stared out at Ravenna from the depths of her hood. Those dark eyes, so like Amaranthe's, gazed upon her with pity.

Ravenna looked away, unable to bear it.

No matter what she did or said, Asta wouldn't heed it. Before long, the scrape of the boat running aground on the sandy southern shore of the strait jarred them all. Asta and the handful of other orcs in their boat jumped off; the others pulled the boat further ashore while Asta grabbed both Ravenna and Leita.

Leita came quietly—Ravenna fought.

"Let me go—Asta—I have to—*please*—!"

But the orcess was merciless, marching them up the slope to the grassy hills overlooking the water where they'd made their camp the day before.

Upon the rise, Ravenna dug in her heels, desperate to see what was happening.

Others stopped along the rise, too, hands shading brows to watch. Unhappy murmurs followed as they watched the orcish boats gain on the fae ships. Suddenly, a great wave caught the orcish vessels, scattering them. Most slid backwards across the water and were able to hold their balance—but two began to teeter dangerously.

A groan of distress went up from the berserkers as they watched two ships capsize. A handful of warriors rushed back to the ships they'd just beached, meaning to go aid their comrades.

Ravenna tried to go with them but was held back by Asta.

"I have to help him!" she wailed. "It's my fault, Asta, it's all my fault!"

She would never, for however long or short she lived, forget the sight of almost a dozen fae warriors piling onto her mate's back to subdue him. She would never forget the way he looked upon her, slumped in the sand. Defeat had lined his eyes, a grim sort of determination making her blood run cold.

Ravenna hadn't quite believed what he'd done even as she sailed through the air. Not until she landed hard on someone was reality knocked into her.

He threw her to safety.

He sacrificed himself.

Absolutely not.

This was Ravenna's fight, Ravenna's fault. If anyone should be taken or killed, it should be her.

She told Asta as much, trying to make her see, to let her go. "It should be me—let her take *me*. Not him, not him, not—"

Warily watching the battered, angry warriors around them, Asta pulled Ravenna in close. "Shut up," she hissed, "and come quickly."

Ravenna and Leita were more carried than walked the rest of the way up the slope and into camp. Asta was heaving by the time she dragged both of them into the king's tent, out of sight.

Setting herself up at the entrance, Asta peered outside, a worried frown now adorning her brow.

Ravenna tried darting past her, but this time was stopped by Leita.

The fae woman threw her manacled arms around her, keeping her within their circle.

"Don't," whispered Leita. "Can't you hear them?"

"Hear what?" She couldn't hear anything past her own racing heart and how it was breaking down the center.

"The warriors. They're angry with you." Leita looked upon her seriously. "They blame you."

Ravenna groaned. "It's my fault," she insisted. "This was my plan, my revenge—it should have been me!"

Her words were drowned out by the commotion outside the tent.

"Let us have her, Asta," said a deep, threatening voice just outside.

"She'll come out and speak with you in a moment. Let her regain her composure."

"Damn what she has to say. This was her bloody doing—give her over."

"My brother knew what he was doing," said Asta. "Hope isn't lost. She'll no doubt send terms soon."

"We shouldn't wait. Let's hand her over. We must free the king."

"My brother wouldn't want—"

"Damn what he wants!" shouted another voice.

"He's our king. We can't allow him to be held captive," said another.

Ravenna could feel Leita's shaking breath on her clammy cheek, and the fae woman drew her further into the shadow of the tent. The anger outside swelled, more and more green bodies looming at the entrance.

Asta stood firm, blocking their way. "We'll think of something. Regroup and see to the injured."

"We already know what to do. Hand over the halfling and—"

"That halfling is your queen." Mattias shoved through the crowd to come and stand alongside Asta. "She is your king's mate. You will respect that."

More grunts and arguing, but, eventually, the crowd outside dispersed. Asta and Mattias remained at the entrance, though, wary to let down their guard.

Dragging Leita along with her, Ravenna approached the wall they made.

"Let them have me," she said, "trade me for him."

"We have to wait for terms," Asta said unhappily.

"Fuck that! Give me a boat and let me—"

"STOP IT!" Rounding on her, Asta loomed above Ravenna—and the unfortunate Leita—her tusks bared in anger. "Just stop it! The plan went to shit. Everything went to shit."

"I know!" Ravenna yelled back. "It was all shit and it's my fault! Let me fix this!"

"I don't exactly trust your plans or your judgement. Not right now." Asta may as well have said she didn't trust Ravenna, for that was how her words felt. A slap to her face.

One Ravenna deserved.

"I'm sorry," she murmured. "I'm so, so sorry, Asta."

The orcess huffed, nostrils flaring, and turned away. "I promised Vallek I'd keep you safe. He valued your life over his own, as any mate would." When Asta looked at her again, it was with a forbidding frown. "*We* will think of something to get him back."

Ravenna didn't know if she was included in that *we*.

She didn't deserve to be. Not after this.

Asta retook her place at the front of the tent, and Leita withdrew her arms.

The fae offered another piteous look. "Amaranthe destroys everything. She's like a plague, heartless and inevitable." With those rousing words, Leita silently slipped to the corner of the tent she'd claimed as her own over the past few days.

Left alone in the center of the tent, Ravenna's legs shook until she finally went down. Her energy crashed along with her, all her confidence and determination left to pool on the packed earth floor.

Fates, what have I done?

Her horror was a shard of ice in her heart. How could she have believed she would best a Fae Queen? Armed with a dagger and a set of manacles—how could she have been so arrogant?

Because she had visions? Because her mate had decided she was a queen herself?

She was nothing. None of that. A scared little halfling girl, alone in the world.

She should have stayed in her bower. Not a bother or burden to anyone anymore. All she did was cause misfortune and harm to others.

She should have been brave enough to stop her parents, to stop Vallek. *I'm not worth it.* They didn't need to protect her, to sacrifice for her. She was nothing.

For the first time since her death, Ravenna *ached* for her mother. She hadn't let herself miss Aine too much, focusing instead on her revenge, but now, with the wreckage of that vengeance surrounding her, Ravenna wept. Drawing her arms around herself, sobs wracking her, she longed for her mother's soft voice, her gentle comfort. Aine's touch wouldn't solve anything, but in her darkest hour, Ravenna wished for nothing more, nothing less.

But Aine was gone. Just like Vallek.

Tears burned her cheeks, but Ravenna didn't wipe them away. She couldn't move from her place on the floor, hunched over on herself. Limbs heavy, rubbery, she didn't want to move, either. Down here was where she belonged. In the dirt. Amongst the worms.

Her breathing grew reedy as failure pressed upon her shoulders. The bond inside her, that precious thing she'd denied for years but foolishly let grow, strained under the distance. He was alive, for now, she could feel that at least. But he was gone. Not here. When he should have been.

He should be here.

Vallek was the one worthwhile. He was the one meant to lead and remake the world. The gods, fates, destiny, whatever it was, had marked him for greatness.

She was but a leech, clinging to him as if she could imbibe some of his easy confidence for herself. He knew his place in the world, and if she was attached to him, belonged to him, then she would have a place in the world, too.

She hadn't meant for that place to be his downfall.

I'm sorry. It's my fault. I'm sorry . . .
Crow? What's happened? Are you—
It's my fault.

Ravenna refused to move from the floor. She couldn't.

She was aware of a handful of others coming and going.

Fenna the healer came to look at her arm. Ravenna was distantly aware of the pain as Fenna dabbed at and cleaned the punctures from Amaranthe's claws.

She almost told the old orcess to leave them. She deserved the wounds. But her voice was gone.

Fenna would hardly look at her, although she felt the occasional press of the healer's assessing gaze. Fenna asked her a few things, but Ravenna said nothing.

Night soon descended across the camp. Ravenna only knew because of the smell of the fires. Someone put a bowl of stew in front of her, but she didn't eat.

Sometime in the night, Oberon ducked inside the tent.

His great body was awkward in the space, navigating the tent poles and low canvas ceiling. Folding his legs, he lay beside her, curling his neck around her back.

Crow, speak to me.
It's my fault. I'm sorry.
It's all right. We'll be all right.
No. It's my fault.
Mistakes are best learned from and then left in the past. We'll get your man back.
She has him. It's my fault.

Oberon's warm breath wafted across her cheek, followed by his velveteen muzzle. *We'll get him back, Crow.*
I'm sorry. I'm sorry.

Ravenna didn't move. Her tears didn't stop.

She remained there, on the floor, clutching desperately at the threadbare bond inside her. She dared not grasp it too tightly for fear it would break, but so long as it lived, so too did Vallek.

It was her only hope, her only focus.

If he was alive, then she could make this right.

She'd let herself believe in his confidence and his vision for their future. She'd let herself be carried away by romantic gestures and delusions of happiness.

She'd let herself forget that, since childhood, she was marked for death. There was no other outcome for one who predicted the downfall of a Fae Queen. All who'd tried to stop it, to thwart her fate, had met horrible ends.

It was time Ravenna stop letting them try to save her. It was time she accept that her destiny was written in magic and blood. It couldn't be denied.

She was destined to die, and she meant to take Amaranthe with her.

Dawn approached before Ravenna regained any feeling in her body. Her tears left salty tracks on her face, and her limbs had long since gone numb with inactivity.

Something happened outside the tent, but she couldn't be bothered to care.

Not until Oberon began nudging her. *Ravenna? Ravenna, you must come back. They need you.*

No one needs me.

Oberon nickered. *Enough of that. Come back to us.*

She didn't want to. There was relief in her numbness, a cold comfort that she could wallow in until the time came. Returning meant pain.

When she still didn't move, Oberon nudged harder.

She stiffly slumped forward, unable to catch herself. Ravenna groaned, finally finding enough will to get her hands beneath her. Pushing up to hands and knees, she slowly regained her feet with Oberon's help.

That's it. Slowly now.

Pinpricks of reality assailed her limbs, and Ravenna grimaced under the onslaught.

You're no use to anyone, most of all your mate, like this. Buck up and find your courage, Crow.

She wanted to snap something smart back, but her mind was too muzzy for that.

Ravenna blinked, refocusing her vision in time to see Mattias reenter the tent. He must have gone somewhere, for he returned with mist clinging to his shoulders. He could only look upon Ravenna for a moment, his expression carefully neutral as he turned to Asta to say, "A messenger has been spotted. They're coming ashore now."

"Best get to them before the warriors do." Asta glanced at Ravenna. "Stay here."

"No." It took a few steps, but Ravenna pushed herself forward. "I will hear what they have to say."

Asta obviously didn't like it, her lips pressed into a line between her tusks.

"Stay behind us," said Mattias.

Ravenna agreed, and with Oberon behind her, she followed Asta and Mattias from the tent.

The camp outside was somber, the fires banked low. Dozens of eyes fixed on her as she emerged into the weak dawn light. Unable to meet any of them, Ravenna kept her gaze on Mattias's back, following him and Asta down the slope to the sandy bank.

A handful of warriors already stood there, surrounding a solitary boat. The front half of the vessel had come ashore, but the back half still bobbed in the water. In the middle stood a fae warrior, his long blonde hair pulled back into a tail.

His severe gaze fell on Asta and Mattias as they approached, although his brows lifted to see a unicorn behind them.

A strange smile touched his lips, although it didn't reach his eyes. "So it's true."

"Your seizure of our king is an outrage," said Mattias. "We came to parley in peace."

"I think the time for lies is over," replied the fae cooly. "It was your king who lured our queen here. It was he who had an assassin lying in wait."

That couldn't be denied, and so no one did.

The fae nodded. "My queen can be magnanimous. She's willing to overlook this insult and restore your king to you. Produce the one your king spoke of and we'll accept her life for his."

Asta and Mattias exchanged looks.

Ravenna's heart sank to her stomach. It could be that simple. Trade Leita for Vallek.

Amaranthe must not have known who Ravenna was. The Fae Queen had never seen Ravenna herself, and Maxim ensured few did, hiding her and Aine away behind anonymity, isolation, and decades of wards. Or if she did recognize Ravenna, the potential of securing her own niece was more important.

Leita for Vallek. Simple.

And yet, she couldn't do it.

This wasn't Vallek's fight. It wasn't Leita's either.

This began and ended with Ravenna. It was time she stopped allowing others to suffer for her own vengeance—and mistakes.

Stepping out from behind Asta and Mattias, Ravenna revealed herself to the fae messenger. Asta hissed, trying to grab for her, but Ravenna eluded her grasp, approaching the boat.

At the shoreline, she looked into the fae's eyes and declared, "We have no such person. But your queen will take me instead."

The fae looked her up and down, suspicion gathering in his expression. "The assassin herself, come to make terms?"

"I'm the one your queen wants. The criminal she's been looking for."

If it was possible, the fae went even paler. "You—"

"My name is Ravenna Illyinia, and I have foreseen Amaranthe's death."

36

It was the longest day of Ravenna's life. As the sun rose over Dyfan Bay, she watched as the solitary fae sailed back across the strait, bringing her offer to Amaranthe. If she thought it could've freed Vallek sooner, she would've happily climbed into the boat with him, but Amaranthe was too tricksy for that.

Ravenna needed to start being smart.

Turning back toward the camp, she walked with Asta, Mattias, and Oberon behind her. At the top, she found berserkers crowded round the central fire. Some watched the water suspiciously, while others regarded her with much the same wariness.

The tension of before had simmered down, and she didn't immediately feel in danger from these warriors. Grief had settled over the camp, the reality of the defeat dampening all heat and noise. These were proud warriors, the most illustrious unit, and they had lost.

But it wasn't their fault.

Moved to speak, Ravenna found a stump to stand upon. It gave her a little height, barely more than Mattias, but it'd have to do.

"I know it isn't a warrior's preference to wait, but, for now, that is what we must do. I expect the Fae Queen to accept the offer to trade. I will gladly take Vallek's place."

The berserkers murmured amongst themselves, some of them nodding.

"Stay ready to move; word may come at any time." Looking out across Vallek's most loyal warriors, Ravenna's heart ached to see their despair. "I'm sorry," she murmured, then, louder, "I'm sorry. This wasn't my . . . this isn't how I wanted the mission to go. I take responsibility, and I will make it right."

She hoped their murmurs were of approval, but Ravenna didn't linger. Stepping down from the stump, she rejoined Asta and Mattias.

She took some heart to see Asta's reluctant nod. It wasn't much, but Ravenna didn't deserve much.

"They'll appreciate your acknowledgement," Asta said.

"I meant what I said. I'll get him back, Asta."

"He wouldn't want you to trade yourself," the orcess admitted. "He'll never forgive either of us."

"He isn't here." Ravenna swallowed back the sudden sob that sprung up her throat. "It's my choice to make." *I shouldn't have involved him at all.*

"We'll take what time we have to plan," Mattias said. "There must be a way."

"I mean to slay her," Ravenna said. "That hasn't changed. I want you both to promise me that when the trade happens, you'll secure Vallek. That's all that matters. Don't worry about me, and don't heed Vallek when he orders you to help me."

Asta shifted uncomfortably, hands on her hips, and Mattias looked troubled.

"We can't promise that," he said.

"Then at least make your best effort. Prioritize him."

A great puff of hot air cascaded over Ravenna's head. *Crow, I think . . .* Oberon moved forward to stand alongside her, his attention focused on the eastern forest.

Ears swiveling, he listened for a long moment before bobbing his head in excitement. Mattias leaned far back, warily watching the sharp tip of Oberon's horn.

Stomping the ground, Oberon told her, *Some good news at last!*

What is it? What's—?

"*Fae!*" The cry rang out from one of the sentries guarding the eastern flank. "Fae approach!"

What? But it was far too soon for them to return from across the water?

Not those fae, Oberon corrected. *Friends!*

Ravenna hurried to the eastern edge of camp, Asta, Mattias, and many berserkers behind her. They gathered along the ridge, peering down the grassy slope toward the line of oak trees to the east. Three sentries stood near the tree line, spears raised at a figure walking forward.

Two figures.

A unicorn and mounted fae.

"It can't be . . ."

The black unicorn came to a halt just out from the trees. His dread-rider, clad in leathers rather than armor and regalia, lifted a hand to his brow, shading his eyes to look up the hill.

"Crow? Is that you?"

Oberon neighed merrily, nudging Ravenna's shoulder. *Allarion and Bellarand have come!*

For a moment, she teetered on the edge of the ridge, not quite believing Oberon or her eyes. It just couldn't be.

It'd been years since he left her in the safety of her bower to take the deep sleep behind the layers of wards set by her father. Their plan had been so simple; she would sleep to dull her powers until Allarion could secure a place in human lands, warding it with his own magic. When it was safe, he would bring her there, hide her away to begin again. That seemed so long ago now, another life.

Before she'd even thought to, her legs were moving. She heard someone call her name, but she didn't heed it. Arms wheeling, she ran down the slope, bending and crushing the tall grass beneath her boots.

Her heart beat wildly, so quickly that she nearly flew to him. The sentries were but blurs as she passed them, avoiding their caution and arms.

Allarion jumped off Bellarand to meet her. Arms thrown wide, he caught her when she threw herself at him.

It wasn't quite the arms of her father, but it was the closest Ravenna would ever get in the living world. So many evenings had been spent round the table with her parents and Allarion, telling stories, joking, playing dice. Her father's closest friend, he'd quickly become something of an uncle to her, a second father.

When her parents perished, it was Allarion who came for her. It was Allarion who comforted her and took her to safety.

A shudder passed through him, and he rocked them back and forth. "Goddesses, I've longed for this day."

Ravenna couldn't pull away for long moments, more tears leaking from the dregs of her soul. Fates, she didn't deserve—she could hardly believe—why now? Her old life and her new one were colliding, and she didn't know if she could bear the impact.

Allarion held her tight for long moments, silently offering his comfort as she wept. Goddesses, fates, the spirits of Maxim and Aine—she didn't care what had sent him, only that he was here.

When she did manage to pull back her tears, she was shocked to look upon him.

No longer the grayish color of a fae reliant on magic, his skin bore a purplish hue and his sclera were white, emphasizing the dazzling amethyst color of his irises. When he smiled, she couldn't help catching his chin in her hand to inspect his gums and tongue. Both were a healthy pink.

"How—?" she choked.

"There's much to share. For both of us." Glancing at the baffled sentries around them, he added, "Because I'm intensely curious about why you find yourself amongst an orc war party."

Fates, where to even start.

"Erm, my queen . . ."

Ravenna looked over her shoulder to find Bellarand teasingly knocking his horn against one of the sentries' spears.

Allarion poked his dread-mount's flank. "Don't scare them."

Whatever the unicorn said back had Allarion rolling his eyes.

"There's no danger," she assured the sentry, wiping at her tears. Stepping between Bellarand and the berserker, she petted the unicorn's gleaming black muzzle. "These are good friends."

Bellarand's head bobbed in greeting, his ruby red eyes laughing with mirth. Such a scamp. When he blew his hot breath in her face, Ravenna couldn't help a small grin.

Oberon joined her, knocking horns with Bellarand. The sight of the known unicorn calmly greeting the new one seemed to relieve the sentries somewhat, all of them slowly lowering their spears.

"I mean you no harm," Allarion told the sentries in orcish. "I am an old friend of Ravenna's, come to help her."

His words had more tears pricking her eyes. "Allarion, something's happened . . ."

Sobering, he put his arm around her in comfort. "Tell me everything, Crow."

"Well fuck." Allarion stood inside the great tent, staring in shock at Leita. "This changes everything."

Letia seemed less than enthused to hear it, her lips pursed as she scowled up at him and Ravenna from her cot in the corner.

It'd taken them quite a while to meander up the hill back into camp, Ravenna explaining through her tears how she'd come to be amongst the orcs and find herself mated to their king. Hardest of all was recounting his loss the day before.

By the time she'd introduced him to Asta and Mattias, as well as re-iterating he and Bellarand were to be welcomed as guests and friends to the berserkers, she'd at least gotten through the salient points of the story. She had so much to tell him that when they walked into the tent, she'd entirely forgotten to prepare him for the sight of a potential fae heir.

Allarion scrubbed a hand over his face, looking understandably overwhelmed. "So you have an orc king for a mate and a royal fae as your captive. Am I missing anything?"

"Amaranthe has my *azai*."

"Yes, that." Allarion pressed his mouth into an unhappy line. "Goddesses, Crow, I worried you'd get into trouble on your own, but I never imagined this much trouble."

"I must get my *azai* back." She hadn't informed him of the trade to do just that. Not yet, at least. He was already cross with her.

Allarion nodded, his gaze straying back to Leita. The two of them assessed one another, and finally it was Leita who said, "You don't look like one of *her* fae."

"Because I'm not," he answered easily. "I broke away from Amaranthe and the faelands. Much as you did, I suspect."

Not taking the bait, Leita said, "That doesn't explain why your blood isn't black."

"Ah. No, that is thanks to my *azai*." Ravenna gasped, not quite believing her ears. Wearing a besotted grin, Allarion told them of his adventures in the human realm of Eirea, how a whole village of otherly folk had established themselves, all looking for human mates. Allarion himself had found his *azai* in a human woman named Molly, who he'd brought back to his new home of Scarborough and helped him seal his bond with the land. "Once that was done, we traveled south, to the bower." Allarion's smile fell as he looked upon Ravenna. "We came for you, but you weren't there."

Ravenna shook her head. She couldn't apologize, for she wasn't sorry. What she could say was, "I regret any distress I caused. But I never intended to stay in that bower."

Allarion seemed troubled by the revelation, but he didn't reprimand her, at least.

"What's done is done," he said finally. "I'm just relieved we found each other again, in the end."

"How did you find me?" It was almost too fantastical to believe. Yes, they had sent word through lines of communication to Eirea, but it sounded as though Allarion wasn't even there to receive it.

A wry grin lifted his lips. "The unicorns. It helped, of course, that Molly and I have been staying secretly on my mother's estate. Word reached Bellarand there. We were led through the herds into orcish territory, where Bellarand was able to make contact with Callistix. She sent us westward to find you."

The mention of her grandmare had Ravenna aching all over again. She could use the matriarch's steely will and guidance right about now. Of course, she could easily guess what Callistix would tell her.

Kill the bitch. Win back your male. Simple.

That does sound like my mother, Oberon chuffed.

"You left your *azai* to find me?" Ravenna whispered.

"Molly understands. She's safe with my kin."

Ravenna didn't know what to say. Her stomach clenched uncomfortably to know someone else had sacrificed for her. She was sick of it, sick of being the cause of so much heartache.

Stealing another glance at Leita, Allarion asked, "Has Amaranthe sent terms?"

"Yes. I sent a counter offer. We're awaiting word back."

He nodded absently. "If it was known that an heir of royal blood lived, you wouldn't march alone." Turning the weight of his gaze onto Ravenna, he said, "The fae live in fear of her. All understand Amaranthe's tyranny but have nowhere else to turn. If given another path, most would choose to walk it."

Ravenna's heart lurched painfully, but she refused to entertain true hope. Such hope had already cost her far too much.

"I'll be honest—the fate of the faelands means little to me. My only wish is to free my *azai*."

"I understand. Your loyalties are to your orc." Allarion smiled sadly. "Mine too are with my Molly and our home in Eirea. And yet . . ." he sighed, striding over to stand before Leita and kneel at her cot, "not all hope is lost for the faelands."

Leita leaned as far back into her cot as she could. "I want no part in your plans. I escaped there once—my luck won't hold for a second time."

"A great destiny is something to fear, it's true. But it will come, one way or another. There must be a reason you escaped the slaughter."

Leita bared her fangs. "That reason was my mother and sister. They died so I might live."

"And what will you do with such a gift?"

"They wanted me to *live,* and so I have done," she spat. "To do anything else would insult their sacrifice."

"Insult—or honor?"

"Falling into *her* hands is exactly what they died to prevent."

"So don't fall," Allarion said. "Rise."

Leita's face darkened in a glower, and she turned away from him.

When it was clear she had nothing else to say, Allarion rose. He turned to find Ravenna gone pale.

They died so I might live.

Her stomach rolled ominously.

Allarion reached out to touch her shoulder gently. "If you can buy me a little time and get me across the water, we may just have a chance."

Much later, after a long day of discussions and planning, Allarion and Bellarand boarded a barge to sail across the strait under the cover of darkness. As the rowers took up their oars, Allarion turned round and lifted his hand, waving farewell to Ravenna.

She waved back, heart in her throat. *Goddesses go with you. And the fates, too.*

Ravenna kept nothing for herself except the hope that her aim this time would be true.

37

So many plans were in motion, it made Ravenna sick. Another night with hardly any sleep passed interminably slow, the tenuous bond inside her strained and dim. The smell of him in their bed only brought silent tears, and so when the camp roused for breakfast, Ravenna was quick to flee the soft place where her mate had lain.

There was only more waiting to do today.

Well, that wasn't entirely true. There was one final important thing she needed to take care of.

Carrying two bowls of porridge, mixed with nuts and berries, Ravenna reentered the tent. Leita watched her approach from her place in the corner, gaze as wary as ever.

Taking a seat beside the cot, Ravenna handed Leita her bowl. The fae regarded her suspiciously, her indigo eyes nearly black in the deep shadows of the tent.

Ravenna got a few bites into her, needing the warm reinforcement, before beginning.

"I suspect we'll receive word today, and move out soon after," she said.

"I see."

"I'll need your help to kill her."

Leita's upper lip curled back in a show of disdain. "That sounds like your own problem."

Ravenna mashed a berry into her porridge until purple juice squirted over the grains. "The plan is—"

"*Your plan* is worthless—it's entirely dependent on me agreeing to become Queen."

"No, it's dependent on you becoming Queen," she spat back. Ravenna made herself sit back in her seat. Take a breath. Calm. Collected. Threatening the woman would get her nowhere. "I would speak with you civilly. Negotiate, queen to queen."

Leita snorted. "Neither of us are queens."

"But we could be." Leaning forward, Ravenna pinned the other woman with a steely stare. "My mate has made me his queen. Your blood declares that you can take Amaranthe's place. Why should we not treat?"

"Over what?" Leita sputtered. "Which of us will die first?"

"Upon Amaranthe's death, the cycle will renew. It will take time, but the fae will hopefully begin to live without the sole need of magic. Your people haven't grown or prepared food in centuries. I can ensure that a steady supply reaches them."

"They aren't my people," grumbled Leita before shoving porridge in her mouth.

"But they could be."

The other woman just spooned more mash into her mouth, brows arched defiantly.

Ravenna took a more prim bite, reassessing.

"Whatever you want, if it's in my power, I will give it to you."

Leita smiled maliciously. "The promise of an almost-queen about to die means little to me. Besides, what I want isn't within your power."

"Try me."

"I want my family," she snarled.

"Ah." Ignoring the ache in her heart, for Vallek, for her parents, Ravenna set down her bowl. "I can't bring your mother and sister back—but I can promise you a family."

Leita's frown was a forbidding thing, hiding the vulnerable way her eyes glittered with unshed tears. A knot formed in Ravenna's throat to see the feral need inside her.

Fates, she truly had been out in the wilderness, all alone.

Take the wildness away, the royal fae blood, the spite, and what was left was a woman yearning for a family.

"Don't be cruel," Leita murmured.

"I'm not. I have visions, remember? It's how I found you. I can look into your future, see if there's a family waiting for you."

The woman sat in brooding silence, and Ravenna had to hope no immediate refusal was promising. Slowly reaching out, she laid her hand gently on Leita's knee. Her eyes slid closed, willing a—

—wings mantled on broad shoulders—you won't be rid of me now, doe—flames licking the night sky—burn it all, and from the ashes—life—a sweet cry—I knew you'd find me—

—vision.

Ravenna sucked in a breath, eyes slowly opening. Her sight was fuzzy for a moment, the image of Leita, her lips parted in shock, eventually coming into focus.

Leita groaned. "You—I saw—I felt—"

Slumping back in her chair, Ravenna took a moment to breathe. It was far more than she usually saw, a whole, busy life spreading before her like unfurling wings.

"You will take the throne and heal the faelands," she said, not proud but not ashamed to embellish, "but you won't have to do it alone."

A stark, desperate hope carved lines across Leita's face. "You're lying."

Ravenna shook her head. "Your future holds so much. An *azai*. A child. And—" this was more speculation than anything, but Ravenna again wasn't ashamed "—I don't think you're the only one who escaped."

"You're as cruel as she is." Leita's words were hardly more than a whisper, but they struck Ravenna with the force of a hammer blow.

"I saw it all. You will just have to live to see it."

A tear escaped Leita's eye. She immediately went to wipe it away, the manacles forcing her to lift both hands.

This time, Ravenna did feel shame. She'd meant it when she told herself she had to stop being the reason for so much suffering. This . . . she could start with this.

Heart heavy, she reached to clasp the manacles. It was a gamble, but one she had to take.

Tracing her finger in a tight pattern, the first manacle clicked and unlocked. "They are spelled to release only by the touch of the one who locked them," Ravenna explained as she traced over the second manacle. She wasn't sure how the scholars had worked that out, only grateful that they had.

When the irons released into her hands, Ravenna tossed them aside.

Leita didn't immediately spring up and run for the tent entrance, and so Ravenna pressed on.

"Now we can speak as equals."

"Because we're queens?" Leita derided. Her hackles were back up, her knees curled to her chest as she rubbed her wrists.

"Because we both know what it is to lose everything." Sliding from her seat onto her knees, Ravenna took Leita's hands in her own. The woman watched on in surprise as Ravenna bent to press her forehead into the backs of Leita's hands, an ancient gesture of supplication and humility.

"What are you . . .?"

"Amaranthe has taken everything from me. My future, my peace, my parents. Now she's taken my *azai,* too, the only good—" Ravenna bit back more tears, pressing her forehead harder into Leita. "I want justice. I want revenge. For my parents, for Vallek, for the girl I could have been. For you, too."

Ravenna raised her head, unable to hold back her tears. Leita stared back at her, glassy eyes searching Ravenna's for deception.

"We've been running our whole lives, the two of us. From her—but from the fates, too. I think . . . it's time we stop running. I think it's time we make our stand."

Leita shook her head slowly, her expression troubled. Uncertain.

A frantic, dangerous kind of fluttering hope seized in Ravenna's chest.

"I've *seen it,* Leita," she said, hearing the desperation in her own voice. Her throat clogged with it, with more tears, with the need to make her understand. "You will live. I swear it. You will live and she will die. I've seen it. All my life, I've seen her fall."

"What about you?" Leita murmured.

"I don't know. I don't care, so long as Vallek is safe." Squeezing Leita's hands, she begged, "Please. Please help me. I know now I can't kill her alone. But together—together we can do it. We can end this."

Leita swallowed hard. "You swear you saw my *azai?*"

"Yes."

"On your mate's life, you swear it?"

"Yes!"

Leita squeezed Ravenna's hands back. "And you swear, on his life, that you have seen Amaranthe die?"

"Yes."

All the breath seemed to rush out of Leita's lungs at once, her back bowing as she leaned over Ravenna. Magic rushed around them, slithering under every blanket, pot, and chair, writhing up every tent post, and wrapping round Ravenna's wrists and ankles. Leita held her there with magic, a tendril winding round Ravenna's throat, as she gazed into her eyes.

Ravenna held still, allowing this powerful fae to do as she liked. She could look and take what she needed.

Leita's eyes glowed eerily, and in their ghoulish light, Ravenna saw the shadow of her kinswoman. The power of a royal fae, even uncrowned, was terrible, a force equaled only by nature itself.

Whatever Leita did to her, Ravenna felt herself scooped out and laid bare. Her innards were spread across the floor, every bone and nerve and secret exposed. Her wings trembled against her back, shuddering as if they wished to curl up beneath her shoulder blades and hide.

But there could be no hiding.

When the magic pressed against her lips and nose, Ravenna let it. She held Leita's awful gaze, and it was like looking at the sizzling white energy of a lightning bolt. It burned her from head to toe, but Ravenna wouldn't look away.

She let Leita see it. Everything. She stared down the inferno of a wildfire, a scared little orphan girl. That was all she was. All she'd ever been was a halfling girl who wished for a different life. A scared little girl who, for a brief, wonderful moment, had had everything she wanted—a mate who loved her, a life worth living.

But scared little girls could hurt people, and that's what she'd done. In her need for vengeance, she'd allowed her *azai* to be put in danger. Her hurts had become the hurts of others, and it was a wound she could never heal from.

But at least she could lance the poison.

"Do you swear it?" Leita asked, her voice gone deeper, as though it was some other, more ancient entity who spoke.

"Yes."

Something burned around her neck—the most pain Ravenna had ever felt—but in a moment, it was gone.

The magic reeled back, rushing home to Leita. It left nothing but a few dust motes whirling through the air, and yet its impact was so profound, it left Ravenna altered. Reshaped.

She sat there for a long moment, unable even to blink.

"You've sworn to it," Leita intoned. "Should this not come to pass, your life is forfeit."

Air rushed into Ravenna's lungs, and she sucked in great gulps to fill her chest. She touched her throat to feel the phantom burn of their bargain.

Fates, she didn't know fae could *do that*.

Perhaps only Queens could.

Meeting Leita's gaze, not quite so terrible now, Ravenna nodded. Very well. Her life was forfeit anyway.

"Then so be it," Leita whispered, sealing their pact.

Ravenna's tears came rushing back, her relief exquisite and agonizing. She thanked Leita in burbling sobs before her face fell to the woman's lap. There she cried, her heart overwhelmed by new, excruciating hope.

The congealed, dried blood on Vallek's chest and arms itched something fierce. In his darker moments, he would've traded his kingdom for someone to scratch the brown flakes off and bring him some relief.

Of course, there was no relief in this dark place.

Even in the daylight, the citadel of Fallorian was shrouded in shadow. Ancient banners hung by threadbare ropes, and moldering curtains spanned the tall, narrow windows. Dust and decay was the only scent, a carpet of muzzy gray obscuring the inlay pattern on the marble floor.

From his place in one of the many niches of the citadel, chained and with his back to the pedestal where a statue had once been, Vallek could clearly see how the great bastion was crumbling away. If he cared to see, at least. Which he didn't.

There was nothing in this dead place save for him—and sometimes a cruel shadow.

"Your people send word."

Vallek didn't bother looking up to witness the Fae Queen's theatrics. She was fond of dissolving in and out of shadows, throwing her voice from across the room, and using her magic to make floorboards creak or curtains flutter somewhere she wasn't. She meant to frighten him, unnerve him, and Vallek took great delight in being neither.

No better than an untamed onager throwing a fit, she had tried for the better part of a day to scare him, break him. For now, she played nice, no doubt aware that too much malice would push them both past the brink of war.

Of course, she was prone to losing her temper. Hence the first set of claw marks.

A cold rush of air battered his face. Vallek sneezed from the dust that rushed up his nose.

"She will trade herself for you."

Damn you, sprite.

Vallek's gaze flicked up to meet the formless shadow lurking above him. Too quickly. The shadow laughed without a mouth.

From the darkness came a withered hand the ashen color of aspen bark. Claws with blackened beds just touched the scar on his bare chest, where his mate had set her fangs. Her claiming mark.

Another laugh in Amaranthe's dull, dusty throat as those claws found familiar tracks. Vallek clenched his teeth as they raked slowly down his chest, reopening the fresh scabs. Blood dribbled down to his abdomen to soak the waistband of his trou.

Chained still in the spelled manacles, he hadn't the strength to do much more than glare defiantly at the faceless shadow.

"An orc king and a halfling fae. How ridiculous. And they say I usurped the natural order." Through the hazy darkness, he could just see the curve of a wicked smile. "I will set the world to rights when she comes to save you."

Vallek turned his face away, bored of her threats. There was nothing she could do that would hurt him more than seeing his mate harmed. And she well knew it.

They came the next day, at dawn. Two fae ships. Skimming the water as elegantly as dragonflies, hardly needing to part the waves. As they neared the shore, Ravenna descended the grassy slope, Asta, Mattias, and a cloaked Leita behind her.

A dozen fae jumped into the shallow water to walk ashore. At their head was the messenger who'd come before, his light hair again pulled back in a long tail.

"Our esteemed queen agrees to your terms," he said in orcish. "You will come with us to Fallorian."

"We will have our king first," countered Mattias.

"He remains in Fallorian."

"Then we'll all sail there," said Ravenna. "Together. When the orcs have their king, Amaranthe will have me."

The messenger didn't like it, his lips thinning as he glanced behind Ravenna to assess the berserkers at her back.

Knowing he and his forces were outnumbered, there was no other answer for him to give than, "Very well. We will escort you."

38

It took the better part of a day to travel up the coast to Fallorian. Aided by a southerly wind and the strong arms of the rowers, the orcish and fae ships cut through the water, foam and spray splashing off the sleek hulls.

By the time the tallest spires of Fallorian rose above the sea cliffs, it was late afternoon. The saturated orange light bathed the city, making it gleam like polished abalone shell. The ships followed the rocky coast, a wall of black cliffs topped in swaying grasses to their right and the vast ocean to their left, until white limestone jutted out from the cliffs.

They followed the harbor walls instead, great curving things that reached out into the sea like open arms. Or pincers.

The sea was something the fae had never been able to control. Although they had several legendary shipwrights, the extent of their maritime adventures was to the Twins and back. Severed from the land, any fae felt unmoored at sea.

Fallorian, with its fae-made harbor, was no exception. Lacking a natural bay, the city instead extended out into the depths, forcing a large pool of calmer water for its docks and ships.

The cliffs too had been carved into submission. The dark stone had been chipped away to accommodate the pale limestone the city was renowned for. Nearly as white as marble, it shone in the late-day sun, a blinding beacon. Flecks of crystal in the stone caught the light, making the city glitter. Most commanding of all was the sight of the palace, layers and layers of it standing as some great bird of prey on the edge of the dark cliffs, just waiting to tip over into the open air and take flight. Its spiraling citadel stood tallest of all, overlooking a dangerous, swirling span of water just outside the harbor, littered with jagged rocks.

Ravenna gazed upon it all, the heritage of her father's people, and saw nothing but exposed ribs, bleached by the sun.

The city's façade was beautiful, to be sure, but in the way crystal or snow was. Pale. Cold. Forbidding.

Her gaze traveled up the many looping levels of the city, fixing on the great citadel at the top. She'd heard of the palace, how its architecture, gardens, and pavilions were rivaled nowhere on the continent. That was where her parents had been slaughtered. It was where she'd find her *azai*.

As the ships sailed into the harbor, the bond inside her drew taut. Just a little longer, a little closer.

There was no one to greet them. The docks were abandoned, the other white oak ships pulled to the perimeter of the seawall, allowing the captains to steer their ships up to the docks for disembarking.

For all the cacophony they made, the full force of berserkers marching from their ships, the city met them with an eerie silence.

Are you ready, Crow?

Ravenna looked up at Oberon solemnly. He'd refused to let her leave without him; he, his younger unicorns, and Thalia had all boarded her ship, determined to protect her for as long as they could.

I'm ready for it to be over.

Oberon buffeted her face with his warm breath, nuzzling her

cheek. *Brave girl. Keep your courage.*

Ducking under his head, Ravenna hugged his neck and buried her face there. His warmth and horsey musk filled her senses, a momentary relief from her terror.

Thank you for being with me.

Always, Crow. To the end.

Wiping at her eyes, Ravenna refused her tears. Instead, she took a running leap, throwing her leg over Oberon's bare back.

Oberon turned to walk down the gangplank, the other unicorns behind him. Along the stone docks, they gathered in a diamond formation around Ravenna and Oberon, a wall of horseflesh to protect her—or at least, to get her to the palace.

It left Asta free to look out for Leita, who discreetly walked alongside Thalia at the rear of the formation.

At the head of the dock, a fae lifted a horn to her lips and blew. A melancholy sound echoed across the water, stealing Ravenna's breath.

The escorting fae fell into formation at the front and back of the column of berserkers. Off the ships, there was nowhere to go but forward.

The fae led the way through their city of winding cobbled streets. Even the main streets were narrow, lined on each side by tall limestone buildings. It forced the berserkers to march just three abreast, making them grumble and exchange unhappy looks.

Ravenna bit her cheek, willing them to stay the course. She'd explained to them, standing atop her stump and shouting so everyone could hear, what Allarion meant to do. She described what she could of the city and what the warriors could expect. And most of all, she emphasized that upon reaching the palace, they were to secure Vallek at all costs. He was their priority.

Their long column snaked up the gentle slope, passing beneath peaked arches crowned in coral. A few curious faces peeked out from otherwise shuttered windows, but no one moved on the side streets or alleyways.

The city almost seemed empty, a ghostly remnant of a civilization that had rotted away long ago. More arches denoted other main thoroughfares, just as narrow. From these they finally found others.

Fae soldiers, armed and helmed, began to fall in line, surrounding their column. Encased in fae escorts, the air grew tense.

Careful to keep her face expressionless, Ravenna turned her head to look at the new arrivals.

Her breath caught in her throat to see a familiar face glancing up at her.

Beneath the brim of his helm, Allarion winked at her.

Ravenna had to bite back a heaving sigh of relief. *He's done it.*

Indeed, confirmed Oberon, *just look how many are his.*

Looking more closely at the fae soldiers, she realized some didn't wear gloves, at least one in three. That had been their agreed upon mark, one she'd advised the berserkers of.

They weren't alone in this fight.

Have Thalia tell Leita, she told Oberon.

It was hard to say exactly with their forces kept to the narrow roads, but Ravenna thought, when it came to the fighting—for this would surely come to fighting—Allarion's recruits and Vallek's berserkers would be at least evenly matched against Amaranthe's forces.

She clung to that hope as they ascended, getting closer and closer to the palace.

As they rounded a corner, a strange noise echoed up from the harbor. Ravenna and others turned to see a heavy chain rise from the water between the two pincers of seawall, effectively barring the way in or out.

Shit.

If the orcs were to sail from Fallorian, Amaranthe would have to be dead.

As if Ravenna needed any more reason.

Up through the city they marched, hundreds of boots the only sound in the white city. No wind stirred, no birds flitted between roofs. Fountains sat dry, workshops closed, and the decorative plum trees stood wilted, their dark red leaves gathering on the cobbles.

It was a city abandoned. Had the citizens fled before the arrival of the orcish force? Or had they been driven away?

She wished she could ask Allarion, but there would be no opportunity. It also didn't matter. The fate of the fae wasn't Ravenna's concern and never had been. She couldn't indulge in empathy now.

The walls of the palace finally rose above them, the gates thrown wide. Great wooden doors had been reinforced with bronze polished to a mirror shine, yet the heavy iron hinges carried flecks of rust. Pavers were missing in the wide promenade leading up to a set of shallow white steps, and the lawns of the front pavilion had been left to grow wild.

Up they went over the stairs, beneath a scallop-edged arch leading into an open-air hypostyle hall. Old wisteria vines snaked up the marble columns, obscuring the worn friezes carved into the rounded surfaces. The air was old and chilly inside, long shadows pooling in the corners and giving the painted figures along the plastered walls an almost ghoulish appearance.

Led through the hall, they found the open sky again. To the right, through a crumbling peaked arch, stood a crystal pavilion. Geodes the size of Ravenna had been artfully laid around the pavilion, as well as bursts of celestine and quartz tetragonal clusters bigger than an onager. They looked like great blooming bushes, warning all not to touch with their pointed edges.

To the left was a pavilion full of ornamental trees and hedges. Some had been cut into figures. Many were some sort of flowering fruit, like cherry and apple and plum, which in spring would fill the space with fragrance and delicate petals.

The beauty of it was marred by two conspicuous dark stains on the white pavers.

A cold weight settled in Ravenna's stomach.

That's where they died.

Keep your focus, Oberon warned gently.

With effort, Ravenna pulled her gaze away. She couldn't think of them now. Even if this had all begun in their name, she couldn't allow their deaths to haunt her in these next critical moments. Nothing could distract her aim.

Through the palace they climbed, more sets of shallow steps leading incrementally upward. They passed through so many halls and pavilions, it was almost a surprise when they finally reached the citadel.

Tall iron doors creaked open, spreading a shaft of light onto the otherwise gloomy floor. The white marble, inlaid with star motifs of different colored stone, looked almost soft with the layers of dust coating it.

Grimy stained-glass windows let in meager shards of colored light, but most of the illumination came from a hole in the far wall, the top of one window and casement broken. It allowed in the sounds of the sea and the late afternoon sun, just enough to see by.

The citadel itself looked to be a great peaked cylinder, rising in a spiral to a point. At the front of the space was a large stained-glass circle above a wide stone dais, with shallow steps leading up to and flanked by ornate marble vases that once held exotic flowers. The walls had been inlaid with crystals, jewels, colorful glass, and lacquered tesserae, all meant to catch the light in a cacophony of color—yet all sat dully in the stone. Fluted columns rose high in the air around the perimeter, creating an aisle between them and the rounded walls. More than one column had toppled, leaving drums of stone littering the floor.

It was near one of these piles of rubble, beneath a rounded niche set into the wall, that Vallek sat.

Ravenna couldn't help it—her hopes and temper flared, and the thread of their bond snapped taut.

He lifted his head with some effort, eyes hazy. Stripped to just his trou, wicked red lines scored his chest, dribbles of dried blood beneath them. Claw marks.

As the fae forces gathered on the far side of the citadel, the berserkers took their formation. All were too well trained to make a false move now, but she could feel how their attention focused on their king, wounded and chained like a diseased dog.

Oberon moved to stand at their head. From atop his back, Ravenna spotted a strange shadow lurking to the side of the dais. She watched as it tumbled like smoke across the dais, finally gathering form as it touched the light.

Iridescent wings the color of a starry night caught the sun more brilliantly than the stained glass behind her. As if emerging from a cloud, Amaranthe glided forward, robes of pale blue silk rippling around her lithe limbs. White hair studded with crystals and delicate chains of diamond hanging between fingers, arms, and neck, she looked like every story of the beautiful, benevolent Fae Queens.

But just as in her city and palace, there was decay.

Folding her hands before her, Amaranthe greeted, "Welcome to Fallorian. It pleases me to see such loyalty for your king."

As Amaranthe began to float down the dais steps, Ravenna dismounted. Sliding onto the marble floor, she took half a moment to catch her breath.

Steady now, Crow. I'm with you.

Ravenna patted her old friend before turning to face the Fae Queen.

She took a few steps forward, separating herself from the group behind her.

The fae soldiers split fluidly to allow Amaranthe to pass between them, reforming their line once she'd taken the center of the space. Ravenna took a few more reluctant steps forward, not quite meeting her there but enough to show she'd come and fulfilled their bargain.

Dark eyes glittering, Amaranthe smiled. "So you are the one who's caused me such trouble."

Ravenna stared at the one who'd murdered her parents in silence. She'd already been stupid—she wouldn't risk Vallek with tempestuous snipes. It didn't matter if she bested Amaranthe with words, only with steel.

The Fae Queen began to walk in slow circles around Ravenna, taking her time to assess her.

"You are both more and less than I expected," mused the Queen. She lifted a lock of Ravenna's hair to rub between finger and thumb. "You have the look of your fae kin, it's true, but you reek of human."

Ravenna said nothing, letting her glare be what spoke for her. Amaranthe was a predator who liked to play with their food, and that was all right. She needed to give Allarion's forces time to spread around the citadel and secure the entrance.

Coming around to stand before her again, Amaranthe's red lips curved with satisfaction. "I must say, I never imagined it would be as easy as having you walk through my door."

"I've come to take his place, as promised," was all Ravenna said.

"Don't." The voice, weary with exhaustion, echoed across the citadel. "Don't, sprite."

Amaranthe turned to regard Vallek, her smile growing, but Ravenna couldn't bear to look at him. Something fundamental inside her was already cracking; seeing him beseech her not to do this would break her.

Let me, she begged him. *Forgive me.*

Watching the Fae Queen gloat and smile over her chained *azai* stoked the fire in Ravenna higher. Vallek was a strong, proud man—he didn't deserve to be brought so low.

"Killing me won't change what I've seen," she said, drawing Amaranthe's attention back to her.

The Fae Queen's fair brows rose in surprise. "Kill you? My dear girl, I've no intention of killing you. To waste a power such as yours— no, no. You will serve me, predict my future."

"I already have," Ravenna growled through bared teeth.

"You will see a new vision. A new future."

"I can't—"

"You *will,*" Amaranthe insisted, raising her arm to gesture at where Vallek sat chained. "Or the consequences will be carved into his flesh."

"You swore to free him, to take me instead."

A patronizing smile spread across those ruby-red lips. "My dear, I don't treat with halfling mongrels. Your offer means nothing to me. Besides, you're here now."

Ravenna bit down on her hatred and rage, feeding them to the flames. Behind her, the berserkers stirred. They might not have understood all of what was said, but the gesturing at Vallek raised their hackles.

The air grew thick, and Ravenna swore a gentle weight pressed on her shoulder. The hand of destiny guided her now—it was time to take it.

Finally, she allowed her own wicked smile to overtake her face. Amaranthe's dark gaze snagged on it, the space between her brows twitching.

"What would you say if I told you I'd come to kill you?"

Amaranthe affected a sigh. "I hardly need foresight to know you won't come quietly. You willful mortals are sadly predictable."

"What if I said that I hadn't come alone?"

The Fae Queen maintained her look of boredom, but a flicker of suspicion darkened her gaze. Those fine brows lowered over her eyes, which strayed past Ravenna.

From somewhere behind her, Allarion shouted, "NOW!"

The call went up—Ravenna charged for Amaranthe, Leita right behind her—the berserkers broke for Vallek—and Allarion's troops fell into formation to bar the citadel door.

From one moment to the next, the end began.

39

Ravenna slipped the dirk from her sleeve, palming the hilt just in time to take an upward swipe. Amaranthe bent backwards to avoid the slashing blade, a furious hiss on her lips.

"Protect the Queen!" cried her fae.

"Secure the king!" called the orc berserkers.

The fae soldiers pulsed forward, moving to encircle Ravenna and Amaranthe, but a blast of force knocked them to the side. They went stumbling to their left, some colliding into columns, some tripping on the steps, and others barely able to defend themselves from the oncoming orcs.

Ravenna felt the force on her back, then a pair of hands on her shoulders. Leita leapt over Ravenna, the brute force of her magic slamming against Amaranthe with the subtly of a battering ram.

The Fae Queen gasped, staggering backwards with her hands out to defend herself. An opposing wave of magic crashed against Leita's, forcing her to a halt.

The two royal fae stood there, arms extended, dueling magic keeping them mere feet apart.

"Hello, auntie," Leita growled, a feral madness glinting in her eye. It was the look of a predator who'd smelled blood.

Amaranthe's fair features contorted with rage. "You should've stayed dead, *velloi*." *Dragonfly,* she called Leita.

"You know me, auntie. I was never good at taking direction."

Ravenna hurried to renew her attack, only to be intercepted by a fae warrior. His sword came swinging for her head to the echoing bellow of her angry *azai* from across the citadel. Ravenna slowed the descent with her magic before catching his blade with her smaller one. Before the warrior could retake his stance, she caught his guts with her shoulder and kicked him in the bollocks. Asta would be proud.

Another soldier took his place, one after the other, until Ravenna almost lost sight of the royal fae. Her blade flashed through the air quicker than she could see, rebuffing attacks. She danced in what little space she had, avoiding grasping hands and kicking heels.

A wild scream pierced the air, and a soldier to her left crumpled to the marble floor, stampeded under a small herd of angry unicorns. Oberon led the charge, lethal horn swinging. He cut through the fae line, big body shoving away soldiers as his horn caught swords and helms. The other unicorns followed right behind, forming a loose ring around Ravenna and Leita.

Together, she and the unicorns disarmed, beat back, or slew the soldiers in their vicinity, the screech of metal ringing in her ears.

Dodging another soldier, Ravenna twirled round her attacker, a path finally cleared for Amaranthe. She pumped her arms and legs, wings flapping behind her to give her speed. Ravenna hurtled through the narrow empty spaces, her vision going red.

Before the final few strides to get at the Queen, Amaranthe swung her right arm to catch Ravenna, the force of her magic hitting like a physical wall.

But splitting her power gave Leita the advantage. With a battle cry that sounded from the depths of her soul, Leita pushed forward, charging the wall of magic with her shoulder as though it was a door to break down.

Huffing, Amaranthe waved a hand at a fallen soldier. As she returned to fending off Leita, the soldier jerked upright, the movements unnatural. Ravenna watched in horror as a dead fae, their face pale and gaze unseeing, shuffled towards her, their sword raised.

Necromancy. Her stomach clenched with disgust.

The undead soldier made for little more than fodder, their movements clumsy, almost reluctant, but it was just enough to keep Ravenna distracted. When one fell, another took its place.

And it wasn't just those soldiers near Amaranthe. All across the citadel, fallen fae rose from pools of blood and gore. Some were still barely alive, their eyes frantically twisting in their sockets as they moved involuntarily. Others moved despite exposed bone or entrails leaking from open wounds. Orcs swore and fae shuddered, horrified at the sight.

We must stop her, declared Oberon, flinging an impaled body off his horn. *Destroy her and the dead will find their peace again.*

With a running leap, Ravenna jumped onto Oberon's back, balancing just long enough to spring off again. Diving into a rolling somersault, she bounced back up beside Leita. Dirk in hand, she rushed Amaranthe again, her own magic gathered right in front of her as a bulwark.

The Queen snarled to see her coming. She tried to stop Ravenna's charge with magic again, but theirs met in a silent percussion. Ravenna got closer than before, swinging her dagger. The blade missed, but the force of the attack sent Amaranthe stumbling backwards.

Leita sprang forward, eyes flashing more dangerously than the blade in her hand.

The stone beneath their feet rumbled ominously, sending them both staggering to the side. The very earth shook, plumes of dust cascading down from the high ceiling.

Shit. Amaranthe was going to bring this place down on all of them before she lost.

Vallek gathered all his strength, standing to meet Mattias. His captain rushed forward, covered by a tight formation of berserkers, stark relief plain in his expression.

"My king!" Mattias reached for Vallek, taking hold of the manacles. His hand jerked back, and Mattias rumbled with disdain. "They're spelled."

"Draining my strength," Vallek confirmed. It nearly winded him to say just that.

Never had Vallek been so tired, so weak. It shamed him how much effort it took just to keep his eyes open as his warriors rallied to him. He'd destroy every last one of these blasted manacles when he returned home, and then he'd destroy whoever made them. Infernal devices they were.

Mattias called for tools and weapons, determined to break the irons. Vallek could do little more than look on, supported by two of his warriors as Mattias and another went to work trying to break the chain, pick the lock, or crack the irons.

His raw wrists protested the strain, but Vallek ignored it. Propped against the bulk of a berserker, Vallek craned his neck to see over the many heads, trying to spot his foolish, damnable, glorious mate.

Gods, when he got hold of her . . .

The scene below was chaotic, bands of fae clashing with his berserkers and . . . what looked to be other fae. One group held a position at the doors of the citadel, barring any from leaving to call for reinforcements. More fae formed a loose circle around a small herd of unicorns, all bravely swinging their horns to keep the soldiers back.

And some . . . they were wrong. Vallek wasn't sure if he could believe his tired eyes or if exhaustion played tricks upon him—a fae went down with mortal wounds only to pick themself up again. His stomach revolted watching his warriors fight undead opponents, felling them only for another wave to attack.

The berserkers launched a grisly strategy—hacking limbs. Even undead soldiers couldn't get back up without legs. Axes slashed and hammers crushed undead legs out from under the unnatural fae, creating a mire of blood and gore mixed with the thick coating of dust on the floor.

It was an awful scene that turned the stomach of even the most hardened warrior. More than one leapt away after smashing an opponent to broken bits, retching up their guts at the sight of mangled flesh.

Still the fae fought on, both alive and undead.

Vallek hated their queen for it.

To do this to her own kind, to make a mockery of their lives and deaths . . .

It couldn't be borne.

Movement caught his eye, and Vallek inhaled sharply as he watched his mate jump onto Oberon's back—and then leap off again right into the fray.

His beast, subdued to the point of silence until then, began to rouse.

Gods, their plans had gone so wrong. Perhaps they had both been arrogant to think they could fool a being as cunning and ancient as Amaranthe.

But he could berate himself—*and her*—later. Now, what mattered was getting to Ravenna, throwing her over his shoulder, and getting *the fuck* out of the faelands.

Vallek grimaced when the piece of iron Mattias tried working beneath the left manacle dug into the back of his hand. Blood oozed from the raw skin, dribbling between Vallek's fingers.

Mattias cursed. "Hardly anything will scratch them, let alone release them."

Vallek nodded at the iron loop set into the wall. "That part may not be spelled."

His captain threw himself into breaking the loop from the wall. More warriors joined him, pulling with all their might on the chain. The metal whined and the stone cracked. Fissures erupted across the face of the wall, then with a final mighty heave, the orcs pulled the loop from the wall. Dust and shards of stone rained down on them, but Vallek was free. Somewhat.

Dragging in a breath, Vallek forced himself upright on his own feet. "Get me to Ravenna," he ordered Mattias.

The captain's lips set in a thin line. "I cannot do that, my king."

Vallek bared his tusks. "That's an order, captain."

"You're the one we must protect." Mattias clapped Vallek's shoulder, leaning close to say more quietly, "We promised her."

A growl reverberated in his chest. His foolish, damnable, selfless mate.

Gods, he was going to throttle her and then kiss her—and maybe throttle her again.

"We *will* secure—"

Vallek's words were lost as the room began to shake. The stones beneath their feet trembled, the mortar crumbling away. A moment of horrible silence followed, then the loudest, most horrible *crack* he'd ever heard.

The center of the citadel split apart, a great chasm opening up like the maw of some hungry beast. The stone gave way, the shattering of marble echoing up the walls. One by one, columns began to shake, and then to topple.

Vallek grabbed Mattias by the collar. "Get me. To her," he bit out desperately.

Face carved in stark lines, Mattias only murmured, "No."

The citadel began to collapse around them. Columns swayed before tumbling down, crushing whatever lay beneath. The dark, cobwebbed chandelier creaked on its last chain before that snapped, sending the mass of crystal and iron down to shatter on the floor below in a cascade of shards and fractals.

Ravenna worked with Leita up the dais steps, trying to corner Amaranthe. The Queen was a vicious opponent, content to send soldiers into battle again and again until they were hacked apart. Her magic sent Ravenna then Leita then Ravenna again backwards, never allowing them close.

When Leita pushed with her magic, Ravenna tried again to rush Amaranthe with her blade. Desperation made her blood slosh and her hands slick. She caught one silk sleeve, but nothing penetrated the Queen's defenses.

Leita was powerful but all brute force—if she'd ever been taught to use a weapon, those memories weren't guiding her. She battered Amaranthe's magic with her own, one brutal wave after another. Centuries of rage and despair buffeted the Queen, tears glittering on Leita's cheeks as she came back from every rebuff to try again.

Their strategy wasn't enough. Even together, it wasn't enough.

A sick dread clutched Ravenna's throat.

What if they couldn't . . .

No, she wouldn't think it. Failure wasn't tenable. This had to end.

Ravenna got her arms up just in time to block a wave of magic.

She went flying backwards, landing hard at the foot of the dais steps. A moment later, Leita landed in a heap near her, rolling across the buckling floor into the gaping hole.

"No!"

Pushing off with her feet, Ravenna slid across the marble, wings pumping to extend the glide. She grabbed Leita's hand, using her magic to reverse their momentum. Her arm strained, nearly pulled from its socket. Ravenna bared her teeth in a grimace as she heaved, reclaiming Leita from the abyss.

"Fuck!" Leita cursed, scrambling away from the edge.

Ravenna shakily retook her feet.

Calls in orcish drew her attention across the destroyed citadel. Every fae left available to Amaranthe rushed, limped, or crawled toward the orcs, converging on the defensive line they'd made around Vallek.

Her heart bounded across the chaotic space, the bond pulling her in his direction.

Go, go to him. He's all that matters.

He was. Fates, she wished she'd realized that sooner. She loved him so damn much.

That was why this had to end. Here. Now. Before the citadel crumbled into the sea with all of them inside it.

Ravenna grabbed for Leita before she could charge back in. "Punches of magic," she rushed to say, "one after the other. Get me an opening."

Understanding pierced the frenetic rage masking Leita's face. She offered a single nod before she leapt back up the steps.

Ravenna followed, gripping her dirk tight.

She'd just made the top of the dais when a horrid screech lanced through her skull. Amaranthe flung her arms and wings back, mouth agape. A percussive wave of magic burst from her lips, rattling the windows.

In a sudden rush of *cracks* and *snaps*, every window in the citadel exploded. Shards of every size rained down upon them, razor edges finding vulnerable flesh. Screams accompanied the tinkling ring of glass shattering into millions of splinters and fragments.

Ravenna threw her arms up to protect her face, cocooning herself in magic as best she could. Large pieces bounced off her protective bubble, but dozens of little slivers bore into the back of her neck and hands. She shuddered with the awful sensation, a hundred little splinters boring deep into her skin.

The silence that followed the shower of glass was almost more horrible.

It was a long moment before she could get any air into her lungs. Carefully, still in a daze, she brushed some of the glass from her hair, not quite believing the sight of her hands. Although bloodied with tiny cuts, her hands almost looked like dragon scales, blanketed in sharp edges.

Dozens of disembodied screams drew her gaze. Glass slid down the slope of ruined floor, a waterfall of shards falling into the darkness below. Bodies lay impaled with reds and greens and blues, glass faces and flowers peeking out from ruined chests. The wounded cried for help and mercy. The dead, finally, didn't get up.

A unicorn lay dead, their horn dark with blood. The others drew round him, withers and flanks shivering around the hundreds of small wounds scoring their coats.

Finish it, Crow, said Oberon bitterly, blood soaking him like some morbid caparison.

Ravenna saw red.

Orcs spoke of it. Their berserker rage. That unstoppable need to fight and win.

Perhaps her *azai* lent her his. Perhaps any being reached their point of no return.

Through her agony, Ravenna clutched her dirk tight. Turning, she mounted the final steps up to the dais.

There, Leita pushed against Amaranthe's magic, throwing her arms in literal punches. The Fae Queen took each blow, her own magic mostly shielding her, but as Ravenna looked, she began to see signs that the battle was taking its toll.

Every time Amaranthe moved, her face took half a moment longer to follow. Glimpses of another one, her true face, peeked out with every strike.

It gave Ravenna vicious pleasure to see it.

Coming alongside Leita, Ravenna added her own magic. Together, they battered against Amaranthe's defenses, allowing her no quarter. Her magic counterstruck wildly, looking for an opening, but Ravenna and Leita held their ground.

Amaranthe staggered back a step, her desperate eyes flicking back and forth, searching for an escape.

"One more," Ravenna whispered to Leita.

The magic surged, one last expelling of rage and grief. It burst across the citadel, devastating punches of power that caught Amaranthe on either shoulder.

Ravenna ran forward, ducking under the Fae Queen's defensive swipe. Leita punched again on the right, and Ravenna went left. Drawn in two directions, Amaranthe snarled, arms wheeling to defend herself against two onslaughts.

With a great flap of her wings, Ravenna jumped forward, closing the distance.

Amaranthe caught the blade of Ravenna's dirk in her clawed fingertips. An audacious grin slid across Amaranthe's two faces, a haggard, horrible thing peeking out from the distorted pale visage she wore. "A blade can't fell me, whelp."

No, Ravenna understood that now.

Only a force of nature could kill a being as ancient and powerful as Amaranthe.

Wind rushed in through the gaping spaces left by the stained glass. The mangled lead framing creaked and groaned, swaying in the breeze.

The sea crashed far below them, hundreds and hundreds of feet.

Another punch of Leita's magic forced Amaranthe to the left, and Ravenna was there. Slashing her blade, she caught the silken sleeve, pulling it down to restrain Amaranthe's arm.

Wings beating at her back, Ravenna put her shoulder into Amaranthe's chest and wrapped her arms round the Queen. A terrible gasp shuddered against her cheek, and her arms squeezed a form far thinner than the one she saw.

Magic at her back, Ravenna shoved forward.

The metal frame groaned under the strain before giving way.

Wind whipped around them. Amaranthe clawed at Ravenna's head, her free wings flapping uselessly. A withered face screamed with no sound, the sharpened yellow teeth stark against gray gums. Collapsed eye sockets glared out, horror coalescing in the black pits.

Together, she and the Fae Queen broke free of the metal frame to plummet to the sea below.

Forgive me, my love.

For the last time, Ravenna fell.

40

"*Ravenna!*"

Her name burst from his lips, shaking the ground as surely as the Fae Queen's magic.

In horror, Vallek watched his mate barrel into Amaranthe and thrust them both through the remains of the central window, out into the open air beyond.

She can't fly.

His heart shattered like so much glass on the floor.

When the two tumbled past the ruined window, the citadel fell silent. The manacles round his wrists *clicking* open then clattering to the floor was deafening. So was his roar.

His strength wasn't suddenly his again the moment the manacles unlocked, but that didn't matter. Arms and legs pumping, his beast shoved him forward, through the gauntlet of grasping hands, warning shouts, and glass-strewn ground. He didn't care, didn't care, all that mattered was getting—

His lungs heaved as he jumped up the dais steps, past a stunned, unmoving Leita.

The gaping hole they'd made in the window cames was the exact size and shape of the hole rent through his soul. He skidded to a halt just before the open air, the metal strips bent outward, beckoning. Before him, the sky was a burnished, rosy gold, the sunset across the sea a brilliant display that lent just enough light to see down, down, down.

The angry sea churned below, studded with conical rocks jutting from the water like fangs ready to gnash and cut. Dark and deep, even so close to the cliffs, waves battered the rocks as seabirds screamed in their whorls above. But there, just there, he swore he saw a ring of bubbles.

He didn't think, didn't hesitate—with a running leap, and a hundred cries at his back, Vallek threw himself out the window.

The wind *whooshed* past him with the force of a thousand daggers, the chill cutting into his skin. His body hurtled downward, air rushing everywhere but into his lungs. He fell hundreds of feet, it took but a moment, but still he wished himself there faster.

Dark waters rushed up to meet him. He'd just gotten himself into position, arms tight to his sides, legs below him at an angle and braced when—the water hit him.

His feet and ankles erupted with agony, but then all he knew was cold.

Vallek plunged deep into the water, the cold burn sparking in shocks across his body. The force of the cold stunned him, but he allowed himself only a moment before making himself move, making his body comply. Up through the water he shot, defying the depths, pushing himself up to the surface.

He had to reach her.

This wasn't how it would end, damn her.

He was king and he refused to let it be!

Gathering just enough breath, he bellowed, "RAVENNA!"

Nothing replied, the waves tossing him between the rocks. Snarling, Vallek pushed off from the nearest rock, ignoring how his ankles protested.

He worked to tread water and gain a little height, trying desperately to see whereabout he'd spotted that ring. She had to be here; there had to be a chance she—

A little pop caught his eye.

As he watched, a sparse stream of bubbles burst on the surface about ten feet away.

Vallek refused to think it a trick of the waning light. He swam hard for the spot and then dove, arms and legs shoving water aside. The saltwater burned his eyes, but he didn't care. There was little to see in the dark depths, but he didn't care.

He kicked, water streaming past, until finally, a pale face materialized before him.

Eyes closed and face slack, Ravenna hung eerily in the water, as if suspended from a string. Her hair streamed around her, a ghoulish banner, and her waterlogged wings had been crushed against her back. One hand clutched at the shoulder buckle of her cuirass, while the other rose above her, reaching for the surface.

Vallek grabbed her under the arms and swung to get his legs below him again. She was heavier in the water, clothes soaked, her armor weighing her down, but he refused to let that stop him.

His mate in his arms, Vallek forced them upwards, using strength he didn't have and a fierce, abiding will to see her again.

The darkening sky beckoned from above, a tantalizing dream distorted by the water. For a few horrible moments, it didn't seem to get any closer, no matter how hard he swam. They hung there together, the sea clutching them tight, and for the first time in a long time, Vallek was terrified.

Colder than the water, the terror cut him down to the bone.

The sea didn't suffer fools and took its sacrifices greedily. Here, he wasn't king. He was nothing but another body struggling to survive.

What the sea did not know, though, was that Vallek's will was greater.

He held his life in his arms, and he refused to give her up. He would have her and their years together. This was not the end, but the beginning. He and Ravenna would remake the world and leave it better than they found it. Their people would sing songs and tell stories of their greatness for centuries to come.

And most of all, they would remember how the orc king loved his faeling queen above all others. How even the tempestuous sea was no match for his sheer will.

Baring his tusks, Vallek reached for the promise of the sky.

His hand broke the surface of the water, and he clawed his way up to the world above.

Vallek gasped and heaved, pulling air into his lungs. His blood burned for want of it, temples pounding and heart stuttering. Coughing and wheezing, he got an arm around Ravenna and swam for an outcropping of rocks.

Digging his nails into a craggy niche, he pulled them into the minimal shelter it provided from the waves.

Ravenna's head lolled to the side, shooting panic down his spine.

Pinning her between him and the rock, he used his free hand to press on her chest.

"Breathe, damn you!"

His soggy hands were clumsy, taking precious moments, but he finally loosened her cuirass, pulling it off her body and letting it sink below. With the metal out of the way, he pressed her chest again, hand spanning her sternum.

With a start, Ravenna jerked, water sputtering from her mouth. She hacked up more, chest shaking. Vallek held her secure as she fought for breath, expelling the water from her lungs.

As she sucked in great gulps of air, her body began to quake. Eyes wide and wild, she searched the sea for something, hand scrabbling frantically at his chest.

"I have you, sprite, I have you," he crooned.

She jerked at the sound of his voice, her white-rimmed eyes finally falling on him. It was as if she saw him for the first time then, a terrible keening sound bursting past her lips.

"No—*no*—" she cried "—you weren't supposed to die, too!"

"I'm not dead," he insisted, "and neither are you. Although you've given it your best try."

"No, I was supposed to fall—I understand now—this was always how it was going to—I had to—"

"You did what you had to, and so did I," said Vallek. Pushing them further against the rock, he pressed his face into hers, clumsily nuzzling her. "You're alive, sprite. We both are. And I intend to keep it that way."

She blinked and blinked, her eyes gone nearly black in the fading light. He ached to see her distress and confusion, and when her hands began to knead against him nervously, he caught them both in his grip, holding on tight.

"But I haven't seen anything," she said breathlessly, "nothing like this, nothing past—"

Something plopped into the water beside them and began to fizz, drawing their attention up the rock.

Ravenna screamed at the horrible face staring down at them.

He curled his lip in disgust at the sight—what was left of Amaranthe was impaled upon and spattered across the rocks. Her corpse looked ancient already, its eye sockets empty, the lips and tongue rotted away. The breeze caught desiccated skin and clumps of white hair, and her small bones joined the limpets and bird droppings to litter the rocks.

Pushing off with his quivering legs, he moved them to another rock, positioning Ravenna so she couldn't see the withered remains. Of course, being the contrary creature she was, Ravenna twisted in his hold, and so together they watched as the Fae Queen broke apart.

A strong wave caught her skeletal arm, dragging the corpse down the rock. It was as though the sea sought a sacrifice, since it couldn't have him and Ravenna. Rotted flesh and bleached bone fell into the water, fizzing and sizzling before turning to foam.

Ravenna made another sound of distress, one Vallek agreed with. He'd never forget that sight, although he already wished he could.

He turned them away. There was no need to see the seabirds swoop to peck at what remained.

Huddled against the rock, they treaded water together, limbs entangled. The sea churned around them, and Vallek no longer felt cold—which wasn't good. Still, he didn't disrupt the silence, giving his mate the time she needed to compose herself.

When she next met his gaze, Ravenna touched his face gently, tracing his cheekbone up to his ear. "I wasn't supposed to survive," she whispered.

Vallek growled at that. "Who says?"

"I've never had a vision beyond this."

"Perhaps your visions led you here. Everything after, though, will be up to you."

A frown began to form on her brow. "I don't think that's how visions work."

"Well, then, you'll make do with my visions," he said, attempting a grin. "And do you know what I see?"

Her lips twitched. "What?"

"I see us getting out of this fucking water, drying off somewhere warm and cozy, and then taking you over my knee for a thorough spanking."

Ravenna spluttered in offense. "You wouldn't dare!"

"Oh, sprite," he purred, "it would be my absolute pleasure. You must learn that I won't ever, *ever* be parted from you. Not by a Fae Queen, not even by death."

A laugh, not quite hysterical, burst from her lips. Her hands rose to cup his face, and she held him still so she could feather kisses along his mouth and tusks and chin. Her arms wrapped around his neck and her legs around his waist to hold onto him tighter than the limpets on the rocks.

"I'm sorry, I'm sorry," she whispered against his check. "I love you so much."

Vallek rumbled with a purr. "Sprite, there's nothing in this world that will take you from me. You are my heart, my life."

"And you're mine." Pressing another cold kiss to his lips, she hurried to say, "I should have understood that sooner. My father was right, Oberon was right, I shouldn't have sought revenge. Not when I'd found you."

"But then you wouldn't be you," he murmured, nuzzling her neck. "I enjoy how bloodthirsty you are. Besides, now you have me and your revenge."

Ravenna shuddered against him. "But at what cost?"

"No price is too much for you, sprite. I would pay anything, give anything."

"That makes me feel worse," she groaned.

"You'll find a way to repay me," he promised. "You can start by not making me jump off any more cliffs to retrieve you."

That pulled a reluctant laugh from her, which Vallek thanked the gods for. Anything to distract her from the cold water and her guilt. There was no need for her to feel ashamed. There wasn't an orc he knew of who wouldn't have sought vengeance and justice for the brutal slaying of their parents.

If anything, it only proved once more that she was a perfect queen to sit beside him. She may have wings and magic, but she was an orc through and through.

Between the rocks, the final sunlight winked out over the horizon in a spark of green, leaving just a few streaks of orange behind. The water grew darker, the sounds of waves crashing louder. Ravenna shivered against his chest, her teeth beginning to rattle.

Damn, he needed to get her out of the water and her soaked clothes.

"Hold onto me," he told her.

His own limbs quivered, gone nearly numb with cold and exertion. He pushed onwards between the rocks, unwilling to surrender to the exhaustion. There would be time to rest later.

Water swirled around them in foamy eddies, receding only to

crash against them and the rocks again. It was slow going, his nails scraping against the slimy underbellies of the rocks to keep purchase. The tide sucked at them, trying to pull them into the open water, but he resisted.

He couldn't feel his hands or feet, but what he did feel was the racing beat of his mate's heart against his chest. It was all the reason he needed to keep going.

Vallek aimed for the smooth limestone heights of the harbor wall. Perhaps there would be rungs set in the side to climb, and at least it would be something to follow back into safer waters.

He braced himself against the nearest rock as a large wave caught them, pressing his back into the craggy surface. His skin had long since gone numb, but he grimaced knowing something had been cut.

"Vallek . . ."

He *hated* the note of fear in her voice.

"I have you, sprite."

They had come this far—he wouldn't be brought down by the tide.

Cutting through the water, Vallek made a last push toward the harbor wall. He timed it with the receding water, letting it pull them further along the wall. There was less for his fingers to catch on the smooth limestone, and he felt several nails break as they scraped against the wall.

The water pulled them further, Vallek fighting to keep near the wall.

He was beginning to truly struggle when, high above, a familiar voice cried out, "They're here!"

Vallek groaned in relief, flipping onto his back to see a waving green figure atop the harbor wall, backlit by dozens of torches. Mattias's voice called down, "Grab hold!"

A coiling line slithered across the sky before falling down to slap the water near them. With the last of his strength, Vallek kicked to close the distance.

Ravenna reached out, grabbing the rope and pulling it towards them. Holding each other with one arm and the rope in the other, they secured it around their waists before Vallek put his foot through the noose at the bottom.

"Ready?" he asked.

She could only nod, her teeth chattering too hard for speech.

Vallek tugged the rope. "Ready!"

"*Heave!*"

They jerked through the water toward the wall.

"Heave!"

They slid up the smooth stone until Vallek got his free leg up against it, pushing to give them a little room.

"Heave!"

Up they went, heave by heave, water sluicing off them back to the sea. Higher and higher they were pulled, their feet skimming the white stone.

Then, with a final heave, a green hand reached down to take his.

Vallek clasped forearms with Mattias, and then there were many arms, grabbing him and then Ravenna by the shoulders, bearing them up onto the wall.

At the sight of their king and queen, the dozens of orcs along the wall cast aside the rope and let out a resounding cheer.

Mattias clapped his shoulder. "You are a sight for weary eyes, my king."

"Thank you, my friend." Vallek nodded at his mate, being helped up by Asta. "See that the queen is tended to and fed," he ordered before exhaustion finally dragged him into oblivion.

4I

Ravenna awoke gradually to a delicious warmth against her back. Still half-asleep, she snuggled back into the warmth—and opened her legs to her *azai*'s seeking hand. A pleased purr rumbled against her cheek as Vallek leaned over her from behind.

Cracking open one eye, Ravenna found the world still dark and quiet. Their tent was cool and dim, and no noise emanated from outside. Although plenty of rooms were available throughout the palace and Fallorian itself, the orcs had chosen to make camp within the outer hypostyle hall and the crystal pavilion. Covered in dust and echoing with the abandoned lives once lived there, the place carried an eerie quality.

Even Leita and Thalia chose to make camp near the orcs. The new Fae Queen refused to enter her predecessor's apartments, not until everything had been cleared away and destroyed.

That work had already begun over the intervening three days, and Ravenna was content to stay out of it. Leita had Allarion and others to rely on now, and so Ravenna saw to much more important matters— the care of her mate.

Vallek slept for the better part of two days, only rising when they woke him to force broth down his throat. Ravenna worked with Fenna to care for his wounds, and as her own strength and magic returned with some rest and food, she used her magic to speed up the healing. The claw marks scoring his chest had already closed, four pink lines left behind. Though she couldn't totally prevent scarring, Ravenna decided she could stomach them fading into silvery lines.

For now, she had to fortify herself for the sight of them. The marks of her own folly, carved into her mate's skin. It wasn't a lesson she'd soon forget.

There were only a few things that took her from his side, one of which she allowed only Oberon to join her in. With a bucket of warm water, a brush, and the strength of her back, Ravenna scraped and washed away the bloodstains in the blossoms pavilion. The stones didn't want to give up their color, but with her magic and tears, Ravenna cleansed them.

Oberon stood guard, ensuring no one would see or disturb her. She needed to do this alone, to rid this place of the last vestiges of her parents' pain. Ravenna had never had bodies to bury, and so this was their funeral, their last rites said by the daughter they'd died for.

It was there, her hands scrubbed raw and her cheeks hot with tears, that Ravenna finally said goodbye. That she was sorry. That she was wrong. In the rust-tinged water, she saw for herself the sacrifice Maxim and Aine had made. Their spilled blood wasn't just sacrifice, though. Not just tragedy. It was love, a love so pure and strong, it defied a tyrant and her awesome power.

Ravenna had known but never truly appreciated the strength of that love. She cherished it now, held it close to her heart, alongside where she kept the bond with her *azai*. As she washed away the dark stains, she understood now what her father had tried to teach her—that they would live on, with her. That she was everything to them, all their hopes and dreams, and that she had been worth it. All the sacrifice, all the tragedy, every challenge and risk—it was all worth it, for her.

Such a gift was precious, and as Ravenna stood from the cleaned floor, she thought she understood now. Such a gift wasn't to be squandered.

She left that place with Oberon, her heart rawer than her hands. She climbed into bed with her healing mate and curled herself around him. Another gift she would never take for granted.

On the third day of his rest, he managed to stay awake for about an hour and eat something more substantial. Ravenna was grateful; after days of captivity and then needed rest, his face had gone gaunt with hunger. His fae captors had hardly remembered to provide drinking water, let alone food. Any chance she got, Ravenna was there pushing food into his mouth.

He bore it amiably, and seeing him awake did wonders for the berserkers' morale. Mattias and several of his sergeants visited, just to reassure themselves of his recovering health, before Asta and Fenna shooed them away.

Once they knew their king was secure and recovering, the berserkers took their strange circumstances and surroundings in stride. The dead were seen to, their bodies placed in coffins that Leita promised would keep them safe from decay during travel until they could be properly interred in Balmirra. Over thirty of the two-hundred berserkers had been lost, with another forty wounded. It kept Fenna busy, but Ravenna was more than happy to shoulder the burden of Vallek's care.

It wasn't a burden but penance. She needed to see for herself that he was healing.

If his lascivious purr and wandering hands were any indication, he was indeed recovering well.

Her smile unspooled as she felt her nightgown rucked up past her waist, allowing one big hand to tease the undersides of her breasts and the other to slide along the length of her thigh to her knee, which he hooked to draw up over his. Exposed to the darkness and his hungry touch, Ravenna bit her lip as pleasure sparked low in her belly.

"You should eat something," she murmured. "And you need to rest."

"Later. After." He nuzzled the crook of her neck, nipping at her throat.

Ravenna lifted her head, mouth seeking his. Their kiss was slow, deliberate, just like his fingers between her thighs. He circled round her clitoris as leisurely as his tongue swirled round hers, an intimate dance of sighs and teasing touches.

She wasn't sure he was recovered enough for this, but who was she to deny the king. Her heart fluttered to think he needed and wanted her so much, he reached for her in the middle of the night. The truth was, she needed him just as badly. To feel him against her, skin to skin, reaffirming the bond that had been strung thin by distance and danger.

She moaned into his mouth when one large hand rolled a nipple and the other teased the hood of her clitoris. It felt indulgent to lay like this, curled into the curve of his body, his hands bringing her such pleasure with just a few touches. He knew her body well by now, knew how to draw out her pleasure, and it seemed that's just what he meant to do, keeping his pace steady.

Ravenna played along. She would indulge in whatever he wished, however fast or hard or wicked. He deserved to have his way—for now. If that meant soft lovemaking or swats across his knee, he would have it.

The hot bar of his cock nearly burned her backside, throbbing in the cleft between her cheeks. Beads of spend leaked across her lower back as he gently rocked up and down, his hips finding an unhurried rhythm.

Clutched to his front, there was little she could do but lay there and receive his attentions. No doubt that was his aim, another show that she was his to have and please. Ravenna smiled against his lips, whispering, "I love you, my king."

Vallek rumbled deeply in approval. "My beautiful mate." A hand slid up her front to gently hold her neck and take the weight of her head. "My fearsome queen." Braced in his hold, she met his passionate kiss, twining their tongues as his purr buzzed against her lips. "My love for you frightens all who see it. Never did a king love his queen more than I love you."

Her cheeks hurt from smiling so wide, and she couldn't help a little wiggle of pleasure. Fates, he made her feel like a blushing maiden, talking like that—even with his hand between her thighs and a finger pushing inside her.

He swallowed down her moan as he began to work her, preparing her for the greedy cock at her back. Skimming her fingers down his flank, she found the side of his shaft, caressing it in light touches.

His purr grew into almost a growl. "You won't rush me, sprite."

"No, never."

His huff spilled across her cheek. The hand at her throat tightened just a little, a warning and a distraction. Reclaiming her mouth, he thrust his tongue inside just as two fingers began to plunge inside her.

Pace still measured, he worked her methodically, mercilessly. His hand was soon soaked in her slick, his fingers making wet noises as they shuttled in and out, in and out.

Ravenna began to tremble, pleasure clenching almost painfully in her belly. Gripping the meat of his hip, she held on as he moved them, unable to do more than receive and enjoy.

When he next lifted his head, allowing her a breath, he whispered at her ear, "Come if you need to. I'm far from done with you yet."

Shuddering in his arms, Ravenna shook her head. "N-no. Together." She couldn't explain further. She just needed to do this together.

Nuzzling her temple, he rumbled, "You would defy me?"

"Sounded like a suggestion—not an order."

His dark chuckle was a rich sound in her ear. "My good girl, how could I ever deny you?"

Her muscles gripped him tight even as he pulled away. A mewl of protest escaped her, replaced on the next breath with a gasp of delight when his cockhead teased against her cunt. Reaching behind her, she dug her hand into his thick mane, needing to hold on lest she fall apart just as he slid inside.

Their few days apart had been awful, interminable, and meant a pinch and stretch she hadn't felt in a long while. Vallek was patient, moving in little rolls of his hips, each bringing him a little deeper.

Scraping her nails along his scalp, Ravenna bore it, head thrown back on the pillow. He hooked his chin over her shoulder, his warm exhale reaching down to tease her erect nipples.

"That's it, sprite, just like that, now. Just a little more and I'll be home."

The breath hissed out of her lungs as she bared her fangs at the darkness. The need to snap her hips back against his, to take him to the hilt in one fell thrust, consumed her. She held out and held on, her other hand reaching down between her thighs to feel his invasion. She shuddered at the burn of his shaft beneath her fingertips, how he was already coated in slick with more gushing between them to ease his way.

Ravenna teetered on the edge, her need cutting deep. There was only a shiver of relief when she felt his root push flush against her cunt. She pulsed around him, stuffed full, pinned there in agony and ecstasy both.

Vallek trembled against her back, his big body beginning to move. At first his thrusts were gentle, introductory. The slide and withdrawal were as delicious as they were maddening, each making her want to claw and pull at his mane. He drew her knee further up and back, creating more room for his rolling hips.

The muffled, wet slap of their bodies echoed dully in the tent, the darkness filled with the scents and sounds of their lovemaking.

He held her still, just where he wanted her. His cock drove up inside her in a relentless rhythm, his thrusts gaining power and speed. Unable to bear it, she rolled her hips, meeting his every upstroke with her own downstroke. They groaned together at the new layer of friction and sensation, and soon, they were nothing but mindless motion, chasing down their orgasm.

She gasped and moaned sweet things, nonsensical things. She wept his name and begged for his mercy. Rumbles and whispers teased her ear, but he had no mercy. Even as his hands trembled, even as she pleaded, he was ruthless, keeping them both at that knife's edge for as long as he could.

There were some things even a king had to bend to, though.

Hurrying to cover her hand with his, he used both their fingers to pinch her clitoris to his thrusting shaft. The unbearable pleasure seared her from the inside out, and Ravenna took flight. With a gasp, she came apart, giving him his prize.

Vallek soared with her, hips pumping in a brutal claiming. His spend lashed and overfilled her, spilling across their fingers.

Even as she came apart at the seams, the tension snapping inside her, Ravenna could feel their bond weaving another thread between them. Strong. Unbreakable. It glowed golden in the dark of the tent, visible in the breath they shared and their harmonized heartbeats. As tangible as it was ethereal, Ravenna held onto it and her mate, heart fuller than it had ever been.

An *azai*. A future. More than a dream and beyond wildest hopes.

They were hers—and she would never let go.

After and later, with Vallek feeling strong enough to dress and meet with Mattias to discuss the aftermath of the battle, Ravenna found herself surveying the damage with Leita. With the loyal, watchful Thalia trailing behind, they made their way to the ruined citadel, not straying much past the doors.

A room of broken floors and windows, it couldn't even be called a shell. It was just . . . ruined.

"Perhaps fitting," Leita mused.

"Will you rebuild it?"

The new Fae Queen shook her head absently. "I don't know. There's so much . . ."

Ravenna understood. As they passed from one part of the palace to another, all they found were things that needed fixing. Not every room was empty or ruined. Some were merely abandoned. Some were stuffed full of furniture and other artefacts from when the palace had once been a home. A whole room of paintings. Another of statuary. Just one after the other of the unused, forgotten detritus of another life.

Leita regarded it with a sort of detached sadness. The woman said little, her arms almost always folded across her narrow chest.

Although she'd been proclaimed Queen, she looked no different from the homespun-clad wildling woman by the stream. Ravenna had no familiarity in what the natural course of power passing from one royal fae to the next looked like, but it didn't surprise her to know that after centuries of corrosion, the magic of the faelands wasn't immediately taking to Leita.

Although caring for Vallek meant that Ravenna had missed much of the formal process of anointing the new Queen, she did witness Leita's brief address to her stunned people.

Many fae had long since fled Fallorian, wishing to be out from under the suspicious eye of Amaranthe. Those who remained gathered in the palace grounds, astounded to learn that not only had a royal heir survived, but that she was here to claim the queenship.

"My aunt was a sickness. A blight. It will take time to heal what she has wrought," Leita had said. *"It starts with returning to the old ways. The magic must be allowed to renew and heal, and so the fae must learn to live as we used to."*

Ravenna hadn't been able to tell which the fae found most surprising—a new Queen or being told they would have to eat and drink again. There was no denying that Amaranthe had disrupted the order of the world, but the fae would now have to contend with a far more difficult truth. Individually and together as a people, they had all become too reliant on magic. It hadn't started with Amaranthe, but it'd only made her usurpation more complete and more devastating.

Every fae would have to bear the consequences of that.

Most of all Leita, the one who now would lead them through it.

The faelands and the fae themselves were at a reckoning.

Ravenna didn't envy her at all. Destruction was painful, horrible, but it was also easy. Surviving, rebuilding, healing, that was the difficult bit.

There was so much to do, so many places to start, it wasn't surprising, either, that Leita found herself paralyzed with the enormity of it all. Seeing her unsmiling face, Ravenna harbored a niggle of shame. They had their bargain, yes, and one day Leita would have her *azai* and family, but that didn't make any of this easier. It was a heavy mantle to lay upon Leita's shoulders.

All Ravenna could do now was offer her support and friendship. Vallek agreed that the orcs would aid the faelands in their recovery. Leita wouldn't be alone—but Ravenna had no doubt that she certainly felt alone now. A throne could be a very lonely place.

"It's yours by rights, you know," Leita said softly.

Ravenna's nerves clenched tightly in her chest. "What do you mean?"

"There were times, very long ago, when sisters and cousins would fight for the throne. Whoever could best the others and defeat the old Queen became the new one. It's how the unicorns decide who will lead, and many other beasts, too. By rights, you could be the Queen."

Ravenna snorted. "No, thank you. I already have a precarious throne. I've no use for another. Besides, the fae would never accept a halfling Queen." And there was the important fact that, with her more unruly grip on magic beyond that which was inherent to her, she'd make a poor conduit. No, what the faelands needed was a young, strong Queen, one of full blood able to manage and command the magic.

Leita herself was all raw power, it was true, but with a little honing, she'd be a fearsome Queen. Ravenna held onto hope that Allarion and those fae like him who'd opposed Amaranthe would be able to aid and guide Leita until she was ready in her own right.

Their walk had brought them to one of the outer pavilions. Decorated in black sand and obsidian flagstones, manicured junipers formed something of a waist-high maze. The path winding through them led out onto a magnificent veranda, shaded by a trellis thick with established wisteria vines.

As they gazed out upon the harbor and the sea beyond, Leita sighed. An autumnal breeze floated up from the water, catching their hair. Ravenna tucked hers behind her ears, but Leita made no move, letting the long white strands dance on the wind.

Eyes hard, Leita told the horizon, "I still have no desire to be Queen."

"I told Vallek much the same thing," Ravenna mused. "I'll tell you what he told me: that it likely means you'll be a good queen. So long as you try."

Leita turned her head, her indigo eyes dark in her pale face. Ravenna realized—she was scared.

"I've no one to teach me. All the other Queens did. Even my aunt."

"You won't make her mistakes."

"No, but I'll make my own."

"That's to be expected. I'm sure every Queen has."

Leita looked away, her lips thinning. Ravenna could feel it, too, how the words weren't nearly enough. Neither were good intentions. It would take a fierce force of will to lead the faelands forward—a will Leita had yet to find.

Her guilt only growing, Ravenna tried to do something she'd little practice with—comforting. Drawing closer, she laid a gentle hand on Leita's shoulder.

"You will succeed, Leita. You will restore the faelands and make your foremothers proud."

"Did you see that in a vision?"

"No." She hadn't had any since Amaranthe's death. But, "I don't need one to know. You will succeed. But it will take time. It will be difficult. There will be days you hate it, resent it even." She squeezed Leita's shoulder. "And that's all right."

A tear escaped Leita's right eye as she gravely met Ravenna's gaze. "I already do."

Ravenna winced. "I can't pretend to understand—but I promise you, you have an ally in Balmirra. And . . . a friend in me, should you want it."

"I haven't had friends before. Thalia has been the only one."

"For a long time, I didn't, either. But from one orphan girl to another, I promise, friends are worth having."

A long moment passed before Leita slowly nodded. "I suppose . . . another friend couldn't hurt."

<h1 align="center">42</h1>

Three Months Later

The royal quarters of the citadel echoed with lively chatter and bursts of giggles. On this most special of days, the king had been banished from his quarters to ready himself elsewhere, as all of the rooms were needed for the true preparations.

Ravenna had bid her handsome mate goodbye early that morning, claiming a lingering kiss that would have to last her until that afternoon. With a wink, Vallek had whispered, *"I'll be waiting for you,"* before bidding farewell to the gaggle of women already gathering in their quarters.

And so Ravenna had handed herself over to Hilde's care. If she'd thought preparing for the day Vallek announced her as his mate had taken time, it was nothing compared to the wedding day.

"Everything has to be perfect," Hilde muttered, not for the first time, as she dabbed a little more opalescent cream across Ravenna's collarbones, stood back to view her progress, and then stepped forward to add a little more.

Eydis grinned patiently. "It will be, love." She and Ravenna exchanged smirks; for all that it was Ravenna and Vallek's wedding day,

Hilde's anxieties outnumbered them all.

Ravenna wasn't quite sure how Eydis had managed to plan and execute a royal wedding so seamlessly in such little time, but then, she'd given up on trying to decipher the spymaster's brilliance. It was an unseen force, like the wind, and Ravenna found it best to be blown along.

Although it had been three months since defeating Amaranthe, Eydis had only really had two to plan, as Ravenna and Vallek had stayed on in Fallorian for some weeks, offering Leita support. They returned to Balmirra only when Leita assured them she had enough allies and protection within both the capital and the faelands. Although, Leita had extracted promises from Ravenna to visit again when she could.

Balmirra had erupted in celebration at the king's return, descending into days of feasting, drinking, and dancing. It'd been almost surreal to return to their lives, something Ravenna hadn't thought she'd see again. Duties resumed, life went on; Vallek easily retook his place within the complex web of government, but Ravenna required a few more days to get her head round the idea that a future, vast and unknown, had been laid at her feet.

Her determined *azai* knew just where to start: it was time to wed. A wedding and coronation both.

Foodstuffs and wine had to be ordered. Banners had to be made, flowers had to be sourced, and commemorative coins had to be struck. Fabric, jewels, lace, it all came flowing into the citadel. Meanwhile, invitations went out, great official scrolls written in gold ink, secured with silk ribbon, and sealed by Vallek's signet ring.

Under Brynhíl's expert leadership, the citadel was scrubbed from top to bottom, preparing to house the great orcish paladins. Kennum and all his daughters. Hrothgar and his whole retinue. The court of Holdur, the chieftains of the eastern tribes, denizens from every village and hamlet—they would all be welcomed to witness the dawning of a new age.

Between resuming the duties she'd begun before leaving for Fallorian and overseeing the tasks delegated by Eydis, Ravenna had caught her stride. Preparations lent a momentum to the days, until they were passing in a blur of fittings, flower arrangements, and council meetings. She and Vallek collapsed into their bed each night, exhausted but satisfied.

There had been so much rush, so much anticipation, that the day finally being here hardly seemed real.

For all the planning and stress, Eydis was the most serene of them all. As Ravenna stood patiently atop a low table, Hilde circling her with dizzying speed, Eydis had taken it upon herself to stand nearby—ostensibly to feed Ravenna but also keep Hilde from working herself into a true fit.

The strategy worked, and as the day lengthened, Ravenna neared being ready—even if Hilde insisted she wasn't even close. The others flitted in and out of the main hall, helping where they could, even if it was just by keeping Ravenna and Eydis company as Hilde worked feverishly.

Brynhíl came in often, monitoring their progress to update Vallek, as well as bringing fortifying plates of finger foods. Although too busy to stay long, she gushed over the vision Ravenna made in her gown. "You'll knock him right over," she promised.

Asta and Molly kept them supplied with food and good cheer—as well as running little errands for Hilde. When Hilde discovered how handy Molly was with a needle, the woman was conscripted into last-minute adjustments, mainly adding a few more loose crystals into Ravenna's train.

The next time the human woman wandered into her sight, Ravenna laid her hand gently on Molly's shoulder to—

—a great house upon a hill—three unicorns butting heads to get the best view of the baby—well done, sweetling, well done—we call her Laniet—

—apologize.

Ravenna's thoughts dissolved into surprise. It was her first vision in months. After fulfilling Amaranthe's fall, Ravenna had begun to believe she wouldn't have visions anymore. It was another new reality she had to grow accustomed to.

Although she'd never relished having visions, something about never having them again brought a touch of sadness. Her visions had been part of her magic, part of her, and being without them was like losing a finger or toe. Not catastrophic, but not comfortable, either.

A smile broke across her lips, a surge of relief overtaking her.

Molly looked up at Ravenna's touch to see her enigmatic smile.

"I'm sorry you've been put to work," said Ravenna.

Molly waved away her concerns. "It's no problem. How many chances will I have to work on something so fine?"

"If you ever want a break from that fae of yours, I'd be happy to offer you a position," Hilde teased.

All of them laughed at the idea of Allarion ever letting Molly out of his sight again.

The weeks they'd spent apart, with Allarion aiding Leita in Fallorian and Molly safely kept with his family at their country estate, had been difficult on the pair. She had finally come to reunite with him not long before Ravenna and Vallek departed the fae capital.

Although she hadn't gotten to spend much time with Allarion's *azai,* Ravenna quickly took to Molly. Lively and sarcastic, she was a perfect complement to Allarion's more serious nature—and wouldn't be bullied by Bellarand. From what Ravenna came to know of Molly's past, she sensed a kindred spirit, and the two of them shared an easy understanding.

And, most importantly to Ravenna, Molly and Allarion made each other happy. Watching them together, bantering back and forth—sometimes silently as they conversed and argued with Bellarand—was something to behold. They were a unit, a family, and Ravenna couldn't be happier for Allarion.

He'd sacrificed so much for her and her family. Even though Ravenna had upended her father's plans, none of this would have been possible without Allarion's help. His loyalty to Maxim and love for

Ravenna was a catalyst, and she would always be grateful.

Molly and Allarion had arrived from the faelands a few days previously, bringing well-wishes from Leita. The new Fae Queen sent her apologies for not being able to attend in person, as her growing bond with the faelands was too fragile to risk.

Ravenna understood and hoped to visit her friend the following spring. Hopefully by then, Leita would have made more progress.

As Molly began to string another crystal bead on her thread, Ravenna warned, "Just don't tire yourself. Not in your condition."

Molly frowned first at the thread and then at Ravenna. "My condition? I'm well, I—" Her eyes widened, a choked sound catching in her throat.

Ravenna's smile was smug as the orcesses squealed in delight. She'd missed this—her visions hadn't always been bad, and being able to offer a little hope, a little glimpse of good times, always pleased her.

Molly was stunned, but within a moment, realization dawned, and a smile drew wider and wider across her face.

Leaning down to kiss her cheeks, Ravenna whispered, "It's early days yet, but know that she will be happy and healthy."

Molly blinked up at her with watery eyes. Her brilliant smile almost blinded Ravenna, and Molly threw her arms around her, catching her in a tight embrace. "Thank you," she whispered back.

"Not the veil!" Hilde yelped.

Molly released her, wiping at a stray tear. Still smiling, she helped Hilde straighten all the nonexistent creases in the long veil.

You see? said Oberon smugly. *I told you it'd return with time. Gifts aren't known to suddenly vanish.*

Yes, I need to stop doubting you.

Exactly right.

One of the more interesting things Ravenna had overseen the past few months was the creation of comfortable stables for Oberon, Callistix, and their herd. Though the danger to her had passed, the unicorns determined they wished to stay near Balmirra and her, and so Ravenna wanted to offer them accommodations whenever they desired to stay in the citadel.

It shocked more than a few orcs, and the distrust between orcs and unicorns wouldn't disappear overnight, but it was a step towards coexistence. And, with the wounds sustained at the battle of Fallorian, it gave her peace of mind to know Oberon had a safe, warm place to continue healing.

Hilde had even taken to sewing more and more elaborate caparisons. She enjoyed the challenge, and Oberon was nothing if not a little vain, and so the two of them had worked out a system to try different fabrics and threads—especially after Ravenna refused to be a mediary whenever they wanted to spend a long afternoon debating colors.

Just wait until you see what she's made me, Oberon teased. *I fear I might outshine even you, Crow.*

We'll see about that.

Ravenna suspected she'd outshine the sun with the wealth of gold and jewels Hilde had managed to pin, place, and sew onto her.

The royal quarters quickly returned to chatter and giggles. Asta kept the jokes and teasing flowing while Eydis dutifully kept Ravenna fed. Molly and Hilde worked their magic, and by the time the afternoon sun began to saturate the rooms, Ravenna was ready.

Heart full, she took a moment to soak in the cheeriness and love.

Had she ever seen what her life would be like now, surrounded by friends and love, she likely wouldn't have believed it. Perhaps that was why she never saw visions beyond defeating Amaranthe. Perhaps, however strangely, her gift knew she had to discover it for herself first.

Whatever the truth, Ravenna was grateful. For her friends. For her new life. And most especially for the handsome orc awaiting her.

The sun blazed through the tall windows of Ninevar's Basilica, drenching the red limestone in shafts of glorious color. Hundreds of orc-kin crowded between the columns, eager for a glimpse of the new queen.

None more so than Vallek. Standing before his throne on the dais, his heart pounded a little harder in his chest as horns blew, announcing her arrival.

A hush fell over the crowd, all leaning forward for that first peek. Orcish paladins and denizens made up most of the ranks, but a few different faces underscored how much Balmirra had evolved. Near the dais, standing with Eydis, Hilde, and Asta, were the fae Allarion and his human mate Molly. To their left, a whole contingent of unicorns, Oberon at their head, all cloaked in velvet and brocade.

It made for an already unprecedented sight—and then, from the far side of the basilica, she emerged.

Shafts of light from the window behind him haloed her in a warm glow, making her shine like the rising moon. A gown of silver silk draped artfully from her lithe form, billowing sleeves reaching almost to the floor and cascading behind her with a long train. Subtly embroidered with flowers and unicorns in white thread, the fabric moved like water, rippling in a current that brought her ever closer to him.

Vallek descended the steps to meet her, entranced by the ethereal beauty come to bless him. Dazzling as a diamond and shining even brighter, her lilac skin shimmered opalescent. Hundreds of crystals sewn into the gown caught the light, as did the teardrop bobs dangling from her ears and the waterfall of diamonds dripping down her elegant neck.

Some of her long tresses had been secured with pearl-encrusted pins, while the rest hung unbound to wave behind her. From the dark cascade fell a long veil, gleaming gossamer lined in the finest lace. The veil spread behind her along the length of the basilica, a slithering wisp of fabric that contrasted her dark hair and iridescent purple wings.

He didn't know how she'd managed it, but little diamond and silver bobs hung from the points of her wings, tinkling as she moved. All-Mother, she was a goddess incarnate, blessing the very stones she walked upon.

All of his breath had fled his lungs by the time she stood before him. He hurried to fill them again, catching her scent of jasmine and cloves. A rumbling purr rattled in his chest as he offered her his hand.

A shy smile touched her rouged lips, and she slid her hand into his.

Vallek watched as her eyes went distant, and for a moment she didn't move. It'd been so long since he saw her have a vision, he'd almost forgotten what it looked like.

After a moment, though, she was back with him. He lifted a brow in question, but she smiled wider, a comely blush stained her cheeks. His purr deepened; he couldn't wait to hear what she'd seen.

Hand in hand, they mounted the dais steps. Her veil swept down behind them, a waterfall of glistening elegance.

They turned to face each other, and Vallek smiled down at his beautiful bride.

Gods, he was the luckiest bastard alive.

The crowd stood silently, anxiously awaiting the rites, but Vallek wasn't hurried by their anticipation. No, he wouldn't be rushed. He intended to savor this day and the sight she made.

Lifting their joined hands, he kissed her knuckles.

"You're more beautiful than the moon," he murmured.

Another lavender blush colored her cheeks. "Do I look like a queen?" she whispered back.

Vallek's answering smile was ferocious. "Oh, yes, sprite. Every bit. Down to your slippered toes."

Taking up a little pot of ochre, Vallek popped off the lid and dipped a finger into the pigment.

Cupping her head so, so gently, he carefully used the ochre to paint a line across one cheek. "For you." Another line on her other cheek. "For your kin." And, with his heart in his throat, the third line across her forehead. "For me. Before the Ever-Father and our kin gathered today, I stand before you, to take as your husband."

Her chest rising with a nervous breath, Ravenna dipped her own finger into the pot. Painting the first line across his left cheek, she said, "For you," and then the second across his right, "For your kin." She lifted onto her toes and Vallek bent so she could mark him with the final line. "For me. Before the All-Mother and our kin gathered today, I stand before you, to take as your wife."

Joining hands again, Vallek asked, "Will you take me, sprite?"

"Yes." Her soft little hands squeezed his. "Will you take me?"

"Oh, yes." And cradling her hands against his chest, he pulled her to him to seal their bargain with a kiss.

The crowd erupted in cheers, filling the basilica with noise. They clapped and stomped and hooted—and although it rang in Vallek's ears, he could hardly hear it past the blood rushing there.

A little peck wasn't enough, he greedily kissed his wife, telling her how he'd missed her today, how proud he was to stand beside her, how he would crawl to her on his belly if she ever asked, and most of all, how grateful he was to be hers.

They'd just begun to earn a few chuffs of amusement at the length and depth of their kiss when Vallek finally pulled back. Satisfied to see her rosebud lips swollen from the kiss—and in no doubt that his were now redder with her rouge—he whispered, "Are you ready?"

Grinning up at him, her violet eyes sparkling, she whispered back, "Make me your queen."

Rumbling with pride, Vallek motioned for an attendant left of the dais to step forward. Lifting the lid of the box the attendant bore, Vallek picked up the crown he'd had made for her. Not a coronet, not a tiara or diadem. This was a crown, made for a queen, to be worn by once and future queens.

Their line, now into the future, crowned by her blood and his.

He presented her with it, a circle of gold with artful spires all studded with amethysts and rubies. Bowing her head, she accepted the weight as he placed the crown upon her head.

When she lifted her gaze to his, her eyes sparkled as brightly as the two ribbons of diamonds that dangled from either side of the crown.

Gods, it almost didn't seem real. All he'd planned, all he'd worked and fought for—he gazed upon it all now, saw everything he could ever want or hope for reflected in her eyes. Be it the gods, fate, destiny, he didn't care who had blessed him, just that he was blessed to have her. A gift, a partner, a wife. She was and would be everything to him.

Together, they turned to face the cheering crowd. Over the din, Vallek proclaimed, "Your queen!"

Thunderous shouts and stomps met his declaration.

"Queen Ravenna!"

"Queen Ravenna!" they cheered back.

"King Vallek!" she cried.

"King Vallek!" they called. "All hail their names!"

Epilogue

Ten Months Later

The pale winter sun had long since set, but still they were trapped in this infernal meeting. Dinner had been brought in and taken out again, one of the ministers had fallen asleep in his chair, and Ravenna was beginning to worry spring would be upon them before the meeting was finished.

Usually, Ravenna relished the chance to debate. It'd become something of a favorite pastime, attending these meetings after learning all she could on the topics. Her father always advised knowing all she could about an enemy or new terrain; Ravenna took this to heart, always prepared with questions for the ministers.

Tonight, however, it was the scholar minister and mining minister whose questions—well, argument—kept them rooted to their seats. The topic was an important one; a new vein of gold had been discovered, but, before delving further into the mountain, the mining minister first had to get Vallek's permission and check the existing records. More gold was all well and good, but not worth bringing the city down to get at it.

As in most things, the scholar minister took a more cautious approach, bringing charts and maps and surveys to argue that the existing information clearly showed that mining where they wanted to could prove dangerous. The mining minister, however, brought up that all the existing information was well out of date, compiled early in Mordis's reign some thirty years ago.

Good arguments abounded on either side, and while Ravenna would have normally delighted in asking questions, tonight, she was ready for this to end.

She'd been cranky long before the meeting began.

Vallek had been called away early that morning, several of the city garrison reporting odd sightings in the sky. It'd taken him the better part of the morning to round up those guards who'd claimed to have seen something unusual on the horizon and then deploy more guards.

That left Ravenna alone in their bed. Of course, she was used to his early mornings. He kept to a strict schedule most days, rising with the dawn to train with his berserkers. However, this morning, he'd been called away well before dawn, so early that they hadn't been able to indulge in their usual morning routines.

It wasn't that she *had* to have his cock in the mornings, it was that she'd gotten used to it. In her time spent as Vallek's mate, wife, and queen, she'd become accustomed to a certain life, and that included starting her day with a delicious orgasm.

She feared she'd been a bit of a beast all day because of the loss.

As the ministers continued to argue the same points, Ravenna stole a glance at her *azai*. Even in her crankiness, she had to hide her grin when she saw just how hard he fought to keep the boredom from his face. She commended him for being judicious; mining was far too important to decide on rashly. Still, he had other important matters to attend to.

Her.

Shifting in her seat, Ravenna let her magic pool at her feet. Keeping half an ear on the debating ministers, she had her magic glide the few feet across the floor to Vallek's boots. The magic spiraled softly up his legs in gentle, teasing caresses.

At first, she wasn't sure he felt it. But when her magic slid beneath his tunic to pool at his cock still hidden under his trou, he sat up straight. Clearing his throat, he threw her a quick, stern frown. She answered with a smirk and raised brow.

Ravenna knew a challenge in her mate's eye when she saw it. Vallek settled back in his seat, spine straight, and gave the ministers his attention again.

Excitement flushed her cheeks. She did so love to tease him.

Moving her fingers under the table, Ravenna's magic followed her subtle directions. It caressed his thighs and abdomen, swirling in warm whorls across his lap. Unseen by the others, it reached up his chest to tease at his nipples and the freshly healed bite she'd left upon him not three days ago.

He bore it all admirably, lasting far longer than she thought he would. Indeed, he sat stoically so long, it was her who began to squirm in her seat. She discreetly crossed her legs, clenching her thighs tight to prevent the whole council from scenting her growing excitement.

Finally, when she'd decided it was time to make a decision, she gathered her magic at his cock again. She could feel through the ephemeral touch how hard he'd grown, a heavy bulge pressing against his trou front. Adding pressure, she let the magic press gently down on his cockhead.

Vallek choked—then cleared his throat.

"I appreciate the care you've both taken in your arguments," he said, "but I think we've said all there is to say. Begin a new survey of the mines, and, if it is found to be safe, we'll open the new shaft in spring."

She flicked his chin with her magic. *There, was that so difficult?*

The ministers bowed, even the scholar and mining ministers agreeing. The matter settled, they and the other ministers began to gather their things and bid goodnight, their overused voices crackling.

Vallek and Ravenna met their bows and farewells with nods and thanks, Ravenna smiling serenely as each orc passed her, one by one. It was difficult, but she tried not to be too smug about getting her way. Even amongst a city of orcs, she often did, one way or another, but the triumph remained sweeter when she had to work for it.

Finally, the door closed behind the last minister, leaving Ravenna alone with her *azai*. She turned to behold him, that serene smile still on her lips.

Vallek pushed his chair back from the table, the legs screeching against the hardwood. "Come here. Now."

Shivering at the command in his voice, Ravenna stood. She took her time flicking her hair over her shoulders and flouncing toward him. When she was close enough to grab, he hauled her forward, pressing the small of her back into the table edge.

"You are an impetuous brat," he rumbled, even as he worked to unbuckle his belt.

"I am only ever your loving, devoted wife," she countered, even as she rucked up her skirts.

Legs planted wide, Vallek leaned back in his seat, one hand freeing his angry cock. Holding it by the root, he told her, "Finish what you start, sprite."

Lip caught between her teeth, Ravenna mounted her bossy mate, knees rested on either side of his thighs. Holding up her skirts for him, she watched as he ran his cockhead over her cunt.

They shuddered at the contact, his palm sliding up her thigh to hold onto her hip, her hand smacking onto his chest for balance.

"Gods, you're burning up," he groaned.

"You left me this way," she pouted, "all day."

Vallek hummed in understanding. "Is that what this is about? Revenge for leaving our bed?"

Ravenna leaned down to catch his lips in a ferocious kiss. Nipping at his bottom lip, she whispered, "I have no need of revenge. Not anymore."

He huffed in amusement. "I'm not sure I can believe that. Not with that cunning mind of yours."

"It's true. Now, will you fuck your long-suffering queen senseless, or do I have to start without you?"

A frenetic purr buzzed in his chest as he set his cockhead at her weeping entrance. Seizing her by the hips, Vallek pressed her down as he pushed up, a merciless invasion that didn't end until he was fully seated inside her.

Ravenna's head fell back, mouth open in a silent scream.

Fates, so full.

She dug her claws into his tunic, scrabbling for purchase as he began to move. There was no gentleness, no finesse. He moved inside her like the brutal warlord he was, thrusting up to stretch her with every stroke. Ravenna bounced in his lap, content just to hold on, hips rolling frantically to try keeping pace.

A growl was her only warning. Surging up, he lifted her under the knees and set her back on the table. Spreading her wide, he took her by the hips again, pulling her to meet every single hard thrust. Those ethereally blue eyes of his glittered with pleasure to see her spread across the table for his enjoyment.

He reached so deep like this, bodies colliding in violent smacks. Ravenna bared her fangs, delighting in the burning pleasure. She would feel him for days after this, a delicious soreness to take with her. Clutching him tight, she beckoned him deeper, called him home. *Give it to me, give it all to me.*

Vallek planted his palms on the table on either side of her. Grinning down at her, he grunted, "Hold on." She'd just enough time to wrap her hands around his taut forearms before he began moving again in earnest.

Without her hold, she would've slid clear across the table from the force of his thrusts. Hips pounding, their bodies made wet smacks as they met, slick dripping between them. She gritted her teeth and bore it, pleasure that bordered on pain, desperately trying to roll her hips for more. Unbearable pressure built low in her belly, tension begging to snap.

He was too tall to kiss like this, so she caressed his lips with her magic, an extra layer of sensation. Chest rumbling, his hungry gaze devoured her—the way her lips parted with every mewl and moan, how she flushed with lust, the wild cascade of her hair across the table.

His arms tensed, and a growl rumbled in his throat. A snarl on his lips, Vallek thrust inside a final time, pinching her clitoris with his shaft.

Sharp sensation severed the tension, and Ravenna came with a shout. Convulsing on the table, she felt how her cunt milked his cock, drawing him further in, sealing them together. He collapsed over her, just catching himself on his elbows as he pulsed inside her, filling her with spend.

For a long while, all Ravenna could do was float. Happiness carried her along, body trembling with aftershocks of pleasure as she lay beneath her mate.

When she had the strength, she lifted a hand to caress his cheek, tracing the broad bone. He purred for her, curling over her and burying his face in her hair.

"Gods, sprite, the throne, the curtain wall, the council room—you'll have me on the basilica floor next."

Ravenna made a noise of interest.

Vallek huffed with laughter, pushing up onto his hands. His eyes glittered with mirth as he smiled down at her, tracing his fingertips over her chin then down her neck.

Fates, she could spend her life just looking at him, especially with that smile. To know she'd put it there, was the glitter in his eye, had her arching her back in pride.

Pulling a kerchief from his pocket, which he'd taken to doing for this very situation, Vallek did his best to clean them up. Having gotten just what she wanted, Ravenna was content to let him move her how he pleased, holding still when he said and climbing into his lap when he was finished. Laying his cheek against the top of her head, he drew his arms around her, cuddling her close.

Ravenna sighed. She could go to sleep just like this, even still in her stays.

"I hope you suffer no more, lady wife," he said.

"I'm satisfied—for now."

"Ah, good, I'm proud to hear it."

Ravenna nuzzled into the side of his neck, taking in a long pull of his scent. Fates, she'd never dreamed it possible to be so happy.

There were challenges, to be sure, and days when their arguments became more than banter. But they never went to sleep angry, and they always began their days in each other's arms. Her favorite days were those she spent all in his company, and she wasn't too proud to admit that if she could, she would've ridden on his back, holding onto him stronger than a limpet as he went about his kingly business.

She didn't know having someone, even a mate, could be like this. Her parents' love had been a beautiful but tragic thing, something of storybooks and bardic poems. Although she and Vallek ruled a kingdom, there were so many moments of domestic simplicity, of quiet intimacy. Ravenna lived for those moments, collected them like the sea glass she used to with her mother.

She had the occasional vision still. They required her to be touching the person whose future she wished to see, as well as a concentrated focus to bring forth the vision. Vallek supposed that these were her true gift; the other visions had been the work of the gods, intervening to right the cycle Amaranthe had upset. She supposed it made as much sense as anything else—but she didn't need them to know her future.

She held it in her arms. Not knowing what exactly the future held was its own kind of thrill, but in the end, she knew that no matter the challenges or bad days, hers would be a life worth living because he was in it.

Ravenna was going positively soft in her new life, but that was all right.

Her parents had taught her to survive. With Vallek, Ravenna was learning to live.

Snuggling against her big, warm mate, Ravenna decided that was as much a gift as her visions.

They were beginning to think about braving the journey up to bed when a knock at the door jarred them awake. After a moment, the door opened to reveal a harried Mattias.

The captain strode quickly into the council room, bowing before hurrying to say, "Forgive the interruption, but you're needed in the basilica."

Even after a few more blinks, Ravenna still couldn't quite believe what she was seeing. From where she stood atop the dais with Vallek, she watched in amazement as the two interlopers bowed low.

One was a human woman, her curls of flaming red hair tied back into a long plait. Her beautiful face was set in hard, determined lines, the rest of her clad in sensible leathers and travel gear. Most intriguing were a pair of goggles dangling around her neck.

Beside her was a bulky male dragon in his bipedal form. Although he kept the hood of his cloak up, the torchlight still managed to catch on the gleam of his red scales. His gold predator's eyes glowed from the shadows of his hood, his slitted pupils careful as he assessed Ravenna and Vallek.

"And what, exactly, is the meaning of this?" Vallek asked. His tone wasn't quite annoyed, not yet, but demanded swift answers.

"Please forgive the surprise," said the woman in careful orcish, "we decided it would be safer to come at night. To scare fewer people."

Vallek looked between the two of them. "You *flew* into my courtyard?"

"Yes, King Vallek."

"*Why?*"

Bowing again, the woman produced a tightly wound scroll. When she moved forward to present it, Mattias intercepted her, plucking the document from her hand to deliver it himself. The dragon rumbled unhappily but bit back the sound when the woman glared at him.

"These are letters of introduction from Allarion Meringor-Dunne, Lord Scarborough, as well as your own Chieftain Kennum of Kaldebrak."

Ravenna's brows lifted to hear such names. They had begun laying plans to travel north and opened negotiations with the kingdom of Eirea several months ago. It was a lot of trouble for one visit, but Ravenna considered nothing too great an ask in order to meet Allarion and Molly's new baby daughter. There were official channels for that, though, all of which she thought were moving along smoothly.

"And who am I being introduced to?" asked Vallek.

"My name is Fia, and this is Theron. We come on behalf of Lady Aislinn Darrow and Queen Ygraine Monaghan."

Vallek and Ravenna exchanged glances.

"We're already in negotiations with Dundúran and Gleanná," said Ravenna. "Why come to us now? This way?"

"The message we bear requires the utmost discretion." Fia nodded at the scroll Vallek now held. "My lady and queen seek more than trade negotiations. I am here to secure promises of friendship for Crown Princess Isolde. The queen hopes to count on your support of the princess, when the time comes."

"And who are we supporting her against?" Vallek wondered.

Lips thin, Fia answered, "The Pyrrossi emperor."

Ravenna's insides clenched. Yes, a play at the Eirean throne wasn't out of the question for the ambitious emperor. The Eirean king himself was half-Pyrrossi, and although he only ruled as regent when Queen Ygraine was indisposed, even they in Balmirra had heard of his maneuverings. There was talk of an illegitimate son or marrying the teenage Isolde to a Pyrrossi cousin.

Should the two human realms unite, particularly under the Pyrrossi banner, it would mean more incursions along the orcish borders.

In the silent moment of surprise, the dragon Theron stepped forward. The berserkers surrounding the pair tensed, but the dragon stopped after just a step. Pushing back his hood, the soft firelight caught on his sharp features, the long dark hair tied in a tail, and the crown of horns atop his head.

Vallek sucked in a breath. "Shit," he rumbled.

"There is something else," said Theron in that hissing cadence of the dragons.

Fia hurried forward, grabbing Theron by the sleeve. "*No,* there's not," she growled. "We *agreed.*"

Laying his hand over hers, Theron shook his head. "No, *agae.* You decided. I merely flew."

Ravenna looked between the pair, sensing far more there than just a messenger and her transport. Glancing up at her mate, she knew he felt the same.

His mouth an exasperated line, Vallek said, "You're already here. Tell us the rest."

As though remembering they had an audience, Theron turned again to face the dais. "I am Theron Princep, second fire of my father's line." Ah. That would explain the horns. Ravenna had read only royal dragons grew more than two, something to do with dominance and hierarchy. But what in all the hells was a dragon prince doing with a human spy in an orcish basilica?

"I see," said Vallek, "and who is it you wish to broker an alliance for? Your brother the *anax?*"

"No," the dragon said gravely, "I want you to help me kill Araxos."

Glossary of People, Places, Pronunciations, and Orcish & Fae Words

Aine Broch (awn-yuh brock)—human mate of Maxim, mother of Ravenna

Aislinn Darrow (ash-lihn)—heiress of the Darrowlands, wife to Hakon Green-Fist

All-Mother—the female goddess in orcish mythology; goddess of feminity, fertility, the sun, the harvest, and bodies of water

Allarion Meringor-Dunne (ah-lar-ee-on mehr-in-gore)—friend of Maxim, rider of Bellarand, mate of Molly Dunne, Lord Scarborough

Amaranthe (am-uh-ran-thee)—Fae Queen, a hag

anax (ahn-acks)—leader of the dragons of the Droplets

Araxos (ah-racks-ohs)—*anax* of the dragons of the Droplets, not having a good time

Asta Broad-Back (ahs-tah)—younger sister of Vallek and Eydis, captain of the eastern guard

azai (ah-zhigh)—faethling for *soulmate, fated mate*

Balmirra (Bahl-meer-uh)—preeminent ancient orcish stronghold, the largest and oldest orcish city

Bellarand the Black (bell-uh-rand)—black unicorn, grumpy, lets Allarion ride him

breddah (breh-duh)—orcish for *little brother*

Brynhíl Broad-Back (brihn-heel)—housekeeper to Vallek

Callistix (cah-liss-ticks)—unicorn mare, mother of Oberon

deep sleep—for the fae, a level of sleep like torpor, when bodily and magical functions shut down almost completely; can last for years

denizen—in the orcish culture, a high-level member of a city, such as the master of a guild or city elders

dread-mount—a stallion unicorn bonded to a fae warrior

Dundúran (dun-dure-un)—capital city of the Darrowlands; can mean the city or the castle itself

Dyfan Bay—bay contested by the orcs in the south and fae in the north

Eirea (eer-ee-uh)—central kingdom of humans, still recovering from brutal wars of succession

Ever-Father—the male god in orcish mythology; god of masculinity, fertility, the moon, battle, and wilderness

Eydis Broad-Back (ay-diss)—older sister of Vallek and Asta, mate of Hilde, advisor and spymaster

faelands—territory claimed and inhabited by the fae; imbued over millennia with their magic

faethling—native language of the fae

Fallorian—fae capital

Fenna Broad-Back—personal healer to Vallek

Fia (fee-uh)—Lady Aislinn's seneschal

Fulk Stone-Skin—chieftain of the Stone-Skin clan

Gleanná (glay-ah-nah)—capital of Eirea

Griegen Mountains (gree-gun)—mineral-rich mountain range in the southwest, occupied by orcs

groff mi tal (grof mee tahl)—orcish for *I've won,* declared at the end of a game of *talfon*

Grogar Broad-Back—an unwise Balmirran noble

Hilde Broad-Back (hill-dee)—mate of Eydis

Hormhím (horm-heem)—Vallek's double-bladed axe

Hrothgar Long-Tusk (roth-ghar)—chieftain of Innrinhom

Innrinhom (ihn-rihn-home)—eastern orcish stronghold, currently ruled by Hrothgar

Isolde Monaghan (ih-zolde mon-uh-han)—Crown Princess of Eirea

Kaldar Stone-Skin (cal-dar)—nephew of Fulk

Kaldebrak (call-dih-brack)—orcish stronghold in the northern Griegen Mountains, currently ruled by Kennum

Kennum Green-Fist (ken-num)—chieftain of Kaldebrak

kone (cone)—orcish for *seer, wisewoman*

Leita (lee-tah)—a mysterious fae woman from Ravenna's visions

long sleep—for the fae, a normal type of sleep taken every few days rather than a nightly rest; can last for a full day or more if the fae is recovering from injury

lord/lady—in the book, honorific of any noble person of any rank, usually attached to the person's given name

Mattias Broad-Back (muh-tie-uhs)—captain of Vallek's elite berserker warriors

Maxim Illyinia (max-ihm ill-ee-eena)—fae warrior, mate of Aine, father to Ravenna

Molly Dunne-Meringor—mate of Allarion Meringor, Lady Scarborough, former barmaid

Mordis Broad-Back—former chieftain of Balmirra, killed by Vallek, uncle of Silvia

Oberon the Starlit (oh-burr-on)—Maxim's unicorn dread-mount, friend to Ravenna, son of Callistix

paladin—in orcish culture, a member of the orcish nobility; historically, a knight

Pyrros (peer-ohs)—southern kingdom of humans, has conquered other lands, countries, and tribes to the south

Ravenna Broch-Illyinia—half-fae, half-human daughter of Maxim and Aine, gifted with foresight, our heroine

Rulf Green-Fist—emissary of Kennum in Balmirra

Scarborough—estate restored by Allarion

Silvia Broad-Back—niece of former chieftain Mordis

skala—orcish for *raven*

stone sleep—for the fae, a type of eternal sleep taken by elder fae when it is time for them to pass on to the afterworld; typically taken on the Twins

talfon (tahl-phon)—orcish strategy boardgame not unlike chess

Thalia—a white unicorn mare

Theron (ther-ohn)—a dragon prince, currently in hiding in the Darrowlands

The Spearhead—a peninsula at the mouth of Dyfan Bay, creating an estuary into the bay

The Twins—the two fae goddesses that represent the sun and moon, life and death, war and love, and all duality, they are believed to bestow azai as a sign of favor; also associated with the two islands off the coast of the faelands

tristah (triss-tah)—orcish for *little sister*

Ulrich Broad-Back (ool-rick)—second in command to Vallek

Vallek Far-Sight (val-eck)—chieftain of Balmirra, new king of the orcish kingdom, brother of Eydis and Asta, our hero

velloi (vel-oy)—faethling for *dragonfly*

vini mun (vee-nee muhn)—orcish for *my friend*

Ygraine Monaghan (ee-grane mon-uh-han)—Queen of Eirea

Yngrid Long-Tusk (eeng-grid)—younger daughter of Hrothgar

Yphella Long-Tusk (ee-fell-uh)—elder daughter of Hrothgar

Author's Note

Hello! Thank you so much for reading *Faeling!* I hope you enjoyed Vallek and Ravenna's story and returning to the Monstrous World!

These two have been cooking in my head for a while now. I knew I wanted to do a monster odd couple with some serious size difference. I also love that each MW book has a different vibe to it; *Halfling* is the fantasy road trip, *Ironling* is the court intrigue, *Sweetling* is the gothic fairytale, and now *Faeling*, to me, feels like the heavy metal story.

I knew exactly who Ravenna and Vallek were the moment they appeared on the page. Characters and their arcs don't always come to me so easily, but this book sprang from my mind like Athena jumping out of Zeus's head, fully formed. It was such a joy to write; I don't think I could have written this at the pace I did without everything going so smoothly. This might be my favorite thing I've ever written, and I'm so happy with how it turned out!

It's been a pleasure exploring the orcs of this world, but I think now we're ready for an expansion. What's going to happen with the faelands? What are those slithery serpents doing down there on their islands? What is Queen Ygraine and Lady Aislinn up to? Those questions and more to be answered! Eventually.

First, for our next MW release, we're headed back to the Darrowlands! With my upcoming publishing schedule with Avon, now is the perfect time for some sweet, fluffy novellas. I'm excited to write some pure fluff, and for that, we can't do better than our fluffy manticore brothers. Yes, we're headed back to the otherly village to see who might be finding their mates!

We'll switch things up a bit with the novellas; due to my publishing schedule, the first will hopefully arrive in ebook late 2025, with the second releasing (as well as an omnibus paperback) in spring 2026. That's the plan, anyway.

Look for more on *Changelings* soon! I can't wait to dive into Balar's story, as well as his broody brother Soren's. Who are their lady loves? What shenanigans will they be getting into? Find out soon!

As for gargoyles, I'm so excited for *Heartsong* paperbacks and audiobooks to release February 2026 from Avon! The second book, *Heartsworn*, will launch Summer 2026. Things are happening in that series, and I can't wait to share.

Lots to come with the MW as well. These novellas are going to be a nice little palette cleanser for me, but don't you worry, in the next book, there will be dragons ;) and a certain feral fae getting far more than she bargained for.

Thank you so much for reading! If you enjoyed this story, I'd appreciate it if you'd consider leaving a review. Reviews are so important in helping spread the word about a book and getting it in front of more eyeballs. Thanks again!

Come say hi on social media or check out my website, www.sewendelauthor.com, for more on my stories and to explore awesome merch!

Thanks so much!

—S. E.

Acknowledgements

I'd also like to take a moment to thank some of the people who made this book possible!

A huge thank you to Lily, my writing bestie and the best beta reader out there!

Thank you to Leah, my awesome PA, who helped me go from hobbyist to big girl author with my own website and everything.

I'm also so grateful to my amazing ARC team, y'all are amazing!

And I have to mention too the amazing artists who helped bring Vallek, Ravenna, and Oberon to life. I know I went full honey-baked ham with this book heh. A huge thank you to Beth Gilbert, my stunningly talented cover artist. I also want to thank Ali, Kels, Line, Flavia, Eva, Jeannine, and more, you're all so amazing and I'm so grateful for the care you've taken with my book babies!

Other Works

A Time of War and Demons (House of the Rising Sun, Book 1), fantasy romance novel

Aerie (Broken Wings Duet, Book 1), fantasy romance novel
Haven (Broken Wings Duet, Book 2), fantasy romance novel

Stone Hearts (War of the Underhill, Book 0), historical monster/fantasy romance novella
Heartsong (War of the Underhill, Book 1), monster/paranormal romance novel, paperbacks Winter 2026
Heartsworn (War of the Underhill, Book 2), monster/paranormal romance novel, Summer 2026

Halfling (Monstrous World, Book 1), monster/fantasy romance novel
Ironling (Monstrous World, Book 2), monster/fantasy romance novel
Sweetling (Monstrous World, Book 3), fae/fantasy romance novel
Faeling (Monstrous World, Book 4), monster/fae/fantasy romance novel
Changelings (Monstrous World, Book 5), monster/fantasy romance novella collection, Autumn 2025

Stay in Touch

If you'd like to stay in touch, come on over to socials and say hi! I'm around on most platforms as se.wendel.author, and I'm most active on Instagram. Come check it out to find out about what I'm working on, get some reading recommendations, and get spammed with pictures of my cat. What's not to love?

You can also check out all my books, commissioned art, and book merch shop on my author website (www.sewendelauthor.com)! Lots of good stuff over there!

I've also started up a monthly newsletter. The first is out now and you can subscribe on my website to keep up with me and my news.

About the Author

S. E. is a California native who grew up with animals; her ginger tabby is her current writing partner and lets her know when it's time to take a break (by laying on her keyboard). She graduated from the University of California, Davis with a master's in creative writing and uses all her available time to build worlds, characters, and their stories. She enjoys animal rescue shows, almost everything in Trader Joe's, and all the beautiful landscapes of California.